L.A. FIELDS &
TYSON KADWELL

FRONT COVER (L-R):
Lizzie Borden, Roy Cohn, Lili Elbe, Alan Turing, Freddie Mercury
Virginia Woolf, Susan Sontag, Quentin Crisp, La Maupin, Rock Hudson,
Marsha P. Johnson, Robert Mapplethorpe, Radclyffe Hall

BACK COVER (L-R):
Maud Allan, Lord Byron, Valerie Solanas, Oscar Wilde, Wilfred Owen,
Gertrude Stein, Elizabeth Bathory, Colette, Tallulah Bankhead
Arthur Rimbaud, Isadora Duncan, James Baldwin, Hannah Höch

INTRODUCTION

The book you're holding began as a sort of bet.

Authors L.A. Fields and Tyson Kadwell were watching the 1997 movie *Love! Valour! Compassion!* based on the play by Terrence McNally, and one of the characters had a book called *Queer America from A to Z.* They wondered if that was a real book, found that it was not, joked that they should do a Gay A Day tear-off calendar or something, and on a lark decided to pitch the idea to Steve Berman at Lethe Press. Berman said a calendar is a cute idea, but why not make it a book? Why not indeed! That's how this project began.

Soon after, it started to evolve.

The original order was for a book half the size of this one, but it was impossible to condense the lives of kings, queens, artists, activists, killers, and movie stars into about 100 words each—we had to make it 200. After that it came time to compile the list of names, which took weeks. We've included only the dead, and when it came to sources, we had to trust what got published before us. Gossip or not, if it was good enough to publish once, it's good enough to repeat. Our stance in choosing the LGBT of distant and recent history was to be CNN about it: we research, you decide. Unauthorized biographies, tell-alls by family members or hangers-on, conflicting historians—we've included it all. The thing about gay history is sometimes the truth is never the 'official' story, so we've had to make do with what little we could find.

All that means for you is: get ready to be scandalized.

As far as our standard goes, three same-sex situations makes a bisexual. The suspiciously and emphatically unmarried with close same-sex companions? They're included too. Transgender, transvestite, and possibly intersex people have been included as well, with care taken not to choose labels or pronouns that they didn't call themselves. Harder than the research itself, however, was trying to fit everyone on some sort of date that mattered to their personal history. If you've read any *Who's*

Who in gay history, either alphabetized or serialized, you still haven't read anything quite like this.

At the end of the day, it's the spectrum that makes the rainbow.

The aim of this project, and the part we find so delightful even after a year of exacting work, is the showcase of diversity. The good, the bad, the beautiful, the tragic, and the talented, across all walks of life, all races, and all fields of expertise—when these stories are concentrated together, the result is a mesmerizing tapestry. We've learned more history putting this book together than any class could teach, and we've fallen in love at least as many times as we've had our hearts broken. There will be names and stories you recognize, as well as secret histories you'll be shocked you've never heard before.

With this book, you can take any year and make it queer, one day at a time.

CONTENTS

JANUARY

FEBRUARY

MARCH

APRIL

MAY

JUNE

JULY

AUGUST

SEPTEMBER

OCTOBER

NOVEMBER

DECEMBER

INDEX

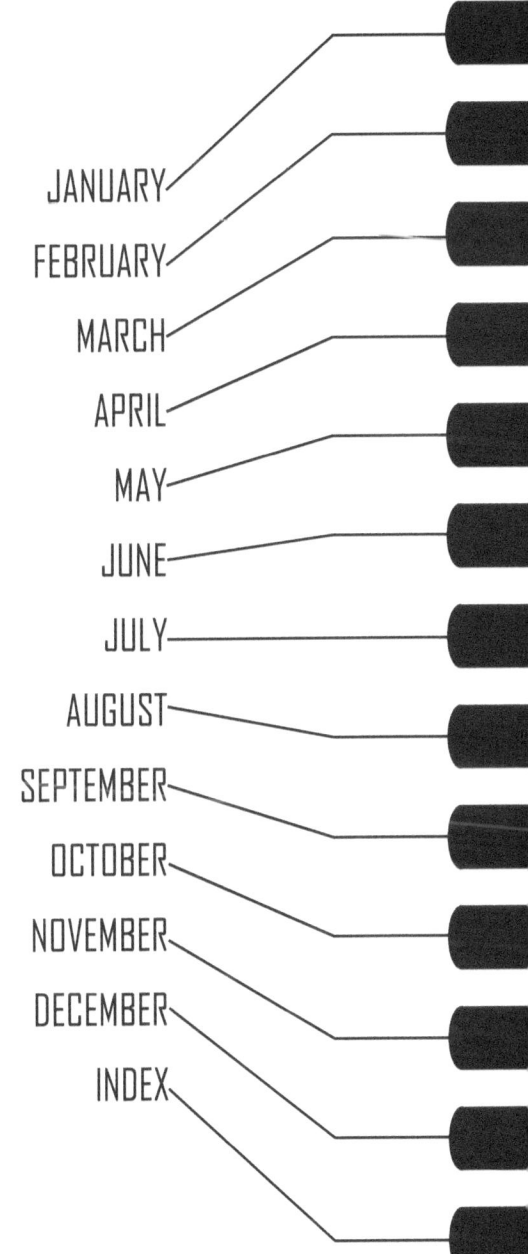

JANUARY

NEW YEAR'S DAY

E.M. FORSTER
(EDWARD MORGAN FORSTER)

JAN 1 1879 – JUN 7 1970
(AGED 91)

E.M. FORSTER was an English novelist, essayist, and librettist. Best known for his novels *A Room with a View* (1908), *Howards End* (1910), and *A Passage to India* (1924), he was nominated for the Nobel Prize in 16 different years.

After repressing his sexuality for the first half of his life, Forster lost his virginity to a wounded soldier in 1917 while working for the Red Cross, which led to a series of romances with working-class men. His only novel about homosexual relationships, *Maurice* ("Finished in 1914. Dedicated to a happier year."), was not published until after his death. A 2010 biography of Forster theorizes the sharp decline in his writing output occurred because he was finally finding physical fulfillment. Forster's own diary states: "I should have been a more famous writer if I had written or rather published more, but sex prevented the latter."

Forster encouraged other young homosexual writers, including Belfast-based novelist Forrest Reid, poet Siegfried Sassoon, and author and memoirist Christopher Isherwood. He was elected an honorary fellow of King's College in 1946, declined a knighthood in 1949, was made a member of the Order of Merit in 1969, and died of a stroke in 1970.

MARTHA "MINNIE" CAREY THOMAS

JAN 2 1857 – DEC 2 1935

(AGED 78)

MARTHA CAREY THOMAS was born to Quakers in Baltimore, Maryland. She attended Sage College at Cornell University, changed her name to Carey Thomas, and studied education, graduating in 1877. She furthered her studies at the University of Leipzig, Johns Hopkins University, the University of Zurich, and the Sorbonne in Paris. Thomas pursued higher education as a means to show that women had the same intellectual capabilities as men.

In 1884, Thomas was made dean and chair of the English department at Bryn Mawr College in Pennsylvania. She helped fund a prep school for Bryn Mawr in Baltimore, and became president of Bryn Mawr College in 1894. Thomas was the first president of the National College Women's Equal Suffrage League, a member of the National American Woman Suffrage Association, and founded a summer school for women workers. Though Thomas made huge advances for women in education, she also actively blocked Jewish students and teachers from entering Bryn Mawr.

Thomas had romantic relationships with childhood friend Mary Mackall "Mamie" Gwinn, and B&O Railroad heiress and philanthropist Mary Elizabeth Garrett. Thomas retired from the college in 1922, and died of a coronary occlusion in 1935.

MONIQUE WITTIG

JUL 13 1935 – JAN 3 2003
(AGED 67)

MONIQUE WITTIG'S first novel *L'Opoponax* (1964) won the Prix Médicis award and received international acclaim when translated in 1966. Her next novel, *Les Guerilleres* (1969), depicts a war of the sexes in which women fight back with bullets, rocket launchers, and laughter. The book's publication is considered to be an important landmark in French lesbian feminism. Wittig was a founding member of the *Gouines rouges* or "Red Dykes," which was the first lesbian group in Paris. Wittig continued to write works on gender theory, lesbianism, and feminism in France and the United States.

Wittig lived with her partner Sande Zeig, an American film director and writer. They met in Paris in 1975, when Zeig was studying mime and teaching karate. In 1976, they moved to the United States, where Wittig worked as a professor at various colleges, including the University of California, Vassar College, and Berkeley University. Zeig's film *The Girl* (2000) was based on an unpublished short story of the same name by Wittig, her first written in English. Wittig died in 2003 of a heart attack in Tucson, Arizona.

5

CHRIS KANYON
(CHRISTOPHER MORGAN KLUCSARITS)

JAN 4 1970 – APR 2 2010
(AGED 40)

Christopher Klucsarits played rugby at the University of Buffalo, and graduated with a bachelor's degree in Physical Therapy, but his real love was professional wrestling. He started in the ring as the masked character Mortis, then fought under the name CHRIS KANYON, or simply Kanyon. He played with the WWF and WCW, winning the WCW United States Championship, the WWF Tag Team Championship, and the WCW World Tag Team Championship twice. He worked as a stuntman and stunt coordinator for the films *The Jesse Ventura Story* (1999) and *Ready to Rumble* (2000).

Kanyon knew he was gay after his first kiss with a girl at 11 years old. He was 17 when he had his first sexual experience with another teenaged boy in the park. Kanyon was eager to present a positive role model as the first openly gay professional wrestler, but was unable to gain traction in the wrestling world. Kanyon sought treatment for multiple concussions, and in 2003 was diagnosed with bipolar disorder after a suicide attempt. He was released from his WWE contract in 2004, and was unable to get rehired despite his attempts. Kanyon committed suicide with a drug overdose of antidepressant medications in 2010.

5th

ALVIN AILEY

❧

JAN 5 1931 – DEC 1 1989
(AGED 58)

Born in Rogers, Texas, ALVIN AILEY was an African-American dancer, choreographer, and founder of the Alvin Ailey American Dance Theater. His most famous piece, *Revelations*, was inspired by his "blood memories" of growing up in Texas, and is said to be the best-known and most often seen modern dance performance.

Raised by his single mother through the Great Depression, Ailey made his Broadway debut in Truman Capote's *House of Flowers* (1954). He started his own dance company in 1958 and took his show on the road, traveling the U.S. and the world. He was awarded the NAACP's Spingarn Medal, the Kennedy Center Honors, and posthumously the Presidential Medal of Freedom, selected for that recognition by President Barack Obama.

Ailey's personal life was marred by failed relationships, untrustworthy business partners, and cocaine addiction. He suffered from arthritis, took lithium to help stabilize his bipolar disorder, and found most of his later-in-life intimacies with street hustlers. Ailey died of AIDS in 1989. Similarly to when he concealed his dance career from his mother for the first two years, he also asked his doctor to disguise his cause of death as "terminal blood dyscrasia," to spare her the truth.

EPIPHANY,
CHRISTIAN OBSERVANCE

BENEDETTA CARLINI

1591 – 1661
(AGED ~70)

When BENEDETTA CARLINI was nine years old, she was placed with Theatine nuns at the Convent of the Mother of God in Pescia, Italy. Carlini quickly stood out amongst her fellow nuns as she experienced visions, fell into trances, and spoke in the voices of angels and Jesus. While in trances, Carlini would be transformed into a handsome young man, known as the Angel Splenditello. Carlini became abbess of the convent at 30, based on her divine revelations and administrative skills.

When Carlini's visions took on a more demonic nature, she was confined to a cell with Sister Bartolomea Crivelli, who was meant to observe her. They began a sexual relationship while Carlini was embodied by Splenditello and Jesus. According to testimony, "Benedetta would grab her [Crivelli] by the arm and throw her by force on the bed. Embracing her, she would put her under herself and kissing her as if she were a man, she would speak words of love to her. And she would stir so much on top of her that both of them corrupted themselves." Carlini was removed as abbess, placed under guard for the remainder of her life, and died in 1661.

DR. SOPHIA LOUISA JEX-BLAKE

JAN 21 1840 – JAN 7 1912
(AGED 71)

SOPHIA JEX-BLAKE campaigned to study medicine, applying directly to colleges at a time when women were unable to seek higher education. She led the charge of the Edinburgh Seven, seven women who sought the right to attend medical classes and examinations at the University of Edinburgh. They faced great hostility from male students: obscene letters, fireworks attached to their doors, and an angry mob blocking their entrance to an anatomy exam, hurling trash, mud, and insults. Due to some influential members persuading the University, the Edinburgh Seven were refused graduation, and many chose to attend college elsewhere in Europe. Jex-Blake continued her studies and became the third registered female doctor in the country.

Jex-Blake helped found the London School of Medicine for Women in 1874, and established the Edinburgh School of Medicine for Women in 1886. She opened an outpatient clinic for poorer women to receive medical care, and the clinic eventually grew into Scotland's first female-staffed hospital for women.

Jex-Blake's longtime partner was Dr. Margaret Todd, 19 years Jex-Blake's junior. After Jex-Blake retired in 1899, they moved to Windydene, Mark Cross, Rotherfield. Jex-Blake died in 1912 after a series of heart attacks.

9

DR. GRAHAM ARTHUR CHAPMAN

JAN 8 1941 – OCT 4 1989
(AGED 48)

Medical doctor, ex-alcoholic, and member of legendary comedy supergroup Monty Python, GRAHAM CHAPMAN spent his free time mountaineering, playing rugby, and attempting extreme sports in formal wear with the Dangerous Sports Club. He appeared in *Monty Python's Flying Circus* (1969-1974), Python stage tours, and four Python films, including starring as Brian in *Monty Python's Life of Brian* (1979). With assistance from colleagues John Cleese, Bernard McKenna, and Douglas Adams, Chapman penned scripts like *Rentadick* (1972), *The Odd Job* (1978), and *Out of the Trees* (1975).

While attending Cambridge, Chapman found with some exper-imentation he was a 4 on the Kinsey scale, meaning "predominantly homosexual, but more than inci-dentally heterosexual." In *A Liar's Autobiography* (1980), Chapman described seeing love of his life David Sherlock on the beach in Ibiza: "I thought, 'Fucking hell, he's a goer if ever I saw one,' which I hadn't (male that is)." Sherlock said, "It was a year before I could believe I wasn't being taken for a ride."

Chapman and Sherlock lived in England and Los Angeles, owned beagles, provided lodging for runaway gay youths, and adopted teen John Tomiczek. Chapman died of cancer that had spread from his tonsils to his spine in 1989.

SIMONE DE BEAUVOIR
(SIMONE LUCIE ERNESTINE MARIE BERTRAND DE BEAUVOIR)

JAN 9 1908 – APR 14 1986
(AGED 78)

SIMONE DE BEAUVOIR was the ninth woman to have received a degree from the Sorbonne. She sat in on postgraduate examination prep classes for the agrégation in philosophy and placed second, becoming the youngest person to pass the exam at 21.

De Beauvoir met fellow philosopher Jean-Paul Sartre in the examination classes and though they did not marry, they maintained a lifelong relationship. She later wrote, "We were two of a kind, and our relationship would endure as long as we did: but it could not make up entirely for the fleeting riches to be had from encounters with different people." De Beauvoir had female lovers,

and would seduce underage female students to pass them off to Sartre in what they called the "trio."

She explored existentialism through philosophical essays, co-edited the political journal *Les Temps modernes*, and wrote *The Second Sex* (1949), a two-volume work of feminist philosophy about the treatment of women throughout history, and the societal impositions placed on women from birth onward. She won the Prix Goncourt for her book *The Mandarins* (1954), wrote short stories and essays, and was at the forefront of France's women's liberation movement. De Beauvoir died in 1986 of pneumonia.

SALVATORE "SAL" MINEO, JR.

JAN 10 1939 – FEB 12 1976
(AGED 37)

Born in New York, SAL MINEO came to acting young, making his first Broadway appearance in 1951 with Tennessee Williams's *The Rose Tattoo*, followed by *The King and I* in 1953 alongside Yul Brynner. Mineo's most famous role was playing opposite James Dean in the 1955 movie *Rebel Without A Cause*, which earned him a Supporting Actor Oscar nomination for the role of 'Plato' Crawford.

Mineo's Plato is often seen as a gay role due to his sensitive devotion towards the James Dean character. Self-professed bisexual, Mineo had a relationship with British actress Jill Haworth starting in 1960 while filming *Exodus*, which ended when she caught him in bed with a boy. A similar circumstance occurred when he met Susan Ladin in 1965, who according to Mineo's biographer, took a handful of sleeping pills after Mineo admitted he was also attracted to men.

In a 1972 interview with Boze Hadleigh, Mineo discussed his bisexuality, and how he was often mistaken as gay. In 1976 Mineo was murdered, stabbed to death by a burglar behind his West Hollywood apartment. At the time of his death, he was in a six-year relationship and living with male actor Courtney Burr III.

BAYARD TAYLOR

JAN 11 1825 – DEC 19 1878
(AGED 53)

American travel writer, translator, literary critic, poet, and diplomat, BAYARD TAYLOR wrote what some consider to be America's first gay novel, *Joseph and His Friend* (1870). Based on poets Fitz-Greene Halleck and Joseph Rodman Drake (known socially as Damon and Pythias, after the Greek legend of ideal friendship), the 'friends' in Taylor's book explicitly show their love for one another: "They took each other's hands. [...] Each gave way to the impulse of his manly love, rarer, alas! but as tender and true as the love of woman, and they drew nearer and kissed each other."

Taylor himself married the sickly Mary Agnew mere months before her death in December 1850. By December 1851, he'd met the dearest friend of his life while traveling, German landowner August Bufleb. Taylor and Bufleb were struck with a mutual ardency so intense that Taylor's 1973 biographer called it "embarrassing." Taylor later married Bufleb's niece, a circumstance he approximated for his groundbreaking novel.

Bufleb built a house on his estate in Germany specifically for Taylor's visits. Taylor died in Berlin in 1878. Henry Wadsworth Longfellow wrote a poem for Taylor after his death, which was read by Oliver Wendell Holmes at his Pennsylvania memorial.

LORRAINE VIVIAN HANSBERRY

❧

MAY 19 1930 – JAN 12 1965
(A G E D   3 4)

Writer and playwright from Chicago, LORRAINE HANSBERRY wrote *A Raisin in the Sun* (1959), its title taken from a Langston Hughes poem ("What happens to a dream deferred? Does it dry up like a raisin in the sun?"). It was the first drama by an African-American woman to be produced on Broadway.

Growing up, Hansberry's family hosted many prominent African-Americans, including professor W.E.B. DuBois, poet Langston Hughes, musician Duke Ellington, and Olympic gold medalist Jesse Owens. Her family deliberately attempted to move into a restricted white neighborhood in 1938, were met with a brick-throwing mob, and took the issue to court. First ordered

to leave, their case was overturned on a technicality, and ultimately opened up South Side Chicago to African-Americans.

Hansberry met Robert Nemiroff, a Jewish writer, at a protest against racial discrimination; they married in 1953. She wrote anonymously to lesbian magazine *The Ladder* in 1957 identifying herself as a "heterosexually married lesbian." She and Nemiroff divorced in 1964, but remained collaborators until her death from pancreatic cancer in 1965.

Her work was praised by James Baldwin for its honesty, and Nina Simone wrote the song "To Be Young, Gifted and Black" in her memory.

KAY FRANCIS
(KATHERINE EDWINA GIBBS)

JAN 13 1905 – AUG 26 1968
(AGED 63)

American actress KAY FRANCIS was known as The Queen of the Lot: the highest paid employee on the Warner Bros. lot between 1932-1937. Best known for her portrayals of intelligent women in movies like *Dr. Monica* (1934), *Living on Velvet* (1935), and *House on 56th Street* (1933), Francis was uninterested in fame, writing in 1938, "When I die, I want to be cremated so that no sign of my existence is left on this earth. I can't wait to be forgotten." She retired from film in 1946.

Regularly socializing with homosexual men, Francis considered a sexual relationship (apparently unconsummated) with longtime friend Kay Johnson, who pledged her love for Francis in 1929. Francis lived for a few months with school chum Katty Stewart, who'd also fallen in love with her, once writing in her diary, "Slept with Katty only because she wanted me to—Damn!" In a 1932 entry, Francis recorded, "Swell time but got very drunk. T[allulah] B[ankhead] called me a lesbian. E[dith] H[ead] and I were very next to getting queer! Damn fool!"

Francis married five times, had no children, and left her fortune to an organization providing guide dogs for the blind. She died from breast cancer.

GERALD "JERRY" SANFORD SMITH

JUL 19 1943 – OCT 15 1986
(AGED 43)

GERALD "JERRY" SMITH was born in Eugene, Oregon. He attended San Lorenzo High School and Arizona State University, playing football from his junior year onward. Smith was a 9th-round draft pick for the Washington Redskins in 1965. He played as tight end for the Redskins from 1965 to 1977, caught 421 passes, set a tight end record of 60 touchdowns, and twice was named All-Pro. Smith played in Super Bowl VII on January 14th, 1973.

Smith never openly discussed his sexuality, but felt protected by Redskins coach Vince Lombardi, who demanded a homophobia-free locker room and would not tolerate players' gay slurs.

Smith and running back David Kopay went out drinking one night and ended up in bed together. Kopay said, "I was sharing something of myself with someone who's close and understood all that I had been through and understood so much of what we hoped for would come. And that's where we left it. And it never happened again."

Smith died of AIDS in 1986. He spoke candidly of his diagnosis months before his death, saying, "I want people to know what I've been through and how terrible this disease is. Maybe it will help people understand."

MAZO DE LA ROCHE
(MAZO LOUISE ROCHE)

JAN 15 1879 – JUL 12 1961
(AGED 82)

Born in Canada near Toronto, MAZO DE LA ROCHE wrote her first short story at nine, and later went on to write the *Jalna* series, or *Whiteoak Chronicles*, about a century of the fictional Whiteoak family's country aristocracy between the years 1854-1954. The 4th novel of the series, *Jalna* (1927), won the $10,000 Atlantic-Little Brown Award, bringing de la Roche huge popular success, though not the serious critical response she would have liked. She wrote more than 25 books, including short stories, a history of Quebec, and two books for children, alongside the 16-book *Jalna* series.

At seven, de la Roche's family adopted her orphaned younger cousin, Caroline Clement, who would become de la Roche's lifelong companion. Living a reclusive life together, they also adopted the two orphaned children of their friends. There is speculation that their relationship was only a passionate friendship, and their household a "Boston marriage" arrangement done to maintain financial independence from men, but de la Roche's biographer points out: "Caroline Clement was almost Mazo's other self. These two dissimilar, but perfectly attuned persons, lived one of the most unusual and certainly most productive partnerships in the history of literature." They are buried alongside one another.

SUSAN SONTAG
(SUSAN ROSENBLATT)

JAN 16 1933 – DEC 28 2004
(AGED 71)

SUSAN SONTAG started self-publishing newspapers at nine years old, which she sold to neighbors for 5¢ each. Sontag wrote fiction, nonfiction, plays, and essays, delving deep into subjects considered controversial. In 1967 she wrote of white civilization being a cancer, then later recanted this saying it slandered cancer patients.

Sontag was a political activist and filmmaker, traveling to war-torn North Vietnam, filming in Israel during the Yom Kippur War, and witnessing the siege of Sarajevo. She believed all writers should "pay attention to the world."

At 15 she wrote in her diary,

"I feel I have lesbian tendencies (how reluctantly I write this)." At 16 she wrote of her first sexual encounter with a woman she named H: "Perhaps I was drunk, after all, because it was so beautiful when H began making love to me." Sontag spoke of being bisexual in 2000, saying she had been in love nine times with five women and four men. She was married to sociologist Philip Rieff from 1950 to 1959, and had a son, David. Sontag had a relationship with photographer Annie Leibovitz from the 1980s until Sontag's death in 2004 from myelodysplastic syndrome, which had developed into acute myelogenous leukemia.

BARBARA CHARLINE JORDAN

FEB 21 1936 – JAN 17 1996
(AGED 59)

BARBARA JORDAN was inspired to become a lawyer after hearing a speech in high school by Edith S. Sampson. Jordan majored in political science and history at Texas Southern University, was a national champion debater, and graduated *magna cum laude* in 1956. She graduated from Boston University School of Law in 1959.

Jordan became the first African-American woman to serve in the Texas Senate in 1966, and was elected to the U.S. House of Representatives in 1972, becoming the first woman to represent Texas in the House. In 1975, she was appointed to the Democratic Steering and Policy Committee. In 1976, Jordan was the first African-American woman

to deliver a keynote address at the Democratic National Convention. She also delivered the opening speech during the impeachment hearings against Richard Nixon. Jordan received the Presidential Medal of Freedom in 1994.

Jordan met educational psychologist Nancy Earl on a camping trip in the 1960s, and they became lifelong partners. Earl occasionally worked as a speechwriter for Jordan, and when Jordan began suffering from multiple sclerosis in 1973, Earl became her caretaker. Jordan died in 1996 of pneumonia complications. She was the first African-American woman to be buried in the Texas State Cemetery.

CARY GRANT
(ARCHIBALD ALEC LEACH)

JAN 18 1904 – NOV 29 1986
(AGED 82)

Born in Bristol, U.K., to an alcoholic father and a clinically depressed mother who was committed to a mental institution when he was nine years old, actor CARY GRANT was told at the time his mother was dead. He wasn't told the truth until he was 31 years old at his father's deathbed. Grant left school at 14 and joined a theater troupe which toured to America. He stayed on in New York City and eventually made it to Hollywood.

Between his five marriages to women, Grant lived for 12 years with fellow actor Randolph Scott. When pressured by studios to marry, Grant would sink into depression and alcoholism until he could return to living at 'Bachelor Hall' with Scott. Grant maintained that he was heterosexual his whole life, from threatening to sue gossip columnist Hedda Hopper for implying he wasn't "normal," to actually bringing a suit against Chevy Chase in 1980 over the joke, "I understand [Grant] was a homo. He was brilliant. What a gal!" Another joke floating around: "Archie Leach was gay, but Cary Grant was straight." Grant died of a massive, protracted stroke at St. Luke's Hospital in Davenport, Iowa at the age of 82.

PATRICIA HIGHSMITH

JAN 19 1921 – FEB 4 1995
(AGED 74)

Born in Fort Worth, Texas but raised primarily in Manhattan, PATRICIA HIGHSMITH had a very fractured relationship with her mother, who once said she'd tried to abort Patricia by drinking turpentine. Highsmith eventually became the author of *Strangers on a Train* (1950), *The Price of Salt* (1952), and the "Ripliad" series begun with *The Talented Mr. Ripley* (1955).

Attracted to women all her life, Highsmith nevertheless tried to cure her homosexuality, noting in her diary: "I like most men better than I like women, but not in bed." Her relationships with women and attempts at heterosexuality with men were all short-lived, and though her literary work was successful, she wrote in 1970 that she was "cynical, fairly rich ... lonely, depressed, and totally pessimistic."

In 1947, she wrote a "New Year's Toast" in her diary: "To all the devils, lusts, passions, greeds, envys, loves, hates, strange desires, enemies ghostly and real, the army of memories, with which I do battle — may they never give me peace." An alcoholic who descended more and more into misanthropy as she grew older, she died from a combination of aplastic anemia and lung cancer in Locarno, Switzerland at age 74.

BARBARA STANWYCK
(RUBY CATHERINE STEVENS)

JUL 16 1907 – JAN 20 1990
(AGED 82)

American actress, model, and dancer, BARBARA STANWYCK was ranked the 11th greatest female star of classic American cinema by the American Film Institute. She received a star on the Hollywood Walk of Fame, was nominated for four Academy Awards, won three Emmys, a Golden Globe, and received honorary lifetime awards from the American Film Institute, the Film Society of Lincoln Center, the Los Angeles Film Critics Association, and the Screen Actors Guild. At one time she was the highest paid woman in the United States. Orphaned at the age of four and partially raised in foster homes, she ultimately appeared in 85 films over 38 years in Hollywood.

Biographer Axel Madsen wrote the consensus on Stanwyck, that "unearthing the truth about her sexuality would remain impossible." However, he also noted that "people would swear she was […] Hollywood's biggest closeted lesbian." Tallulah Bankhead claimed she slept with Stanwyck, and Stanwyck's most intimate relationship was with publicist Helen Ferguson, who was sometimes a live-in companion. Several of Stanwyck's roles made her a lesbian icon, but she categorically refused to answer Boze Hadleigh's questions about bisexuality.

Stanwyck married and divorced twice, had a son, and died of congestive heart failure.

DIANE ALEXIS WHIPPLE

JAN 21 1968 – JAN 26 2001
(AGED 33)

DIANE WHIPPLE played lacrosse in high school and earned a scholarship to Penn State, where she was a two-time first team All-American, and received the NCAA Final Four MVP Midfielder in 1989. She was named the Penn State Female Athlete of the Year, and the NCAA National Player of the Year in 1990. Whipple played for the World Cup lacrosse team, coached lacrosse for a private high school, and later for St. Mary's College in Moraga.

Whipple met partner Sharon Smith through a mutual friend, and a few months later they moved in together. They traveled across Europe, Hawaii, and Puerto Rico, and exchanged rings in a private ceremony. In 1999 they moved into an apartment in the Pacific Heights neighborhood of San Francisco where they lived with their two cats, Shadow and Bootie.

Whipple was returning home with bags of groceries when she was attacked by two large dogs in the hallway of her apartment building. She was viciously mauled, receiving 77 wounds in the attack and succumbing to blood loss and traumatic injuries at the hospital. The dogs were euthanized and legal proceedings were taken against the owners. Smith has since become an advocate for gay rights.

ROY FRANKLIN SIMMONS

NOV 8 1956 – FEB 20 2014
(AGED 57)

ROY SIMMONS played football at Alfred E. Beach High School in Savannah, Georgia when he was recruited to play for Georgia Tech. In 1979, Simmons was an 8th-round draft pick for the New York Giants, and became a regular on the offensive line. His performance declined with drinking and drug abuse, and he left the Giants citing mental fatigue. Simmons briefly had a stint as an airport baggage handler before being signed to the Washington Redskins as a backup lineman in 1983. His final game was Super Bowl XVIII with the Washington Redskins on January 22nd, 1984.

Simmons often visited bathhouses near his college campus, and during his time at the NFL he maintained relationships with women while also having affairs with men. He was the second player in the NFL to come out as gay, and the first to disclose his HIV-positive status. At one point Simmons became homeless and struggled with drug addiction, but he recovered enough to work in drug treatment clinics, and live in an apartment in the Bronx. Simmons died in 2014 from pneumonia-related complications. Simmons was inducted into the National Gay and Lesbian Sports Hall of Fame in 2015.

ALAN MATHISON TURING

JUN 23 1912 – JUN 7 1954
(AGED 41)

Mathematician, computer scientist, cryptanalyst, and logician, ALAN TURING is best known for breaking the Nazi Enigma code on January 23rd, 1940, giving the Allies the winning edge in WWII. He also invented the Turing test for determining whether artificial intelligence is equivalent to human intelligence, and contributed to mathematical biology with his 1952 essay on morphogenesis, the development of patterns and shapes in biological organisms. He's considered the father of computer science, and godfather of all modern computers.

Turing was prosecuted in 1952 for "gross indecency," i.e. homosexual activity, under the Labouchere Amendment, the same law which convicted Oscar Wilde in 1895. Turing submitted to chemical castration treatment as an alternative to prison, hormone injections that rendered him impotent and caused him to grow breasts. The conviction also meant he was stripped of the security clearances for governmental intelligence work.

In 1954, Turing died of cyanide poisoning, possibly by accidental inhalation of cyanide fumes, or by intentional suicide. A bitten apple was found beside him, but not thoroughly tested to prove whether or not it was laced with cyanide. At the time of his death, Turing's contributions to the war effort were unknown. Turing wasn't officially pardoned until 2013.

CALIGULA
(EMPEROR GAIUS JULIUS CAESAR AUGUSTUS GERMANICUS)

AUG 31 12 AD – JAN 24 41 AD
(AGED 28)

The third of Rome's emperors, CALIGULA is best known for the degree of waste and carnage during his four-year reign (37-41 AD). The third son of Roman general Germanicus, Gaius earned the nickname "Caligula" (meaning "little boots") in reference to the miniature uniform he wore as a child. After his father's death in 17 AD, the emperor Tiberius eventually adopted Caligula; he relished bringing out the worst in his great-nephew, saying that he was "nursing a viper in Rome's bosom."

Caligula was emperor by 25, and quickly came to reign with terrible whimsy. He executed the allies that put him into power, spent money on bizarre structures (such as a legendary two-mile floating bridge he could gallop across), and is attributed with often saying, "Remember that I have the right to do anything to anybody."

He had brazen affairs with the men of his court and the wives of his allies, and was also rumored to have had incestuous relationships with his sisters. He wore women's shoes, lavish accessories, and wigs. He allegedly would roll in piles of money and drink precious pearls dissolved in vinegar. In January of 41 AD, Caligula was stabbed to death by Praetorian Guard officers.

VIRGINIA WOOLF
(ADELINE VIRGINIA STEPHEN)

JAN 25 1882 – MAR 28 1941
(AGED 59)

VIRGINIA WOOLF was the author of the novels *Mrs Dalloway* (1925), *To the Lighthouse* (1927), and *Orlando* (1928), as well as the book-length essay *A Room of One's Own* (1929) which stated, "A woman must have money and a room of her own if she is to write fiction."

Born to a privileged household, Woolf suffered from severe bouts of depression. Writing from a very young age, she became associated with a group of writers and artists collectively known as the Bloomsbury Group, which included herself, John Maynard Keynes, Lytton Strachey, and E.M. Forster. The group held modern attitudes towards feminism, pacifism, and sexuality.

In 1912, she married fellow author Leonard Woolf, a happy and enduring union. In 1937, she wrote, "After 25 years can't bear to be separate […] our marriage so complete." Sexually open, in 1922 she also began an affair with writer Vita Sackville-West, who worked to encourage Woolf's self-esteem. According to Sackville-West in a letter to her husband, the relationship was only twice consummated, yet the intimacy continued into the early 1930s.

During a depression, Virginia drowned herself by filling her pockets with stones and walking into the River Ouse near her home in 1941.

PAUL LEONARD NEWMAN

JAN 26 1925 – SEP 26 2008
(AGED 83)

American actor and Academy Award-winner PAUL NEWMAN is known for his roles in *Cat on a Hot Tin Roof* (1958), *Cool Hand Luke* (1967), *Butch Cassidy and the Sundance Kid* (1969), and many others. Newman married twice, first to Jackie Witte, with whom he had a son and two daughters, then to actress Joanne Woodward, with whom he had three daughters during a marriage that lasted 50 years. When asked about his devotion to Woodward, Newman once quipped, "Why go out for a hamburger when you have steak at home?"

A 2009 biography by Darwin Porter recounts Newman's many youthful affairs with male and female stars, including (but not limited to) Marilyn Monroe, Grace Kelly, Judy Garland, Lana Turner, Natalie Wood, Marlon Brando, Montgomery Clift, Steve McQueen, James Dean, Tony Perkins, and Sal Mineo (an affair which Porter says ended badly, with Mineo calling up Newman later to say he was in bed with Newman's also bisexual son, Scott).

Scott died of an overdose in 1978, at age 28. Newman said, "It was the saddest day of my life." Newman started a charity in his son's memory, one of his many philanthropic endeavors. Newman died of cancer at age 83.

BEATRICE HASTINGS
(EMILY ALICE HAIGH, BEATRICE TINA, D. TRIFORMIS, ALICE MORNING, ROBERT Á FIELD)

JAN 27 1879 – OCT 30 1943
(AGED 64)

BEATRICE HASTINGS was born in England, grew up in South Africa, moved to Paris where she fell in with bohemian circles, and found a career in journalism. Hastings was a socio-political writer with most of her work being featured in the literary magazine, *The New Age*. Hastings published three novels, several short stories and poems, as well as books on literary criticism and the double standard in society for women. Hastings also posed for Amedeo Modigliani, becoming his muse for 14 paintings and countless sketches.

Hastings had relationships with men and women, including A.R. Orage, Wyndham Lewis, and Modigliani. Hastings also had a relationship with fellow writer and collaborator Katherine Mansfield. Mansfield's nickname for Hastings was Biggy B.

Hastings was known to drink a considerable amount of whiskey, admitted to having a "temper not to be trifled with," and published the pamphlet "The Old New Age" in 1936 as a vicious takedown of Orage and the literary circles of Britain. In late October of 1943, Hastings burned all of her letters, stuffed a towel under the door of her apartment, took her pet mouse in her hand, and turned on the gas to commit suicide.

RICHMOND BARTHÉ
(JAMES RICHMOND BARTHÉ)

JAN 28 1901 – MAR 5 1989
(AGED 88)

African-American sculptor RICHMOND BARTHÉ began drawing as soon as he was crawling, and he was painting by age six. He first exhibited his work at age 12 at the Bay St. Louis Country Fair. Barthé had typhoid fever at 14 and was unable to complete school, but he was admitted to the Art Institute of Chicago in 1924.

Barthé's debut as a professional sculptor was in 1927 at *The Negro in Art Week* exhibition. From this he won critical acclaim and commissions for work, including a bust of painter Henry O. Tanner and a 40ft tall monument to Toussaint L'Ouverture in 1928. Barthé worked without models, relying on his sharp visual memory to create the human form. He often sculpted black, nude men in sensual poses. He left Chicago for New York, then lived abroad in Jamaica, Switzerland, Spain, and Italy.

In a letter to the recognized "Dean" of the Harlem Renaissance, Alain Locke, Barthé wished for a long-term relationship with a "Negro friend and a lover." He had short affairs with poet Richard Bruce Nugent, fellow sculptor John Rhoden, photographer Carl Van Vechten, writer Lyle Saxon, as well as with Alain Locke. Barthé died in 1989 in Pasadena, California.

GIA MARIE CARANGI

JAN 29 1960 – NOV 18 1986
(AGED 26)

American fashion model and arguably the world's first supermodel, GIA CARANGI appeared on the covers of *Cosmo* and *Vogue* across America and Europe, and in advertising campaigns for fashion houses like Armani, Christian Dior, Versace, and Yves Saint Laurent.

Carangi's first major fashion shoot was with photographer Chris von Wangenheim in October of 1978. After wrapping the shoot, he asked her to pose nude behind a chain link fence with Sandy Linter, a makeup assistant. This scene was later reproduced in HBO's 1998 film, *Gia* (starring Angelina Jolie), and sparked an attraction between Carangi and Linter. However,

Carangi's modeling schedule, wild personality, and escalating drug addiction did not leave much room for a relationship.

By 1980, Carangi was using heroin. In 1981, she underwent surgery to treat an infected vein on her hand (the result of repeated drug injections). As her habit increased, her modeling jobs decreased. She entered a drug rehab facility in 1984, but returned to using by 1985. In June of 1986, she was admitted to a hospital with bilateral pneumonia, and diagnosed with AIDS-related complex (an early term for the symptoms of HIV infection). By November she was dead from AIDS-related complications, at 26 years old.

ANGELA "ANGIE" CALOMIRIS
(ANGELA COLE)

❧

AUG 1 1916 – JAN 30 1995
(AGED 78)

ANGIE CALOMIRIS fell in love with photography at a young age, and after studying at Brooklyn College and Hunter College, she moved to Greenwich Village, bought a camera with her money instead of food, and joined the Photo League, a New York photography group committed to social change.

In 1942, Calomiris was approached by the FBI to become an informant, and was asked to infiltrate the Communist Party of America (CPUSA) to gather information. She agreed to their offer, later saying she "kind of wanted to be a hero." Her undercover name was Angela Cole.

Calomiris helped compile a case which led to 12 arrests, and gave testimony during the trial. The defendants were convicted, and Calomiris capitalized on her celebrity with the autobiography *Red Masquerade: Undercover for the FBI* (1950). Calomiris continued to report to the FBI and had Yetta Cohn, a lesbian policewoman with supposed Communist ties, fired.

Calomiris had a relationship with Myrtis Johnson, the sister-in-law of her FBI handler. When the New York gay community disowned her for the Cohn firing, she moved to Provincetown, Massachusetts, bought beachfront condominiums, and ran the property as Angel's Landing. She died in San Miguel de Allende, Mexico.

HILDA MARIA KÄKIKOSKI
(HILDA MARIA SJÖSTRÖM)

JAN 31 1864 – NOV 14 1912
(AGED 48)

At age 14, HILDA KÄKIKOSKI moved alone to Helsinki to study at a girls' school on scholarship. She tutored prior to her enrollment in university, where she completed a PhD in Finnish and Nordic history in 1895.

Käkikoski taught history and Finnish language in Helsinki until 1902. Käkikoski became a member of the Finnish Women's Association, writing articles for their magazine *Home and Society*. She was elected the Vice President of the FWA in 1895, and held that position until 1904. Käkikoski ran for a position in the Parliament of Finland in 1906, and became one of the first women elected to Parliament. Käkikoski also wrote short stories, poetry, children's songs, and was working on a four-volume set of Finnish history until her death in 1912.

Käkikoski was a vegetarian, gymnast, and cyclist who wore mannish clothing. She lived with fellow schoolteacher Fanny Pajula and her son for six years, later becoming involved in a complicated affair with Hildi Ennola, a married colleague. In 1902, Käkikoski met American Frances Weiss with whom she started a correspondence and relationship. She also had affairs with activist Helmi Kivalo and deaconess Hanna Masalin. Käkikoski is buried near Ennola in Karjalohja.

FEBRUARY

LANGSTON HUGHES
(JAMES MERCER LANGSTON HUGHES)

FEB 1 1902 – MAY 22 1967
(AGED 65)

START OF BLACK HISTORY
MONTH, U.S. AND CANADA

Born in Joplin, Missouri, LANGSTON HUGHES was a poet, novelist, playwright, columnist, and social activist. Best known as the leader of the Harlem Renaissance, which spanned the 1920s in New York City, Hughes was one of the earliest innovators of jazz poetry.

Hughes was greatly influenced by the work of Walt Whitman. His poems "Cafe: 3 AM" and "Poem (To F.S.)" (thought to be Ferdinand Smith, a sailor from Jamaica whom Hughes met in the 1920s and kept in touch with for over 30 years) are believed by academics and biographers to be signifiers of Hughes' closeted homosexuality.

Likewise with his posthumously published short story "Blessed Assurance," in which a man frets about his overly intelligent, probably queer son. It begins: "Unfortunately (and to John's distrust of God) it seems his son was turning out to be a queer." The son, Delmar, is criticized by his father for smoking effeminately ("like a woman"), and goes on to sing a female part in the church choir, during which the male choir director faints, and the father keeps yelling for Delmar to "Shut up!" Delmar does not stop singing.

Hughes died from complications after surgery related to prostate cancer at age 65.

OLIVER WELLINGTON "BILLY" SIPPLE

NOV 20 1941 – FEB 2 1989
(AGED 47)

Decorated former Marine BILLY SIPPLE came to national notice on September 22nd, 1975, when he grabbed the arm of Sara Jane Moore as she fired a pistol at President Gerald Ford, saving him from assassination. In this incident's aftermath, Sipple was outed to the *San Francisco Chronicle*, in part by his friend, openly gay San Francisco Board of Supervisors member Harvey Milk, who believed all gay people should be outed to help normalize the community.

Sipple sued seven newspapers for invasion of privacy, saying, "My sexuality is a part of my private life and has no bearing on my response to the act of a person seeking to take the life of another." The suit was dismissed on the basis that Sipple's sexual orientation had been known to "hundreds of people" prior to the news reports. However, Sipple had been closeted in his hometown of Detroit. He was subsequently disowned by his parents, and barred from attending his mother's funeral.

Wounded in Vietnam, Sipple's only form of income was from Social Security Disability Insurance. Depressed and isolated, Sipple began to drink heavily, and was found dead on the floor of his apartment in 1989 from "natural causes." He was 47.

EMILE ALPHONSE GRIFFITH

FEB 3 1938 – JUL 23 2013
(AGED 75)

EMILE GRIFFITH worked at a hat factory when his physique was noticed by the owner, and he was encouraged to get into boxing. In 1958, Griffith won the New York Golden Gloves 147lb Open Championship. Griffith became a World Champion in several different weight classes, and later was the coach for the Danish Olympic boxing team from 1979 to 1980. After his retirement, Griffith became a corrections officer for the Secaucus, New Jersey Juvenile Detention Facility.

In his 1962 Madison Square Garden televised fight against Benny Paret, Paret groped Griffith during weigh-in and called him an anti-gay slur.

Griffith won by technical knockout, but Paret died 10 days later. Griffith had nightmares about Paret from then on.

Griffith addressed his bisexuality in *Sports Illustrated* in 2005, saying, "I will dance with anybody. I like men and women both. But I don't like that word: homosexual, gay or faggot. I don't know what I am. I love men and women the same, but if you ask me which is better...I like women." He married dancer Mercedes "Sadie" Donastorg in 1971. Griffith suffered from *dementia pugilistica* (or "punch-drunk syndrome") and died in a Hempstead, New York care facility in 2013.

LIBERACE
(WŁADZIU VALENTINO LIBERACE, WALTER "LEE" LIBERACE, THE GLITTER MAN, MR. SHOWMANSHIP)

MAY 16 1919 – FEB 4 1987

(AGED 67)

WŁADZIU LIBERACE started playing piano at the age of four and could memorize difficult pieces of music by seven. His first breakthrough of "classical music with the boring parts left out" came at the end of a concert in 1939, when he encored with "Three Little Fishies" in the style of several different composers.

Liberace worked in extravagant costumes, adorned himself with rings and jewelry, and performed on ornate pianos. He had his own television program, *The Liberace Show* (1952-1969), and made appearances on other popular shows of the time, as well as in movies. He performed live in Las Vegas, co-authored cookbooks, owned an antiques store and a restaurant, and sued any magazine for libel that suggested he was homosexual.

While linked to actresses like Mae West and Betty White, Liberace had live-in male lovers, the most vocal of which was Scott Thorson, who worked as Liberace's secretary/chauffeur. Thorson sued for palimony after he was let go and received a cash settlement, cars, and dogs.

Liberace's death was initially attributed to anemia, emphysema, and heart disease, but after an autopsy was performed by the coroner, it was discovered the true cause of death was cytomegalovirus pneumonia from AIDS-related complications.

WILLIAM S. BURROUGHS
(WILLIAM SEWARD BURROUGHS II)

FEB 5 1914 – AUG 2 1997

(AGED 83)

WILLIAM S. BURROUGHS was a core figure in the Beat Generation literary movement, along with Jack Kerouac and Allen Ginsberg. His best-known work is *Naked Lunch* (1959), which was banned after an obscenity trial in Boston in 1962 for being "morally corrosive material," a decision that was overturned in 1966. His other works include *Junky* (1953), *Queer* (written 1951-1953, published 1985), and *The Nova Trilogy* (1961-1967) of 'cut-up' narratives, written with the technique of cutting up newspapers, rearranging them, and reading across to find unique sentences.

Burroughs lived a chaotic life, once killing his common-law wife, Joan Vollmer, in Mexico in 1951, during a game of William Tell: instead of shooting a highball glass off her head, Burroughs shot her. Fleeing to Tangiers, he abandoned their son with his parents. William S. Burroughs Jr. took after his father, accidentally shooting his own friend in the neck at age 15 (though that incident wasn't fatal), becoming a writer, a speed addict, and dying of cirrhosis of the liver in 1981, at age 33.

Burroughs died from a heart attack at age 83, and is buried in St. Louis, Missouri. The marker bears his name and the simple epitaph, "American Writer."

RAMON NOVARRO
(JOSÉ RAMÓN GIL SAMANIEGO)

FEB 6 1899 – OCT 30 1968
(AGED 69)

When RAMON NOVARRO was 14, he and his family moved to Los Angeles to escape the Mexican Revolution. Novarro took bit parts in films and worked as a singing waiter until he found success in the silent film *Scaramouche* (1923). Novarro is best known for playing Ben-Hur in the 1925 silent epic of the same name, becoming a sex symbol, and earning the moniker of "Latin lover." After his contract with MGM Studios expired and was not renewed, Novarro struggled to continue working in movies and television.

Novarro was unable to reconcile his religion with his homosexuality. He leaned on alcohol to blot out his troubles, and lost his driver's license after multiple DUIs. Novarro had a relationship with composer Harry Partch, but ended it when his film career began. He was also linked to his publicist, journalist Herbert Howe.

Later in life, Novarro relied on male prostitutes for company. Novarro was beaten during an encounter and choked to death on his own blood. His killer and the attacker's accomplice were sentenced to life in prison, idolized in the tabloids, interviewed by Truman Capote, and were paroled within seven years. Novarro is buried in Calvary Cemetery in East Los Angeles.

G.H. HARDY
(GODFREY HAROLD HARDY)

FEB 7 1877 – DEC 1 1947
(AGED 70)

G.H. HARDY's mathematical talent was obvious at a young age, when he amused himself during church service by factoring the hymn numbers. He studied at Winchester and Trinity College, lectured and taught at Cambridge, Oxford, and Princeton. Hardy made multiple advances in number theory and mathematical analysis, as well as changing the teaching methods of British mathematics from applied mathematics toward the concept of pure mathematics. After being introduced to a population genetics problem by his cricket partner, Hardy formulated a theorem now known as the Hardy-Weinberg principle, which is still used in testing population stratification.

Of his work Hardy said, "I have never done anything 'useful.' No discovery of mine has made, or is likely to make, directly or indirectly, for good or ill, the least difference to the amenity of the world."

Hardy's mathematical collaborator John Edensor Littlewood called Hardy, a "non-practising homosexual." He formed close relationships with younger men over the love of cricket. Hardy spoke of his discovery, collaboration, and mentoring of Indian mathematician Srinivasa Ramanujan by saying it was "the one romantic incident in my life." In 1947, Hardy attempted suicide by barbiturate overdose. Though he survived the attempt, he died later that year.

OPERA DAY

JULIE D'AUBIGNY
(LA MAUPIN)

1670/1673 – 1707
(AGED 34/37)

JULIE D'AUBIGNY'S father trained King Louis XIV's court pages, so d'Aubigny was able to train alongside them. She learned fencing, dancing, and drawing, all while dressing as a boy. D'Aubigny once kissed a woman at a society ball, and dueled three men who objected to her behavior, defeating them all. She was mistress to Count d'Armagnac, married off to Sieur de Maupin, and became involved with Sérannes, an assistant fencing master. When Sérannes killed a man in an illegal duel, they fled the city.

D'Aubigny joined an opera company and began an affair with a young woman before the woman was sent to a convent in Avignon. D'Aubigny sneaked into the convent, stole the body of a dead nun, put it in the woman's bed, and set the room on fire. They escaped into the night and lived together for several months before the woman returned to her family. D'Aubigny was charged as a male for kidnapping, body snatching, arson, and failing to appear; she was sentenced to death by fire. D'Aubigny contacted Count d'Armagnac to persuade a pardon from the king, which she received, and she continued to sing with the opera until her eventual retirement and death.

AMY LAWRENCE LOWELL

FEB 9 1874 – MAY 12 1925
(AGED 51)

Born to a wealthy family in Brookline, Massachusetts, AMY LOWELL was first educated by an English governess who failed to teach spelling. While attending private schools, Lowell was known as a terror to both faculty and fellow students.

Lowell discovered a love of free verse poetry, and wrote her first adult poem after seeing Italian actress Eleanora Duse perform. Her first collection, *A Dome of Many-Coloured Glass*, was published in 1912. Lowell published her own books of poetry, re-worked translated poems of ancient Chinese poets, she assisted in the publication of other writers and poets, wrote essays on contemporary poets, and wrote a biography on John Keats. She smoked cigars, dressed in men's shirts and suits, and wore her hair in a bun. T.S. Eliot described Lowell as a "demon saleswoman of poetry."

Lowell found a muse and love in actress Ada Dwyer Russell. They met in 1909 and began a relationship in 1912, living together until Lowell's death in 1925 of a cerebral hemorrhage. As executor of Lowell's estate, Russell burned all personal correspondence, but poems inspired by Russell indicate their closeness. In 1926, Lowell was posthumously awarded the Pulitzer Prize for Poetry for *What's O'Clock* (1925).

WILLIAM "BIG BILL" TATEM TILDEN JR.

FEB 10 1893 – JUN 5 1953
(AGED 60)

BILL TILDEN took up tennis at a young age, but wasn't known for it in prep school, and wasn't good enough to play on his college team at the University of Pennsylvania. Tilden dropped out to dedicate his time to tennis and started winning tournaments. His first national title was the mixed doubles championships with Mary Browne in 1913, a title he successfully defended the following year. He won six consecutive U.S. Championships and became the first American male to win the Wimbledon singles championship in 1920, winning again in 1921 and 1930.

Tilden was arrested twice for soliciting underage males,

receiving shortened prison and parole sentences. Tilden believed the commuted sentences were due to his status, and influence from friends like Charlie Chaplin. In his autobiography *My Story* (1948), Tilden wrote, "Greater tolerance and wider education on the part of the general public concerning this form of sex relationship is one of the crying needs." Tilden was expelled from his hometown tennis club, and the University of Pennsylvania scrubbed his name from the alumni files. Tilden died from heart complications in 1953, his packed bags were found at the door, ready to head to another tournament.

LEE ALEXANDER MCQUEEN

MAR 17 1969 – FEB 11 2010
(AGED 40)

ALEXANDER MCQUEEN received a master's degree in Fashion Design, and his graduation collection was bought out by magazine editor and fashion aficionado Isabella Blow, who then helped McQueen launch his career. McQueen, under his label Alexander McQueen, became known as "the hooligan of English fashion" for his unconventional and shocking runway shows. Credits include reviving low-rise jeans or "bumsters," and designing wardrobes for David Bowie. He received four British Designer of the Year awards and CFDA's International Designer of the Year award in 2003.

McQueen realized he was gay when he was six years old, and came out to his family when he was 18. He said, "I was sure of myself and my sexuality and I've got nothing to hide. I went straight from my mother's womb onto the gay parade." In 2000, McQueen and partner documentary filmmaker George Forsyth were married in an unofficial ceremony aboard a yacht in Ibiza. Their relationship ended the next year, but they remained close friends.

On February 11th, 2010, days after his mother's death, McQueen's body was found by his housekeeper, having hanged himself in his wardrobe. A note was discovered that read: "Look after my dogs, sorry, I love you, Lee."

ABRAHAM "ABE" LINCOLN
("THE GREAT EMANCIPATOR")

FEB 12 1809 – APR 15 1865

(AGED 56)

Lawyer and 16th President of the United States, ABRAHAM LINCOLN successfully preserved the Union through the Civil War (1861–1865) before being assassinated in Ford's Theater by John Wilkes Booth.

Lincoln's most intimate friendship was with a man named Joshua Speed, who ran a general store when he met Lincoln in 1837. Lincoln could not afford a bed, so Speed invited him to share his own: "I have a very large room, and a very large double-bed in it; which you are perfectly welcome to share with me if you choose." They shared that bed for four years until Speed married, and on his departure Lincoln fell into a deep depression that has puzzled many scholars.

Elmer Ellsworth, the first Union soldier killed in the Civil War, was deeply mourned by Lincoln, who had what one author called a "schoolboy crush" on the younger Ellsworth. David Derickson, Lincoln's presidential bodyguard, as two contemporaries noted, "frequently spent the night at [President Lincoln's] cottage, sleeping in the same bed with him, and—it is said—making use of his excellency's nightshirt!" Furthermore, after spotting Walt Whitman through the White House windows, Lincoln once strangely commented, "Well, *he* looks like a *man*."

LINO BROCKA
(CATALINO ORTIZ BROCKA)

APR 3 1939 – MAY 22 1991
(AGED 52)

After his father died, LINO BROCKA was raised by his mother in her hometown of San Jose in the Philippines. He directed his first film *Wanted: Perfect Mother* in 1970, which won Best Screenplay at the Manila Film Festival.

Brocka became one of the most influential Filipino filmmakers. His film *Insiang* (1976) was the first film from the Philippines to be shown at Cannes Film Festival. His film *Macho Dancer* (1988), about a gay teenager involved in prostitution, required smuggling out of the country to avoid censorship.

In 1983, he founded Concerned Artists of the Philippines, a progressive organization that represented artists to address issues in the country. Brocka and other petitioners were arrested in late January of 1985 for the illegal assembly of a public transportation drivers' strike. They were released on February 13th of that same year.

Brocka came out as gay in 1975, and his films often spoke to the underground of the city, of loneliness and love. Brocka died in an auto accident in 1991, when the driver of his car, actor William Lorenzo, swerved to avoid a tricycle and smashed into a concrete post. Brocka was posthumously made a Philippines National Artist for Film.

MARTHA MAY ELIOT

Apr 7 1891 – Feb 14 1978
(AGED 86)

MARTHA ELIOT was born into the Boston upper-class, and had poet T.S. Eliot for a cousin. She studied at Bryn Mawr College and enrolled at Johns Hopkins University School of Medicine, graduating medical school in 1918. From 1921-1935 Eliot taught at Yale University's department of pediatrics, and was director and later bureau chief of the National Children's Bureau Division of Child and Maternal Health.

Eliot was responsible for drafting most of the language in the maternal and child health portions of the Social Security Act, helped establish programs for maternity care and child health services, and researched the prevention and reversal of rickets. She was also the only woman to sign the World Health Organization's constitution on behalf of the United States.

Eliot met partner Ethel Collins Dunham at Bryn Mawr, and they enrolled at Johns Hopkins together. Both were groundbreaking pediatricians whose relationship spanned nearly 60 years. Their letters captured their romantic domesticity, with lines like, "Ever and ever so much love, my darling." Eliot died in Cambridge, Massachusetts.

CESAR JULIO ROMERO JR.

FEB 15 1907 – JAN 1 1994
(AGED 86)

Cuban-American actor CESAR ROMERO stood at 6'3" and owned over 500 suits. He played a wide range of roles from Latin lovers, to rogue bandit *The Cisco Kid* (1939-1941), to the Joker in the 1960s *Batman* series. Grandson of Cuban national hero José Martí, Romero was a natural dancer, and served during WWII on the USS Cavalier. He refused to shave his mustache to play the Joker, leaving it visible under the makeup, and said in 1984, "When I started in motion pictures in 1934, they said I was going to be the next Valentino. […] I was saddled with the label because I had a Latin name. My background is Cuban, but I'm from New York City. I'm a Latin from Manhattan."

Romero never married and was consistently described as a 'confirmed bachelor.' He spoke openly once to Boze Hadleigh (*Hollywood Gays*, 1996) about close friend Tyrone Power, the joys of glory holes, and a single hook-up with Desi Arnaz: "[T]o make a very pleasant story short, one day Desi said to me, 'All right, we both know what you want. Let's get it over with.' We did. End of story."

Romero died a confirmed bachelor at age 86.

LESLEY GORE
(LESLEY SUE GOLDSTEIN)

MAY 2 1946 – FEB 16 2015
(AGED 68)

LESLEY GORE was a singer, songwriter, actress, and activist. Her song "It's My Party" was recorded when she was 16, and was a certified gold record. The 1964 feminist anthem "You Don't Own Me" was also recorded before Gore was 18, and has been repeatedly covered by performers like Dusty Springfield, Joan Jett, and the cast of *The First Wives Club* (1996).

Gore won an Academy Award for composing songs for the 1980 movie *Fame* with her brother, Michael Gore. Her song "Sunshine, Lollipops and Rainbows" from the 1965 movie *Ski Party* was nominated for a Grammy. She hosted an LGBT-focused public television show called *In the Life* between 1992 and 2012.

Gore said that though the music industry was "totally homophobic," she was never particularly closeted: "I just kind of lived my life naturally and did what I wanted to do. I didn't avoid anything, I didn't put it in anybody's face." In 2005, Gore came out publicly in an interview on *After Ellen*, revealing that she had been in a long-term relationship with luxury jewelry designer Lois Sasson. By the time of Gore's death in 2015 from lung cancer, she and Sasson had been together for 33 years.

JACK COLE
(JOHN EWING RICHTER)

APR 27 1911 – FEB 17 1974
(AGED 62)

JACK COLE ran away from boarding school to study dance for six weeks at the Denishawn School of Dancing and Related Arts before joining the company in August 1930. He then traveled the world to study and master various forms of authentic, ethnic dances.

On New Year's Eve in 1937 at the Rainbow Room, Cole premiered his unique juxtaposition of East Indian dances to jazz music and the result was dubbed "Hindu Swing." Cole found success drawing from various forms of dance to create theatrical jazz dance, though Cole preferred the term, "urban dance."

Cole and his dancers headlined at nightclubs. Cole performed in Broadway musicals and was choreographer for several Broadway shows, before moving over to choreographing for films with *Moon Over Miami* (1941). He was known for working with Rita Hayworth, Betty Grable, assistant and collaborator Gwen Verdon, and coaching Marilyn Monroe through several films, including *Gentlemen Prefer Blondes* (1953).

Jack Cole was openly gay and was known as "a terrible genius," with angry outbursts directed toward his regular dancers in service of his drive for perfection. Cole played up his image in *Designing Woman* (1957) as the flamboyant choreographer Randy Owens. He died of cancer in 1974.

AUDRE LORDE
(AUDREY GERALDINE LORDE)

FEB 18 1934 – NOV 17 1992
(AGED 58)

When a young AUDRE LORDE was asked how she was feeling, she would respond in recitation of a relevant verse of poetry. She began writing her own poems at 12. Lorde attended the National University of Mexico and Hunter College, began working as a librarian in Greenwich Village, and completed a master's degree in Library Science in 1961.

Lorde was nominated for the National Book Award for Poetry in 1973. Her book *The Cancer Journals* (1980) won the American Library Association Gay Caucus Book of the Year Award in 1981. She was the New York State Poet Laureate from 1991 until her death. Lorde's poetry focused on the layers of self, her personal struggles, and racial injustice. She knew that "as a Black lesbian mother in an interracial marriage, there was usually some part of me guaranteed to offend everybody's comfortable prejudices of who I should be."

Lorde married attorney Edwin Rollins, had two children, and divorced in 1970. She met longtime partner Frances Clayton, a psychology professor, while in Mississippi, and had a short affair with sculptor/painter Mildred Thompson. Lorde lived with partner and fellow feminist warrior Gloria I. Joseph in St. Croix until her death from liver cancer.

SYLVIA RAE RIVERA
(RAY RIVERA MENDOZA)

JUL 2 1951 – FEB 19 2002
(AGED 50)

Drag queen, trans activist, and founding member of the Gay Liberation Front, SYLVIA RIVERA was present at the Stonewall riots in 1969. Born in a taxicab in the parking lot of Lincoln Hospital, Sylvia later said, "The old queen couldn't wait, ready to hit the streets [...] you see why I'm always out standing on the street corner; I came out feet first." She left home at age 10 and became a street walker to make money.

Sylvia insisted the Gay Rights movement not forget the trans members of the community, the butch women, the effeminate men, and those in drag. In 1973, Sylvia gave a speech calling out some activists' privilege: "I have been beaten. I have had my nose broken. I have been thrown in jail. I have lost my job. I have lost my apartment for gay liberation and you all treat me this way? What the fuck's wrong with you all?"

In 1970, Rivera and fellow Stonewall-starter Marsha P. Johnson co-founded STAR (Street Transvestite Action Revolutionaries) to aid homeless youth. In 2002, to carry on Sylvia's legacy, The Sylvia Rivera Law Project (SRLP) was founded to help end poverty and gender identity discrimination for marginalized people.

ROY MARCUS COHN

FEB 20 1927 – AUG 2 1986
(AGED 59)

ROY COHN was always good at getting what he wanted. The day he was admitted to the bar, he used his family's connections to obtain a position at the United States Attorney's office in Manhattan. Cohn was Joseph McCarthy's chief counsel, prosecutor at Julius and Ethel Rosenberg's 1951 espionage trial, and attorney for the occasional mob boss or steak salesman.

Cohn's fierce patriotism was seen in a friend's recollection: "Roy sang three choruses of 'God Bless America,' got a hard-on and went home to bed." A registered Democrat, he supported conservative ideals.

He had an Irish wolfhound named Disraeli, a llama or two, and was said to have jumped into a river to save a stranded dog.

Cohn kept his life private, often alluding to made-up relationships for the press, like a fake engagement to Barbara Walters that she quickly denied. His real companions were men he introduced to others as office managers or secretaries. He contracted AIDS and fought to keep the diagnosis hidden under the guise of liver cancer, all while using his connections to gain access to AZT clinical trials. In June of 1986, Cohn was disbarred for unethical conduct; in August he died of AIDS complications.

W.H. AUDEN
(WYSTAN HUGH AUDEN)

FEB 21 1907 – SEP 29 1973
(AGED 66)

Poet W.H. AUDEN, winner of a 1948 Pulitzer Prize, was born in York, England in 1907.

He became a collaborator and friend-with-benefits to author Christopher Isherwood in 1925, and after spending time in pre-WWII Berlin, married Erika Mann, daughter of author Thomas Mann, exclusively to secure her English citizenship. Isherwood refused her hand first, suggested Auden, and was affectionately called the "family pimp" by the Manns. Auden went to help at the Spanish Civil War front in 1937, and traveled through China with Isherwood during the Sino-Japanese war in 1938, about which they produced *Journey to a War* (1939). Auden and Isherwood expatriated to the United States together in 1939.

It was in the U.S. that Auden met poet Chester Kallman, calling their relationship a marriage that began with the "honeymoon" of a cross-country journey, though Kallman could not abide Auden's insistence on mutual fidelity, and ended their sexual relationship in 1941. However, they remained friends and lifelong companions, living together from 1953 until Auden's death.

Auden went from a youth of socialist ideals to deep Christian faith in his later life. He died in Vienna in 1973 of congestive heart failure, a leading figure in 20th-century poetry.

EDNA ST. VINCENT MILLAY

FEB 22 1892 – OCT 19 1950
(AGED 58)

American poet, playwright, and essayist, EDNA ST. VINCENT MILLAY won the Pulitzer Prize for Poetry in 1923. Named after St. Vincent's hospital in New York (which had saved her uncle's life), Millay came to national attention in 1912 when her poem "Renascence" was included in *The Lyric Year*, winning 4th place in a poetry contest. However, even the 1st place winner (among many others) felt that Millay's poem was the best entry. The 2nd place winner offered Millay his $250 prize money, and the poem ultimately prompted a benefactor to pay for Millay's attendance at Vassar College.

Bisexual, Millay once answered a personal question by responding, "Oh, you mean I'm homosexual! Of course, I am, and heterosexual too." While at Vassar, Millay was inspired by her love for her friends, one of whom (Dorothy Coleman) died prematurely, prompting the poem "Memorial to D.C." (1920) about friendship and Sapphic love.

Millay married retired importer Eugen Jan Boissevain in 1923, and dedicated her poem "The Pioneer" (1923) to his deceased first wife, feminist Inez Milholland. They maintained an open marriage until Boissevain died of lung cancer in 1949. Millay lived alone until her own death by heart attack the next year.

MALCOLM X
(MALCOLM LITTLE,
EL-HAJJ MALIK EL-SHABAZZ)

MAY 19 1925 – FEB 21 1965
(AGED 39)

A fiery orator for black nationalism, after studying the teachings of Elijah Muhammad in prison, MALCOLM took the name "X" to symbolize his stolen African identity. After prison, Malcolm advocated the liberation of African-Americans "by any means necessary." In 1964 he made a pilgrimage to Mecca and returned with a more moderate philosophy. In 1965, he was shot to death by Nation of Islam rivals. His funeral began on February 23rd and lasted five days.

Recent biographies state Malcolm had sexual encounters with other men, usually for money. Bruce Perry's documents boyhood mutual-masturbatory behavior, maturer nights spent with gay transvestite Willie Mae in Flint, Michigan, and servicing "queers" for money in NYC. Malcolm was also paid by white millionaire William Paul Lennon to rub Lennon with talcum powder until he orgasmed.

The relationship with Lennon is also relayed in historian Manning Marable's book, who cites a memoir by Malcolm's nephew which states Lennon would pay both Malcolm and his friend to rub powder on him. The incident is also present in Malcolm's own autobiography, but with another man doing the massaging (not Malcolm himself). Malcolm later married, and Marable states there's no evidence that he was actively homosexual after 1952.

COLE ALBERT PORTER

JUN 9 1891 – OCT 15 1964
(AGED 73)

COLE PORTER learned the violin at six and the piano at eight. Porter moved to Paris, threw extravagant and scandalous parties, studied at the Schola Cantorum, married Linda Lee Thomas, and wrote songs on commission. His first Broadway hit was *Paris* (1928), and he found success in composing scores to musicals like *Anything Goes* (1934) and *Kiss Me, Kate* (1948), as well as films including *High Society* (1956). Porter's lyrics had style and wit, and he often started with the title of a song and built from there. Porter received a tribute on Ed Sullivan's *Toast of the Town* on February 24th, 1952.

Other meaningful relationships of Porter's included dancer Nelson Barfeld and Californian Robert Bray. He had a love of chorus boys, and an affair with actor Jack Cassidy.

In 1937, while riding in New York, Porter's horse rolled on him and crushed his legs. Crippled and in constant pain, he consistently refused amputation. In 1958, his right leg required amputation due to ulcers from the injury, and after this surgery was performed, Porter never wrote another song. He lived in seclusion, visited occasionally by close friends. He died of kidney failure in 1964.

"TENNESSEE" WILLIAMS
(THOMAS LANIER WILLIAMS III)

MAR 26 1911 – FEB 25 1983
(AGED 71)

"TENNESSEE" WILLIAMS was a Pulitzer Prize-winning American playwright. When Williams was first able to put on a play with an amateur theater group in Memphis, he wrote of the experience, "Then and there the theatre and I found each other for better and for worse. I know it's the only thing that saved my life." It was around this time that he adopted "Tennessee" as his professional name.

During the winter of 1944-1945 his "memory play" *The Glass Menagerie* was produced; it was an instant hit. His next play was another success, *A Streetcar Named Desire* (1947), and from there Williams went on to write multiple Broadway plays,

including *Cat on a Hot Tin Roof* (1955).

His personal life was shadowed by his sister's diagnosis of schizophrenia. She was lobotomized and institutionalized for the majority of her life. Williams also had issues with profound substance abuse. Williams had many relationships with men, including Pancho Rodriguez, Williams's lover from 1946-1948 and the model for the Stanley Kowalski in *A Streetcar Named Desire*, and Frank Merlo, an occasional actor who was the most enduring love of his life. Merlo died of lung cancer in 1963. Williams died from accidental choking in 1983.

CHRISTOPHER "KIT" MARLOWE

FEB 26 1564 (BAPTIZED) – MAY 30 1593
(AGED 29)

English playwright, poet, translator, and contemporary of Shakespeare, CHRISTOPHER MARLOWE'S career was cut short, along with his life, under mysterious circumstances. There are homosexual instances in his poem *Hero and Leander* (c.1593), as well as support for male sexual relationships in his play *Edward II* (c.1592), which depicts a love story between Edward II and Piers Gaveston:

The mightiest kings have had their minions; / Great Alexander loved Hephaestion, / The conquering Hercules for Hylas wept; / And for Patroclus, stern Achilles drooped.

Marlowe was killed in a knife fight over drinks that may have been nothing but a bar brawl, or may have been an assassination ordered by Queen Elizabeth I to silence his alleged atheist rhetoric. Elizabeth I did pardon Marlowe's killer a month after his death, and she is not the only figure who may have wanted Marlowe dead (only the most powerful). There are even thinner conspiracies that speculate Marlowe's death was faked, and that a portion of Shakespeare's output was produced by him in secret. Regardless, his official grave bears a modern headstone inscribed with a quote from his play *The Tragical History of Doctor Faustus* (c.1589): "Cut is the branch that might have grown full straight."

ANGELINA WELD GRIMKÉ

FEB 27 1880 – JUN 10 1958
(AGED 78)

ANGELINA GRIMKÉ was born into a biracial family. Her father Archibald was the second African-American to graduate from Harvard Law School, and her mother Sarah Stanley returned to the Midwest with Angelina after struggling with the strong racial opposition they faced. At the age of seven, Angelina was sent back to remain with her father, and Stanley committed suicide some years later.

In 1902, Grimké began teaching English at the Armstrong Manual Training School, then in 1916 at Dunbar High School, revered for its academic excellence in teachers and students. In her off time, Grimké took classes at Harvard University.

Grimké wrote poems, essays, and short stories, and is counted among the players of the Harlem Renaissance. She wrote *Rachel* (1920), a three-act drama which was one of the first racial violence protest plays, where the character Rachel refuses to marry and have children, as it would only provide more black children for white communities to torment.

Grimké's journals and letters tell of her sexuality and sorrow. At 16 she wrote to her friend Mary P. Burrill, "I hope, darling, that in a few years you will come to me and be my love, my wife!" She died in 1958.

JING OF HAN
(EMPEROR, LIU QI)

188 BC – 141 BC
(AGED 47)

On February 28th, 202 BC, the coronation ceremony of Liu Bang as Emperor Gaozu of Han took place, initiating four centuries of the Han Dynasty's rule over China. As 5th emperor of the Han dynasty, EMPEROR JING's reign was from 157 BC to his death in 141 BC.

Emperor Jing sought to limit the power of feudal kings and princes, causing the Rebellion of the Seven States in 154 BC, an attempt to resist a centralized government. That revolt was crushed by Emperor Jing, who subsequently denied lords the power to appoint/dismiss ministers, or to consolidate their domains in one son (their holdings would be divided amongst all sons). This move centralized authority and led to the glorious reign of Emperor Jing's son, Emperor Wu, 141-87 BC.

Emperor Jing had two Empresses, many Consorts, and even more children. He also had certain male favorites, the most famous of which was Zhou Ren, whose talents at "secret games" played in the bedroom brought him and his family honors, gifts, and aristocracy.

After his death, Emperor Jing was given the title Emperor Xiaojing, meaning "filial and decisive." He is buried in the tomb mound at the Yangling mausoleum in the Shaanxi Province.

VIOLET TREFUSIS
(VIOLET KEPPEL)

JUN 6 1894 – FEB 29 1972
(AGED 77)

Violet Keppel and her sister grew up around royalty and nobility, as their mother Alice was the favorite mistress of King Edward VII. In 1919, Violet married Denys Trefusis, an officer in the Royal Horse Guards, and they were together platonically until his death from tuberculosis in 1929. VIOLET TREFUSIS was awarded the Legion of Honour for her work in broadcasting on behalf of the liberation of France during WWII. She also wrote popular novels, plays, poems, memoirs, and essays, in addition to appearing as a character in other writers' novels.

At age 10, Trefusis met Vita Sackville-West at a party, and the two bonded over their loves of horses and books. They wrote romantic letters to each other, and were together in Italy as teenagers when Trefusis gave Sackville-West a ring as a token of their relationship. They continued to correspond, and found time for occasional weekend getaways from their spouses. Their relationship was the basis for the characters of Orlando and Sasha in Virginia Woolf's novel *Orlando* (1928). Trefusis later had a relationship with sewing machine heiress Winnaretta Singer. As journalist Joseph Alsop asserted in rhyme, "Mrs. Trefusis never refuses."

Trefusis died of starvation from a malabsorption disease.

MARCH

1st

START OF WOMEN'S HISTORY
MONTH, U.S., U.K., AUSTRALIA

MERCEDES HEDE DE ACOSTA

MAR 1 1893 – MAY 9 1968
(AGED 75)

MERCEDES DE ACOSTA was a playwright as well as a screenwriter. She had poems published in *Poetry* magazine, and her published poetry collections spoke to sexual desires, love, and life. She was a vegetarian and refused to wear furs, campaigned for women's suffrage, and studied Hinduism. Actress Tallulah Bankhead named de Acosta 'Countess Dracula' for her slicked-back black hair, her red lips, and her penchant for wearing capes.

Alice B. Toklas wrote, "Say what you will about Mercedes, she's had the most important women of the twentieth century." Mercedes de Acosta was called "a professional lesbian," "that furious lesbian," and "a lover to the stars." She had relationships with actresses Eva Le Gallienne, Alla Nazimova, Greta Garbo, Marlene Dietrich, Ona Munson, Russian ballerina Tamara Platonovna Karsavina, and dancer Isadora Duncan. Her memoir *Here Lies the Heart* (1960) implies some of these relationships, and though nothing was explicit, de Acosta was still called a liar and her friendships with Le Gallienne and Garbo were severed. She was married to painter Abram Poole from 1920-1935. Mercedes de Acosta died in 1968 and is buried in Trinity Cemetery in Washington Heights, New York City.

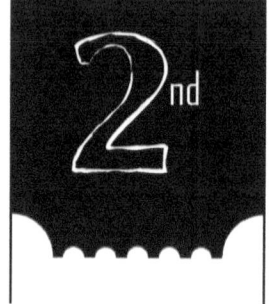

LAURENCE MICHAEL DILLON
(LAURA MAUD DILLON, LOBZANG JIVAKA)

MAY 1 1915 – MAY 15 1962
(AGED 47)

British physician LAURENCE MICHAEL DILLON was the first trans man to undergo phalloplasty, and is often dubbed "the first man-made man."

Educated at the all-girls St. Anne's College, Dillon worked as a garage hand until a doctor agreed to administer male hormone pills. In 1942, Dillon underwent a mastectomy, and in 1944 amended his birth certificate to read Laurence Michael, son. Quickly disinherited by his father, Dillon entered medical school at Trinity College Dublin in 1945. During holidays he underwent surgeries to complete his physical transition with plastic surgeon Sir Harold Gillis, who along with Dillon would later perform surgeries for the U.K.'s first male-to-female transsexual, Roberta Cowell.

Medically and socially, Dillon's surgeries were disguised under hypospadias, a condition in males where the urinary opening is not at the usual location on the head of the penis. When it was discovered that Laura Maude had been replaced by Laurence Michael as heir to his brother's baronetcy, Dillon avoided attention by fleeing to India. There he was later ordained as a Tibetan Buddhist monk on March 2nd, 1959, one of the first Westerners granted the honor. At Rizong Monastery, he wrote and studied until his death from ill health at 47.

ADRIAN
(ADRIAN ADOLPH GREENBERG, GILBERT ADRIAN)

MAR 3 1903 – SEP 13 1959
(AGED 56)

ADRIAN studied at the New York School for Fine and Applied Arts in 1920, and transferred to the Paris campus in 1922. His first costume designing credit was for Irving Berlin's *Music Box Revue* (1921). Adrian then designed costumes for the films *A Sainted Devil* (1924) and *What Price Beauty* (1925), before becoming head costume designer for Cecil B. DeMille's studio, then chief costume designer for Metro-Goldwyn-Mayer in 1928. He created costumes for over 200 films.

His regular screen credit read "Gowns by Adrian." He created extravagant evening gowns for stars including Greta Garbo, Jean Harlow, and Joan Crawford. His style influenced fashion trends, with large shoulder pads on many of Crawford's outfits, as well as Garbo's Eugénie hat in the film *Romance* (1930). Adrian famously costumed *The Wizard of Oz* (1939), and created Judy Garland's red-sequined ruby slippers. Adrian left MGM to start his own fashion house, only returning to the studio to design for *Lovely to Look At* in 1952.

Adrian lived as an openly gay man, but married actress Janet Gaynor in 1939, a relationship that benefited both of them during Hollywood's anti-gay Hays Code. They had one son. Adrian died of a heart attack in 1959.

JEAN O'LEARY

MAR 4 1948 – JUN 4 2005
(AGED 57)

Founder of the Lesbian Feminist Liberation, and co-founder of National Coming Out Day, JEAN O'LEARY ran away from a marriage proposal after high school to live in a convent. At the Sisters of the Holy Humility of Mary, according to Jean, she was "always in love" and involved in at least eight affairs, including a particularly deep one with a postulant mistress. O'Leary left the convent as a Religious Sister, never completing the training.

In 1971, she moved to Brooklyn and got involved with the gay rights movement. In 1973, O'Leary's aim for feminist liberation put her at odds with Sylvia Rivera at the Christopher Street Liberation Day, when she opposed the idea of men dressing as women for entertainment. O'Leary later came to see that effort as misplaced: "How could I work to exclude transvestites and at the same time criticize the feminists who were doing their best back in those days to exclude lesbians?"

O'Leary served on the Democratic National Committee for 12 years, and in the 1980s worked with the National Gay Rights Advocates, which used aggressive litigation to the benefit of AIDS patients. She died of cancer in 2005, survived by her partner and their children.

LILI ELBE
(EINAR MAGNUS ANDREAS WEGENER, LILI ILSE ELVENES)

DEC 28 1882 – SEP 13 1931
(AGED 48)

Danish painter LILI ELBE was one of the first documented recipients of sex reassignment surgery. Her autobiography, *Man into Woman*, was posthumously published in 1933, and inspired another book, *The Danish Girl* (2001), and the 2015 movie of the same name.

Born Einar Wegener, she studied at the Royal Danish Academy, and married fellow artist Gerda Gottlieb in 1904. While modeling women's clothes for Gerda, Einar felt the presence of Lili, and eventually lived openly as a woman. On March 5th, 1930, Lili began a series of operations to remove her male organs, construct a female appearance, and implant ovaries. A female passport was granted that same year, and the Wegener's marriage was dissolved.

Lili began a relationship with a French art dealer, with whom she wanted to marry and have children. Her final surgery involved a uterus transplantation, which caused rejection of the foreign tissue, infection, and eventual death from cardiac arrest. Aware she was dying, Lili wrote, "That I, Lili, am vital and have a right to life I have proved by living for fourteen months. It may be said that fourteen months is not much, but they seem to me like a whole and happy human life."

KARL FRIEDRICH ALEXANDER,
KÖNIG VON WÜRTTEMBERG
(CHARLES I, KING OF WÜRTTEMBERG)

MAR 6 1823 – OCT 6 1891
(AGED 68)

Born in the Kingdom of Württemberg, KARL married Grand Duchess Olga Nikolaievna of Russia in 1846, but produced no children. He succeeded his father in 1864.

In 1888, he became the subject of scandal. International papers published a story about American men being granted titles and gifts by the King, one of whom was Richard Mason Jackson (known as "Mase"). The *New York Herald* reprinted a story from its European edition, saying these men had the king in thrall, were spending his money lavishly, and referred to Jackson as "one of the three gentlemen who are now playing Piers Gaveston parts in Germany" (Gaveston being the lover of English King Edward II). The article stated: "The story is so sensational that it reminds one of the late unfortunate Bavarian King Ludwig" (also homosexual).

One of the other Americans, Charles Woodcock, was elevated to Baron in 1888. Karl and Charles would often appear in public together, dressed identically. Eventually the publicity forced Woodcock to return to America. Years later, Karl found masculine companionship again with the technical director of the royal theater, Wilhelm George.

Karl died in 1891, and was succeeded as King of Württemberg by his sister's son, William II.

LORD BYRON
(BARON GEORGE GORDON BYRON)

JAN 22 1788 – APR 19 1824
(AGED 36)

British poet and politician, LORD BYRON was born with a clubfoot, about which he was always sensitive. He's best known for his autobiographical *Childe Harold's Pilgrimage* (1812-1918), his satiric *Don Juan* (1819-1824), and as a notorious figure in the Romantic movement.

Byron's first love was the already-engaged Mary Chaworth. He next experienced "a violent, though pure, love and passion" for a young chorister, John Edleston. In 1811, both Byron's mother and Edleston died. On March 7th, 1812, Byron published "Lines to a Lady Weeping" anonymously, a political criticism in lyric form, his specialty.

Byron married in 1815 for long enough to sire a daughter, before his affairs caused an acrid separation. He left England in 1816 in self-imposed exile, and took up with the Shelleys—Percy Bysshe, Mary Shelley, and Claire Clairmont, Mary's step-sister. In Switzerland, Mary began *Frankenstein* (1818), their friend Dr. Polidori produced *The Vampyre* (1819, first of the romantic vampire genre), and Claire conceived Byron's second daughter, Allegra.

In 1822, Allegra and Percy Bysshe Shelley both died. Byron attended Shelley's funeral before sailing to Greece to assist their revolution against Turkish rule. His final infatuation was with Greek page Lukas Chalandritsanos, before his death from fever in 1824.

SOFIA VASILYEVNA KOVALEVSKAYA
(SONIA KOVALEVSKY)

JAN 15 1850 – FEB 10 1891
(AGED 41)

Born in Moscow, SOFIA KOVA-LEVSKAYA was a mathematician, writer, and women's rights proponent who contributed significantly to analysis, partial differential equations, and mechanics. She was the first woman to receive a doctorate in Mathematics in Europe, to edit a scientific journal, and to be appointed as a professor of Mathematics. She's regularly honored on March 8th in Russia on International Women's Day.

Kovalevskaya entered a "fictitious" marriage to young paleontologist Vladimir Kovalevsky in 1868, at age 18. This was done so that her husband could grant her permission to study abroad. They agreed to live together as no more than fellow students, but nevertheless had a daughter in 1878, separated in 1881, and Vladimir committed suicide in 1883. After their separation, Sofia moved to Sweden, changed her name to Sonia, and began writing, including her coming-of-age novel *Nihilist Girl* (1892).

Her writing inspiration was Swedish actress, novelist, and playwright Anne Charlotte Leffler, whose brother helped to secure Kovalevskaya a professorship. They collaborated on plays, Kovalevskaya's memoir *A Russian Childhood* (1890), and maintained a close "romantic friendship" until Kovalevskaya's death from influenza. Leffler's final book was a biography of Kovalevskaya, written before her own death from appendicitis in 1892.

ROBERT MAPPLETHORPE

Nov 4 1946 – Mar 9 1989
(AGED 42)

A giant of 20th century photography, ROBERT MAPPLETHORPE is best known for his large black-and-white captures of celebrities, flowers, self-portraiture, athletes, and nudes. His most controversial photos were those depicting New York City's underground BDSM scene.

Born in Queens, Mapplethorpe was an intimate companion of singer Patti Smith, living with her for a time in Manhattan's Chelsea Hotel, and taking what eventually became the cover photo for her 1975 album, *Horses*. As his success rose, Mapplethorpe worked as a photographer for Andy Warhol's *Interview* magazine. In 1972, he met millionaire Sam Wagstaff, initially Mapplethorpe's lover, then his patron and lifelong friend.

In 1977, Mapplethorpe became lovers with *Drummer* magazine editor Jack Fritscher, who introduced him to the Mineshaft, a member's-only BDSM club that was considered the "definitive S&M club" of New York's Meatpacking district. During this time, Mapplethorpe was also being sought after as a portrait photographer for cultural luminaries such as fashion designer Carolina Herrera, bodybuilder Arnold Schwarzenegger, actress Susan Sarandon, singers Iggy Pop and Grace Jones, writers William S. Burroughs and Truman Capote, among others.

Mapplethorpe went public with his 1986 AIDS diagnosis, and died in 1989 of AIDS-related complications. He was 42 years old.

FELICE RAHEL SCHRAGENHEIM

MAR 9 1922 – MAR 1945
(AGED ~23)

A Jewish resistance fighter in Berlin during WWII, FELICE SCHRAGENHEIM is known for her tragic love affair with Elisabeth "Lilly" Wust, wife of a Nazi officer and mother of four sons. Their story inspired the book (1994) and German film (1999), *Aimée and Jaguar*.

Orphaned before the war, Schragenheim intended to emigrate to Chicago, but several ships failed to set sail, trapping her in Berlin. She met Wust through Inge Wolf, Wust's nanny and Schragenheim's lover. Dressed always in pants, she wooed Wust, confided to her that she was Jewish, and was sheltered by Wust until the Gestapo dragged her from Wust's apartment on August 21st, 1944. She was eventually deported to Auschwitz, from which she presumably died on a death march. The grave her family chose lists her death as March, 1945. March 10th is the day after her birthday.

Wust later said she never loved again: "I was like a snail climbing back into its shell." Wust was given the Order of the Federal Republic of Germany for helping shelter Schragenheim and three other Jewish women after her deportation. In 1995, Wust received one of Israel's highest honors, the same awarded to Oskar Schindler, "Righteous Among the Nations."

SYLVESTER
(SYLVESTER JAMES, JR.)

Sep 6 1947 – Dec 16 1988
(AGED 41)

After performing in the drag troupe The Cockettes, SYLVESTER found success as a solo artist, becoming known as the "Queen of Disco." His album *Step II* in 1978 was certified gold, and his falsetto tones topped the charts worldwide. His hit songs include "You Make Me Feel (Mighty Real)" and "Dance (Disco Heat)."

During a San Francisco performance, Sylvester was awarded the key to the city by Mayor Dianne Feinstein, along with the proclamation that March 11th was Sylvester Day.

Sylvester's style was flamboyant, colorful, and chic, with attire gendered male and female. Of his gay icon and spokesman status, Sylvester said, "I realize that gay people have put me on a pedestal and I love it." He had relationships with model John Maley, hairdresser Tom Daniels, and architect Rick Cranmer, who died of AIDS-related complications in 1987. Sylvester died the following year, suffering the same fate.

Sylvester planned his funeral to take place at the Love Center church. His body was dressed in a red kimono, music was performed by Jeanie Tracy, and his makeup applied by friend Yvette Flunder. In his will, Sylvester had all future music sales donated to Project Open Hand and the AIDS Emergency Fund.

EDWARD ALBEE
(EDWARD FRANKLIN ALBEE III)

MAR 12 1928 – SEP 16 2016
(AGED 88)

EDWARD ALBEE was given up for adoption two weeks after he was born. He was expelled and dismissed from high school, military school, and college, though he graduated from a private prep school in 1946. Albee left home as a teen and moved to Greenwich Village, where he held odd jobs and wrote plays.

His first play, *The Zoo Story* (1958), was written in three weeks and won the 1960 Obie award. He received three Pulitzer Prizes for Drama, his play *Who's Afraid of Virginia Woolf?* (1962) won the Tony Award for Best Play, and was also selected for the Pulitzer Prize, though

trustees overruled the decision, objecting to its profanity; no Pulitzer was awarded that year. Albee's prolific playwriting gained him numerous accolades, including the National Medal of Arts in 1996.

Albee knew he was gay at the age of 12-and-a-half. He never considered himself a gay writer, but "a writer who happens to be gay." He met playwright Terrence McNally while sharing a cab ride, and they spent the next four years together. His longtime partner was sculptor Jonathan Thomas; they were together from 1971 to Thomas's death in 2005. Albee died after a short illness in 2016.

SPRING DELL BYINGTON

Oct 17 1886 – Sep 7 1971
(AGED 84)

After a brief stint of newspaper journalism, SPRING BYINGTON started acting in New York City, stating "I can't do anything else very well." Byington worked in repertory theater, touring Argentina with American plays translated into Spanish. Her first performance on Broadway was in 1924, and she continued to work onstage, in films, and in radio. She was perhaps best known for her starring television role of the widow Lily Ruskin in her sitcom, *December Bride* (1954-1959), as well as Mrs. Jones in the Jones Family movies between 1936-1940, starting with *Every Saturday Night* which premiered on March 13th, 1936.

Byington was married to her theater troupe manager, Roy Chandler. They had two children together, and divorced in 1920. Her later engagement to an Argentinian industrialist ended with his unexpected death. Byington was reported to have had an affair with the actress and writer Maude Adams, and had a long-term relationship with actress Marjorie Main. Main and Byington lived together in Los Angeles. When asked in an interview about Byington's sexual orientation, Main stated, "It's true, she didn't have much use for men." Byington died of colorectal cancer in 1971.

SYLVIA BEACH
(NANCY WOODBRIDGE BEACH)

MAR 14 1887 – OCT 5 1962
(AGED 75)

SYLVIA BEACH lived in Paris and Bridgeton, New Jersey as a child. She returned to Europe to study languages, to work for the Balkan Commission of the Red Cross, and to study French Literature at the Sorbonne. Beach entered the Paris bookshop La Maison des Amis des Livres while conducting some research, and met the owner Adrienne Monnier, who quickly became the love of her life and business partner.

Monnier helped Beach open an English language bookshop and lending library named Shakespeare and Company, where Beach offered hospitality, encouragement, and books.

Beach published James Joyce's *Ulysses* in 1922, was awarded a Knight of the Legion of Honour in 1937, and kept the bookshop running during Nazi occupation in 1939.

After refusing to sell a Nazi the last copy of *Finnegan's Wake* (1939) and him threatening to confiscate all books, she and her friends hid the books, dismantled the shop, and painted over the sign. She spent six months in a Nazi internment camp in Vittel until her secured release in 1942. She wrote the memoir *Shakespeare and Company* in 1956, had a relationship with Camilla Steinbrugge, whom she met in Vittel. She died in 1962.

JOHN B. MCLEMORE
(JOHN BROOKS MCLEMORE)

❦

MAR 15 1966 − JUN 22 2015
(AGED 49)

The instigator and eventual subject of the record-breaking serial podcast *S-Town* (2017), JOHN B. MCLEMORE was a lifelong resident of Woodstock, Alabama, an antique horologist and clock restorer, as well as a considerable character.

After sending emails to the staff of *This American Life* asking for an investigation into an alleged murder in his hometown, which he called "Shit Town," the murder was disproved. However, while the story about Woodstock and its mysteries was still under production, McLemore committed suicide. From there the story became an exploration of his life, the aftermath of his death, and the small town he railed against so verbosely while alive.

Describing himself, McLemore said he was "unmarried, sort of, ahem, like ahem—let's just say I might be a fan of David Sedaris." His friend put it another way, saying McLemore "might have had a little sugar in his tank." According to interviewer Brian Reed, McLemore never called himself "gay," but instead used terms like semi-homosexual, semi-practicing homosexual, or celibate homosexual. McLemore ended his life by drinking potassium cyanide at age 49, leaving his mother, his estate containing a newly planted hedge maze, and his legacy to be tended to by his survivors.

SYBILLE BEDFORD
(FREIIN SYBILLE ALEID ELSA VON SCHOENEBECK)

MAR 16 1911 – FEB 17 2006
(AGED 94)

SYBILLE BEDFORD was living in Italy when she wrote an article criticizing the Nazi regime in Klaus Mann's literary magazine *Die Sammlung*. Bedford's German bank accounts were frozen and she was unable to renew her passport, but Aldous Huxley's wife Maria had a plan for escape. She proposed a marriage of convenience by saying, "We need to get one of our bugger friends," and Sybille married English Army officer Walter "Terry" Bedford to obtain a British passport and flee to safety.

After spending a year traveling in Mexico, Bedford produced her first published book, *The Sudden View: a Mexican Journey* (1953). Her second book, *A Legacy* (1956), was a semi-autobiographical novel about her and her father's life in Germany. She continued to write novels, nonfiction books, and travelogues, as well as work as a legal reporter, covering the Jack Ruby trial and the "most hilarious" trial of *R v. Penguin Books Ltd* regarding the obscenity charges against D.H. Lawrence's *Lady Chatterley's Lover* (1928).

Bedford had many relationships with women, including one with Evelyn W. Gendel, who left her husband for Bedford. Bedford died of natural causes at a hospital near her London home in 2006.

JOHN WAYNE GACY JR.

MAR 17 1942 – MAY 10 1994
(AGED 52)

JOHN WAYNE GACY gave children a legitimate reason to fear clowns. Gacy managed fried chicken restaurants, had a family, did charity work, started his own construction company, shook hands with First Lady of the United States Rosalynn Carter, and dressed as a clown for fundraisers and children's hospitals. "Pogo" was his main clown persona.

Gacy lured young men and boys to his house where he would handcuff, rape, and torture them before strangling them to death. He buried their bodies in the crawl space of his house, dumping some in the river when they no longer fit. Authorities investigated Gacy after victim Robert Piest's disappearance, and learned of Gacy's previous sodomy and battery charges. Gacy became friendly with his police surveillance, inviting them to dinner and telling them of his businesses and clowning activities, saying on one occasion to officers, "You know…clowns can get away with murder."

Gacy's crimes were discovered when an investigator stopped for a bathroom break at Gacy's house, and after flushing the toilet, found a distinct rotting corpse smell. Gacy was found guilty of 33 murders and sentenced to death. He died by lethal injection and his reported last words were, "Kiss my ass."

WILFRED OWEN
(WILFRED EDWARD SALTER OWEN)

MAR 18 1893 – NOV 4 1918
(AGED 25)

WILFRED OWEN was one of the leading poets of the First World War. He was virtually unknown at the time of his death on the battlefield, exactly one week (almost to the hour) before the signing of the Armistice that ended the war. Owens was promoted to the rank of Lieutenant the day after his death, and awarded the Military Cross for participating in the breaking of the Hindenburg Line at Joncourt in October, 1918. Some of his best-known poems are "Dulce et Decorum est," "Insensibility," and "Anthem for Doomed Youth." Most of his poems were published posthumously.

Owen's poems highlighting the horrors of trench and gas warfare were heavily influenced by his mentor, Siegfried Sassoon, whom he met while undergoing shell-shock treatment at the Craiglockhart War Hospital in Edinburgh. Owen was homosexual, and through his hero-worship of Sassoon, was introduced to a sophisticated homosexual literary circle which included Oscar Wilde's friend Robbie Ross. Owen and Sassoon met for the last time in August of 1918, after Sassoon was shot in the head and sent back to England to recover. They had what Sassoon called the "whole of a hot cloudless afternoon together," and never saw each other again.

ELLEN GATES STARR

MAR 19 1859 – FEB 10 1940
(AGED 80)

ELLEN GATES STARR attended the Rockford Female Seminary from 1877-1878, but was forced to leave due to financial problems. Starr went on to teach in Chicago for 10 years. During a visit to London, Starr witnessed the success of the English Settlement movement and became interested in setting up a similar movement in Chicago.

Starr and her partner Jane Addams, whom she met at Rockford, founded Hull House in 1889. Hull House provided continuing education and social opportunities for working-class citizens, as well as daycare and education for children. All who passed through their doors were treated with respect, and there was no discrimination as to age, language, race, or creed.

Starr campaigned to reform child labor laws, was a member of the Women's Trade Union League, founded the Chicago Public School Art Society and was president of the organization until 1897, when she founded the Chicago Society of Arts and Crafts.

Starr and Addams lived together, and their friendship lasted many years. Addams later struck up a relationship with Starr's former student, Mary Rozet Smith. Starr retired to a Roman Catholic convent in 1931, where she was cared for until her death in 1940.

LORD ALFRED DOUGLAS
(ALFRED BRUCE "BOSIE" DOUGLAS)

OCT 22 1870 – MAR 20 1945
(AGED 74)

ALFRED DOUGLAS was the third son of the 9th Marquess of Queensberry (of the Queensberry boxing rules) and his first wife, who nicknamed her favorite son "Bosie" (a derivative of "boysie"), an endearment that would follow Douglas for the rest of his life. Douglas is best known as the lover of Oscar Wilde, and for the phrase he coined in 1894, "the love that dare not speak its name."

Douglas met Wilde in 1891, beginning a tempestuous relationship that would provoke a fight with Douglas's father and eventually end Wilde's career. They reunited occasionally after Wilde's release from prison but never fully reconciled. Douglas got into an altercation with Robbie Ross at Wilde's funeral, beginning a bitter rivalry between these former lovers of Wilde that would last until Ross's death.

Douglas married bisexual poet and heiress Olive Eleanor Custance in 1902 and had one son, Raymond, who would ultimately die in a mental asylum, diagnosed with schizoaffective disorder. Douglas converted to Roman Catholicism in 1911, which further strained his marriage and sent him on a campaign against homosexuality, Robbie Ross, and the memory of Wilde. Douglas died of congestive heart failure in 1945 and was buried alongside his mother.

JOAN ANN WERNER LAURIE

NOV 17 1920 – MAR 21 1964
(AGED 43)

JOAN LAURIE was born in Marylebone, London. She attended finishing school in Switzerland and married Paul Clifford Seyler in May of 1942. They had a son, Nicholas, in 1946, after which Paul Seyler left Britain and disappeared. Laurie worked at her father's publishing company, T. Werner Laurie Ltd, as a production editor. She also joined the Women's Royal Naval Service during World War II, working as a clerk and as a driver. After the war, Laurie worked at a Society for Promoting Christian Knowledge bookshop.

Laurie then became editor of the periodical *She*. From the first issue in March 1955, the magazine's motto was "young,

gay, elegant." It promoted risqué, unconventional portraits of women, and tackled subjects like abortions and hysterectomies, along with carpentry and cooking recipes.

Laurie met broadcaster and journalist Nancy Spain in 1950, and they were regulars at the lesbian nightclub, Gateways or "The Gates" in Chelsea. Spain and Laurie lived together and raised their sons in a house they shared with rally driver Sheila Van Damm. Laurie and Spain were traveling by plane to the Aintree racecourse for Spain to cover the 1964 Grand National when their plane crashed. They were cremated in London.

LÁSZLÓ ALMÁSY
(LÁSZLÓ EDE ALMÁSY DE ZSADÁNY ET TÖRÖKSZENTMIKLÓS, COUNT ALMÁSY)

AUG 22 1895 – MAR 22 1951
(AGED 55)

LÁSZLÓ ALMÁSY was a Hungarian pilot during WWI, shot down over Northern Italy in March of 1918. He spent the rest of the war working as a flight instructor, and afterwards became the personal secretary of the Bishop of Szombathely, where he was mistaken by the King of Hungary as Count Almásy, a made-up title Almásy then used to his advantage. Almásy raced cars for Steyr Automobile, was reported dead after surviving another plane crash, and organized multiple expeditions to seek the mythical city Zerzura.

Almásy discovered and catalogued prehistoric rock art sites (including the Cave of Swimmers), reestablished contact with the Magyarab tribe, smuggled Nazi agents through the Libyan Desert, and received the Iron Cross. He was arrested for war crimes based primarily on his own book, *With Rommel's Army in Libya* (1943), but was acquitted when it turned out neither the judge nor prosecutor had read it.

After correspondence was discovered in Germany in 2010, it was learned Almásy had a loving and sexual relationship with the soldier Hans Entholt, who later died by stepping on a landmine. The letters also confirmed Almásy had relationships with a number of Egyptian princes. Almásy died of amoebic dysentery in 1951.

POPE JULIUS III
(GIOVANNI MARIA CIOCCHI DEL MONTE)

SEP 10 1487 – MAR 23 1555
(AGED 67)

POPE JULIUS III started life as Giovanni Maria Ciocchi del Monte, born in Monte San Savino, Tuscany. He studied law, served as bishop of Pavia, was twice governor of Rome, and barely escaped execution while a hostage in the Sack of Rome in 1527. In 1536 he was made Cardinal-bishop of Palestrina by Pope Paul III, and when Paul III died, del Monte was elected Pope and took the name Julius III. Pope Julius III spent most of his time and papal money on entertaining at Villa Giulia, a villa he had commissioned.

Pope Julius III came across a teenaged beggar he named Innocenzo Ciocchi del Monte, a good-looking illiterate boy between the ages of 14-17. Julius III originally put del Monte in charge of his pet monkey, later adopting him as his nephew, and bestowing upon him the rank of cardinal. Julius III and del Monte shared a bedroom. Italian historian and cardinal librarian Onofrio Panvinio characterized Julius III as *"puerorum amoribus implicitus"* or entangled in love for boys. Julius III died in 1555. Innocenzo was less than innocent in the end, murdering two men in Nocera Umbria who spoke ill towards him, and raping two women in Brevia.

JAMES CHARLES STUART
(KING JAMES I OF ENGLAND AND IRELAND, KING JAMES VI OF SCOTLAND)

JUN 19 1566 – MAR 27 1625
(AGED 58)

On March 24th, 1603, KING JAMES VI OF SCOTLAND became King James I of England, uniting the English and Scottish crowns. The only son of Mary Queen of Scots, he commissioned the Bible translation that bears his name, married Anne of Denmark in 1589, and produced seven children whose descendants still wear England's crown.

Evidence of the king's homosexuality comes from letters written to three male favorites, most remarkably those to George Villiers, 1st Duke of Buckingham, whom James greets as "my sweet child and wife." Commentators throughout the ages have called the letters indecent and repulsive, but James stated publicly, "You may be sure that I love the Earl of Buckingham more than anyone else, and more than you who are here assembled. I wish to speak in my own behalf and not to have it thought to be a defect, for Jesus Christ did the same, and therefore I cannot be blamed. Christ had John, and I have George."

Ill of health, King James died during a bout of dysentery, with Villiers at his side. A portrait of the handsome Villiers by Peter Paul Rubens was rediscovered in 2017, after it had been missing for 400 years.

GERALD CLERY MURPHY

MAR 25 1888 – OCT 17 1964
(AGED 76)

Born in Boston to the Mark Cross leather goods family, GERALD MURPHY married Sara Sherman Wiborg of the manufacturing Wibogs in 1915. They moved to Paris with their three children in 1921, and soon after the French Riviera, to live as expats and inspirations. Their influence is portrayed in many works of art, including Pablo Picasso's painting *Woman in White* (1923), Ernest Hemingway's short story "Snows of Kilimanjaro" (1936), Archibald MacLeish's play *J.B.* (1958), but most conspicuously in F. Scott Fitzgerald's novel *Tender Is the Night* (1934).

Art historian John Richardson writes, "Murphy had a repressed homosexual side, which he called his 'defects' in a 1931 letter to Archibald MacLeish, saying that his post-adolescent life 'has been a process of concealment of the personal realities.'" He struggled with his desires while remaining married throughout his life.

In 1929, the Murphy's son Patrick developed tuberculosis. Gerald gave up painting and unhappily took up the family business again in 1934. In 1935, their older son, Baoth, died suddenly of spinal meningitis developed from a case of measles. Patrick died in 1937. The Murphys never lived in Europe again. Gerald died in 1964, and Sara in 1975. Only their daughter, Honoria, survived them.

A.E. HOUSMAN
(ALFRED EDWARD HOUSMAN)

MAR 26 1859 – APR 30 1936
(AGED 77)

Born in Worcestershire, England, A.E. HOUSMAN attended Oxford to study the classics. At university, he met his greatest friends, brothers Moses and Adalbert Jackson. He also unexpectedly flunked his final exams after years of stellar performance.

After Oxford, he moved in with the Jackson brothers and took a job as a Patent Office clerk in London. Living frugally, Housman continued to translate and publish scholarly papers, eventually becoming so prolific he secured a job as a professor. Housman's unrequited love for Moses Jackson never ended, and caused him great pain when Moses married, moved abroad, and eventually died.

A stern Latin professor, Housman is best known for his sentimental and neatly rhyming poetry collection, *A Shropshire Lad* (1896). After A.E. Housman's death, his brother Laurence (also homosexual) revealed, "I doubt whether Moses ever kissed AEH: but I have no doubt that AJJ did." Adalbert Jackson died even younger than Moses, leaving Housman alone. Housman kept their portraits hanging together in his rooms at Cambridge until his own death. When Laurence asked who Moses was, the incredibly private Housman gave his most revealing answer: "That was my friend Jackson, the man who had more influence on my life than anyone else."

FARLEY GRANGER
(FARLEY EARLE GRANGER JR.)

JUL 1 1925 – MAR 27 2011
(AGED 85)

FARLEY GRANGER is known for his roles in Alfred Hitchcock's movies *Rope* (1948), a fictionalized retelling of the Leopold and Loeb crime, and *Strangers on a Train* (1951), based on the novel by Patricia Highsmith. Granger began acting during WWII, saying later, "The war was on, and men were in short supply." Not yet 18, he was cast in 1943's *The North Star*.

Granger's career paused when he enlisted in the Navy. "Chronically seasick," he served on shore in Honolulu. Granger's 2007 memoir *Include Me Out*, written with partner Robert Calhoun, states that in Honolulu at age 21, "I lost my virginity twice in one night," first with a female prostitute, and then before leaving the premises with a male Navy officer. He went on to have affairs with Shelley Winters and Ava Gardner, as well as with Arthur Laurents and Leonard Bernstein, the writer and composer respectively of *West Side Story* (1957).

Granger ultimately bought out his studio contract to study acting and perform live theater. He met production assistant Robert Calhoun while working with Eva Le Gallienne's repertory troupe. They were together until Calhoun's death from cancer in 2008. Granger died of natural causes in 2011.

DIRK BOGARDE
(SIR DEREK JULES GASPARD ULRIC NIVEN VAN DEN BOGAERDE)

MAR 28 1921 – MAY 8 1999
(AGED 78)

British leading man of the 1950s, DIRK BOGARDE made his stage debut in 1939, but his career was put on hold with the outbreak of WWI. Bogarde served as an intelligence officer, was eventually awarded seven medals, and rose to the rank of Major. He was present at the liberation of the Bergen-Belsen death camp, likening the experience to "peering into Dante's Inferno."

Bogarde signed a long-term contract with Britain's J. Arthur Rank studio in 1948. He worked there for 12 years, starring in three of their popular "Doctor in The House" comedies. When his contract ended, Bogarde decided to pursue more challenging roles in arthouse films. He played a blackmailed gay lawyer in *Victim* (1961), the pederastic Gustav von Aschenbach in *Death in Venice* (1971), and a former SS officer in a sexual relationship with a Holocaust survivor in *The Night Porter* (1974).

Bogarde started writing in the late 1970s, penning a series of novels, essays, and memoirs. He was knighted in 1992. He lived with his longtime companion and manager Anthony Forwood for years, publicly insisting that their relationship was platonic. Forwood died in 1988 of liver cancer, and Bogarde died in 1999 from a heart attack.

JEANNE-PAULE MARIE "JEANNINE" DECKERS
(SISTER LUC-GABRIELLE, THE SINGING NUN, LUC DOMINIQUE)

OCT 17 1933 – MAR 29 1985
(AGED 51)

JEANNE-PAULE DECKERS was born in a Brussels suburb and planned on becoming a nun from a young age, though she also trained as a teacher. In 1959 Deckers entered a convent in Waterloo and took the name Sister Luc-Gabrielle. Deckers played the guitar from her days as a Girl Scout, and she wrote and performed her own music in the convent. She became so popular that her superiors had Deckers record an album in 1961 that could be purchased by visitors to the convent.

Her album sold close to two million copies in 1962. She appeared on television and performed concerts. Deckers reported she had been forced out of the convent in 1966 due to personality clashes and financial issues. Due to her recording contract, Deckers was unable to perform under her former names, so her musical career continued as Luc Dominique.

Deckers met Anne Pécher while she was working as a camp counselor and Pécher was a camper. Pécher visited Decker's convent often, and they later lived together in an apartment. According to Deckers' diaries, a sexual relationship began between them around 1980. Citing financial difficulties, Deckers and Pécher committed suicide with an overdose of barbiturates in 1985.

PAUL-MARIE VERLAINE

MAR 30 1844 – JAN 8 1896
(AGED 51)

PAUL VERLAINE was a French poet in the Decadent movement of the late 19th century, along with Stéphane Mallarmé and Charles Baudelaire. In 1869, he fell in love with Mathilde Mauté, aged 16, and they married in 1870. After the birth of his son in 1872, Verlaine abandoned his family to tramp through northern France and Belgium with poet Arthur Rimbaud, with whom he carried on a volatile sexual affair.

After briefly attempting a reconciliation with his wife, Verlaine ran off with Rimbaud again. In 1873, a quarrel with Rimbaud in Brussels ended with Verlaine firing two shots, wounding Rimbaud in the wrist. Verlaine served over 18 months in prison as a result of this incident. A plaque commemorates the spot where the fight took place, and the gun Verlaine used sold for £368,000 ($460,000) at auction in 2016.

After separating from both his family and Rimbaud, in 1877 Verlaine fell in love with a student of his, Lucien Létinois, who died of typhus in 1883. In his final years, Verlaine lived in slums and spent his days drinking absinthe in Paris cafes until his death in 1896. His notable works include "Sagesse," "Confessions, notes autobiographiques," and "Les Poètes maudits."

LUCY HICKS ANDERSON
(LUCY, TOBIAS LAWSON)

1886 – 1954
(AGED ~68)

LUCY HICKS ANDERSON was born Tobias Lawson in Waddy, Kentucky. She took the name Lucy in high school and wore dresses. After a doctor's visit, Lucy's mother was advised to raise Lucy female. At the age of 15, Lucy moved to Pecos, Texas and worked at a hotel for 10 years. She later owned and operated a brothel while living in Oxnard, California.

She married Clarence Hicks in 1920, divorcing in 1929. In 1944, Lucy married soldier Reuben Anderson. After the Ventura County district attorney learned that Lucy was biologically male, she was tried for perjury for her marriage license. During the trial Lucy stated, "I defy any doctor in the world to prove that I am not a woman, I have lived, dressed, acted just what I am, a woman." She was convicted of perjury, and the judge chose to sentence her to 10 years under probation instead of a jail sentence.

The federal government later prosecuted Reuben and Lucy for fraud in 1946, as Lucy had received military spousal support. Both were found guilty and sentenced to prison. After her release from prison, Lucy lived in Los Angeles until her death in 1954.

APRIL

LESLIE CHEUNG
(LESLIE CHEUNG KWOK-WING)

SEP 12 1956 – APR 1 2003
(AGED 46)

Born in Hong Kong and later gaining Canadian citizenship, LESLIE CHEUNG broke records as a pop singer before pursuing a career in acting. He won awards for his roles in *Days of Being Wild* (1990), *Ashes of Time* (1994), and *Farewell My Concubine* (1993).

Openly bisexual, Leslie Cheung said in an interview that he was essentially married to his work: "In terms of lover, I think I can be a better friend than a lover. Because I am a workaholic. To share my romance, that person has to compromise something." He also stated in an interview, "My mind is bisexual. It's easy for me to love a woman. It's also easy for me to love a man, too," and, "I believe that a good actor would be androgynous, and ever changing."

Leslie Cheung committed suicide by jumping from the 24th floor of the Mandarin Oriental hotel in Hong Kong. After a lifetime of battling depression, he left a note thanking his therapist and his sister for their support and saying, "This year has been so tough. I can't stand it anymore. [...] In my life I have done nothing bad. Why does it have to be like this?"

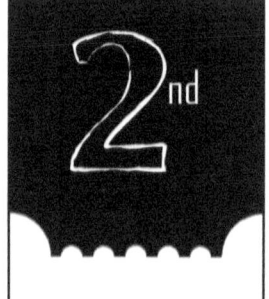

HANS CHRISTIAN ANDERSEN
(H.C. ANDERSEN)

APR 2 1805 – AUG 4 1875
(AGED 70)

HANS CHRISTIAN ANDERSEN was first captivated by stories when his father read him *Arabian Nights* (1706). He studied soprano at the Royal Danish Theatre program until his voice changed. He then moved into writing. Best known for fairy tales, Andersen adapted stories he recalled from childhood and created new ones, including "The Little Mermaid," "The Ugly Duckling," and "Thumbelina." Andersen also penned novels, travelogues, plays, and poems. Andersen had a correspondence with Charles Dickens, which ended after Andersen overstayed his welcome at Dickens' house and was asked to leave.

Andersen had a deep, un-requited love of childhood friend Riborg Voigt, and a letter of hers was found on Andersen's person when he died. He proposed to opera singer Jenny Lind by letter, who turned him down. He wrote to friend Edvard Collin, "I languish for you as for a pretty Calabrian wench... my sentiments for you are those of a woman. The femininity of my nature and our friendship must remain a mystery." He was close with hereditary duke Carl Alexander, and described his time with Danish dancer Harald Scharff as his "erotic period," frequently writing of their love and his longing. Anderson died in 1875 of liver cancer.

MARLON BRANDO, JR.

APR 3 1924 – JUL 1 2004
(AGED 80)

American actor and film director, MARLON BRANDO is known for his Academy Award-winning roles in *On the Waterfront* (1954) and *The Godfather* (1972), as well as his performances in *A Streetcar Named Desire* (1951), *Guys and Dolls* (1955), *Last Tango in Paris* (1972), and *Apocalypse Now* (1979).

Brando had a turbulent love life, with numerous wives, girlfriends, children, and male lovers as well. In a 1976 interview Brando said, "Homosexuality is so much in fashion, it no longer makes news. Like a large number of men, I, too, have had homosexual experiences, and I am not ashamed. I have never paid much attention to what people think about me." He had relationships with Marilyn Monroe, Rita Moreno, and Shelley Winters, as well as affairs with Cary Grant, Montgomery Clift, and James Dean, according to a 2006 biography. His close friendship with Wally Cox was summed up by Brando's saying: "If Wally had been a woman, I would have married him and we would have lived happily ever after."

After Cox's death in 1973, Brando kept his ashes until his own death in 2004 from respiratory and congestive heart failure. Their ashes were mingled together and scattered in Death Valley.

ANTHONY "TONY" PERKINS

APR 4 1932 – SEP 12 1992

(AGED 60)

ANTHONY PERKINS felt suffocated by his mother's controlling and inappropriate affection. His father, film and theater actor Osgood Perkins, died when he was five, and Anthony found a refuge in the same profession. He later said, "There was nothing about me I wanted to be, but I felt wonderfully happy being somebody else."

Perkins was first noticed when he replaced the lead of the Broadway play *Tea and Sympathy* in 1954. He received a Golden Globe for New Star of the Year – Actor, and an Oscar nomination for his supporting role in the film *Friendly Persuasion* (1956). He received Tony nominations for his roles in *Greenwillow* (1960) and *Look Homeward, Angel* (1957), and released three pop albums under the name Tony Perkins.

Perkins is best known for his performance of Norman Bates in Alfred Hitchcock's *Psycho* (1960), a role that affected the rest of his career. He reprised the character in three sequel films.

Perkins had relationships with actors Rock Hudson and Tab Hunter, photographer Christopher Makos, and actress Victoria Principal. Perkins met photographer Berinthia "Berry" Berenson at a party in 1972. They married in 1973 and had two children. Perkins died of AIDS-related pneumonia in 1992.

FRANCES POWER COBBE

DEC 4 1822 – APR 5 1904
(AGED 81)

FRANCES POWER COBBE was descended from Archbishop Charles Cobbe, Primate of Ireland. She worked at Red Lodge Girls' Reformatory in Bristol and lived with Mary Carpenter, superintendent. Cobbe moved out in 1859 and went on to found the first organization against animal experimentation in 1875, the Society for the Protection of Animals Liable to Vivisection (SPALV), as well as the British Union for the Abolition of Vivisection (BUAV) in 1898.

Cobbe also served as a member of the executive council of the London National Society for Women's Suffrage. She initiated legislation for women to legally separate from abusive husbands as well as retain custody of their children. She successfully campaigned for the release of a woman sentenced to death for killing her husband in self-defense. She advocated for women being allowed into university examinations to earn degrees.

In 1861, Cobbe met sculptor Mary Lloyd in Rome, who became her longtime partner. In published work as well as letters, Cobbe referred to Lloyd as "wife," "husband," and "dear friend." Cobbe is buried next to Lloyd in a cemetery in Wales, and her name is also listed on the Reformers Memorial in London's Kensal Green Cemetery.

CHARLES REGINALD JACKSON

APR 6 1903 – SEP 21 1968
(AGED 65)

American author CHARLES JACKSON is best known for *The Lost Weekend* (1944), a novel about a sexually conflicted alcoholic on a five-day bender. Raised in Arcadia township, Newark, at age 13 his brother and sister were killed in a car-meets-express-train accident, after which his father abandoned the family. Before exiting childhood, Jackson and his other brother were molested by the church's piano player (incidents referenced in *The Sunnier Side*, 1950).

Jackson was forced to leave university after a "furtive sexual encounter" with another boy. He spent years in Swiss sanatoriums for tuberculosis, struggled with alcoholism, married magazine writer Rhoda Booth, and had two daughters. He sold *The Lost Weekend*'s movie rights to Paramount for the paltry sum of $35,000; the 1945 film, directed by Billy Wilder, was nominated for seven Academy Awards (and won four). Jackson's Hollywood fame was unsustainable; he never delivered another *Lost Weekend*, but he did fall "in love" with Judy Garland, and add pills to his addiction roster.

Jackson attended Alcoholics Anonymous, but struggled with addiction all his life. He ultimately resided in New York's Chelsea Hotel with a male companion— young Czech immigrant Stanley Zednik—where he repeatedly overdosed until it killed him in 1968.

VIOLETTE LEDUC

APR 7 1907 – MAY 28 1972

(AGED 65)

Author VIOLETTE LEDUC was born illegitimate to a serving girl and the son of a rich family in Arras, France. She would go on to create her own scandals, from a boarding school love affair that would later inspire her writing, to a relationship at age 18 with her music instructor, which would end with the teacher's dismissal. She wrote several books that were obscured, censored, or ignored during her lifetime.

Considered a writer's writer, Violette Leduc found advocates for her novels in Simone de Beauvoir, Albert Camus, Jean-Paul Sartre, Jean Cocteau, and Jean Genet, but her treatments of female and lesbian sexuality never found a wide enough audience. Her novella *Thérèse and Isabelle* (1966), about a lesbian affair between girls in boarding school, was written as part of her earlier novel, *Ravages* (1955), but had to be removed and published separately. Leduc came closest to commercial success when her memoir, *La Bâtarde (The Bastard)* (1964), nearly won the Prix Goncourt, and led to a second installment of autobiography, *La folie en tête (Mad in Pursuit)*, in 1970. However, *Thérèse and Isabelle* would not be published completely uncensored until 2000, nearly 30 years after Leduc's death from breast cancer.

JAMES BYRON DEAN

FEB 8 1931 – SEP 30 1955
(AGED 24)

American actor and enduring cultural icon, JAMES DEAN is best known for the role of Jim Stark in *Rebel Without a Cause* (1955). His other credited film roles were in *East of Eden* (1955) and *Giant* (1956), those three films making up the near entirety of his short career.

Dean was helped into acting by Rogers Brackett, a radio director of an advertising agency, who met Dean when he worked as a parking lot attendant and invited him home. When Dean's agent confronted the young actor about his housemate's homosexuality, Dean's only response was, "I have my own room."

An early girlfriend, Liz Sheridan, revealed that Dean told her he'd slept with Brackett. Dean's close friend and first biographer, William Bast, said their friendship also included sexual intimacy. A recent biography claims a long sexual relationship between Dean and actor Marlon Brando. Actress Elizabeth Taylor has named James Dean as one of her close gay friends, along with Rock Hudson, who apparently won a bet with Taylor on the set of *Giant* over who would bed Dean first.

Dean was cast in his first movie role on April 8th, 1954. He died on September 30th, 1955 in a car accident.

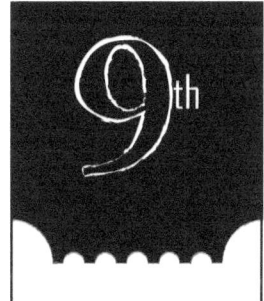

SIR FRANCIS BACON
(VISCOUNT SAINT ALBAN)

JAN 22 1561 – APR 9 1626
(AGED 65)

SIR FRANCIS BACON was an English Renaissance statesman, philosopher, and scientist, best known for creating the ubiquitous "scientific method" still in use today. Bacon served as attorney general and Lord Chancellor of England, ultimately resigning amid charges of corruption and bribery. He was spurned by his first potential wife, who broke their engagement for a wealthier match, and he eventually married late in life at age 45, to the 14-year-old Alice Barnham, daughter of a London alderman. That marriage was unhappy, with Alice Barnham ultimately disinherited in Bacon's will.

Contemporary writings show Bacon was primarily attracted to "masculine love," with a particular preference for young Welsh serving-men. There was Francis Edney who received "£200 and my rich gown" after Bacon's death from pneumonia; a Mr. Bushell, "gent. usher," who came to his household in 1608 at age 15 and remained until Bacon's death; "that bloody Percy," so-called by Bacon's mother, Lady Ann, in a letter to her other son, and referred to as "a coach companion and a bed companion," yet another of Bacon's "Welchmen one after another." Above all others was Tobie Matthew, who became Sir Tobie through Bacon's efforts, and was the inspiration for Bacon's essay, "Of Friendship."

EVELYN WAUGH
(ARTHUR EVELYN ST. JOHN WAUGH)

OCT 28 1903 – APR 10 1966
(AGED 62)

English writer of novels, biographies, and travel books, EVELYN WAUGH is best known for *Brideshead Revisited* (1945), which follows army officer Charles Ryder from the 1920s to the early 1940s. Exploring Ryder's nostalgic memories of the Flyte family, former occupants of Brideshead Castle where he is unexpectedly billeted, it focuses on his intimate relationships with brother and sister, Sebastian and Julia.

Known as "Wuffles" at home and at school, Waugh arrived at Oxford in 1922, and within a year had fallen in with a crowd of avant-garde students known as the Hypocrites—artistic, heavy-drinking, and homosexually inclined. Waugh entered into several homosexual relationships while at school, the longest-lasting ones with Richard Pares and Alastair Graham, both inspirations for Sebastian Flyte.

Waugh went on to teach, to marry Evelyn Gardner (they were known together as "He-Evelyn" and "She-Evelyn"), to divorce, convert to Catholicism, and to travel. After his first marriage was annulled, Waugh married a cousin of Gardner's, Laura Herbert, with whom he had seven children. He served unhappily during WWII. Frustrated by his circumstances, he wrote *Brideshead Revisited* during unpaid leave, which brought him fame and fortune after the war. Ill of health, he died on Easter day in 1966.

CHANTAL ANNE AKERMAN

JUN 6 1950 – OCT 5 2015
(A G E D   6 5)

Belgian film director CHANTAL AKERMAN is best known for *Jeanne Dielman, 23 quai du Commerce, 1080 Bruxelles* (1975), a movie depicting a mother's regimented schedule of cooking, cleaning, caring for her son, and having sex with male clients to earn money. The breakdown of those rituals culminates in the murder of one of Jeanne's clients with a pair of scissors. It is considered one of the great feminist films for its hypnotic depiction of a middle-aged widow's stifling routines. It directly influenced Gus Van Sant's films *Gerry* (2002) and *Elephant* (2003). Akerman's work also influenced Todd Haynes, director of the Patricia Highsmith

adaptation, *Carol* (2015).

Akerman appeared in her movies, even performing a naked wrestling match with her lover at the time, Claire Wauthion, in 1976's *Je Tu Il Elle*, which featured one of the first lesbian sex scenes on film.

Akerman was born in Belgium to Polish Holocaust survivors. Her 2015 film, *No Home Movie*, is a series of conversations between Akerman and her ailing mother recorded shortly before the latter's death in April, 2014. It was Akerman's last film. Bereaved over the loss of her mother, and despite being hospitalized for depression, Akerman committed suicide the next year.

JOSEPHINE BAKER
(FREDA JOSEPHINE MCDONALD)

JUN 3 1906 – APR 12 1975
(AGED 68)

JOSEPHINE BAKER left the United States for Paris as the U.S. was "only a country for white people." Baker became known for erotic dancing, vaudeville performances, wearing a skirt made of fake bananas, and performing with her pet cheetah, Chiquita. Ernest Hemingway called Baker "the most sensational woman anyone ever saw."

Baker was the first person of color to star in a major motion picture, and appeared in several films. After the Germans invaded France, Baker worked as a spy, transporting top-secret information written with invisible ink on her sheet music. She later received the Croix de guerre, the Rosette de le Résistance, and was awarded the Legion of Honour from Charles de Gaulle.

Baker refused to perform for segregated crowds, worked with the NAACP, spoke at the March on Washington in 1963, and was requested to become the Civil Rights Movement's leader after Reverend Martin Luther King Jr.'s death, but declined on behalf of her children.

Baker was married four times and adopted 12 children from diverse ethnicities and religions, forming "The Rainbow Tribe." Baker also had affairs with artist Frida Kahlo, blues singer Clara Smith, and other talented women. Baker died from a cerebral hemorrhage in 1975.

WHITNEY ELIZABETH HOUSTON

AUG 9 1963 – FEB 11 2012
(AGED 48)

WHITNEY HOUSTON grew up in Newark, New Jersey and performed as a soloist in the New Hope Baptist Church's gospel choir. Houston signed with Clive Davis and Arista Records in 1983 and quickly rose to fame, becoming a best-selling music artist and award-winning icon. Her film debut in *The Bodyguard* (1992) also gave Houston her hit song, "I Will Always Love You."

At the Soul Train Music Awards on April 13th, 1989, Houston was booed when her nomination was announced, as the crowd considered her a sellout to white America's marginalizing culture. That same night she met New Edition's Bobby Brown. They were married in 1992,

and their daughter Bobbi Kristina Brown was born in 1993. A highly toxic couple, with multiple incidents of drug use and violence, they divorced in 2007.

Houston met Robyn Crawford in 1979 at a New Jersey community center. Crawford became Houston's best friend, assistant, and later creative director. Crawford had a romantic relationship with Houston, and they sometimes lived together, including during Houston's marriage to Brown. Both Bobby Brown and stylist Ellin Lavar confirm Houston's bisexuality.

Houston was discovered drowned in her bathtub, with cocaine and other drugs in her system, in 2012.

SIR ARTHUR JOHN GIELGUD

APR 14 1904 – MAY 21 2000
(AGED 96)

JOHN GIELGUD's first paid acting job was working as a junior member for his cousin's theater company in 1922. He studied at the Royal Academy of Dramatic Art, and went on to Oxford Playhouse's repertory company, the Old Vic, the West End, Broadway, and film.

Gielgud played Hamlet over 500 times, as well as Shakespeare's other leads including Macbeth, Romeo, and King Lear. He directed, acted, wrote six autobiographical works, and won dozens of awards. He was knighted in 1953, and outside of his work enjoyed reading "trashy" American novels and listening to opera.

In 1953, Gielgud was arrested and fined for "importuning for immoral purposes," or cruising for sex in a men's bathroom in Chelsea. At the time the news broke, Gielgud was performing in a new play in Liverpool, and was too terrified to go on. Fellow actress Sybil Thorndike grabbed him and led him onto the stage, where he received a standing ovation.

He met partner Martin Hensler at a Tate Gallery exhibition in the 1960s, and they shared a love of gardening. They were together until Hensler's death in 1999. Gielgud died in 2000. Both of their ashes were spread over their rose garden.

BESSIE SMITH

APR 15 1894 – SEP 26 1937
(AGED 43)

Nicknamed the Empress of Blues, BESSIE SMITH was born in Chattanooga, Tennessee. Orphaned at a young age, Smith began to perform as a street singer, eventually becoming a dancer with the Rabbit Foot Minstrels, where she met singer "Ma" Rainey and started singing the Blues. She signed with Columbia Records in 1923, the same year she married Jack Gee, and her recording of "Downhearted Blues" sold over 800,000 copies, propelling her to fame. Smith was the highest-paid performer of her day.

Her marriage with Jack Gee was stormy, and Smith had affairs with women on the side.

There is speculation that "Ma" Rainey initiated Bessie Smith into bisexuality, but regardless, Smith kept mistresses and became deeply involved with women like Lillian Simpson, a chorus girl in her touring show, with whom she had a particularly intense affair. Also like Rainey, Smith sang songs with explicit lesbian content, such as "It's Dirty But Good" (1930) with the lyrics, "I know women that don't like men. The way they do is a crying sin. It's dirty but good."

Smith eventually entered a common-law marriage with old friend Richard Morgan, and stayed with him until her death by car accident in 1937.

APHRA BEHN

Dec 14 1640 (baptized)
– Apr 16 1689
(AGED 48)

British playwright, poet, and translator, APHRA BEHN was one of the first women to earn a living by writing professionally. In Virginia Woolf's *A Room of One's Own* (1929), she wrote of Behn saying, "All women together ought to let flowers fall upon the tomb of Aphra Behn […] for it was she who earned them the right to speak their minds." Behn's novel *Oroonoko: or, the Royal Slave* (1688), based on her friendship with an enslaved African prince she met in Surinam, is considered an early foundation for the development of the English novel.

From unknown origins, Aphra Behn returned to England from South America, became associated with a Dutch merchant named Ben, Bene, or Behn, and wrote publicly as "Mrs. Behn" from then on, to support herself after his death in 1665. Further indebted as a spy to King Charles II, she produced the play *The Forc'd Marriage* (1670) to escape debtor's prison. She continued writing until her death to maintain her income.

She was known as "the English Sappho" for her explicitly lesbian and androgynous poems, like 1688's "To the Fair Clarinda, Who Made Love to Me, Imagin'd More than Woman," addressed to a hermaphroditic figure.

TAMOTSU YATŌ

1928? – 1973
(*AGED ~45*)

Born around 1928, TAMOTSU YATŌ was a Japanese photographer responsible for pioneering Japanese photography of the male form. In his short career, he shot fervently, taking photographs of men (including author/political militant Yukio Mishima) that he published in three books: *Young Samurai: Bodybuilders of Japan* (1967), *Naked Festival: A Photo-Essay* (1969), and *Otoko: Photo-Studies of the Young Japanese Male* (1972). Mishima introduced the first two volumes, while the third was dedicated to his memory.

Yatō was a long-term romantic partner of Meredith Weatherby, a Texas-born American publisher known for his English translations of Mishima's works. According to American author Donald Richie's diaries, in an entry dated April 17th, 1994, Yatō was banished from his mentor Weatherby's house in the end, but kept returning. Weatherby, "in bed with his new friend," would wake up to find "the black and baleful Tamotsu" standing over him, or the maids would find Yatō sleeping under the house with matches in his pocket, as if he might burn the place down while Weatherby slept. Ultimately it was Yatō who died in his sleep of an enlarged heart, in an apartment paid for by Weatherby. Like his birth, the exact date of his death is unknown.

INTERNATIONAL DAY FOR
MONUMENTS AND SITES

GENERAL HUO GUANG
(ZIMENG)

❧

DIED 68 BC
(AGE UNKNOWN)

GENERAL HUO GUANG was a Western Han politician who honorably deposed an emperor, not to usurp the throne, but for the good of the state.

Huo served in high government office under several emperors. In 74 BC, Emperor Zhao died without children, and Huo decided that Zhao's nephew should take the throne. Once installed however, the nephew spent money incessantly and disregarded the period of mourning for Emperor Zhao. Finding him unfit, Huo worked to depose him just 28 days into his reign, and replace him with a titleless commoner. It was an unprecedented move in Chinese history, and during the next few years, Huo and the new Emperor Xuan shared imperial powers.

In his personal life, Huo was enamored of a slave master named Feng Zidu, whom he included in all his official activities, and who later maintained an affair with Huo's widow after his death from illness. Emperor Xuan personally attended Huo's wake, built him a mausoleum, and included him in a portrait of great statesmen in 51 BC. Huo's descendants, conversely, were entirely wiped out by Xuan due to political intrigue and conspiracy. It is only the tomb of Huo Guang which has survived to this day.

DR. PRINCESS VERA IGNATIEVNA GEDROITZ
(SERGEI GEDROITZ)

APR 19 1870 – 1932
(AGED ~62)

VERA GEDROITZ was born into Lithuanian royalty, and trained to be a surgeon at the University of Lausanne in Switzerland. Due to her family's illness and her sister's death in 1900, she returned home and became the first female surgeon in Russia. During the Russo-Japanese War, she perfected a technique for laparotomies which was highly successful. The Russian army adopted her procedure, thus changing how abdominal wounds were treated for the better. In 1909, Gedroitz was transferred to work as surgeon for the imperial family and taught first aid to the Tsar's daughters.

Gedroitz joined the Poets' Guild and published poetry and prose under the name Sergei Gedroitz. She also wrote research on oncology, endocrinology, and pediatric surgery, and in 1921 taught at the Kiev medical institute, becoming one of the first female professors of surgery in the world. She became chair of faculty surgery in 1929.

Large and overweight, Gedroitz dressed in men's hats, ties, and jackets, and wore her hair short. She referred to herself with masculine pronouns, and fell in love with the countess Maria Nirad. They lived together with Nirad's children, who did not like Gedroitz at all. Gedroitz died of cancer in 1932.

BILLIE HOLIDAY
(ELEANORA FAGAN, "LADY DAY")

APR 7 1915 – JUL 17 1959
(A G E D   4 4)

Considered one of the greatest jazz vocalists of all time, BILLIE HOLIDAY dropped out of school by age 11, and began working for a brothel. Her mother moved them to Harlem at age 12, and Holiday went looking for work as a dancer.

She found work as a singer, and by 1933 an 18-year-old Holiday was discovered by record producer John Hammond. By 1935, she was working with some of the best musicians in NYC: Lester Young, Benny Goodman, and Ben Webster. On April 20th, 1939 she recorded "Strange Fruit," a dirge about lynching. Performing this song brought theater into her act; she would dim the lights, sing the song on a stool in a pinpoint spotlight, then disappear into the darkness.

Bisexual, Holiday carried on a number of lesbian relationships while serving prison sentences for drug possession, and is rumored to have dated notorious actress Tallulah Bankhead. Ultimately addictions ate away at her and her fortunes. Holiday's drug use became unmanageable after the death of her mother and old friend Lester Young.

In 1957, she married abusive Mafia enforcer Louis McKay. In 1959, she was diagnosed with cirrhosis of the liver. She died from cirrhosis complications at age 44.

LORD JOHN MAYNARD KEYNES
(BARON KEYNES OF TILTON, IN THE COUNTY OF SUSSEX)

JUN 5 1883 – APR 21 1946

(AGED 62)

JOHN MAYNARD KEYNES received a first class bachelor's degree in Mathematics, was a member of the secret society The Cambridge Apostles, was President of the Cambridge Union Society, and the Cambridge University Liberal Club. Perhaps his biggest delight at Cambridge was captured in his diary when he wrote, "Practically everybody in Cambridge is an open and avowed Sodomite!"

Keynes kept detailed accounts of his early sexual experiences, such encounters included the "Stable Boy of Park Lane," "the Grand Duke Cyril of the Paris Baths," and "the young American near the British Museum." He had relationships with male and occasionally female

Cambridge students and scholars.

The British government consulted Keynes on currency exchanges and suspensions during WWI, and he was appointed financial representative for the Treasury to the Versailles peace conference in 1919. He was rewarded for his macroeconomic strategy work in WWII by receiving a hereditary peerage in 1942 from the King. He advocated for free markets and capitalism, and his economic applications became known as Keynesian economics.

He married Russian ballerina Lydia "Loppy" Lopokova in 1925, with his former great love Duncan Grant standing as best man. Keynes died after a series of heart attacks in 1946.

ALLEN GINSBERG
(IRWIN ALLEN GINSBERG)

JUN 3 1926 – APR 5 1997
(AGED 70)

Jewish-American poet, ALLEN GINSBERG was prominent in the Beat Generation of the 1950s. Close friends with Jack Kerouac and William S. Burroughs, Ginsberg contributed to a counterculture literary movement with his views against militarism, materialism, and sexual repression.

During the San Francisco Renaissance, Ginsberg participated in the iconic Six Gallery reading of 1955, where he presented his poem "Howl" for the first time. It begins, "I saw the best minds of my generation destroyed by madness, starving hysterical naked […]." It was during that time when Ginsberg met and fell in love with Peter Orlovsky, who

remained his partner in a lifelong open relationship. On April 22nd,1958, Orlovsky wrote to Ginsberg, "I miss the shoe shine you'd give my cock!—God—you know I've layd nobody since we last made it together—God for all I know my cock may be getting rusty like a dusty kings crown in dewy dungen—I'm sick of all this crying […]"

After suffering two small strokes, Ginsberg developed liver cancer brought on by hepatitis. He died in NYC's East Village at 70, surrounded by friends and family, and not before placing calls to all the names in his address book, to say goodbye.

APRIL

JAMES BUCHANAN, JR.

APR 23 1791 – JUN 1 1868
(AGED 77)

JAMES BUCHANAN was the 15th President of the U.S. and the sole bachelor, with his niece serving as First Lady. Buchanan lived for 13 years with his inseparable friend and colleague Senator William Rufus King of Alabama, and together they were often called the Siamese twins, "Miss Nancy" and "Aunt Fancy," Mr. and Mrs. Buchanan, and King specifically was referred to as Buchanan's "better half" and "wife." A contemporary newspaper noted their relationship had a "conspicuous intimacy."

In a letter to Cornelia Roosevelt in 1844 while King was away in France, Buchanan wrote, "I am now 'solitary and alone,' having no companion in the house with me. I have gone a wooing to several gentlemen, but have not succeeded with any one of them. I feel that it is not good for man to be alone, and [I] should not be astonished to find myself married to some old maid who can nurse me when I am sick, provide good dinners for me when I am well, and not expect from me any very ardent or romantic affection."

As President, Buchanan is counted among the worst for failing to prevent the Civil War. He died of respiratory failure at 77.

WILLA CATHER
(WILELLA "WILLIE" SIBERT CATHER, WILLIAM CATHER)

Dec 7 1873 – Apr 24 1947
(AGED 73)

At the age of nine, WILLA CATHER moved with her family to Nebraska to avoid tuberculosis outbreaks back in Virginia. Though she initially studied medicine while attending the University of Nebraska, she changed her studies to English after she saw her school essay published. While a student, Cather cut her hair short, dressed as a man, and went by William.

Her first collection of short stories, *The Troll Garden*, was published in 1905. Cather worked on the editorial staff of *McClure's Magazine* from 1906-1911, before leaving to pursue her own writing. Cather's novels featured strong female heroines and presented landscapes of Nebraska, the Southwest, Quebec, and France, capturing the dialects and characters of immigrants and bohemians. Cather won the Pulitzer Prize for Novel in 1923 for her book *One of Ours* (1922), and received the American Academy of Arts and Letters Gold Medal for Fiction in 1944.

Cather had close relationships with Pittsburgh patroness Isabelle McClung, college pal and American folklorist Louise Pound, opera singer Olive Fremstad, and musician/artist Yaltah Menuhin. Cather met editor and copywriter Edith Lewis while in Lincoln, and they lived together for nearly 40 years until Cather's death in 1947 of a cerebral hemorrhage.

MICHIYO FUKAYA
(MICHIYO CORNELL)

APRIL 25 1953 – JULY 9 1987
(AGED 34)

Japanese-American poet, writer, and activist, MICHIYO FUKAYA was born in Japan to a Japanese mother and a white American G.I. father. Born with her father's surname, Michiyo changed it back to her mother's family name as an adult. She was raised in Massachusetts.

Herself a single mother to a biracial daughter (whose father was African-American), through writing and activism Michiyo exemplified the interstices of oppressions she faced, including rape, sexism, homophobia, childhood sexual abuse, poverty, and mental illness. In 1981, she self-published a collection of poems, *Lesbian Lyrics*. In 1979, she gave a speech entitled "Living in Asian America: An Asian American Lesbian's Address Before the Washington Monument" at the First National Third World Lesbian and Gay Conference. Michiyo called attention to both the racism in the lesbian and gay movement, and the heterosexism/homophobia in the growing Asian American community.

Most of her work is out of circulation. *A Fire Is Burning It Is in Me: The Life and Writings of Michiyo Fukaya* is the only collection still in print, and was published as a memorial by Gwendolyn L. Sherington in 1996. Michiyo died of a self-inflicted gunshot wound to the head in 1987, aged 34.

WILLIAM SHAKESPEARE
("THE BARD")

APR 26 1564 (BAPTIZED) − APR 23 1616
(AGED 52)

English poet, playwright, and actor, largely considered the world's leading English dramatist, WILLIAM SHAKESPEARE invented words and phrases that still permeate the English language.

Shakespeare's Sonnets (1609) have led to speculation of affairs with a "Dark Lady" and a "Fair Youth," perhaps the "Mr. W.H." of the book's dedication. Even Oscar Wilde weighed in with his story "The Portrait of Mr. W.H." (1889), which theorizes that the dedicatee was a boy actor who specialized in playing women with Shakespeare's company, Willie Hughes, a speculation brought about by puns on the words "Will" and "Hues."

Scholars dispute whether the ardor of the poems was based on platonic loving friendship or sexual love, but it remains that the first 126 Sonnets are addressed to a man, including, "Shall I compare thee to a summer's day…" (Sonnet 18) and "When, in disgrace with fortune and men's eyes…" (Sonnet 29). They detail the beauty of this man, urge him to have children so his beauty will pass into future generations, and discuss the author's jealousy that the "Fair Youth" might prefer another poet over himself.

Husband to Anne Hathaway and father of three, Shakespeare died at 52. No surviving source explains how or why.

HAROLD HART CRANE

JUL 21 1899 – APR 27 1932
(AGED 32)

Between 1917-1924, HART CRANE worked as a copywriter in New York, and as an employee at his father's candy factory in Cleveland. Crane had several poems published in literary magazines before his first volume, *White Buildings*, was published in 1926. *The Bridge*, Crane's epic poem inspired by the Brooklyn Bridge, was published in 1930.

Crane sought to provide "a mystical synthesis of America" with his highly stylized poetry. Tennessee Williams said of Crane's poetry that he could "hardly understand a single line—of course the individual lines aren't supposed to be intelligible. The message, if there actually is one, comes from the total effect."

Crane cruised for sex in public parks, and enjoyed "educating" truck drivers and sailors with his poetry. He wrote the poem "Voyages" for Emil Opffer, a Danish ship's purser with whom he lived. He had a single heterosexual dalliance with painter Peggy Cowley. Crane drank heavily, was crushed by bad reviews, and landed in jail after fighting with waiters over his bar tab. While aboard the steamship Orizaba, Crane attempted to pick up a crewman and ended up being severely beaten. He then exclaimed, "Goodbye, everybody!" before throwing himself overboard. Crane's body was never recovered.

DAVID HAMPTON

APR 28 1964 – JUL 18 2003
(AGED 39)

American con artist, DAVID HAMPTON became infamous when he swindled people by claiming to be the son of Sidney Poitier. The incident inspired the Pulitzer and Tony-nominated play *Six Degrees of Separation* (1990), that was later made into a movie of the same name, starring Will Smith.

As David Poitier, Hampton would tell people he'd just been mugged or missed his plane, and needed a place to stay. At least a dozen people were taken in, including Melanie Griffith, Gary Sinise, and Calvin Klein. One of the deceived's son recalled, "Before going to sleep [he] asked my mom to wake him early so he could go jogging. The next morning she knocked on his door and found him in bed with a scruffy young man. But he told her not to worry, that it was Malcolm Forbes's nephew, who had gotten locked out of his place."

Eventually arrested, he was ordered to make financial restitution to his victims. Hampton failed to pay, violated a court order banning him from NYC, and continued to use the name David Poitier. He ultimately served 21 months in prison.

Sidney Poitier had six daughters and no sons. Hampton died of AIDS-related complications in 2003.

EDWARD MONTGOMERY CLIFT

OCT 17 1920 – JUL 23 1966
(AGED 45)

MONTGOMERY CLIFT started acting as a teenager, his stage career culminating on April 29th, 1940 with his appearance on Broadway in the Pulitzer Prize-winning *There Shall Be No Night*. At 25 he moved to Hollywood, subsequently earning four Academy Award nominations and starring in 17 films, including *Red River* (1948), *A Place in the Sun* (1951), *From Here to Eternity* (1953), and *Suddenly, Last Summer* (1959).

In 1956, he crashed his car while leaving Elizabeth Taylor's home, later requiring extensive plastic surgery. After the accident, he began what was called "the longest suicide in Hollywood history." Writer Christopher Isherwood's diaries state he was "drinking himself out of a career." Biographers say that on the set of *Raintree* (1957), the crew used code words to describe Clift's drunkenness: "bad was Georgia, very bad was Florida, and worst of all was Zanzibar."

Bisexual, Clift's orientation was concealed until after his death in 1966 from a heart attack. Clift largely hid from Hollywood's social scene, but had affairs with choreographer Jerome Robbins and actor Roddy McDowall, who attempted suicide after their breakup. In 2000, Liz Taylor referred to Clift (along with Rock Hudson and James Dean) as gay men whom she'd loved.

ALICE B. TOKLAS
(ALICE BABETTE TOKLAS)

APR 30 1877 – MAR 7 1967
(AGED 89)

After surviving the San Francisco earthquake of 1906, ALICE B. TOKLAS moved to Paris in September of 1907, and on her first day in the city, she met the love of her life, Gertrude Stein. Among their numerous nicknames, Stein called Toklas "wifey," "baby precious," and "lobster," and Toklas called Stein "Mr. Cuddle-Wuddle," "husband," and "Mount Fattie."

Toklas was uninterested in writing her memoirs, so Stein wrote them for her with *The Autobiography of Alice B. Toklas* (1933), her best-selling book. Toklas later wrote the part-autobiographical, part-recipe book *The Alice B. Toklas Cook Book*

(1954), which contained friend and artist Brion Gysin's recipe for "Hashish Fudge," and became wildly popular. Her second cookbook, *Aromas and Flavors of Past and Present* (1958), was unapproved by Toklas after too much interference from her editor.

Stein died from stomach cancer in 1946, and though she willed her estate to Toklas, without legal recognition, Toklas was unable to claim it. Relatives of Stein's stole the women's art collection while Toklas was away on holiday. She lived off donations from friends, and died from a long illness in 1967. Toklas is buried next to Stein in Père Lachaise Cemetery in Paris.

MAY

ROMAINE BROOKS
(BEATRICE ROMAINE GODDARD)

MAY 1 1874 – DEC 7 1970
(AGED 96)

ROMAINE BROOKS escaped her unhappy childhood of abusive, absent parents and traveled to Rome to study figure drawing. When a fellow student sexually harassed her by leaving a pornographic book on her stool, Brooks picked up the book and hit him in the face with it. She moved to St. Ives where she refined her color palette to grayer tones, and had her first solo exhibition in 1910.

In 1911, Brooks found a muse and romantic partner in Russian dancer Ida Rubinstein, whom she painted and was involved with until 1914. At the start of World War I, Brooks painted *La France Croisée* (1914) which featured a Red Cross nurse with a burning city behind her. This painting was reproduced in a Red Cross booklet, and Brooks received the Legion of Honour for her fundraising efforts. In 1930, Brooks experimented with drawing in continuous curved lines. Though she was believed to have stopped painting over the years, Brooks insisted she drew all her life.

Brooks met Natalie Barney in 1916 and became involved in a *ménage à trois* with Barney and Élisabeth de Gramont for the rest of their lives. Brooks is buried with Natalie Barney in a Paris cemetery.

LORENZ "LARRY" MILTON HART

MAY 2 1895 – NOV 22 1943
(AGED 48)

After their first creative meeting, Richard Rodgers had "acquired in one afternoon a career, a partner, a best friend, and a source of permanent irritation." That was LORENZ HART.

Hart translated German plays at $50 a week for the Shubert brothers. His joining up with Richard Rodgers led to Broadway songwriting success. The duo created music and lyrics for 26 Broadway musicals and several films, and Hart's lyrics were touted for their cleverness, wit, sorrow, and their technical sophistication. Hart's memorable lyrics make up lasting hits like "My Funny Valentine," "The Lady is a Tramp," and "Bewitched, Bothered, and Bewildered."

Hart disappeared for days on drunken binges. Rodgers once offered that they both be committed to a sanitarium so Hart could get help and work at the same time, but Hart wouldn't budge, urging Rodgers to forget about him. When asked about his love life, Hart reported he hadn't any, and that "nobody would want me." George Balanchine reported that on a trip to London, he would have to get his friend out of brawls when Hart "would pick up sailors and get beat up." Hart died of pneumonia brought on by exposure during a drinking binge in 1943.

BARON FRANZ NOPCSA VON FELSŐ-SZILVÁS

MAY 3 1877 – APR 25 1933
(AGED 55)

Hungarian-born aristocrat, scholar, and paleontologist, BARON FRANZ NOPCSA'S sister discovered dinosaur bones on the family estate in Transylvania in 1895, which inspired him to study fossils at the University of Vienna. He also took an interest in Albanian nationhood, venturing into mountainous areas of northern Albania, learning Albanian dialects and customs, and aiding their efforts for independence by smuggling weapons. When Albania was established as a state, Nopcsa was considered for the throne.

With Austria-Hungary's defeat at the end of WWI, Nopcsa's family estate was part of the Transylvanian land ceded to Romania. Nopcsa lost all his possessions. Searching for work, he and his Albanian secretary and lover, Bajazid Elmaz Doda, moved to Vienna so he could return to studying fossils. However, his financial difficulties continued, forcing him to sell his fossil collection. Deeply depressed, in 1933 he drugged Doda and fatally shot him, before killing himself. In a letter left behind, he stated: "The reason that I shot my long-time friend and secretary, Mr. Bajazid Elmaz Doda, in his sleep without his suspecting at all, is that I did not wish to leave him behind sick, in misery and without a penny, because he would have suffered too much."

JANE BOWLES
(JANE SYDNEY AUER)

FEB 22 1917 – MAY 4 1973
(AGED 56)

JANE BOWLES fell in love with literature while in traction in Switzerland during adolescence, being treated for tuberculous arthritis of the knee. She began writing on her return to New York City, where she spent her time in Greenwich Village. She liked drinking, smoking cigars, and jokingly referring to herself as "Crippie, the Kike Dyke."

Jane met composer Paul Bowles in 1937, and they married in 1938. Both enjoyed each other's company, and sought bisexual relationships outside the marriage. In a letter to Paul, Jane wrote, "Men are all on the outside, not interesting. They have no mystery. Women are profound and mysterious—and obscene." Jane Bowles had relationships with divorcée Helvetia Perkins, torch singer Libby Holman, and a Moroccan grain seller by the name of Cherifa.

Bowles's novel, *Two Serious Ladies*, was published in 1943. Her play *In the Summer House* was first performed in Pennsylvania in 1951, then at the Playhouse Theatre on Broadway in 1953. Though her work received mixed reviews, she was praised among other writers, such as Truman Capote and John Ashbery. Tennessee Williams considered Bowles to be the most underrated writer of fiction in American literature. Bowles died in 1973 from stroke complications.

JAMES ANDREW BEARD

MAY 5 1903 – JAN 21 1985
(AGED 81)

JAMES BEARD's first memory of food formed when he was two years old, attending the World's Fair-esque Lewis and Clark Exposition in Oregon, where he watched Triscuits being made. According to Beard, "By the time I was seven, I knew that I was gay." He attended Reed College, but was expelled for engaging in same-sex activity. Beard went on to pursue a theater career in New York, and opened a catering company with his friend Bill Rhodes on the side.

In 1940, Beard's first cookbook *Hors D'Oeuvre and Canapes* was published. From 1946-1947 he hosted the first network cooking show *I Love to Eat* live on NBC. Beard created the James Beard Cooking School in 1955, traveled and taught for 30 years, and in his spare time wrote and revised over 20 cookbooks. Beard's longtime partner Gino Cofacci was an architect-turned-pastry chef who co-authored a cookbook with him. James Beard died of heart failure in 1985. He left much of his estate to an AIDS charity in Key West.

The James Beard Foundation was formed in 1986 to honor Beard's memory, and the annual awards presented to chefs and journalists are considered to be the Oscars of the food world.

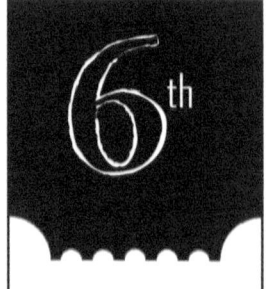

MARLENE DIETRICH
(MARIE MAGDALENE DIETRICH)

DEC 27 1901 – MAY 6 1992
(AGED 90)

German-American motion-picture actress of the 20th century, MARLENE DIETRICH was known for her sophisticated glamor, sensual voice, and languid beauty. Her films included roles in *The Blue Angel* (1930), *Morocco* (1930), *Shanghai Express* (1932), and *Desire* (1936). In *Morocco*, which introduced Dietrich to America, she wore a tuxedo, kissed another woman, and essentially made the leading man (Gary Cooper) her girlfriend, thus making fluid sexuality part of her image and appeal. Critic Kenneth Tynan wrote, "She has sex but no positive gender. Her masculinity appeals to women and her sexuality to men."

Dietrich was bisexual, and her lovers included John F. Kennedy, Frank Sinatra, Edith Piaf, writers Mercedes de Acosta and Erich Maria Remarque, and very likely Greta Garbo (who flatly refused to acknowledge Dietrich's existence after the affair ended—the feeling was largely mutual). She learned to box, married once, and had a daughter. She also had endless romances, with actors Gary Cooper, Jimmy Stewart, John Wayne, Yul Brynner, and actresses Claudette Colbert and Dolores del Río, whom Dietrich thought was the most beautiful woman in Hollywood.

Dietrich's career spanned over 50 years. She died of renal failure in her Paris apartment at age 90, while sleeping.

PYOTR ILYICH TCHAIKOVSKY

MAY 7 1840 – NOV 6 1893
(AGED 53)

PYOTR TCHAIKOVSKY began piano lessons at age five, and could read sheet music as well as his tutors by eight. He studied music at the Saint Petersburg Conservatory, graduating in 1865 to a low-paying teaching job at the Moscow Conservatory. Tchaikovsky composed in his spare time, creating music that was popular, but critically panned. His works include *The Nutcracker* (1892), *Swan Lake* (1875–1876), and the *1812 Overture* (1880).

Tchaikovsky was romantically linked to fellow music students, both pupils and colleagues, as well as his valet. He also had an intimate relationship with his nephew Vladimir "Bob"

Davidov, to whom he dedicated his *Symphony No. 6* (1893), or "The Passionate Symphony." In a letter to Davidov in 1892, Tchaikovsky wrote, "I often think of you and see you in my dreams, usually looking sad and depressed. This has added a feeling of compassion to my love for you and makes me love you even more. Oh God! How I want to see you this very minute."

Tchaikovsky had plans to live together with Davidov before his death. Though on record Tchaikovsky died of cholera after drinking unboiled water, one of his doctors later confirmed Tchaikovsky had poisoned himself.

TOM OF FINLAND
(TOUKO VALIO LAAKSONEN)

MAY 8 1920 – NOV 7 1991
(AGED 71)

Finnish artist Touko Laaksonen is best known as TOM OF FINLAND, and for his highly masculinized homoerotic art.

When the Soviets invaded Finland in November of 1939, Laaksonen was conscripted as an anti-aircraft officer, second lieutenant. He pursued anonymous sex in the streets during the WWII blackouts, and attributed his fetishistic interest in uniformed men to these nighttime encounters with jackbooted Germans: "In my drawings I have no political statements to make, no ideology. I am thinking only about the picture itself. The whole Nazi philosophy, the racism and all that, is hateful to me, but of course I drew them anyway—they had the sexiest uniforms!"

In 1953, Laaksonen met Finnish dancer Veli "Nipa" Mäkinen in the park and invited him home; they lived together for the rest of Mäkinen's life. In 1956, Laaksonen sent his artwork to American muscle magazine, *Physique Pictorial*: the Spring 1957 cover features a pair of log-drivers at work, drawn by "Tom of Finland."

Even with censorship opposition, Laaksonen still found avenues for his work with the biker and leather subcultures, eventually quitting his full-time Helsinki advertising job in 1973, and living full time off his drawings. He died in 1991 of emphysema-induced stroke.

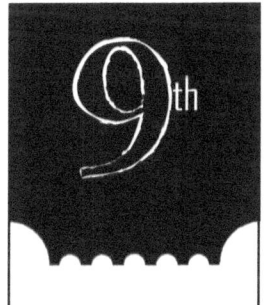

BRENDA NOKUZOLA FASSIE

NOV 3 1964 – MAY 9 2004
(AGED 39)

BRENDA FASSIE was born near Cape Town in South Africa. She learned to sing along with her mother's piano playing, and at age five she was singing for paying tourists. Johannesburg producer Koloi Lebona called her "the voice of the future," and placed her in the singing group, Joy. After her contract ended, Fassie created her own group, Brenda and the Big Dudes. Her 1983 record became a hit with the single "Weekend Special." She continued to release multi-platinum albums in South Africa, and toured around the world.

Fassie had a son with a fellow Big Dudes musician, later marrying and divorcing Nhlanhla Mlambo, a businessman. Fassie's drug and alcohol abuse, money troubles, and bisexuality were widely documented in the tabloids. Fassie went to rehab in 1995, after her lover Poppie Sihlahla died of an overdose in their hotel room. Fassie met a new lover, Sindisiwe Khambule, after accidentally stepping on her toes at a nightclub's dance floor.

Fassie was reported to have died of cardiac arrest after an asthma attack led to a collapse and a coma, but the post-mortem revealed there had been a fatal level of cocaine in her system. She was 39 years old.

FRIEDA BELINFANTE

MAY 10 1904 – APR 26 1995
(AGED 90)

FRIEDA BELINFANTE began studying the cello at age 10, and graduated from the Amsterdam Conservatory at 17. She became the first female conductor of a professional orchestra in Amsterdam, and after WWII conducted the Orange County Philharmonic in California.

When the Netherlands was under Nazi occupation, Belinfante joined up with the Dutch resistance and began forging identification documents for Jews. To obscure their fake ID efforts, she created a plan to blow up the Amsterdam population registry at City Hall, and assisted with the bombing. Afterwards she went into hiding, disguising herself as a man and living with friends for three months before escaping through Switzerland, crossing the Alps on foot.

Belinfante lived openly as a lesbian, once saying, "I just lived my life and I never explained anything." She married fellow musician John Falcone in 1931 with the understanding she could never love a man as she did a woman; they later divorced in 1936. In 1987, The City of Laguna Beach declared February 19 "Frieda Belinfante Day" to honor her contributions to music. In 1994, The United States Holocaust Memorial Museum recognized her contributions to the Dutch Resistance during World War II. Belinfante died of cancer in 1995.

11th

JANE HEAP

❧

1883/1887 – 1964
(A G E D ~ 7 7 / 8 1)

JANE HEAP was born in Topeka, Kansas, and grew up on the grounds of a mental asylum where her father worked as the warden. She studied at the Art Institute of Chicago, and became an art teacher at the Lewis Institute.

Heap met the founder of *The Little Review* magazine, Margaret Anderson, in 1916, and Anderson was immediately taken with her. Heap became co-editor of the magazine, as well as Anderson's romantic partner. After serially publishing James Joyce's *Ulysses* between 1918-1920, Anderson and Heap were convicted of obscenity charges, fined $100, and were forced to discontinue the serialization. Heap later became the main editor, and also helped found Maurice Browne's Chicago Little Theatre in 1912.

Heap wore her hair short and dressed in men's trousers. She met student Florence Reynolds at the Lewis Institute in 1908. Together they traveled to Germany in 1910, and were friends and lovers throughout their lives, though at times they lived apart. Fashion designer and British *Vogue* editor Elspeth Champcommunal lived with Heap in London for a time, and Heap, Champcommunal, and Reynolds traveled every summer throughout Europe from 1929-1939. Heap died in 1964 from diabetes complications.

DAVID BOWIE
(DAVID ROBERT JONES)

JAN 8 1947 – JAN 10 2016
(AGED 69)

British singer, songwriter, and actor best known for his 1970s glam rock persona Ziggy Stardust, DAVID BOWIE's world-famous songs include "Fame" (1975) with John Lennon, "Under Pressure" (1982) with Freddie Mercury and Queen, and "Dancing in the Street" (1985) with Mick Jagger.

Bowie came out as gay in a 1972 interview for *Melody Maker*, saying, "I'm gay, and always have been, even when I was David Jones." According to first wife Angela, he was sexually involved with The Rolling Stones' Jagger, whose song "Angie" is rumored to be about that love triangle.

Bowie's public sexuality evolved as much as his image. In a September 1976 interview with *Playboy*, Bowie said, "It's true—I am a bisexual. But I can't deny that I've used that fact very well. I suppose it's the best thing that ever happened to me." Then, in a May 12th, 1983 interview with *Rolling Stone*, Bowie said his declaration of bisexuality was "the biggest mistake I ever made," that he "was always a closet heterosexual."

Of his second wife, Iman, Bowie said, "I was naming the children the night we met." They were married from 1992 until his death from cancer in 2016.

DAME DAPHNE DU MAURIER
(LADY BROWNING)
❧
MAY 13 1907 – APR 19 1989
(AGED 81)

DAPHNE DU MAURIER was an English author and playwright, daughter of actor Gerald du Maurier, granddaughter of artist and writer George du Maurier, and cousin to the Llewelyn Davies boys who served as J.M. Barrie's inspiration for the Lost Boys in the Peter Pan stories. Her works include the short stories "Don't Look Down" and "The Birds," as well as the novels *Jamaica Inn* (1936) and *Rebecca* (1938), all of which were adapted for film and television, three of them by Alfred Hitchcock. *Rebecca* is her best-known book, and the character of the housekeeper Mrs. Danvers is seen as particularly lesbian due to her obsession with her deceased mistress, the titular Rebecca.

In 1932, du Maurier married Major Frederick Browning (later Lieutenant-General) and had three children. Their marriage was chilly, her children ignored in favor of her writing, and after du Maurier's death, her bisexuality was suggested by biographer Margaret Forster, based on her passionate letters to women. An affair with performer Gertrude Lawrence, and an attraction to the wife of her publisher, were gleaned from these letters. Du Maurier's written objections to the label of lesbianism were pointed to as evidence of internalized homophobia. She died at age 81.

MAGNUS HIRSCHFELD

MAY 14 1868 – MAY 14 1935
(AGED 67)

MAGNUS HIRSCHFELD studied philosophy, philology, and medicine. In 1897, he founded the Scientific Humanitarian Committee, which defended gay rights and worked to repeal a section of the German penal code which criminalized homosexuality. During testimony in the Harden-Eulenburg affair, Hirschfeld said "homosexuality was part of the plan of nature and creation just like normal love," a comment that sparked outrage throughout Germany. Newspaper editorials cited it as propaganda from "a freak who acted for freaks."

In 1921, Hirschfeld formed the First Congress for Sexual Reform, became known as "the Einstein of Sex" during sexologist speaking tours, coined the term transvestite, campaigned for women's rights and the decriminalization of abortion, and created the Institute of Sexual Research, the extensive research library of which was burned by the Nazis in 1933.

Hirschfeld met Karl Giese after a lecture in Munich, and they had what Hirschfeld described as a "physical-mental connection." Giese moved in with Hirschfeld and headed the Institute's archive. Hirschfeld then met medical student Li Shiu Tong while abroad, and the three men lived together in a *ménage à trois* in Paris. Hirschfeld died of a heart attack in 1935, with Giese and Tong as his heirs.

THOMAS JEFFERSON WITHERS

❧

1804 – NOV 7 1865
(AGED ~61)

THOMAS J. WITHERS was born in York County, South Carolina. He attended South Carolina College where he studied law, and later worked as a journalist, a lawyer, and a judge of the South Carolina Court of Appeals. In 1861, Withers represented South Carolina in the Provisional Confederate Congress, and signed the Confederate States Constitution.

While at college, Withers had a relationship with future governor, senator, and state representative James Henry Hammond. Withers' letters to Hammond included the following correspondence on May 15th, 1826:

"…and whether you yet have the extravagant delight of poking and punching a writhing Bedfellow with your long fleshen pole–the exquisite touches of which I have often had the honor of feeling? Let me say unto thee that unless thou changest former habits in this particular, thou wilt be represented by every future Chum as a nuisance. And, I pronounce it, with good reason too. Sir, you roughen the downy Slumbers of your Bedfellow–by such hostile–furious lunges as you are in the habit of making at him–when he is least prepared for defence against the crushing force of a Battering Ram."

Withers died at his Kershaw County, South Carolina home in 1865.

ADRIENNE CECILE RICH

MAY 16 1929 – MAR 27 2012
(AGED 82)

In her last year at Radcliffe College, ADRIENNE RICH's first collection of poetry *A Change of World* (1951) was selected by W.H. Auden for the Yale Series of Younger Poets Award. After graduation, Rich received a Guggenheim Fellowship to study at Oxford, but chose to travel through Europe instead.

In 1955, Rich published her second poetry collection, *The Diamond Cutter*, and received the Ridgely Torrence Memorial Award. In 1960, she received her second Guggenheim Fellowship and the National Institute of Letters award. Rich continued to publish poems and novels as well as nonfiction books, teaching at several colleges,

and receiving many accolades for her work. In 1997, Rich declined the National Medal of Arts in protest of the House of Representatives' vote to end the National Endowment of the Arts.

Rich married economics professor Alfred Conrad in 1953, "in part because I knew no better way to disconnect from my first family." Rich moved out of their house in 1970, and shortly thereafter Conrad shot himself. Rich met novelist Michelle Cliff in 1975, while Cliff worked as an editor of history books. They became partners in 1976, and were together until Rich's death in 2012 of rheumatoid arthritis complications.

SANDRO BOTTICELLI
(ALESSANDRO DI MARIANO FILIPEPI)

1445 – MAY 1510
(AGED ~65)

Nicknamed after his brother Botticello, meaning "little wine barrel," SANDRO BOTTICELLI entered the studio of artist Fra Filippo Lippi as a teenager around 1462, and began his career painting frescoes for Florentine churches and cathedrals. By 1470, he had his own workshop.

Botticelli spent most of his life working for the Medici family, for whom he painted some of his most magnificent secular paintings, including *La Primavera* (1470s/1480s). In 1481, he was summoned to Rome by the Pope to help decorate the walls of Sistine Chapel, and on returning to Florence he began the most prolific stage of his career.

Between 1478-1490 he produced his most famous works of mythological depiction, including *The Birth of Venus* (1480s). After the death of his patron Laurentius (Lorenzo) de' Medici, however, Botticelli was swept up by religious fervor, reportedly going so far as to throw some of his own paintings onto Florence's famed Bonfire of the Vanities in 1497.

Botticelli never married, and was anonymously charged with sodomy in 1502, at age 57. A common charge, Leonardo da Vinci, Benvenuto Cellini, and Michelangelo were also accused at various times. Botticelli died in May of 1510, and was buried in Ognissanti on May 17th.

R.H. BARLOW
(ROBERT HAYWARD BARLOW)

MAY 18 1918 – JAN 2 1951
(AGED 32)

ROBERT HAYWARD BARLOW studied at the Kansas City Art Institute, San Francisco Junior College, the Escuela Nacional de Ciencias Biológicas, and the University of California. Barlow moved to Mexico permanently around 1943, and taught as a professor at several colleges, becoming chairman of the anthropology department at Mexico City College. He made huge contributions to the discovery, collection, and preservation of Mexican artifacts, including colonial manuscripts and Maya codices. He was an expert in Nahuatl, the Aztec language, and in 1950 he published a Nahuatl language newspaper, *Mexihkatl itonalama*.

He collaborated with H.P. Lovecraft on at least six stories, and was Lovecraft's correspondent, transcriber, and typist. After Lovecraft's death, Barlow was named his literary executor. Barlow was also a talented sculptor and experimental poet.

Barlow was known to have relations with Mexican youths. A disgruntled student approached Barlow, threatening to reveal his homosexuality, and rather than be blackmailed or risk exposure, Barlow locked himself in his room and overdosed on 26 capsules of Seconal. His suicide note, made up of Mayan pictographs, was pinned to his door. The translation read, "Do not disturb me. I want to sleep a long time."

T.E. LAWRENCE
(THOMAS EDWARD LAWRENCE, LAWRENCE OF ARABIA)

AUG 16 1888 – MAY 19 1935
(AGED 46)

T.E. LAWRENCE was a British archaeologist, military officer, diplomat, and writer, best known for his role in the Arab Revolt against the Ottoman Empire during WWI, which was depicted in the 1962 film *Lawrence of Arabia*.

Upon his return to England, Lawrence exhibited masochistic tendencies, hiring men to whip and humiliate him while he exercised, a predilection he may have gained after his experiences abroad, specifically a self-reported flogging and sexual assault perpetrated upon Lawrence by soldiers in Deraa (the veracity of which is often questioned by scholars). He also wrote of homosexual coupling among the men and boys in the desert when the

"raddled meat" of female prostitutes was deemed too unappealing:

"[O]ur youths began indifferently to slake one another's few needs in their own clean bodies—a cold convenience that, by comparison, seemed sexless and even pure. Later, some began to justify this sterile process, and swore that friends quivering together in the yielding sand with intimate hot limbs in supreme embrace, found there hidden in the darkness a sensual co-efficient of the mental passion which was welding our souls and spirits in one flaming effort."

Lawrence died from injuries sustained during a motorcycle accident in 1935.

LIBBY HOLMAN
(ELIZABETH LLOYD HOLZMAN)

MAY 23 1904 – JUN 18 1971
(AGED 67)

Jewish-American LIBBY HOLMAN graduated from the University of Cincinnati, shaved two years off her age, and moved to New York City to pursue theater work. She found success as a torch singer with her signature blues number "Moanin' Low." Holman is also credited with popularizing the strapless dress.

When her son died in a rock climbing accident, she created the Christopher Reynolds Foundation in his name. It was through this foundation that Holman secured the funds for Martin Luther King Jr. and Coretta Scott King to travel to India and meet with the followers of Gandhi.

Holman married tobacco heir Zachary Smith "Smitty" Reynolds in November 1931, though their marriage was not announced until May 20th of the following year. At a friend's birthday party, Reynolds died of a gunshot wound to the head, and Holman was arrested for murder. She was bailed out by DuPont heiress and lover Louisa d'Andelot Carpenter. Charges were later dropped at the Reynolds family's request, to avoid scandal.

Other lesbian lovers include writer Jane Bowles and actress Jeanne Eagels. Holman's second husband died of a barbiturate overdose. After past suicide attempts, Holman died in 1971 of carbon monoxide poisoning in her Rolls Royce.

NATHAN FREUDENTHAL LEOPOLD JR.

NOV 19 1904 – AUG 29 1971
(AGED 66)

Young ornithologist and linguist NATHAN LEOPOLD started attending the University of Chicago at age 15, where he befriended another teenaged prodigy, Richard Loeb. Leopold became enthralled with Loeb, and began trading participation in Loeb's petty crimes (robbery, vandalism, arson) for sexual favors. This reciprocity escalated to the murder of 14-year-old Bobby Franks on May 21st, 1924. At the time it was dubbed "the crime of the century."

Leopold and Loeb pleaded guilty, with famed defense lawyer Clarence Darrow presenting their mental states as mitigating circumstances, a legal watermark made to avoid the death penalty.

Both boys were sentenced to life plus 99 years.

Loeb was murdered by a fellow inmate in 1936. Leopold helped the WWII effort by volunteering for malaria testing. Leopold was released in 1958 after serving 33 years. Once paroled, he moved to Puerto Rico and married a local widow, though his letters reveal he still pursued sexual relationships with young men. He kept Richard Loeb's picture on his bedroom dresser, and once noted it, saying, "Dickie Loeb was the guy who ruined my life. Still, [...] he was really a swell guy, the best friend I ever had."

Leopold died of a heart attack at 66.

HARVEY BERNARD MILK

MAY 22 1930 – NOV 27 1978
(AGED 48)

HARVEY MILK was known as "a man's man." He studied Mathematics at the New York State College for Teachers in Albany, played football, basketball, and wrote for the college newspaper. He served in the U.S. Navy during the Korean War as a diving officer aboard the rescue sub USS Kittiwake (ASR-13). Milk worked as a high school teacher, an insurance actuary, a Wall Street firm researcher, and a theater associate producer before finding a home in San Francisco, where he opened a camera store on Castro Street with Joseph Scott Smith, his partner and later campaign manager.

Milk turned Castro Camera into a social center, a polling center, and a refuge. He became involved in politics, campaigning for gay rights, and was deemed the "Mayor of Castro Street" for organizing labor coalitions and helping found the Castro Village Association. Milk served as the first openly gay city commissioner in 1976, and was elected to the San Francisco Board of Supervisors as City Supervisor for District 5.

Milk was assassinated by former District 8 Supervisor Dan White in 1978. His ashes were spread in the San Francisco Bay and beneath the sidewalk of 575 Castro Street, the location of Castro Camera.

MARGARET WISE BROWN
(TIMOTHY HAY, GOLDEN MACDONALD, JUNIPER SAGE)

MAY 23 1910 – NOV 13 1952
(AGED 42)

MARGARET BROWN received a bachelor's degree in English from Hollins University in 1932, and started writing children's books while she worked at the Bank Street Experimental School in New York City. Her first book, *When the Wind Blew*, was published in 1937, and she continued to write while employed at children's publisher W.R. Scott as an editor. She wrote over 100 children's books and picture books, including the notable *Goodnight Moon* (1947) and *The Runaway Bunny* (1942). Brown also fought for equal payment for her illustrators at a time when illustrators only received a flat payment on their artistry.

Brown had been engaged while attending university, and had affairs with men. In 1940, Brown began a relationship with playwright, poet, and actress Blanche Oelrichs, formerly married to John Barrymore. In 1943, they moved in together in Manhattan, and remained together until Oelrichs's death in 1950. Brown became engaged again to James Stillman Rockefeller Jr., but died prior to the wedding of an embolism. She was 42.

STORMÉ DELARVERIE

DEC 24 1920 – MAY 24 2014
(AGED 93)

Biracial butch lesbian STORMÉ DELARVERIE rode jumping horses with Ringling Brothers Circus as a teenager. She worked the black theater circuit as an emcee and drag king of the *Jewel Box Revue*, the first integrated drag revue, from 1955-1969. She performed at the Apollo Theater, Radio City Music Hall, and the Copacabana.

DeLarverie was referred to as "the gay community's Rosa Parks" and identified herself as the "Stonewall Lesbian." During the 1969 police raid of Greenwich Village gay bar The Stonewall Inn, DeLarverie fought with four policemen, escaped several times, and was hit with a police baton for complaining about the tightness of her handcuffs. As DeLarverie bled from a head wound, she yelled to bystanders, "Why don't you guys do something?" and was chucked into the paddy wagon. This was the moment the rebellion started, later known as the "Stonewall Riots."

DeLarverie was Chief of Security, Ambassador, and later Vice President of the Stonewall Veterans' Association. She became a volunteer street patrol worker, a "guardian of lesbians in the Village." DeLarverie had a relationship with a woman named Diana, a dancer who died in the 1970s; DeLarverie always carried her photograph.

DeLarverie died of a heart attack in 2014.

ROBBIE ROSS
(ROBERT BALDWIN ROSS)

MAY 25 1869 – OCT 5 1918
(AGED 49)

Canadian journalist and art critic ROBBIE ROSS is best known for his relationship with Oscar Wilde. After his family's move to London, Ross attended King's College, Cambridge until he caught pneumonia after a fountain-dunking bullying incident encouraged by Junior Tutor Arthur Augustus Tilley. Ross demanded an apology, managed to force Tilley's resignation, but dropped out before graduating.

Ross was involved with Wilde before Cambridge, and is believed to have been Wilde's first male lover. In 1893, he and Wilde's more tempestuous lover, Lord Alfred Douglas, were frantic after a 16-year-old boy they'd had sexual relations with confessed to his family.

The parents were dissuaded from involving the police for fear their son would also be prosecuted.

After Wilde's 1895 conviction for gross indecency, Ross remained a loyal friend until Wilde's death in 1900, later becoming his literary executor. A vindictive Douglas repeatedly attempted to have Ross prosecuted for homosexual activity, but nevertheless Ross lived openly, mentoring other young homosexual artists like Siegfried Sassoon and Wilfred Owen.

Ross died of a heart attack in 1918. His ashes were interred at Wilde's tomb in Paris. Sassoon remarked of Ross's death, "It was the only time that his heart had ever failed him."

SALLY KRISTEN RIDE

MAY 26 1951 – JUL 23 2012
(AGED 61)

Astronaut and physicist from California, on June 18th, 1983, SALLY RIDE was the first American woman sent into space. A crew member on the space shuttle *Challenger*, she was preceded into space by two Soviet women (cosmonauts Valentina Tereshkova in 1963, and Svetlana Savitskaya in 1982), but was still put under scrutiny for her gender, receiving questions about how her reproductive organs would be affected by spaceflight, or if she cried when things went wrong on the job. Sally insisted that she saw herself only as an astronaut.

But Sally Ride was also a lesbian, a fact kept private until her obituary stated that she was survived by her partner of 27 years, Tam O'Shaughnessy. In collaboration with O'Shaughnessy, Ride wrote several books, including *The Third Planet* (1994), which won the American Institute of Physics Children's Science Writing Award.

After leaving NASA in 1987, Dr. Ride worked at the University of California San Diego as a Professor of Physics, and served as Director of the California Space Institute. In 2001, she founded Sally Ride Science, a company that aimed to motivate girls and young women to pursue careers in science, math, and technology.

Ride died of pancreatic cancer at 61.

JOHN WILLIAM CHEEVER
("THE CHEKHOV OF THE SUBURBS")
MAY 27 1912 – JUN 18 1982
(AGED 70)

American novelist and short story writer, JOHN CHEEVER'S life's work earned him the Pulitzer Prize, a National Book Award, and the National Medal for Literature just weeks before his death. Born in Quincy, Massachusetts to a family that fell in status during the Great Depression, Cheever married in 1941, joined the army during WWII, and very narrowly missed being present with his old infantry during the D-Day invasion of Normandy, 1944.

Cheever lived an unhappy life: from his family's early poverty, to his failure to prove an IQ high enough for Officer Candidate School in the army, to his unsatisfying marriage and late-surprise third child, to his nearly suicidal alcoholism. He had a difficult time accepting his homosexual yearnings. His letters revealed that he had a few affairs with men, some dalliances with male prostitutes, and eventually found a lover and a caretaker in his former student, Max Zimmer, before dying of cancer.

In one of Cheever's later stories, "The Leaves, the Lion-Fish, and the Bear" (1974), two men come together in a motel during a snowstorm, where they drink whiskey and make love. He wrote, "These men were what they were—bewildered, naked, carnal and content."

ANNE SEYMOUR DAMER
(ANNE SEYMOUR CONWAY)

NOV 8 1748 – MAY 28 1828
(AGED 79)

ANNE DAMER was an English sculptor born in Sevenoaks, Kent in 1748. She married John Damer in 1767, whose extravagant spending led him to debt and suicide. After his death, Anne traveled (and was once kidnapped by privateers while doing so), before she began studying modeling, anatomy, and sculpture, to great success. She created sculptures of King George III, Horatio Nelson of the Royal Navy, and of the god Apollo for installation at the Drury Lane Theatre.

Damer went around in male dress even during her marriage, and later did so with a cane she needed after a fall from some scaffolding, which earned her the nickname 'Stick.' She was "a Lady much suspected for liking her own Sex in a criminal Way," according to her contemporaries, a woman of "Sapphick" tendencies. The women in her life included actresses Sarah Siddons and Elizabeth Farren, as well as author and playwright Mary Berry, with whom she lived for several years. Together they once visited Paris in 1802, where they were given a diamond-encrusted snuffbox by Napoleon himself.

Damer died in 1828. She was cremated, and buried in Sundridge, Kent along with her sculptor's tools and the ashes of her favorite dog.

SIR NOËL PEIRCE COWARD

Dec 16 1899 – Mar 26 1973
(AGED 73)

NOËL COWARD had little formal schooling, and was placed in a dance academy in London by his mother. He first appeared as Prince Mussel in a children's play *The Goldfish* in 1911, and continued to work as a child actor. He wrote and starred in his first full-length play in 1920, and went on to produce more than 50 plays, over 300 songs, as well as screenplays, poems, a novel, short stories, a three-volume autobiography, operettas, comic revues, and musical comedies.

Coward spied for England during WWII, worked the British propaganda office in Paris, and was on the Third Reich's kill list for a British invasion. Coward had his knighthood blocked by Winston Churchill, but was eventually knighted by Queen Elizabeth. Coward became known for his silk smoking jacket and long cigarette holder, his flamboyance, and his wit.

Coward's sexuality wasn't publicly discussed. As he said in the 1960s, "There are still a few old ladies in Worthing who don't know." Coward saw actor Graham Payn in the show *Gaities* in 1945, and they remained together until Coward's death of heart failure in March of 1973. His memorial service was held in London on May 29th, 1973.

30th

ALBERT D.J. CASHIER
(JENNIE IRENE HODGERS)

DEC 25 1843 – OCT 10 1915
(AGED 71)

Born in Ireland, Jennie Hodgers began dressing as a boy at a young age, for better ease while herding sheep. Stowed away to the U.S. as a teenager, in 1862 Hodgers joined the 95th Illinois Infantry as ALBERT D.J. CASHIER after a very cursory medical examination.

Private Cashier was enlisted for the duration of the Civil War, fought at Vicksburg, the Siege of Atlanta, and the Battle of Kennesaw Mountain throughout a full service. Brave and unwounded, Cashier was honorably discharged, and thenceforth worked on farms, in hardware stores, and as a handyman. Cashier received a soldier's pension, and lived in a small house that stands as a monument today. For a time, Cashier led the Decoration Day parade in uniform every year.

Cashier was moved to the Soldier's and Sailor's home in old age, where it was discovered that he was born female. Cashier was then transferred to a mental asylum and forced to wear women's clothing. Cashier died after a fall caused by tripping on a dress's hem. The Grand Army of the Republic arranged for a burial with full military honors. There are two headstones marking the grave today, honoring both of Cashier's names.

WALTER "WALT" WHITMAN

MAY 31 1819 – MAR 26 1892
(AGED 72)

WALT WHITMAN was an American poet, essayist, and journalist, best known for his book *Leaves of Grass*, containing the poems "Song of Myself," "I Sing the Body Electric," and "O Captain! My Captain!" Though he did not fight in the American Civil War, he did tend the hospitals long after the conflict ended, bringing requested items and writing letters for "the boys" as a self-described "Soldiers' Missionary."

Derided and once fired for being the author of sexually frank poetry, Whitman nevertheless was a beacon for fellow artists and "camerados," receiving letters and pilgrimage-like visits from men such as Edward Carpenter, Bram Stoker, and Oscar Wilde. A lover of working-class men, Whitman was also a great admirer of President Lincoln, and was quite pleased to hear that Lincoln once remarked approvingly of his gait.

Whitman's most significant relationship was with Irish bus conductor Peter Doyle, who met Whitman one stormy night: "We were familiar at once—I put my hand on his knee—we understood." Whitman's letters to Peter offered him a great deal of affection: "a good smacking kiss, & many of them—& taking in return many, many, many, from my dear son—"

Whitman died of bronchial pneumonia.

JUNE

MARY ANN TALBOT
(JOHN TAYLOR)

FEB 2 1778 – FEB 4 1808
(AGED 30)

Born in London, the sole survivor of twins, and soon to lose her mother during another childbirth, MARY ANN TALBOT believed she was the illegitimate child of Lord William Taylor, Baron of Henson. At 14, Mary Ann was given to the care of Captain Essex Bowen, who stole the money intended to educate Mary, and dressed her as a boy for use "in the menial capacity of his foot-boy." That was when she was first known as John Taylor.

After Bowen's death, Mary Ann remained John Taylor. She fought for the British against the French in what became known as "The Battle of the Glorious First of June," the first and largest fleet action during the French Revolutionary Wars. Mary Ann was significantly wounded by a musket ball to the thigh, and a grapeshot that lodged above her ankle.

At times imprisoned, more often freely employed as a ship's officer, Mary Ann at last revealed her gender to avoid being taken into service against her will. Uncomfortable in female presentation, she worked until her death from illness in the household of Robert S. Kirby, who published her autobiographical story posthumously in 1809, in his magazine, *Kirby's Wonderful and Eccentric Museum*.

VITA SACKVILLE-WEST
(VICTORIA MARY SACKVILLE–WEST, LADY NICOLSON)

MAR 9 1892 – JUN 2 1962
(AGED 70)

VITA SACKVILLE-WEST was born into English aristocracy, and was educated by a governess until she was 13. She then attended Helen Wolff's school for girls, where she met her longtime loves Violet Trefusis and Rosamund Grosvenor. A poem written in French from Sackville-West to Trefusis contains the lines, "I search on your lip for a madder caress / I tear secrets from your yielding flesh." On her affair with Grosvenor, Sackville-West wrote, "Oh, I dare say I realized vaguely that I had no business to sleep with Rosamund, and I should certainly never have allowed anyone to find it out, but my sense of guilt went no further than that."

Sackville-West became an established poet, novelist, and journalist. She twice received the Hawthornden Prize for Imaginative literature, in 1927 and 1933. She and her husband Sir Harold Nicolson created a celebrated garden at their home, Sissinghurst Castle, which became one of the most famous English gardens. Sackville-West had a decade-long affair with Virginia Woolf, and was the inspiration for the protagonist of Woolf's novel *Orlando* (1928). She died in 1962 of abdominal cancer. In 1973, her son Nigel Nicolson published Sackville-West's autobiography, *Portrait of a Marriage*.

ALLA NAZIMOVA
(MAREM-IDES LEVENTON)

JUN 3 1879 – JUL 13 1945
(AGED 66)

Russian-born Broadway and silent film actress, ALLA NAZIMOVA was especially noted for her performances in classic plays by Turgenev, Ibsen, and Chekhov. After becoming a naturalized citizen of the United States, Nazimova began producing and writing the films she starred in, bringing Ibsen's *A Doll's House* (1922) and Oscar Wilde's *Salomé* (1923) to film.

Nazimova's house on Sunset Boulevard was known as "The Garden of Alla," a place of lavish parties. Nazimova had relationships with men and women: a secret husband, a child of suspect paternity, and a "lavender marriage" of convenience that,

when revealed to be a sham, harmed her reputation. She helped start the careers of Rudolph Valentino's two wives, Jean Acker and Natacha Rambova, who were her lovers and his shams, and even coined the phrase "sewing circle" as a code for lesbian and bisexual actresses. Her relationships included affairs with Eva Le Gallienne, Mercedes de Acosta, Dorothy Arzner, and the niece of Oscar Wilde, Dolly Wilde.

Toward the end of her career, Nazimova's mansion was sold, and turned into The Garden of Allah Hotel. She died there, while renting a room with longtime companion Glesca Marshall, from a coronary thrombosis.

VALERIE JEAN SOLANAS

APR 9 1936 – APR 25 1988
(AGED 52)

American radical feminist and author, VALERIE SOLANAS is best known as author of the *S.C.U.M. Manifesto* (1967), and the woman who shot Andy Warhol. Describing herself as a "garbage-mouthed dyke," Solanas was indeed an openly opinionated lesbian.

Born in New Jersey to a volatile home life, by 1965 she was living in New York. Supporting herself with prostitution and begging, Solanas was also working on a play titled *Up Your Ass*, about a young prostitute. In 1967, she met Andy Warhol outside his studio, The Factory, and asked him to produce the play. After giving him the script to read, Solanas was told that he'd lost it. The next year she came to believe that Warhol was working in conspiracy with publisher Maurice Girodias to steal her work. On June 3rd, 1968, she shot and critically wounded Warhol before turning herself in to police. On June 4th she was famous.

Solanas was declared mentally unfit to stand trial, and by 1969 was diagnosed with chronic paranoid schizophrenia. She pleaded guilty to reckless assault and was sentenced to three years in prison. She spent the rest of her life homeless or institutionalized, before dying of pneumonia in San Francisco in 1988.

FEDERICO GARCÍA LORCA
(FEDERICO DEL SAGRADO CORAZÓN DE JESÚS GARCÍA LORCA)

JUN 5 1898 – AUG 19 1936
(AGED 38)

FEDERICO GARCÍA LORCA was a Spanish poet and dramatist. During the 1920s, he became part of the Generation of '27, a group of artists including Salvador Dalí and Luis Buñuel. Lorca was infatuated with Dalí, but though the friendship was mutual, Dalí rejected Lorca's sexual advances, stating in 1969, "He tried to screw me twice. I was extremely annoyed, because I wasn't homosexual, and I wasn't interested in giving in. […] But I felt awfully flattered vis-à-vis the prestige. Deep down I felt that he was a great poet and that I owe him a tiny bit of the Divine Dalí's asshole."

With the success of Lorca's *Gypsy Ballads* (1928) came an estrangement from Dalí and the breakdown of an affair with sculptor Emilio Aladrén. Lorca traveled to New York in 1929, writing *Poet in New York* (1940), published posthumously.

Returning to Spain in 1930, Lorca produced plays for La Barraca, the traveling theater company sponsored by the country's progressive new Republican government. By 1936, a rising right-wing faction assassinated Lorca's brother-in-law within a week of him becoming Mayor of Granada. Lorca was executed by a Nationalist militia the next day. His body was never found.

LONNIE RAY FRISBEE

JUN 6 1949 – MAR 12 1993
(AGED 43)

LONNIE FRISBEE liked to read the Bible on acid. After a baptizing session with friends in Tahquitz Falls, California, and hallucinating hordes of people who'd come to hear him preach on two separate LSD trips, Frisbee was inspired to forge a path as the premier hippie preacher. He was said to "party on Saturday night and preach on Sunday morning." Frisbee set up a commune known as The House of Acts, and in 1968 he and his wife Connie joined up with Chuck Smith of Calvary Chapel to minister to new converts.

Self-described as a "nudist, vegetarian hippie," Frisbee brought thousands of people into the church with his charismatic, Pentecostal style, and was a major proponent in the Jesus movement, creating "Jesus People" and "Jesus Freaks" across the nation. Frisbee's sexuality wasn't entirely public knowledge, and though his early testimonies in preaching included the concept of leaving homosexuality behind for the church, he later dropped it from his narrative. Smith's son, Chuck Smith Jr., recalled a conversation with a pastor who'd heard a young man's confession about being in a six-month relationship with Frisbee, which Frisbee admitted to. Frisbee died in 1993 of AIDS-related complications.

AI OF HAN
(EMPEROR, XIAOAI)

27 – 1 BC
(AGED ~26)

Famous for being the most fulsome homosexual emperor of China's Han Dynasty, EMPEROR AI's relationship with Dong Xian (and homosexual desire itself) became known as "the passion of the cut sleeve," because it was told that after taking a nap together, Emperor Ai cut off his sleeve rather than disturb the sleeping Dong Xian, whose head was resting upon it.

Ai became emperor in 7 BC, and met Dong around 4 BC. After receiving many honors and gifts, Dong and his wife moved into the palace while Ai ordered a luxurious residence built for them. He ignored any protests against the bestowing of these favors, including opposition from his prime minister Wang Jia, whom Ai eventually forced to commit suicide on false charges to silence his dissent. Dong was ultimately appointed the supreme commander of the armed forces at age 22, and on Ai's deathbed he ordered that Dong should take possession of the imperial throne, but this command was ignored.

Dong and his wife were forced to commit suicide after Ai's death, and the throne passed to Ai's cousin, Emperor Ping. "The passion of the cut sleeve" is still a known euphemism for male same-sex desire.

MARGUERITE YOURCENAR

(MARGUERITE ANTOINETTE JEANNE MARIE GHISLAINE CLEENEWERCH DE CRAYENCOUR)

JUN 8 1903 – DEC 17 1987

(AGED 84)

MARGUERITE YOURCENAR was born in Brussels, Belgium and grew up in her grandmother's home, as her mother died days after giving birth. Yourcenar became a poet, playwright, and writer. Her novels include *Alexis* (1929), *The Abyss* (1968), and the highly popular *Memoirs of Hadrian* (1951). She was interested in creating authentic historical works while exploring gender and sexual struggles in her characters. Her novel *Coup de Grâce* (1939) captured in fiction her love and pursuit of a man she discovered was homosexual. Yourcenar also worked as a translator for James Baldwin and Virginia Woolf.

Yourcenar was the first woman elected to the Académie française, received several French literary prizes, and in 1983 was awarded the Erasmus Prize for contributions to European literature and culture.

Literary scholar Grace Frick invited Yourcenar to the U.S. to escape the outbreak of World War II. Yourcenar accepted, and found in Frick a researcher, translator, companion, and lover. They lived in Hartford, Connecticut and Mount Desert Island, Maine, in a house they named Petite Plaisance, remaining there for the rest of their lives. Frick died in 1979, Yourcenar in 1987, and they are buried alongside one another in Mount Desert's Brookside Cemetery.

"BUNNY" ROGER
(NEIL MUNRO ROGER)

JUN 9 1911 – APR 27 1997
(AGED 85)

"BUNNY" ROGER was an English couturier, war hero, social ornament, and the inventor of Capri pants.

Roger was a lifelong bachelor and flamboyantly effeminate. He was expelled from Oxford after a single year for homosexual activities, but it did not shame him. He opened his own dressmaking establishment in Great Newport Street in 1937, catering to the likes of Vivien Leigh and Princess Marina, Duchess of Kent. He served in the Rifle Brigade during WWII, and described the Battle of Anzio by saying, "There were pieces of people flying past my nose and I thought, 'This is perfectly awful but not as bad as being at school.'" He claimed he went into battle rouged, with a mauve chiffon scarf around his helmet.

He invested well after the war and threw a lot of parties. In 1953, he hosted a Coronation Ball dressed as Queen Alexandra, a Fetish Party in 1956, and for his 60th, 70th, and 80th birthdays he held the Diamond, Amethyst, and Flame Balls.

"Bunny" Roger is credited with inventing the tight-cut Capri pants while vacationing there in 1949. According to his obituary, "to onlookers [he was] a passing peacock, to intimates a life enhancer and exemplary friend."

RAINER WERNER FASSBINDER

MAY 31 1945 – JUN 10 1982
(AGED 37)

As a child in Munich, RAINER FASSBINDER was often sent to the cinema while his mother worked, where he might see up to four films a day. In 1963, he began experimenting with 8mm cameras and started making his own movies. Fassbinder joined the Munich Action-Theater in 1967, working as an actor, director, and script writer. Fassbinder found international success and acclaim with his avant-garde filmmaking, often portraying gay relationships and individuals on screen.

Fassbinder's acting ensemble was made up of friends, family, former members of the Munich Action-Theater, as well as his lovers. For a time he was involved with his secretary, Irm Hermann, and later fell for Günther Kaufmann, attempting to buy his love with film roles and Lamborghinis. Fassbinder married Ingrid Caven in 1970, who later explained, "Rainer was a homosexual who also needed a woman. It's that simple and that complex." He also had a relationship with Moroccan actor El Hedi ben Salem, former butcher Armin Meier, and his editor Juliane Lorenz.

Fassbinder died of a lethal combination of cocaine and barbiturates. He was found with a cigarette between his lips and notes for a future film at his side.

YUKIO MISHIMA
(KIMITAKE HIRAOKA)

JAN 14 1925 – NOV 25 1970
(AGED 45)

Born in Tokyo, Japan, Kimitake Hiraoka began writing fiction at 12 years old. He had to write in secret, as his father forbade it and would rip up any manuscript he found. His teachers gave him the pen name YUKIO MISHIMA when they submitted one of his stories to a literary magazine, and he continued to assume the name for the rest of his writing career.

Mishima married Yoko Sugiyama on June 11th, 1958. He was known to visit gay bars, but claimed it was research for his novel, *Forbidden Colors* (1951). He wrote several novels that featured homosexual overtones.

Mishima was also a play-wright, an actor, a model, and eventually formed his own private militia. On November 25th, 1970, Mishima and four other members of his militia barricaded the office of a military building as part of an attempted *coup d'état*. While Mishima addressed the audience of troops below, the crowd began to mock him, and it was clear that his *coup* had failed. Mishima finished his speech, went back inside, and committed ritualistic suicide (*seppuku*), dying at 45. In 1998, writer Jiro Fukushima published a book that contained private correspondence between Mishima and himself, revealing their romantic relationship.

DJUNA BARNES

JUN 12 1892 – JUN 18 1982
(AGED 90)

DJUNA BARNES was a freelance journalist and illustrator. Her illustrated volume of poetry, *The Book of Repulsive Women*, was published in 1915, and she continued to publish stories, plays, and novels throughout her life. She often referred to herself as "the most famous unknown of the century," bemoaning that people knew her reputation better than her writing.

Barnes's novel *Nightwood* (1936) was one of the earliest to portray lesbians. Main characters Nora Flood and the androgynous Robin Vote were based on Barnes and her former lover, sculptor Thelma Wood. Wood was unhappy with her portrayal in the book and broke off all contact with Barnes after its publication.

Barnes was briefly engaged to Ernst Hanfstaengl, lived with philosopher Courtenay Lemon whom she referred to as her common-law husband, and had relationships with the aforementioned Thelma Wood, as well as reporter Mary Pyne. Not the biggest fan of labels, Barnes once claimed, "I'm not a lesbian, I just loved Thelma."

A recluse later in life, her Greenwich Village neighbor, poet E.E. Cummings, would yell out his window from time to time to check if Barnes was still alive. She died in 1982 in New York City.

DR. JOHN FORBES NASH, JR.

JUN 13 1928 – MAY 23 2015
(AGED 86)

JOHN NASH was an American mathematician who made significant contributions to the understanding of game theory, differential geometry, and the study of partial differential equations. In 1994, he earned a Nobel Memorial Prize in Economic Sciences, along with fellow game theorists Reinhard Selten and John Harsanyi. He later became the subject of the 1998 film *A Beautiful Mind*, starring Russell Crowe. He suffered from paranoid delusions which caused erratic behavior throughout his life.

Nash fathered an illegitimate son, John, with Eleanor Stier, whom he met while she was his nurse. He later had another son named John with the wife he married twice, Alicia Lopez-Harrison de Lardé. In between these relationships, in 1954, Nash was arrested for indecent exposure during a sting targeting homosexual men who sought sex in public bathrooms. Along with his first son, this incident was left out of the biographical film, as was Nash's assertion that his mental illness had cleared away naturally. Addressing a colleague in the mid-1990s, he wrote, "I emerged from irrational thinking, ultimately, without medicine other than the natural hormonal changes of aging."

Nash's second son has since developed schizophrenia. Nash and his wife were killed in a car accident in 2015.

EMMA STEBBINS

Sept 1 1815 – Oct 25 1882
(AGED 67)

EMMA STEBBINS moved to Rome to pursue her love of art. There she lived with sculptor Harriet Hosmer, and studied under Welsh neoclassical sculptor John Gibson. Stebbins was commissioned to make a portrait bust of actress Charlotte Cushman between 1859-1860. Her bronze statue of education reformer and U.S. Representative Horace Mann was installed outside Boston's State House in 1865.

Stebbins is best known for her sculpture *Angel of the Waters* (1873), which is also known as Bethesda Fountain in Central Park. It was created to celebrate the completion of the Croton Aqueduct, and is considered to be one of the great works of American sculpture in the 19th century.

Stebbins was in love with Charlotte Cushman, whom she met in Rome. They traveled together frequently, and their circle of friends included fellow artists and bohemians, like Harriet Hosmer and Edmonia Lewis. Stebbins and Cushman were together until Cushman's death from pneumonia in 1876. Stebbins released their correspondence in 1878 as *Charlotte Cushman: Her Letters and Memories of Her Life.* Stebbins died in 1882.

On June 14th, 2014, Stebbins' grave was featured in the first gay tour of Green-Wood Cemetery in Brooklyn, New York.

ADAH ISAACS MENKEN

❧

JUN 15 1835 – AUG 10 1868
(AGED 33)

Actress, painter, and poet ADAH ISAACS MENKEN told many versions of her origins, so little is known for sure. A leading theory is she was a Louisiana-born Creole Catholic of mixed race, another is she was Jewish, based on her knowledge of Hebrew and her refusal to perform on High Holidays. She married several times, and had a habit of keeping her new names.

Menken was friends with the likes of Walt Whitman, Charles Dickens, Dante Gabrielle Rossetti, George Sand, and possibly more-than-friends with Alexandre Dumas. Though she had ambitions as a writer, Menken was best known as an actress, particularly for her starring role in *Mazeppa* (1861), based on a play by Lord Byron. During the show she would be stripped on stage to a flesh-colored body stocking, and strapped to a live horse.

Bisexual, Menken once wrote to poet Hattie Tyng, "We find the rarest and most perfect beauty in the affections of one woman for another... The electricity of the one flashes and gleams through the other, to be returned not only in degree as between man and women, but in kind as between precisely similar organizations."

Menken died of an unconfirmed illness after collapsing in Paris.

ONA MUNSON
(OWENA WOLCOTT)

JUN 16 1903 – FEB 11 1955
(AGED 51)

ONA MUNSON came to fame starring in the title role of *No, No, Nanette* (1925) on Broadway. From there she worked in stage and radio. Her first starring role onscreen was *Going Wild* in 1930. The film was originally produced as a musical, but nearly all numbers were cut prior to its release. Munson retired in 1931, but returned to the screen in 1938. Her other films include *Wagons Westward* (1940) and *Lady from Louisiana* (1941). Her most well-known role was playing Belle Watling in the epic film *Gone with the Wind* (1939), a part that would typecast her in later films.

Munson was married three times and had affairs with women, including filmmaker Dorothy Arzner. Munson also had a relationship with the playwright Mercedes de Acosta and wrote that they "shared the deepest spiritual moment that life brings to human beings." Munson severed her relationship with de Acosta in fear that her sexuality would be exposed. She suffered from depression and committed suicide by overdosing on barbiturates in 1955. Her suicide note read, "This is the only way I know to be free again…Please don't follow me." Munson posthumously received a star on the Hollywood Walk of Fame.

CARL VAN VECHTEN

JUN 17 1880 – DEC 21 1964
(AGED 84)

American writer and photographer, CARL VAN VECHTEN was a patron of the Harlem Renaissance, and literary executor of Gertrude Stein. His books include *Peter Whiffle* (1922), the controversial *Nigger Heaven* (1926, named after a slang term for the segregated balcony of a theater, used by Van Vechten as an analogy for Harlem itself), and his autobiography *Sacred and Profane Memories* (1932). As a photographer, he captured the likenesses of countless notable artists and influencers.

Often a newspaper correspondent, Van Vechten became the first American critic of modern dance. He married and divorced friend Anna Snyder, then married actress Fania Marinoff in 1914, who remained his wife until his death in 1964. He nevertheless had open relationships with men, most notably with Mark Lutz, a journalist from Virginia, to whom Van Vechten sent thousands of letters during their three decades of friendship, and all of which were destroyed after Lutz's death, as per Lutz's wishes. Van Vechten's masculine desires can also be seen in his homoerotic portraits of working-class men.

Edward White's 2014 biography of Van Vechten dubbed him *The Tastemaker*, a man who dabbled widely. Van Vechten said of himself, "I don't think I've ever lost interest in anything."

JANIS LYN JOPLIN

JAN 19 1943 – OCT 4 1970
(AGED 27)

Best known for her song covers of "Me and Bobby McGee," "Piece of My Heart," and "Cry Baby," JANIS JOPLIN's final recording was an original song, "Mercedes Benz," written as a birthday gift for John Lennon. After a short life, Joplin was posthumously inducted into the Rock and Roll Hall of Fame (1995), awarded a Lifetime Achievement Grammy (2005), and is still one of the top-selling musicians in the U.S.

Joplin was launched into stardom the weekend of June 17-18th in 1967, on the strength of her blistering performance at the Monterey International Pop Festival. During her first attempt at a music career in San Francisco in 1963, Joplin dated a woman, Jae Whittaker, became engaged to a man, Peter de Blanc, but was sent home to Texas to sober up within three years. After her success in 1967, her drug and alcohol abuse returned.

Joplin had many significant relationships with both men and women, the last of each were Seth Morgan and Peggy Caserta, who both coincidentally decided to abandon Joplin one Friday night in October. Joplin mentioned her heartache to her drug dealer on Saturday, while buying the dose of heroin that would kill her on Sunday.

ELISABETH "BESSIE" MARBURY

JUN 19 1856 – JAN 22 1933
(AGED 76)

BESSIE MARBURY came from a prominent New York family, and parlayed her contacts into the theatrical and literary world, becoming an agent for high-profile clients including Oscar Wilde, George Bernard Shaw, Vernon and Irene Castle, and Jerome K. Jerome. Marbury and other agents formed the American Play Company in 1914, which produced and established musical comedies for Broadway, most notably *See America First* (1916) and *Love O' Mike* (1917).

Marbury wrote *Manners: A Handbook of Social Customs* in 1888, which offered advice like which servants to tip, whether or not you should let a stranger into your house, and the usual number of bridesmaids for a wedding (answer: six). Her autobiography, *My Crystal Ball: Reminiscences*, was published in 1923, where she wrote that she never married because she "never had a really good offer." During World War I, Marbury provided aid in French military hospitals.

Marbury met interior designer Elsie de Wolfe at a party, and they were together for decades, living in houses de Wolfe restored in Gramercy Park, the Upper East Side, and the Villa Trianon, a mansion in Versailles. Though de Wolfe married Sir Charles Mendl, she returned to Marbury weeks after the wedding. Marbury died in 1933.

LIZZIE ANDREW BORDEN

JUL 19 1860 – JUN 1 1927
(AGED 66)

LIZZIE BORDEN was an American woman who gained notoriety when she was tried for the axe murders of her father and stepmother. She was acquitted on June 20th, 1893.

The murders occurred on August 4th, 1892. In contradiction to the popular rhyme, the Bordens were not 'whacked' 40 and 41 times; Abby had been struck 19 times and Andrew 11, his face nearly split in half, an eye cut open, and his nose partially severed from his head. Lizzie was brought to trial on circumstantial evidence, specifically: she and the maid, Bridget Sullivan, were the only people in the house when the bodies were found; Lizzie would inherit her father's wealth and so had financial motive; Lizzie had been seen burning a dress three days after the murders.

One theory is that Lizzie Borden was discovered to be having an affair with Bridget, and the Bordens were killed to keep that secret. Lizzie never married, though Bridget Sullivan later did. Lizzie was also enthralled with actress Nance O'Neil, who remained unmarried until well into her forties, and for whom Lizzie would host lavish parties.

After the trial, Lizzie remained in Fall River, Massachusetts until her own death from pneumonia.

OWEN VINCENT DODSON

NOV 28 1914 – JUN 21 1983
(AGED 68)

As a student at Bates College and later the Yale School of Drama, African-American OWEN DODSON directed, wrote, and acted in plays. While enlisted in the U.S. Navy, Dodson wrote naval history plays, as well as the poems "Black Mother Praying in the Sun 1943" and "The Ballad of Dorie Miller" (1943). Dodson became chair of the Drama Department at the historically black Howard University, and went on to be a successful playwright, poet, and novelist, often writing about religion and sexuality. His novels *Boy at the Window* (1951) and *Come Home Early, Child* (1967) are seen as partially if not fully autobiographical.

Dodson's relationships included the writer and theater critic Hilton Als, and a brief engagement to his classmate at Bates, Priscilla Heath. Close friendships and admirers include authors Carl Van Vechten and James Baldwin; his correspondence with Van Vechten continued for 25 years.

He treated his rheumatoid arthritis with alcohol, and continued to write out poems however illegibly on any available surface: brown paper bags, napkins, and handbills. Dodson lived with his sister Edith until her death in January of 1983 from stroke-related complications. Dodson died later that year of cardiovascular disease.

M.F.K. FISHER
(MARY FRANCES KENNEDY)

JUL 3 1908 – JUN 22 1992
(AGED 83)

Preeminent American food writer M.F.K. FISHER had a career spanning 60 years, made up of hundreds of stories for *The New Yorker*, over 25 books, and an enduring translation of Brillat-Savarin's *The Physiology of Taste* (1825). She was a founder of the Napa Valley Wine Library, a "poet of the appetites" according to John Updike, and in W.H. Auden's opinion, "America's greatest writer."

Keeping his name, Fisher left her first husband for the second, her already-married neighbor, Dillwyn Parrish. Parrish developed Buerger's disease, a progressive clotting disorder, which required a leg amputation. He shot himself in 1941 rather than undergo a second amputation. In 1943, Fisher became pregnant. She listed a fictional father's name on her daughter's birth certificate and passed her off as adopted. She never identified the true father. Fisher's third husband was a publisher, Friede, with whom she had her second child.

A 2005 biography by Joan Reardon revealed a significant romance never mentioned in print, a live-in relationship with drama teacher Marietta Voorhees in the 1950s. By that time Fisher had found a "midlife lesbianism," and all her later-life sexual relationships were with women.

Fisher died after a long battle with Parkinson's disease at age 83.

ALFRED CHARLES KINSEY

JUN 23 1894 – AUG 25 1956
(AGED 62)

An American biologist, zoologist, then sexologist, ALFRED KINSEY founded the Institute for Sex Research at Indiana University in 1947. He wrote both *Sexual Behavior in the Human Male* (1948) and *Sexual Behavior in the Human Female* (1953), and created the Kinsey scale of sexuality that goes from 0 – Exclusively heterosexual to 6 – Exclusively homosexual, with varying stages in between.

Kinsey married in 1921 and had four children, the first of which died young due to juvenile diabetes. He was bisexual, and he and his wife agreed they could have sexual relationships outside of their marriage. Kinsey had affairs with men, including his student, Clyde Martin. For a long time Kinsey was so troubled by his homoerotic feelings that he would punish himself while masturbating by inserting straws and then toothbrush handles into his urethra. He continued that sort of abusive behavior for so long that during a particularly dark episode, he was able to circumcise himself without anesthesia, in a bathtub with a pocketknife.

His research was taboo, controversial, and often mischaracterized, but he gathered enough behavioral data to skew sexual labels, and reveal just how normal being 'abnormal' truly is. He died from a heart ailment complicated by pneumonia.

OLIVE YANG
(YANG KYIN HSIU, YÁNG JĪNXIÙ)

JUN 24 1927 – JUL 13 2017
(AGED 90)

OLIVE YANG was born into Burmese royalty, forced into an arranged marriage with her younger cousin, and reportedly threw a urine pot at him when he attempted to consummate the union. Yang bore a child, abandoned her newborn, and left home. By 19, she had organized an army (nicknamed "Olive's Boys") to consolidate control of opium trade routes. She dressed in men's fatigues, "packing a pair of Belgian army pistols on her hips," and as an opium trafficker/warlord, struck deals with the newly-formed CIA to trade opium for arms under "Operation Paper." Yang was arrested, and successfully negotiated a two-decade-long peace agreement in exchange for her release.

Yang had affairs with actresses, musicians, and singers, including actress Wah Wah Win Shwe, to whom she deeded her property. She also fell for beauty queen Louisa Benson, and fought her brother for Benson's attention. Her favorites were showered with gifts, including Kokang tea, valuable fabrics, and bacon from her family's pigs.

Yang's appearance earned her the nickname Miss Hairy Legs, though Yang preferred to be called Uncle Olive. Survived by her son, Duan Jipu, whom she called Jeep after the American vehicles she saw during World War II, Yang died in 2017.

THORNTON WILDER

APR 17 1897 – DEC 7 1975
(AGED 78)

THORNTON WILDER is the only writer with Pulitzer Prizes for both fiction (*The Bridge of San Luis Rey*, 1927) and drama (*Our Town*, 1938 and *The Skin of Our Teeth*, 1942). *Our Town* was inspired by Gertrude Stein's novel *The Making of Americans* (1924), the enduring influence of which can be seen in a telegram Wilder sent Stein, postmarked June 25th, 1937: "JUST FINISHED LONGER MAKING AMERICANS WONDERFUL GLORIOUS LOVE THORNTON." Wilder's many honors include the Presidential Medal of Freedom, and for his WWII service, the Legion of Merit Bronze Star and the Order of the British Empire.

Discreet about his personal life, Wilder was nevertheless close friends and initially lovers with the writer/pornographer/tattoo artist and former college professor Samuel Steward. They met through Stein in 1937, who corresponded regularly with both, once writing to Steward, "And Sammy, do you know how he liked you? He was writing *Our Town* in Zurich and was stuck at the end of the second act, and you walked all night in the rain with him and he struck a match on you, he said, and wrote the whole third act the next day while you were sleeping." Wilder died of heart failure.

"BABE" DIDRIKSON
(MILDRED ELLA DIDRIKSON ZAHARIAS)

JUN 26 1911 – SEP 27 1956
(AGED 45)

Born in Texas, "BABE" DIDRIKSON was an all-American basketball player, an Olympic track and field gold medalist twice over, and winner of 82 golf tournaments, including an astounding 14 in a row. She was a founding member of the LPGA, and the first woman to play against men in a PGA Tour event. She once won a team track meet single-handedly, running from heat to heat, winning enough events to claim the championship against teams with 12, 15, and 22 competitors. She was also an accomplished baseball, softball, and tennis player. She set multiple Olympic records.

Didrikson dropped out of high school to become an athlete. She withstood sexist insults from men and women alike. In 1938, she married professional wrestler George Zaharias and began remaking her image as more "graceful" and feminine. In 1950, she met 20-year-old golf protégée Betty Dodd of San Antonio, and began an immediate intimate friendship that endured for the rest of Didrikson's life. Dodd lived with the Zahariases as the marital bond declined, and cared for Didrikson when she was diagnosed with rectal cancer in 1953. Didrikson won the U.S. Women's Open again in 1954, despite her terminal cancer. She died in 1956.

ALTHEA FLYNT
(ALTHEA LEASURE)

NOV 6 1953 – JUN 27 1987
(AGED 33)

Born in Marietta, Ohio, ALTHEA FLYNT is best known as the 4th wife of Larry Flynt, and co-publisher of Flynt's pornography magazine, *Hustler*.

At age eight, Althea's father shot and killed her mother and two others, before fatally shooting himself. Afterwards, Althea and her siblings were sent to an orphanage, from which Althea frequently ran away to avoid abuse by potential adopters. She met Larry Flynt at 17 when she applied to be a go-go dancer at his Hustler club in Columbus, Ohio. They married in 1976, and stayed married through Flynt's bipolar episodes, a near-fatal shooting in 1978 which left him paralyzed and wheelchair-bound, and the legal battles over obscenity charges that were portrayed in *The People vs. Larry Flynt* (1996). According to Flynt himself, "She made me feel she loved me as much at the end—she kissed me goodnight the night before she died—as the day we were married."

Openly bisexual, Althea struggled with drug addiction, and after a 1982 hysterectomy, was soon found to be suffering from a pre-AIDS condition. With her health in decline and her addictions untreated, she slipped into a bathtub in the couple's Los Angeles mansion and drowned. She was 33.

DOLLY WILDE
(DOROTHY IERNE WILDE)

JUL 11 1895 – APR 10 1941
(AGED 45)

DOLLY WILDE was born three months after her uncle Oscar was convicted of gross indecency. Dolly was often told she was a female version Oscar: the same soft, pale hands, elongated face, melancholy wit... and the same sexual orientation.

Dolly Wilde had a long series of what she called "emergency seductions." In 1914, she went to France to be an ambulance driver during WWI, and had affairs with Standard Oil heiress Marion "Joe" Carstairs, actress Alla Nazimova who brought her uncle's play *Salomé* to the silent screen in 1923, and salon hostess Natalie Clifford Barney, an American expatriate and multi-millionaire. Wilde entered the Barney household on June 28th, 1927, and remained involved with Barney until her death.

Wilde was suicidal, alcoholic, and addicted to heroin. She was written into and out of F. Scott Fitzgerald's *Tender is the Night* (1934) after she made a drunken pass at his wife. Barney financed Wilde's drug detoxifications, but they were unsuccessful. In 1939, Wilde was diagnosed with breast cancer, refused surgery, and was forced to leave Paris at the outbreak of WWII. She died of "causes unascertainable" according to autopsy, three months shy of the same age both her uncle and father died.

FRITZ HAARMANN
(FRIEDRICH HEINRICH KARL HAARMANN, "THE BUTCHER OF HANOVER")

OCT 25 1879 – APR 15 1925
(AGED 45)

Also known as the Butcher of Hanover, the Vampire of Hanover, and the Wolf Man, FRITZ HAARMANN escaped from a mental institution and took up life as a con artist and thief. He got on the good side of the German police by informing on other criminals. This enabled him to cloak his more unsavory activities.

Haarmann liked to lure young boys to his place where he'd rape them, strangle them, and bite through their Adam's apples in a fit of passion. He dismembered the bodies and most likely sold their flesh as mincemeat on the black market. Haarmann and his lover/accomplice Hans Grans were prime suspects after a suspicious number of skulls were found on the banks of the local river.

On June 29th, 1924, police searched Haarmann's apartment and found a number of items belonging to missing victims. Haarmann attempted to talk his way out of the evidence, but eventually confessed to killing and dismembering "somewhere between 50 and 70" victims in what he described as a "rabid sexual passion." Haarmann was sentenced to death and beheaded by guillotine. On the day of his execution, Haarmann received religious counseling, smoked an expensive cigar, and drank some Brazilian coffee.

EVA SELINA LAURA GORE-BOOTH

MAY 22 1870 – JUN 30 1926
(AGED 56)

EVA GORE-BOOTH was the third child of Lady Georgina and Sir Henry Gore-Booth of Lissadell. Her privileged upbringing allowed her to survive the Irish Famine of 1879, though she was forever haunted by the inequalities and injustices of wealth disparity. Gore-Booth learned several languages, found a love of poetry, and traveled with her father through the West Indies and North America.

Gore-Booth met her lifelong companion, women's rights leader Esther Roper, while recovering from a respiratory illness in Italy. Gore-Booth and Roper started the journal *Urania*, which spoke to sexual politics, feminism, and the elimination of gender and sexual distinctions. Gore-Booth fought for women's suffrage, helped establish representation committees for female workers, and was a member of the Women's Peace Crusade and the Committee for the Abolition of Capital Punishment.

Gore-Booth was encouraged by W.B. Yeats to pursue poetry and Irish tales. Her work promoted the female form, and women rather than men in heroic Irish folklore. Roper published a collection of her work after Gore-Booth's death from cancer in 1926. Gore-Booth's sister Constance wrote of Roper, "I feel so glad Eva and she were together, and so thankful that her love was with Eva to the end."

JULY

LUTHER VANDROSS
(LUTHER RONZONI VANDROSS JR.)

APR 20 1951 – JUL 1 2005
(AGED 54)

LUTHER VANDROSS was lead singer of the group Change, with its gold-certified debut album *The Glow of Love* (1980). He pursued a career as a solo artist in 1981, and found success with R&B tunes like "Never Too Much," and "Here and Now." Vandross and his "Velvet Voice" sold over 35 million records worldwide and won eight Grammy Awards. Vandross also wrote and sang national commercial jingles, and contributed back-up vocals for artists including Chaka Khan, Diana Ross, and Barbra Streisand.

Vandross suffered a severe stroke in 2003 and fell into a coma for two months. After his stroke, Vandross was confined to a wheelchair and struggled with speaking and singing. He appeared at the Grammys in a pre-taped segment in 2004. Vandross died in 2005.

Vandross was very guarded about his private life and sexuality. It wasn't until after his death that his sexuality was discussed, and his status as a gay artist recognized. Vandross confided to close friend Bruce Vilanch, "No one knows I'm in the life." He had few sexual contacts. Vandross's longest romantic relationship was with a man, while he was living in Los Angeles from the late 1980s to the early 1990s.

RICHARD BRUCE NUGENT
(RICHARD BRUCE, BRUCE NUGENT)
❧

JUL 2 1906 – MAY 27 1987
(AGED 80)

After his father's death, African-American artist RICHARD BRUCE NUGENT was sent to live in Washington D.C. with his grandmother. There he connected with poets Georgia Douglas Johnson and Langston Hughes, and followed them to Harlem.

Nugent lived with writer Wallace Thurman from 1926-1928, who wrote Nugent into his novel, *Infants of the Spring* (1932). Nugent's short story "Smoke Lilies and Jade" appeared in the only issue of *Fire!!* in 1926. His poem "Shadows" appeared in Countee Cullen's *Caroling Dusk: An Anthology of Verse by Negro Poets* (1927). His prose piece "Sahdji" and its accompanying drawing appeared in the anthology *The New Negro*

in 1925. Nugent acted, painted, and explored sexuality and black identity through his stories, poems, and drawings. Nugent co-founded the Harlem Cultural Council, and served as chair of the Program Committee until 1967.

Nugent married nurse/professor Grace Marr in 1952. Though their marriage was never consummated, they were together until her death in 1969. Nugent was openly gay and had a relationship with Hank Fisher, to whom he wrote the poem "Bastard Song (for H.F.)" which includes the line, "My love for you is love for you though neither black nor white."

Nugent died of congestive heart failure.

THELMA ELLEN WOOD

Jul 3 1901 – Dec 10 1970

(AGED 69)

THELMA WOOD was described as sexually magnetic, boyish-looking, and almost six feet tall, with a love for cooking, dancing, and a good rum and coke. Author Emily Coleman captured Wood in her diary by writing, "I've never seen a more attractive woman. Even on the stage, they don't often have such a compelling face as that. She makes one want to make love."

Wood attended the St. Louis School of Fine Art at Washington University, where she perfected her technique at silverpoint drawing. Wood continued her studies in sculpting, painting, and drawing in Paris, and her work was exhibited in Milch Galleries in New York City in 1931. She frequented Berlin, and fell in love with its open sexual lifestyle.

Her partners included photographer Berenice Abbott, poet Djuna Barnes, poet Edna St. Vincent Millay, and the wealthy Henriette McCrea Metcalf, who supported her art. Wood was fictionalized in Barnes's novel *Nightwood* (1936) as Robin Vote, a portrayal Wood objected to before breaking off all contact with Barnes. Around 1943, Wood moved in with antique dealer Margaret Behrens, and they lived together for 27 years until Wood's death from breast cancer in 1970. Her ashes were interred at the Behrens plot.

KATHARINE LEE BATES

AUG 12 1859 – MAR 28 1929

(AGED 69)

KATHARINE LEE BATES graduated with a bachelor's degree from Wellesley College in 1880. She taught at high schools and Wellesley for several years, briefly studied at Oxford University, and received a master's degree in English Literature. Bates was a poet, travel writer, and children's book author. In her poem "Goody Santa Claus on a Sleigh Ride" from *Sunshine and Other Verses for Children* (1889) she popularized Mrs. Claus as an active character in the Santa Claus narrative.

After a trek to the top of Pikes Peak, she felt a great joy from seeing the expanse of America, and jotted down a draft of "America the Beautiful," later featured in weekly journal *The Congregationalist* for Independence Day, 1895. Bates's words were set to composer S. A. Ward's "Materna," the tune to which Americans sing them today.

At age nine, Bates wrote in her diary, "I like women better than men." She met Katharine Coman, teacher at Wellesley College and founder of the school's Economics department, in 1887, and they lived and traveled together until Coman's death (1915). Bates's book *Yellow Clover: A Book of Remembrance* (1922) was a collection of poems for and about Coman. Bates died at home in 1929.

WANDA ALEKSANDRA LANDOWSKA

JUL 5 1879 – AUG 16 1959
(AGED 80)

WANDA LANDOWSKA was born to Jewish parents in Warsaw, Poland, and began playing the piano at four years old. She studied at the Warsaw Conservatory, under the tutelage of Heinrich Urban in Berlin, and with Moritz Moszkowski in Paris. She taught piano at the Schola Cantorum, harpsichord at the Berlin Hochschule für Musik and the Curtis Institute of Music, and founded the École de Musique Ancienne, a center for study and performance. Landowska also frequented lesbian Natalie Clifford Barney's salon, to socialize and perform.

Landowska and husband Henry Lew published *Musique ancienne* (1909), a book on the harpsichord. After being captured while teaching in Berlin in 1913, Landowska and Lew were prisoners on parole during WWI. Lew died in an automobile accident after their release. Landowska remained in France until the outbreak of WWII, when she and student Denise Restout fled to the United States.

Landowska famously was the first to record Bach's "Goldberg Variations" on its intended instrument of the harpsichord. She acquired old instruments and had French piano company Pleyel et Cie manufacture replicas for collection and performance.

Restout became Landowska's assistant, editor, biographer, and domestic partner. They lived together in Lakeville, Connecticut until Landowska's death in 1959.

FRIDA KAHLO
(MAGDALENA CARMEN FRIDA KAHLO Y CALDERÓN DE RIVERA)

JUL 6 1907 – JUL 13 1954
(AGED 47)

Born in Coyocoán, outside of Mexico City, FRIDA KAHLO was a painter mainly of self-portraits, and is celebrated for her depictions of gender, class, and race in Mexican society. Kahlo began painting after she was severely injured in a bus accident in 1925. A pole pierced her from stomach to pelvis, she endured numerous operations throughout her life, and was often corseted for the purpose of mechanical stretching. Many of her works were painted while lying in bed.

Kahlo was unable to have children due to her injuries, suffering miscarriages and abortions. She had a turbulent relationship with Diego Rivera, whom she married twice. Openly bisexual, Kahlo also had affairs with Leon Trotsky, André Breton's wife Jacqueline Lamba, singer/dancer/actress Josephine Baker, and singer Chavela Vargas, to whom Kahlo once said, "I live only for you and Diego."

Kahlo's right leg was amputated in 1953 due to gangrene. She died of pulmonary embolism in 1954. A few days before her death, Kahlo wrote in her diary, "I hope the exit is joyful—and I hope never to return." Rivera wrote it was the most tragic day of his life. Kahlo remains an enduring icon for Chicanos, feminists, and the LGBT movement.

KITTY GENOVESE
(CATHERINE SUSAN GENOVESE)

JUL 7 1935 – MAR 13 1964
(AGED 28)

KITTY GENOVESE is famous for the circumstances surrounding her horrifying murder. She was stabbed outside of her apartment building in Kew Gardens, New York City, and staggered into the building's entryway, where she was stabbed again and raped by the returning attacker. Sophia Farrar emerged from a neighboring apartment to try to help her friend, and held Genovese in her final moments. Genovese died in an ambulance on the way to a hospital at 4:15 AM.

The *New York Times* reported that 38 witnesses to Genovese's attack did nothing to help, a psychological phenomenon later dubbed "The Bystander Effect,"

where no one person in a crowd will help because they assume someone else will.

In 2015, a documentary called *The Witness* explored Genovese's case via her brother Bill Genovese's efforts to understand why his sister's distress was ignored. This documentary dispels the myth that so many people knew a woman was being murdered and did nothing; it also states that Genovese's body was identified by Mary Ann Zielonko, who was her live-in lover and partner. The day of Kitty's death was a Friday the 13th, and was also the one-year anniversary of when she and Mary Ann first met.

EDITH ELLIS
(EDITH MARY OLDHAM LEES ELLIS)

1861 – SEP 14 1916
(A G E D ~ 5 5)

After her mother's death, EDITH ELLIS was sent to live in a convent in 1873. She joined the Fellowship of the New Life in 1883, a group with the objective of cultivating "a perfect character in each and all," a philosophy influenced by Tolstoy, Thoreau, and Emerson. Ellis wrote novels, plays, and delivered speeches on feminism, sexuality, and gender roles.

Though openly lesbian, Edith Ellis married another Fellowship member, sexologist Havelock Ellis, in 1891. Edith had a nervous breakdown in March 1916, and attempted to commit suicide by throwing herself off the 4th floor of a building. She died of diabetes complications later that year.

Havelock wrote of their unique relationship in his autobiography, *My Life*, published in 1939, prior to his death on July 8th. In it he wrote of his wife's love for an Irish artist who died from Bright's Disease in June, 1903: "Lily was for Edith a star, a star to which for all the rest of her life the chariot of her spirit was attached." Havelock also wrote, "[Edith] craved something more gracious, less prudish, pure by natural instinct rather than by moral principle. In Lily she found the ideal embodiment of all her cravings."

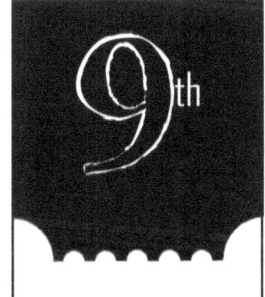

JAMES B. POLLACK

JUL 9 1938 – JUN 13 1994
(AGED 55)

As a child, JAMES POLLACK'S parents were concerned about his learning ability, until a psychologist discovered that Pollack was thinking so quickly that his verbalization couldn't keep up. Pollack learned to speak slowly, so slowly that his NASA colleagues found him nearly impossible to interrupt. He graduated from Princeton with High Honors in Physics, received a master's degree at Berkeley in Nuclear Physics, and went on to Harvard to study Astronomy, where he met up with Carl Sagan.

Pollack was a key player in nearly every NASA planetary mission after Apollo. He helped create the first detailed models on the formation of giant gas planets, formed the foundation for the study of evolutionary climate change on all terrestrial planets, studied nuclear winter, and examined the asteroid impact that led to extinction of the dinosaurs. He received many awards for his research including the esteemed Gerard P. Kuiper Prize in 1989.

Pollack was openly gay. He played tennis, read science fiction, and subscribed to the San Francisco opera. His longtime friend Bruce Hassell noted his favorites were anything by Wagner and Puccini's *Turandot*. Pollack died in 1994 of Chordoma, a rare spinal cancer. A Mars crater was named in his honor.

LOUISE ABBÉMA

OCT 30 1853 – JUL 10 1927
(AGED 73)

LOUISE ABBÉMA was born in France and cited lesbian painter Rosa Bonheur as the person who "decided me to become an artist." With her family's connections to the art community, Abbéma was able to study painting under Charles Joshua Chaplin, Carolus-Duran, and Jean-Jacques Henner. Abbéma's work included etchings, pastels, oil portraits, watercolor, impressionist paintings, engravings, and sculpture. Some of her best-known works are *The Seasons* (1883) and *Among the Flowers* (1893).

Abbéma was featured at the Paris Salon, the 1893 World Columbian Exposition in Chicago, received a bronze medal at the 1900 Exposition Universelle in Paris, and contributed as a writer to several journals and gazettes on art. She also received the Legion of Honour in 1906 with the decorated distinction of Chevalier.

She had a close relationship with film actress Sarah Bernhardt, and Bernhardt was a featured subject in Abbéma's art. It was a portrait of Bernhardt that first brought Abbéma fame at the age of 23, and Abbéma spent holidays at Bernhardt's summer home with her family. In her small biographical book, *Louise Abbéma* (1879), Bernhardt's portrait is featured in the preface of the book, not Abbéma's. She died in 1927 and was buried in a Paris cemetery.

VITO RUSSO

JUL 11 1946 – NOV 7 1990
(AGED 44)

VITO RUSSO was an American author, film historian, and LGBT activist, best remembered for his book *The Celluloid Closet* (1981, revised 1987), about the hidden history of homosexuality in movies.

The first gay movie Russo saw was *Advise and Consent* (1962), where the main character played by Don Murray commits suicide "only because he's accused of being gay," being blackmailed over one experience he had in the army. The second gay movie Russo saw was a British film, *Victim* (1961), starring Dirk Bogarde, with the opposite plot: the hero works with police to hunt down the blackmailers, "a tremendous thing to say in 1961," according to Russo.

Russo was diagnosed with HIV in 1985 and died in 1990. He lost his boyfriend to the virus first, and while grieving still had to take care of himself: "He's been gone three years now, and I'm still sick, and I'm very lonely. It's hard to live alone, and be sick alone, and as many of your friends as you have—and I have good, loving friends and a great support system—people cannot be sick for you, and they can't suffer for you, and they can't be with you all the time."

GEORGE EASTMAN

JUL 12 1854 – MAR 14 1932
(AGED 77)

Father of modern photography and inventor of motion picture film, GEORGE EASTMAN left a bank job in 1881, eventually founding the Eastman Kodak Company in 1888, which produced easy-to-use film and cameras for people around the world. The company's impact was so prevalent, the phrase "a Kodak moment" entered the common lexicon to describe an event so momentous it ought to be photographed.

A lifelong philanthropist in technology, medicine, music, and arts, Eastman's company was among the first to offer employees retirement, insurance benefits, and profit sharing. In 1930 Eastman was awarded the American Institute of Chemists Gold Medal, and on July 12th, 1954 the U.S. issued a commemorative stamp marking the 100th anniversary of his birthday.

Attributed with saying, "What we do during our working hours determines what we have; what we do in our leisure hours determines what we are," as far as Eastman's 'leisure hours' go, most of his biographies say Eastman "never married" and leave it at that. At age 77, afflicted with an unspecified nerve or spinal disease and suffering from depression, Eastman killed himself with a gunshot to the heart. He left a note reading, "To my friends, my work is done—why wait?"

DANITRA VANCE

❧

JUL 13 1954 – AUG 21 1994
(AGED 40)

Though DANITRA VANCE didn't receive a role in her high school play, she got up during the performance to act the part anyway, and stole the show. Vance attended the National College of Education in Evanston, graduated with honors at Roosevelt University in Chicago, and attended the Webber-Douglas Academy of Dramatic Art in London. In 1981, Vance moved to New York, and in 1985 she found success with her off-Broadway revue *Danitra Vance and the Mell-o White Boys*.

Vance became the first African-American woman and lesbian to become a repertory player on *Saturday Night Live* from 1985-1986, but was

frustrated by the stereotypical black roles she was playing, and had trouble with the cue cards due to her dyslexia. Vance received the 1988 NAACP award for Best Actress in the play *The Colored Museum*, and was awarded an Obie performance and 1989 Drama-Logue award for her roles in the George C. Wolfe play *Spunk*.

Vance underwent a mastectomy for breast cancer in 1990, and created the solo performance piece *The Radical Girl's Guide to Radical Mastectomy*. Her longtime companion was Jones Miller, who played an alternate in her original off-Broadway show. Vance died in 1994 of a breast cancer recurrence.

HOWARD HUGHES
(HOWARD ROBARD HUGHES JR.)

Dec 24 1905 – Apr 5 1976
(AGED 70)

American manufacturer, aviator, and film producer, HOWARD HUGHES was born in Houston, Texas, and quickly inherited the family business, Hughes Tool Company. Financially independent, he moved to Hollywood in 1926 to make movies, including the Academy Award-winning *Two Arabian Knights* (1927). Active in aviation, Hughes designed his own planes, and set and broke records, including on July 14th, 1938, when he flew around the world in 91 hours (3 days, 19 hours, 17 minutes). He was the subject of 2004's film, *The Aviator*.

The 2013 biography *Howard Hughes: The Secret Life* details his romances with Hollywood stars like Katharine Hepburn, Bette Davis, Tyrone Power, and Cary Grant. Introduced to Grant by mutual lover and Grant's long-term partner Randolph Scott, Hughes was best man at one of Grant's more hurried weddings, to his third wife.

After a nearly-fatal plane crash in 1946, Hughes became a shut-in and manifested profound eccentricities, like sorting his peas by size with a special fork, storing his urine in jars, and watching the movie *Ice Station Zebra* (1968) starring Rock Hudson in a continuous loop. He ultimately became addicted to codeine, and died of kidney failure on his plane, en route to the hospital in 1976.

MARIE DIANA EQUI

APR 7 1872 – JUL 13 1952
(AGED 80)

American doctor, abortion provider, and anarchist, MARIE EQUI became radicalized when a cannery workers' strike at the Oregon Packing Company was violently stormed by police on July 15th, 1913. Equi herself was clubbed by an officer, and witnessed a pregnant woman being dragged away by police.

While protesting what she saw as capitalist profiteering in WWI "preparedness" efforts, Equi carried a banner that began, "Prepare to die, workingmen." She was eventually charged and convicted of sedition under the Espionage Act, and served 10 months of a three-year sentence in San Quentin Prison between 1920-1921.

Equi's longest relationship was with Harriet Speckart, niece of Olympia Brewing Company founder Leopold Schmidt, who had to fight her family in court after she was disinherited over the relationship with Equi. In 1915, Equi and Speckart adopted an infant girl, Mary, who went on to become Oregon's first female pilot. Speckart died in 1927.

Equi also had an affair with birth control advocate Margaret Sanger, and lived with labor advocate Elizabeth Gurley Flynn, who later became a leader of the Communist Party. Equi fractured her hip in 1950, and spent the rest of her life in care. She is buried next to Speckart in Portland.

MAY SARTON
(ELEANORE MARIE SARTON)

MAY 3 1912 – JUL 16 1995
(AGED 83)

MAY SARTON's family fled from Belgium to England and then to Boston after the assassination of Archduke Franz Ferdinand. Sarton graduated Cambridge High and Latin School in 1929, the same year her series of sonnets were published in *Poetry* magazine. Her first poetry collection, *Encounter in April*, was published in 1937. She wrote poetry, memoirs, novels, plays, short stories, essays, and two children's books. In 1958, Sarton was elected a fellow of the American Academy of Arts and Sciences, and has received many accolades and honorary doctorates for her work.

With her novel *Mrs. Stevens*

Hears the Mermaids Singing in 1965, Sarton came out as a lesbian. She met her muse Judith "Judy" Matlack in Santa Fe in 1945, and they were together for several years. Sarton wrote, "Judy was the precious only love with whom I lived for years, the only one. There have been other great loves in my life, but only Judy gave me a home and made me know what home can be."

May Sarton suffered a stroke in 1990, and after several months worked with a tape recorder to dictate her work. She continued to write up until her death from breast cancer in 1995.

BERENICE ABBOTT
(BERNICE ALICE ABBOTT)

JUL 17 1898 – DEC 9 1991
(AGED 93)

Born in Ohio, BERENICE ABBOTT moved to New York in 1918, where she studied sculpture, and made important connections with avant-garde artists Marcel Duchamp and Man Ray. She moved to Paris worked as a darkroom assistant for Man Ray Studio in 1923, and there fell in love with photography. After viewing some of her work, Ray allowed Abbott to use his studio for her own photography. According to memoirist Sylvia Beach, "To be 'done' by Man Ray or Berenice Abbott meant you rated as somebody."

Abbott returned to New York City in 1929. She began photographing the city, and her work is a historical chronicle of buildings and locations long since destroyed by time. Abbott worked to portray the diversity of people and the stability of place. Abbott also invented camera technology, including the one-legged camera stand and the telescopic lighting post.

Abbott lived with her partner, art critic Elizabeth McCausland, in Greenwich Village for 30 years. McCausland wrote captions for Abbott's collections and wrote many newspaper articles in support of her. Together McCausland and Abbott traveled down the Eastern coast and photographed small towns and automobile architecture in the 1950s. Abbott died in 1991 of congestive heart failure.

LAURENCE HOUSMAN

JUL 18 1865 – FEB 20 1959
(AGED 93)

English artist, writer, and brother of poet A.E. Housman, LAURENCE HOUSMAN wrote prolifically throughout his long life. Housman's first literary success came with the novel *An Englishwoman's Love-letters*, published anonymously in 1900, and his most successful play was *Victoria Regina* (1934), part of a series about the Victorian era. He created illustrations for Christina Rossetti's *Goblin Market* (1892 edition), as well as works of satire, children's literature, and political pamphlets. He supported women's suffrage, was a pacifist and socialist, and a member of the Order of Chaeronea, a secret society for homosexual advancement.

Housman wrote very little about his own homosexuality in his autobiography *The Unexpected Years* (1937), but six years after his brother's death in 1942, he delivered a packet of his papers to the British Museum which included his essay "De Amicitia" ("On Friendship") which discussed his brother's homosexual love for Moses Jackson. Both Housman brothers were among the few who maintained correspondence with Oscar Wilde after the playwright's release from prison, with Laurence once visiting him and writing a remembrance of Wilde called "Echo de Paris; a study from life" (1923).

Laurence Housman lived with his sister from the end of WWI until his death in 1959.

ALICE DUNBAR NELSON
(ALICE RUTH MOORE)
JUL 19 1875 – SEP 18 1935
(AGED 60)

ALICE DUNBAR NELSON was the first generation of her family to be born free in the South after the Civil War. She was biracial, bisexual, and graduated from Straight University at a time when less than 1% of all Americans went to college.

Her collection of short stories and poems, *Violets and Other Tales* (1895), is considered to be the first short story collection to be published by an African-American woman. Dunbar Nelson wrote essays, poetry, short stories, and a was writer and coeditor for many newspapers, circulations, anthologies, and other journalistic endeavors. Dunbar Nelson campaigned for women's suffrage and for the passage of anti-lynching legislation.

Dunbar Nelson was married three times, twice to poets and once to a doctor. While teaching at Howard High School, she had a relationship with school principal Edwina B. Kruse that continued for several years despite their 27-year age difference. She also had relationships with artist Helene Ricks and activist Fay Jackson Robinson, whom she called her "little blue dream of loveliness," and the day they met her "One Perfect Day."

Dunbar Nelson died from a heart ailment in 1935, at age 60.

ALEXANDER THE GREAT
(KING ALEXANDER III OF MACEDON)

JUL 20 356 BC – JUN 10 323 BC
(AGED 32)

King of Macedonia, ALEXANDER THE GREAT led his military to conquer the known world during his short lifespan. Taught by philosopher Aristotle until the age of 16, Alexander never lost a battle. He named over 70 cities after himself, the most well-known being Alexandria, Egypt. He called Alexandria Bucephalous after his beloved horse. He adopted customs, clothing styles, and wives from the lands he conquered to make his rule more agreeable. He overthrew the Persian empire, took the Egyptian and Mediterranean coasts, and invaded India with his military campaigns.

Alexander's dearest friend and probable lover was Hephaestion, a lifelong trusted companion and general in his army. Hephaestion's death in 324 BC devastated Alexander, and he ordered a massive funeral pyre and a period of public mourning in response to it. Alexander had another favorite, a young Persian eunuch named Bagoas, whom Alexander kissed—tenderly and openly—during a celebration after Bagoas won a prize for song and dance.

Within a year of Hephaestion's death, Alexander fell ill, dying of undetermined circumstances, possibly poison, at age 32. It is written that on his deathbed, Alexander was asked to whom he would bequeath his vast kingdom. The king replied, "To the strongest."

HUBERT LYAUTEY
(LOUIS HUBERT GONZALVE LYAUTEY)

NOV 17 1854 – JUL 21 1934
(AGED 79)

HUBERT LYAUTEY grew up in French military training programs, and by December 1877 he achieved the rank of Lieutenant. He served in Algiers, Indochina, Madagascar, France, and Morocco. He received the Legion of Honour in 1897, and was promoted to general de brigade in 1902.

Lyautey was made Marshal of France in 1921, which was the highest rank in the French army. In May of 1931, Lyautey appeared on the cover of *Time* magazine with the title of "Empire-Builder." He served as the Minister of War for three months in 1917, was commissioner of the Paris Colonial Exposition in 1931, and after his governmental resignation, became associated with Mussolini-led fascism.

Lyautey claimed he couldn't work with a man unless he had sex with him first. In an 1886 diary entry he tells of an encounter with "this sub-lieutenant, who pleases me so much and came from ten p.m. to two a.m. to warm up my thirty-year-old self with his hot and rich sap...what a young, vigorous and generous nature! I regret his departure."

After his state funeral and burial in Morocco, his remains were later laid to rest near Napoleon Bonaparte in the Dôme des Invalides in Paris.

MANUEL PUIG
(JUAN MANUEL PUIG DELLEDONNE)

Dec 28 1932 – Jul 22 1990
(AGED 57)

As a young boy living in General Villegas, Buenos Aires, MANUEL PUIG attended the cinema five nights a week to escape his life. In 1956, he was awarded a film school scholarship, and in 1963 he abandoned his unsuccessful film career to begin writing novels.

Puig wrote in a variety of forms and styles, mixing medias and genres to tell stories of sexual and political repression. His novel *Kiss of the Spider Woman* (1976) was made into a film in 1985 starring William Hurt and Raul Julia, and became a Broadway musical in 1992. Puig snidely said of the movie, "La Hurt is so bad she probably will win an Oscar." In fact, William Hurt's Oscar win in 1986 was the first time an Academy Award was given to an actor playing an openly gay role.

Puig was arrested and convicted in Argentina for soliciting a police officer. After his release, he chose to live abroad in self-imposed exile. His relationships consisted of one-night-stands and the occasional week-to-month-long affair. He also named Yul Brynner as one of his conquests. He died in 1990 of a heart attack during a gallbladder operation.

CHARLOTTE SAUNDERS CUSHMAN

JUL 23 1816 – FEB 18 1876
(AGED 59)

CHARLOTTE CUSHMAN was known for her operatic singing voice with a full contralto register, the lowest of female vocal ranges. Cushman and her younger sister Susan Webb Cushman became famous for a production of *Romeo and Juliet* where Charlotte played Romeo and Susan Juliet. Cushman retired from the stage in 1852, but delivered up to seven farewell performances, and in 1861 played the titular role in *Hamlet* at the Washington Theater.

Cushman was involved with Rosalie Sully, daughter of the artist who painted her portrait. In 1844, Cushman gave Sully a ring, noting the day in her diary as, "R Saturday, July 6, Married."

Cushman met journalist Matilda Hays in 1848, and together they were known as a couple that enjoyed dressing alike. Hays started up a relationship with sculptor Harriet Hosmer, and Cushman with sculptor Emma Stebbins. Hays and Cushman's relationship was irrevocably damaged by the affairs, ending with Hays suing Cushman for an unknown sum of money on the claim that her career was sacrificed to support Cushman's. Cushman remained with Stebbins for the rest of her life, but at one point had an affair with an 18-year-old actress she called "my little lover." Cushman died of pneumonia.

DOROTHY STRACHEY BUSSY

JUL 24 1865 – MAY 1 1960
(AGED 94)

DOROTHY STRACHEY married painter Simon Bussy in 1903, despite her family's horror at his low-class habits and station. The son of a shoemaker, the sight of Bussy cleaning up his dinner plate with pieces of bread "shook the regime of Lancaster Gate to its foundations." Despite their disapproval, Dorothy insisted on marrying him, an act her brother Lytton said took "extraordinary courage." The Bussys lived near Monaco in a small house they named Le Souco, which became a haven for entertaining writers, artists, and intellectuals.

Dorothy Bussy published her novel *Olivia* (1949) anonymously with Virginia Woolf's publishing house. The novel relates the life and sexual exploration of a 16-year-old girl in an all-girls' French school, who confesses a romantic attachment to her headmistress. The subject matter was somewhat autobiographical, as Bussy attended a French girls' school as a child, and later taught at the school to students who included the future First Lady, Eleanor Roosevelt.

Bussy had an affair with Lady Ottoline Morrell, a British aristocrat who ran in artistic circles. She was a friend, pen pal, and translator to the Nobel Prize-winning author André Gide. Bussy died of natural causes at the age of 94.

DR. JAMES MIRANDA STEUART BARRY
(MARGARET ANN BULKLEY)

1789 – JULY 25 1865
(AGED ~76)

JAMES BARRY was born Margaret Ann Bulkley and first presented as a man on November 30th, 1809 when boarding a ship to Edinburgh. Barry attended medical school at the University of Edinburgh, qualified in 1812 as an MD, and in 1813 passed the Royal College of Surgeons of England exam.

Barry joined the army as hospital assistant and was only forcibly retired at the rank of Inspector General of Hospitals. During his time with the army, Barry performed one of the first Caesarean sections where both mother and child survived, improved sanitation and water systems in Cape Town, South Africa, bettered conditions for the imprisoned and the mentally ill, and created a sanctuary for those suffering from leprosy.

Barry was close to the Governor, Lord Charles Somerset, and rumors of their intimacy circulated throughout Cape Town. Appearing on a bridge post was even a statement that someone had "detected Lord Charles buggering Dr Barry." Barry died of dysentery in 1865, and his physician Major D. R. McKinnon listed Barry's sex as male on the death certificate. When pushed to reveal Barry's true sex, McKinnon said, "It was none of my business whether Dr Barry was a male or a female."

DR. JOHN BODKIN ADAMS

JAN 21 1899 – JUL 4 1983
(AGED 84)

While working in an Eastbourne, Sussex hospital, DR. JOHN BODKIN ADAMS frequently fell asleep during operations, ate cakes during them, and would mix up the anesthetic gas tubes. Adams became one of the wealthiest general practitioners in England, inheriting a considerable amount of money from his dying patients.

Scotland Yard was wary of Adams's dead patient count and determined that between 1946-1956, 163 out of 310 patient deaths were suspicious. When arrested in December of 1956, Adams stated, "I didn't think you could prove it was murder." Adams was correct in his assumption, and was acquitted from the "murder trial of the century" in 1957. Adams was convicted on July 26th, 1957 of forging prescriptions and other offences for which he was fined and his prescription privileges limited.

Adams was close to Sir Roland Gwynne, Mayor of Eastbourne, whom he vacationed with and visited every morning. Rumors of their sexual relationship were known to both police and journalists, but no case was pursued.

Adams died from heart failure after a chest infection. He left some of his estate to crime reporter Percy Hoskins, the only journalist who thought Adams innocent. Embarrassed by this inheritance, Hoskins gave the money to charity.

GERTRUDE STEIN

❧

FEB 3 1874 – JUL 27 1946
(AGED 72)

Avant-garde American writer, GERTRUDE STEIN'S Paris home was a salon for leading artists and writers between World Wars I and II, among them Pablo Picasso, Ernest Hemingway, F. Scott Fitzgerald, Ezra Pound, and Henri Matisse.

Stein's works include "Q.E.D." (1903), one of the earliest coming-out stories ever published, *Fernhurst* (1904), *Three Lives* (1905-1906), and *The Making of Americans* (1902-1911). Her essay "Miss Furr and Miss Skeene" is possibly the first published use of the word "gay" referring to same-sex relationships.

Stein abandoned university and moved to London and then Paris with her brother in 1902. She met her partner Alice B. Toklas on September 8th, 1907, Toklas's first day in Paris. Toklas moved into 27 Rue de Fleurus with Stein and her brother in 1910, and they lived together for the rest of Stein's life. Toklas was thought of as Stein's wife, and hosted the other wives during Stein's salons.

Stein died after surgery for stomach cancer at age 72. The most widely accepted version of her final words is that Stein asked Toklas before her surgery, "What is the answer?" and when Toklas said there was no answer, Stein replied, "In that case, what is the question?"

JILL ESMOND
(JILL ESMOND MOORE)

JAN 26 1908 – JUL 28 1990
(AGED 82)

Born to stage actors Henry V. Esmond and Eva Moore, JILL ESMOND also caught the acting bug, and made her London stage debut at age 14 as Nibs in Gladys Cooper's *Peter Pan* (1904). She met Laurence Olivier in June of 1928 when they appeared together in John Drinkwater's play *Bird in Hand* (1927). They married in 1930, appeared together on Broadway in 1931 with Noël Coward and Gertrude Lawrence, and had a son, Tarquin, in 1936. They divorced in 1940 amidst Olivier's affair with Vivien Leigh, who became his second wife.

Esmond was known to be attracted to women, and

Olivier had affairs with men during their marriage as well: the night before their wedding with his best man, actor Denys Blakelock, and with Noël Coward during their production of *The Green Bay Tree* (1933), itself a drama about homosexual lust that had slipped by Lord Chamberlain's censorship. Actress Phyllis Konstam said of Esmond and Olivier, "She preferred women to men. He was, at the very least, bisexual. They must have known that the marriage could never last."

Esmond never remarried. She received alimony from Olivier until his death in 1989, and died the next year.

FELIPA DE SOUZA

~ 1556 – 1600
(AGED ~44)

FELIPA DE SOUZA was a Portuguese-born woman who lived most of her life in 16th century Bahia, Brazil. She was condemned to whipping, a hefty fine, and exile by the Catholic Inquisition in 1591, for the "nefarious crime of sodomy," or *sodomia feminarum*: sexually intimate relationships with other women. The Portuguese Inquisition (which included Brazil), had consequences extending over five centuries, until July 29th, 2013, when Portugal became the second country after Israel to enact a Jewish Right of Return law for the descendants of those who were expelled during the 16th century.

Felipa's name was adopted by OutRight Action International for its annual human rights prize. According to OutRight: "The Felipa de Souza Award recognizes the courage and activism of grassroots groups and individuals working for the fundamental human rights of all people. The Award embodies the spirit and story of Felipa de Souza who endured persecution and brutality after proudly declaring her intimacy with a woman during a 16th century inquisition trial in Brazil." Since 1994, OutRight has presented the award to advocates who advance the human rights of lesbian, gay, bisexual and transgender (LGBT) people.

Felipa was exiled to Angola in 1591, and died in 1600.

30th

ANNE STUART, QUEEN OF ENGLAND AND IRELAND

FEB 6 1665 – AUG 1 1714
(AGED 49)

Last of the Stuart monarchs, QUEEN ANNE married Prince George of Denmark in 1683, and was pregnant 18 times before 1700. The only child to survive was a son, the Duke of Gloucester, who died at age 11 on July 30th 1700.

The Queen's earliest intimacy with a woman was Mary Cornwallis, about whom Anne's uncle reportedly said, "no man ever loved his Mistress as his niece Anne did Mrs Cornwallis." However, it was Anne's relationship with Sarah Jennings Churchill (ancestor to Winston) that swayed history. Anne wrote to Sarah with sentiments like, "I hope I shall get a moment or two to be with my dear […] that I may have one dear embrace, which I long for more than I can express." Sarah convinced Anne to side with William of Orange in his 1688 "Glorious Revolution" that ultimately deposed her father.

When William and Anne's sister, Mary, assumed the thrones, they named Anne their successor. With no living heir, Anne designated the Hanoverian descendants of King James I as her successors in 1701. She assumed the throne in 1702. Rendered speechless by a stroke on the anniversary of her son's death in 1714, she died the next morning.

BARBARA GITTINGS

❧

JUL 31 1932 – FEB 18 2007
(AGED 74)

Born in Austria while her father was serving as a U.S. diplomat, BARBARA GITTINGS formed a close relationship in college with a female friend, thus discovering the name for herself: a homosexual. In researching homosexuality, most of what she found centered on men, and didn't mention happiness or love.

She failed out of school due to her side research, and left home after her father discovered a copy of *The Well of Loneliness* (1928) in her room. After cross-dressing, hitchhiking, and searching through the bar scene for a community, she joined the Daughters of Bilitis group, edited the organization's magazine *The Ladder*, but was always restless with the group's tendency to conform to traditional femininity, to the scientific labels of the times (which named homosexuals as 'variants'), and to the heterosexual standards of what being 'normal' meant.

After meeting and becoming inspired by Frank Kameny, an activist discharged from the U.S. Army because of his homosexuality, Gittings was famously pictured marching in Washington D.C. protests, speaking on panels at the American Psychiatric Association, and kissing in Dallas at the American Library Association in a gay kissing/hugging booth. Gittings lent her face to the movement until her death from breast cancer.

AUGUST

YVES SAINT LAURENT

(YVES HENRI DONAT MATHIEU-SAINT-LAURENT)

❧

AUG 1 1936 – JUN 1 2008
(AGED 71)

As a teenager, YVES SAINT LAURENT was already designing dresses for his mother and sister. At 17 he enrolled at the Chambre Syndicale de la Haute Couture in Paris. He was hired by Christian Dior, and was named Dior's successor, becoming the head designer of the House of Dior in 1957.

Saint Laurent was conscripted to serve in the French army in 1960, but was admitted to a military hospital after 20 days from stress, having received severe hazing from fellow soldiers. There he was treated with electroshock therapy and learned he'd been fired from Dior. After his release, Saint Laurent sued Dior for breach of contract, won, and started the fashion house Yves Saint Laurent YSL with his partner Pierre Bergé, a firm that popularized the beatnik look, safari jackets, tuxedo suits for women, and was the first French designer to create a ready-to-wear line.

Saint Laurent met Bergé in 1958. They amicably split in 1976, but continued to work together. As Bergé put it, "The divorce was inevitable but the love never stopped." Saint Laurent was diagnosed with brain cancer in 2008. Days before his death, he and Bergé were joined in a same-sex civil union in France.

JAMES ARTHUR BALDWIN

AUG 2 1924 – DEC 1 1987
(AGED 63)

JAMES BALDWIN was an African-American writer who grew up in the church, and for a short time was a junior minister in the Pentecostal faith. Baldwin became disillusioned with religion and pursued writing instead: essays like those collected in *Notes of a Native Son* (1955), plays, and novels including *Go Tell It on the Mountain* (1953) and *Giovanni's Room* (1956), which depicts black and white characters—some gay, some straight, some bisexual—bohemians, artists, and expats, all living and loving.

Baldwin was part of the civil rights movement and lived significant portions of his life in France, Harlem, Greenwich Village, and Switzerland. The 2016 documentary *I Am Not Your Negro* draws from Baldwin's unfinished manuscript on civil rights leaders, *Remember This House*.

Baldwin wasn't interested in categorizing himself, and believed that human sexuality was fluid. In an interview, Baldwin spoke of recognizing his feelings of loving another boy at the age of 14 at the pulpit. He said that loving people "had nothing to do with these labels. Of course, the world has all kinds of words for us. But that's the world's problem."

He died of stomach cancer at his home in Saint Paul de Vence, France, in 1987.

COLETTE
(SIDONIE-GABRIELLE COLETTE,
SIDONIE GABRIELLE CLAUDINE COLETTE
GAUTHIER-VILLARS DE JOUVANEL GOUDEKET)

JAN 28 1873 – AUG 3 1954
(AGED 81)

COLETTE worked as a mime, an actress, a journalist, and a music hall dancer. Her first four novels, known as the *Claudine* series and consisting of a young girl's diaries and experiences, were initially published under her first husband's name as a ghostwriter. Colette later went to court to have his name removed. Her novella *Gigi* (1944) was turned into a French film, a play, an Academy Award-winning musical film, and a stage musical. Colette was nominated in 1948 for the Nobel Prize in Literature, and in 1949 was elected as the first woman president of the French literary organization, Académie Goncourt.

Colette married author Henry "Willy" Gauthier-Villars in 1893. He encouraged her writing as well as extramarital affairs. Upon discovery that they were both having affairs with the same woman, they turned it into a *ménage à trois*. They were divorced in 1910. Colette had relationships with women and men, including fellow actress and stage partner Mathilde "Missy" de Morny, and their onstage kiss during a pantomime nearly caused a riot. Colette married twice more and had a daughter, Colette de Jouvenel. She also had an affair with her 16-year-old stepson. Colette died at 81 in her Paris apartment.

ESTHER ROPER

AUG 4 1868 – APR 28 1938
(AGED 69)

ESTHER ROPER was one of the first women to receive a degree from Owens College in Manchester. Roper and a fellow student founded and edited *Iris*, a newsletter for female students. She received a degree with first class honors in Latin, English Literature, and Political Economy from Owens College in 1891.

Roper worked as secretary of the Manchester National Society for Women's Suffrage from 1893-1905, and was credited with re-energizing the campaign, and broadening the scope of the effort to include working-class women. Roper fought for women's rights, helped form unions and

committees to protect women workers, and spoke out for pacifism in WWI as well as prison reform.

Roper met Irish poet Eva Gore-Booth on holiday in Italy in 1896. Roper later wrote, "For months illness kept us in the south, and we spent the days walking and talking on the hillside by the sea. Each was attracted to the work and thoughts of the other, and we soon became friends and companions for life." Gore-Booth wrote of their love in a poem, describing it as "the world's great song." Roper died in 1938 of heart failure and was buried next to Eva.

JACK CASSIDY
(JOHN JOSEPH EDWARD CASSIDY)

MAR 5 1927 – DEC 12 1976
(AGED 49)

JACK CASSIDY worked as a bellhop at the Waldorf-Astoria and developed his rich taste from guests. His public persona he based off John Barrymore, and he was known for his spotlight-seeking wit and charm. Cassidy found success on Broadway with *It's a Bird...It's a Plane... It's Superman* (1966) and won a Tony Award for his role in *She Loves Me* (1963). He received two Emmy nominations for television roles, played the villain on several episodes of *Columbo* (1971-1978), and the character of Ted Baxter on *The Mary Tyler Moore Show* (1970-1977) was based off him.

He married actress Shirley Jones on August 5th, 1956, the same year his divorce to actress Evelyn Ward was finalized. Jones described Cassidy as a "sexual Svengali" and that, "He wanted it all: swinging, pornography, drugs, group sex." Cassidy also had an affair with composer Cole Porter.

Cassidy was an alcoholic and suffered from bipolar disorder. Jones recalled finding Cassidy naked, reading a book, when he casually mentioned, "I know now that I'm Christ." Cassidy died after falling asleep drunk with a lit cigarette in his apartment. The cigarette fell and lit the couch on fire, then the apartment. His body was discovered in the doorway.

ANDY WARHOL
(ANDREW WARHOLA)

AUG 6 1928 – FEB 22 1987

(AGED 58)

American artist, filmmaker, and performer, ANDY WARHOL led the Pop art movement of the 1960s. He blurred the lines between fine art and mainstream popular aesthetics, and had a following of underground artists and hangers-on who operated out of The Factory, his silver-painted studio in Manhattan.

Warhol's pop paintings depicted hamburgers, Coca-Cola bottles, and Campbell's soup cans, as well as garishly colored portraits of stars like Elizabeth Taylor, Mick Jagger, and Marilyn Monroe. His silkscreen painting *Eight Elvises* (1963) resold for $100 million in 2008, making it one of the most valuable paintings

in world history at the time. His *Silver Car Crash (Double Disaster)* (1963) broke that record when it sold for $105 million in 2013.

Warhol was gay, but the details are uneven. In 1980, he implied that he was still a virgin, with his biographer Bob Colacello agreeing that what little sex Warhol had was probably "a mixture of voyeurism and masturbation—to use [Andy's] word, *abstract*." However, Warhol underwent hospital treatment in 1960 for a sexually transmitted case of anal warts, and his list of lovers includes John Giorno, Billy Name, and his boyfriend of 12 years, Jed Johnson. He died after gallbladder surgery in 1987.

7th

COUNTESS ELIZABETH BÁTHORY DE ECSED
(BÁTHORY ERZSÉBET, "THE BLOOD COUNTESS")

AUG 7 1560 – AUG 21 1614
(AGED 54)

Born to nobility in the Kingdom of Hungary, COUNTESS ELIZABETH OF BATHORY holds the Guinness World Record for the most prolific female serial killer. Responsible for the deaths of dozens if not hundreds of young girls between 1585-1609, Elizabeth is said to have believed that bathing in the blood of virgins would keep her skin youthful.

Married at the age of 15 to a Count Nadasdy, Elizabeth's vampiric torture methods were said to involve jamming pins under the fingernails of her victims, smearing them with honey and leaving them to insects, and biting off chunks of their flesh. She would visit her lesbian aunt Karla to participate in orgies, and after her husband's death, took up with her maidservant, accomplice, and lover Anna Darvulia, marking a time period when her sadism escalated. Once caught, Elizabeth was not put to death along with the servants who aided her, nor was she ever put on trial thanks to her family's powerful influence, but she was imprisoned in 1611 until her death in 1614.

There is a wooden statue erected of Elizabeth in what is now Slovakia, and her former torture dungeon is currently used to store Bathory "Blood" wine.

GLADYS ALBERTA BENTLEY

AUG 12 1907 – JAN 18 1960
(AGED 52)

African-American GLADYS BENTLEY was born in Philadelphia and felt rejection from her mother, who wanted to raise a boy. Bentley believed that her family troubles may have led to her wearing boys' clothes, and to an early attraction to a female teacher who let Bentley comb her long hair and help out in the classroom.

Bentley moved to New York to pursue a singing career, and found a job opening at Harry Hansberry's Clam House for a male pianist, performing as Barbara "Bobbie" Minton. The club was later named Barbara's Exclusive Club once she became successful, and was renamed again when Bentley began performing under her own name.

Bentley recorded some songs for an agent early in her career, but her first album with Okeh Records was recorded on August 8th, 1928. Bentley was known for her risqué comical lyric twists and deep, growling voice. Bentley lived openly as a lesbian, flirting with female audience members during shows, and occasionally mentioning that she'd been married for a time to a white woman in New Jersey.

During the McCarthy era, Bentley claimed to have been cured through hormonal treatments and started wearing dresses. Bentley died during a flu epidemic in 1960.

JOE ORTON
(JOHN KINGSLEY ORTON)

JAN 1 1933 – AUG 9 1967
(AGED 34)

Playwright and author JOE ORTON was known for his black comedies, like *The Ruffian on the Stair* (1964) and *Entertaining Mr. Sloane* (1964).

While attending the Royal Academy of Dramatic Arts (RADA) in 1951, Orton met partner Kenneth Halliwell, who was seven years older and of independent means. They quickly became lovers. After graduating, they collaborated on novels that never saw publication, living frugally off Halliwell's inheritance and unemployment benefits, saving up for a flat in Islington where they would ultimately die.

Their collaborations defiling library books sent them to prison for six months each, for malicious damage. There, Orton developed an independent voice, and as his personal success grew, Halliwell felt increasingly threatened. In 1967, Halliwell murdered Orton in his sleep, with nine hammer blows to the head, before taking an overdose of Nembutal. Halliwell's suicide note pointed to Orton's diaries as explanation, presumably referring to Orton's prolific records of anonymous sex.

Orton's biography, *Prick Up Your Ears* (1978), was made into a movie of the same name starring Gary Oldman in 1987. It's a title Orton once considered for another project, though his original idea was *Prick Up Your Erse*, erse being a pronunciation of arse.

LOUISE PEARCE

MAR 5 1885 – AUG 10 1959

(AGED 74)

Born in Winchester, Massachusetts, American pathologist LOUISE PEARCE, of the Rockefeller Institute, is best remembered for developing a treatment for African sleeping sickness (*trypanosomiasis*), a fatal epidemic which killed over 60% of the population of the Uganda protectorate between 1900-1906. When a severe outbreak occurred in the Belgian Congo in 1920, Dr. Pearce volunteered to go alone to test their new compound, and ultimately managed a cure rate of 80%. For this work, Pearce received the Ancient Order of the Crown in 1920, and received the King Leopold II prize in Brussels, along with a check for $10,000, in 1953.

Pearce also worked developing treatment protocols for syphilis, and studying animal models of cancer. She retired in 1951 to Trevenna Farm in Skillman, New Jersey, a home she shared with New York City public health physician Sara Josephine Baker, and author Ida A. R. Wylie. All were members of Heterodoxy, a feminist biweekly discussion luncheon with many lesbian and bisexual members.

After Baker's death in 1945, Pearce and Wylie continued living together until their deaths in August and November respectively of 1959. They are buried alongside each other at Henry Skillman Burying Ground, Trevenna Farm's cemetery.

SOPHIA PARNOK
(SONYA YAKOVLEVNA PARNOKH, SOFÍIA IÁKOVLEVNA PARNOK, ANDREI POLIANIN)

AUG 11 1885 – AUG 26 1933
(AGED 48)

SOPHIA PARNOK began writing poetry at six years old. She studied at the Mariinskaya Gymnasium, the Geneva Conservatory abroad, and Saint Petersburg Conservatory before marrying pen pal and poet Vladimir Volkenstein in 1907 to escape her father.

Parnok worked as a journalist under the name Andrei Polianin, had poems published under her own name in Russian journals, and divorced Volkenstein in 1909. Her first collection, *Poems*, was published in 1916, and she continued to produce books of poems, essays, translations, articles, and librettos throughout her life. She became known as "the

Russian Sappho" for her poems on lesbian desire and the love of women. Parnok's relationships include early muse Nadezhda "Nadya" Pavlovna Polyakova, poet Marina Tsvetaeva, and physicist Nina Vedeneyeva. She dedicated works to her lovers and spoke openly of her affairs, as well as of her Russian Jewish identity.

Parnok had Graves' disease and died in 1933 of a heart attack, with a picture of Tsvetaeva at her bedside. After her death, her work was not wildly available until 1979, when a book of collected works by Parnok was released in the United States. A plaque was placed at her birthplace and home in Taganrog, Russia in 2012.

RADCLYFFE HALL
(MARGUERITE RADCLYFFE HALL)

AUG 12 1880 – OCT 7 1943
(AGED 63)

RADCLYFFE HALL was the author of *The Well of Loneliness* (1928), about an upper-class Englishwoman whose love for a female ambulance driver is met with societal backlash. The novel portrays "congenital inversion" (Havelock Ellis's phraseology) as natural, and makes this plea for equality: "Give us also the right to our existence."

Hall had multiple affairs with women throughout her life. Married Mabel Batten, an amateur singer, moved in with the 24-years-younger Hall after the death of her husband. Hall also had a relationship with Una Troubridge, Mabel's cousin, who was seven years younger than

Hall. After Batten's death, Hall and Troubridge lived together, raised show dogs, and though Hall continued having affairs (one with Russian émigré Evguenia Souline beginning in 1934), the relationship with Troubridge lasted until the end of Hall's life.

The Well of Loneliness brought notoriety and controversy, was found obscene by a British judge in 1928, and ordered to be destroyed. A United States court disagreed with that ruling in 1929, finding that the subject and discussion of homosexuality was not in itself obscene, which allowed public access to the book. The British ban would not be overturned until after Hall's death due to cancer in 1943.

GLUCK
(HANNAH GLUCKSTEIN)

AUG 13 1895 – JAN 10 1978
(AGED 82)

British painter, born to a wealthy Jewish family in London in 1895, GLUCK used her trust fund to buy a studio at age 21, cut her hair short, and begin dressing exclusively in men's attire. She went simply by Gluck, "no prefix, suffix or quotes," and once resigned from a job after being referred to as 'Miss Gluck.'

In 1923, she met American painter and lesbian Romaine Brooks, whose painting of Gluck, *Peter (a Young English Girl)* (1923-1924), was controversial for its androgyny. Gluck made floral studies based on flower arrangements by designer Constance Spry, who became her lover in 1932. Spry introduced Gluck to her greatest love, married socialite Nesta Obermer, who inspired Gluck's best-known work, a dual portrait of them both at a performance of *Don Giovanni* that Gluck called *YouWe* (1937). This painting was later used as the cover of Radclyffe Hall's 1928 lesbian novel *The Well of Loneliness*.

Obermer didn't leave her husband, and broke off her relationship with Gluck in 1944. Gluck lived with another lover, journalist Edith Shackleton Heald, the first female reporter in the House of Lords and final mistress of W.B. Yeats. Gluck died two years after Heald, at 82.

ERROL FLYNN
(ERROL LESLIE THOMSON FLYNN)

JUN 20 1909 – OCT 14 1959
(AGED 50)

Australian-born actor who became an American citizen on August 14th, 1942, ERROL FLYNN is best known for his swashbuckling roles in films like *Captain Blood* (1935) and *The Adventures of Robin Hood* (1938). With a notorious reputation as a ladies' man, he became associated with the phrase "in like Flynn" when accused (and acquitted) of statutory rape by two under-age women. During the trial, Flynn met and later married the county sheriff's 18-year-old daughter. She was his second of three wives, and produced two of his four children.

Since Flynn's death from heart attack in 1959, biographies have brought further controversies. *The Secret Life of Tyrone Power* (1979) introduced gossip of a Power/Flynn affair. *Errol Flynn: The Untold Story* (1980) reports dalliances with young boys and girls, reveals a one-nighter with 18-year-old Truman Capote (who said of the incident, "If it hadn't been Errol Flynn, I wouldn't even have remembered it"), and suggests another such encounter with Howard Hughes.

The book also accuses Flynn of being a German operative with Nazi sympathies. Members of Flynn's family sued the author, but the case was dismissed on the grounds that one cannot sue for libel on a dead person's behalf.

LAUREL ANNE HESTER

AUG 15 1956 – FEB 18 2006
(AGED 49)

LAUREL HESTER received a bachelor's degree in Criminal Justice and Psychology from Stockton State College, where she was co-president of the first LGBT group on campus, Gay People's Alliance. At the start of her career, she was one of only two women working at Morris police department in New Jersey. She later served as a detective for the Ocean County New Jersey Prosecutor's Office, becoming one of the first women to rise to the rank of lieutenant in her department.

Hester met mechanic Stacie Andree at a volleyball game in 1999, and they quickly fell in love. Andree and Hester bought a house in Point Pleasant, and registered their domestic partnership in 2004. When Hester was diagnosed with rapidly spreading lung cancer, she appealed to local authorities to change the pension benefits policy to allow for same-sex partners. She was supported by the local Policemen's Benefit Association, and though the county board initially voted against the proposal, a rally of supporters and the unfavorable news coverage led them to reverse their decision.

Hester died in 2006, weeks after the board's reversal. The Laurel Hester Memorial Scholarship was set up in her name to honor young leaders through the LEAGUE Foundation.

RICHARD PRYOR
(RICHARD FRANKLIN LENNOX THOMAS PRYOR)

DEC 1 1940 – DEC 10 2005
(AGED 65)

African-American comedian RICHARD PRYOR was the son of a prostitute and a pimp, grew up in a brothel, was raped at age six by a teenaged neighbor, and became one of the greatest humorists of all time. He won an Emmy, five Grammys, and the first Kennedy Center Mark Twain Prize for American Humor.

Married seven times to five women and the father of seven children, Pryor joked about same-sex affairs, saying in 1977, "I fucked a faggot, I just wanna say it now so no one else can tell." In 2018, record producer Quincy Jones stated Marlon Brando would "fuck anything," including, "James Baldwin. Richard Pryor. Marvin Gaye." Pryor's fourth and ultimately final wife, Jennifer Lee, whom he first married on August 16th, 1981, confirmed the story succinctly: "It was the '70s!"

Pryor's and Brando's children denied the affair, but Pryor's romances include film stars Pam Grier, Margot Kidder, and "a dead ringer for a young Josephine Baker" whom Pryor discovered "was actually a *he*. [...] I never kept him a secret. My best friend for instance, knew I was fucking a dude, and a drop-dead gorgeous one at that."

Suffering from multiple sclerosis, Pryor died of a heart attack.

RICHARD HUNT

AUG 17 1951 – JAN 7 1992
(AGED 40)

At 18, RICHARD HUNT called up Henson Associates from a Manhattan payphone and asked about a job. As it turned out, Jim Henson and Frank Oz were auditioning people that day. Hunt easily won them over at the audition, and joined the ranks of the Muppets.

Hunt puppeteered the right arm of many Sesame Street characters as well as the hindquarters of Snuffleupagus, and went on to perform and voice many beloved Muppet characters such as Scooter, Statler, Janice, and Beaker. Hunt's Muppeteering appeared in *The Muppet Show* (1976-1981), *Fraggle Rock* (1983-1987), *The Muppet Movie* (1979), and many other Muppet projects. He also got behind the camera, directing *Elmo's Sing-Along Guessing Game* (1991) and *Sing-Along, Dance-Along, Do-Along* (1998).

Hunt met his partner Nelson, an abstract painter and ad agency artist, through a mutual friend. Nelson died in 1985 of AIDS complications, and Hunt suffered the same fate in 1992. At Hunt's memorial, fellow Muppeteer Dave Goelz said that around the time Richard started getting sick, he had truly begun accepting himself and his sexuality. *Muppet Christmas Carol* (1992) was dedicated to the memory of Richard Hunt and Jim Henson, as both had passed away prior to production.

LESLIE "HUTCH" HUTCHINSON
(LESLIE ARTHUR JULIEN HUTCHINSON)

MAR 7 1900 – AUG 18 1969
(AGED 69)

West Indian LESLIE HUTCHINSON was one of the biggest cabaret stars of the 1920s and 1930s. He moved to New York City for medical school, but found music instead, joining a black band led by Henry "Broadway" Jones, which enraged the Ku Klux Klan when they played for white millionaires like the Vanderbilts.

Hutchinson moved to Paris with his wife and daughter in 1924. There he met Cole Porter, with whom he collaborated musically and sexually. He next moved to London in 1927, encouraged by English heiress Edwina Mountbatten, with whom he was having a secret-in-plain-sight affair. His lovers included actresses Tallulah Bankhead and Merle Oberon, as well as West End's leading male matinee idol, Ivor Novello. He ultimately fathered eight children with seven different women, including British debutante Elizabeth Corbett, who quickly married an army officer to legitimize the pregnancy. When the child was born of mixed race, the baby was put up for adoption.

Despite the magnitude of his stardom, Hutchinson was still made to enter the places he performed through servant's entrances. When his style of music fell out of fashion, Hutchinson fell on hard times. He died of pneumonia in 1969, hardly remembered.

MALCOLM STEVENSON FORBES

AUG 19 1919 – FEB 24 1990
(AGED 70)

MALCOLM FORBES served in the Army as a machine gunner and was later promoted to the rank of staff sergeant, receiving a Purple Heart and a Bronze Star for his service. After some time in the New Jersey Senate and a run for Governor, Forbes joined up with the family business, *Forbes* magazine.

With money to burn, Forbes amassed expensive collections of yachts, art, Fabergé Eggs, motorbikes, and hot air balloons, one of which was shaped like a motorbike. He wrote a book about his hobbies, *More Than I Dreamed: A Lifetime of Collecting* (1989), which also mentioned the unique possession of President Lincoln's opera glasses, used at Ford's Theater on the night of his assassination. Though married with two children, Forbes also liked to spend his money on men. As a multimillionaire, he had his pick of the masses, but preferred waiters, house boys, magazine coworkers, and chauffeurs, paying for their time from his roll of $100 bills.

Forbes died in 1990 of a heart attack in his New Jersey home. It wasn't until after his death that Forbes was outed by a cover story in *OutWeek Magazine*, written by Michelangelo Signorile, "The Secret Gay Life of Malcolm Forbes."

HANNAH SNELL
(JAMES GRAY)

APR 23 1723 – FEB 8 1792
(AGED 68)

Orphaned at 17, HANNAH SNELL married James Summs in 1744, a Dutch seaman who beat and abandoned her during pregnancy. The child died within a year, and Snell borrowed her brother-in-law's name and clothing, enlisting as a soldier to search for Summs. Snell joined the Royal Marines as James Gray in 1747, fought in the East Indies, took part in the siege of Araapong, and was wounded several times. She once went so far as to have a native woman remove a bullet shot to her groin rather than risk discovery with the regimental surgeon.

While in Lisbon she learned her husband had been executed for murder. Returned to England, Snell revealed her true identity to her shipmates in a London pub in June, 1750. Afterwards she gave exhibitions in military uniform, sold her story to publishers as *The Female Soldier, or the Surprising Adventures of Hannah Snell* (1750), and by November of 1750, the Royal Chelsea Hospital officially recognized Snell's military service, granting her a lifetime pension.

Snell lived another 40 years, married twice, raised two sons, and ended her adventures on August 20th, 1791, when she was admitted to Bethlem asylum. She died six months later, at 68.

EDITH JEMIMA SIMCOX

AUG 21 1844 – SEP 15 1901
(AGED 57)

EDITH SIMCOX worked to establish trade unions, promoted women's suffrage, and was one of the first female delegates to attend the Trades Union Congress. She wrote articles, essays, and books on ancient civilizations and their relations to modern day society. She started the shirtmaking co-operative Hamilton and Company with her friend Mary Hamilton, which only employed women, and offered decent wages and working conditions.

Simcox considered herself "half a man," and signed her name E.J. Simcox to be called mister on occasion. She had a mostly unrequited relationship with older novelist George Eliot (Mary Anne Evans), and in a journal entry two months prior to Eliot's marriage wrote, "I kissed her again and playfully expressed the hope that she did not mind having holes kissed in her cheek." Eliot returned her kisses, but with less enthusiasm. Still, after Eliot's death Simcox wrote, "It is folly not to allow myself to believe that my love was real to Her when She spoke of it more than once in words which She had before appropriated only to Her most loving husband."

Simcox died of respiratory problems. Though she wished to be buried near Eliot, Simcox was buried along with her mother.

JOHN STANLEY WOJTOWICZ

MAR 9 1945 – JAN 2 2006
(AGED 60)

JOHN WOJTOWICZ is best known for a failed bank robbery he attempted on August 22nd,1972, which inspired the movie *Dog Day Afternoon* (1975) starring Al Pacino, and three follow-up documentaries, including *The Dog (or Storyville: The Great Sex Addict Heist)* (2013).

In 1967, Wojtowicz married Carmen Bifulco, and had two children before separating in 1969. In 1971, after meeting Elizabeth Eden (born Ernie Aron), they held a public marriage ceremony. In 1972, along with Salvatore Naturale and Robert Westenberg (another sex partner), Wojtowicz attempted to rob a Chase Manhattan bank to pay for

Eden's sex reassignment surgery. The selling of the movie rights ultimately helped pay for Eden's surgery, though the movie also put Wojtowicz's life in danger in prison, since it implied he'd betrayed his partner, Naturale, who was killed by police. After her surgery in 1973, Eden chose to never see Wojtowicz again. After serving five of a 20 year sentence, Wojtowicz left prison in 1978 with his third spouse, George Heath, and moved in with his mother.

After his release, Wojtowicz cheekily applied for a guard position at Chase. He instead sold autographs outside wearing an "I ROBBED THIS BANK" T-shirt. He died of cancer in 2006.

RUDOLPH VALENTINO
(RODOLFO ALFONSO RAFFAELLO PIERRE FILIBERT GUGLIELMI DI VALENTINA D'ANTONGUELLAINO)

MAY 6 1895 – AUG 23 1926
(AGED 31)

Italian actor of the silver screen and international sex symbol, RUDOLPH VALENTINO starred in many silent films, his best-known being *The Four Horsemen of the Apocalypse* (1921), *The Sheik* (1921), and *Blood and Sand* (1922). Those who imitated his slick-backed hair style were called "Vaselinos."

Valentino came to America in 1913, worked menial jobs in New York City, joined a traveling musical act, and eventually arrived in Los Angeles for a film career.

In 1919, Valentino entered a "lavender marriage" of convenience with actress Jean Acker, herself involved in a lesbian triangle with actresses Grace Darmond and Alla Nazimova. She locked Valentino out on their wedding night; the marriage was never consummated. Valentino married Natacha Rambova in 1922, another protégée (and paramour) of Nazimova, but divorced her in 1925, bitterly leaving her only $1 in his will.

Professor/pornographer/tattoo artist Samuel Steward recorded a sexual encounter with Valentino: in Steward's 'Stud File' of sex partners was an entry reading, "Guglielmi, R." and the brief comment, "Nuf sed." He kept a souvenir of Valentino's pubic hair in a reliquary on his nightstand.

At first misdiagnosed, Valentino died suddenly of perforated ulcers that mimicked appendicitis, what's now known as "Valentino's syndrome."

MARSHA P. JOHNSON
(MALCOLM MICHAELS, JR.)

AUG 24 1945 – JUL 6 1992
(AGED 46)

Born in New Jersey, it's widely agreed that MARSHA P. JOHNSON was one of the first people to start fighting back against the police raids that kicked off the Stonewall riots of 1969. She was a sex worker, drug user, mental illness sufferer, advocate, activist, and transvestite.

After Stonewall, she started STAR House (Street Transvestite Action Revolutionary) with Sylvia Rivera hoping to turn it into a refuge for homeless LGBT youth, though it never truly got off the ground. She continued doing activist work against the AIDS epidemic with ACT UP (AIDS Coalition to Unleash Power) throughout the 1980s.

In 1992, her body was found in the Hudson River. At the time, her death was ruled a suicide, though the New York police department reopened the case in 2012 as a possible homicide. Marsha's friends maintain that while she could have easily come to harm or accident, she was not suicidal.

Her gender identity, expression, and pronouns were fluid throughout her life. When asked in court what the 'P' in her name stood for, she answered as she often did with, "Pay It No Mind." She spent her life adapting to survive as long as possible.

LUDWIG II OF BAVARIA
(LUDWIG OTTO FRIEDRICH WILHELM, MAD KING LUDWIG)

AUG 25 1845 – JUN 13 1886
(AGED 40)

LUDWIG II was the oldest son of Maximilian II of Bavaria, and was only 18 when he ascended the throne. He disliked large social events and wasn't very prepared for policymaking, but was so good-looking it didn't raise any red flags. Then he ran Bavaria into 14 million marks in debt, and was declared mentally ill by rebelling ministers.

Ludwig was briefly engaged to a Duchess, but broke off the engagement and blamed her "cruel father" for their split. He never married, and had close relationships with his Master of the Horse, Richard Hornig, and Hungarian actor Josef Kanz.

He was patron to composer Richard Wagner; when Wagner wrote to his brother-in-law of his relationship with Ludwig, he said, "What he is to me no one can imagine. My guardian! In his love I completely rest and fortify myself towards the completion of my task." Ludwig wrote to Wagner, "My enthusiasm and love for you are boundless. Once more I swear you faith till death!"

Ludwig II was found dead in 1886, having drowned in waist-deep water. As he was a strong swimmer, and the autopsy revealed no water in his lungs, his true cause of death remains under suspicion.

CHRISTOPHER ISHERWOOD
(CHRISTOPHER WILLIAM BRADSHAW ISHERWOOD)

AUG 26 1904 - JAN 4 1986
(AGED 81)

British writer CHRISTOPHER ISHERWOOD is best known for *The Berlin Stories* (1935-1939), books based on his time in Weimar Republic Germany, which inspired the musical and film, *Cabaret* (1972). His gay novel *A Single Man* (1964) also became a movie in 2009.

His longtime friend-with-benefits, poet W.H. Auden, introduced Isherwood to Berlin. Along with meeting the inspiration for Sally Bowles, Jean Ross, in 1931, Isherwood fell in love with a young German, Heinz Neddermeyer, whom he tried to rescue from the conflicted country. Neddermeyer was eventually apprehended in 1937, convicted of "reciprocal onanism" for his relationship with Isherwood, and

sentenced to six months in prison and compulsory military service during WWII. Neddermeyer survived, later naming his son Christoph.

Isherwood and Auden expatriated to the United States in 1939. Isherwood worked as a scriptwriter for movie studios, putting him in contact with Truman Capote, Gore Vidal, and the crowd of closeted Hollywood actors. Isherwood met 16-year-old Don Bachardy on the beach in 1953 (at age 48) and during a partnership that lasted the rest of Isherwood's life, encouraged and supported Bachardy's painting career. Bachardy is now best known for his portraits of movie stars. Isherwood died of cancer in 1986.

MAUD ALLAN
(BEULAH MAUDE DURRANT)

AUG 27 1880? – OCT 7 1956
(AGED ~76)

MAUD ALLAN changed her name to escape from her brother's crimes, the murder of two women in San Francisco in April, 1895. She moved to Germany to study piano. With little training, Allan began dancing professionally, and designed and sewed her own costumes. She was best known for her take on the "Dance of the Seven Veils" from Oscar Wilde's *Salomé* (1893) and was billed as "The Salomé Dancer." In 1908, she published her memoirs *My Life and Dancing* (1908), and toured performing modern dance.

Member of British Parliament Noel Pemberton Billing published a scathing article in his journal titled "The Cult of the Clitoris" on Allan. He implied that she had a lesbian affair with the wife of the Prime Minister, and that all of it was orchestrated by a German conspiracy to lure the wives of powerful men into a lesbian cult.

Allan sued Billing for libel. Charges were brought against her for her dancing being too sexually charged, and she was also accused of practicing necrophilia. Allan lost her case against Billing, left England, and moved to Los Angeles where she taught dance and lived with her secretary/partner Verna Aldrich. Allan died at the age of 83.

NANCY KULP

AUG 28 1921 – FEB 3 1991
(AGED 69)

NANCY KULP received a bachelor's degree in Journalism from Florida State College for Women in 1943. She studied for a master's degree in English and French at the University of Miami, wrote feature pieces for a Miami newspaper, and joined the United States Naval Reserve during WWII, where she rose to the rank of lieutenant junior grade, and received several decorations for her service.

Kulp later worked at MGM's publicity department, and found character work in television and film, becoming best known for her role as secretary Jane Hathaway in *The Beverly Hillbillies* (1962-1971). She also worked for Pennsylvania's Democratic State Committee, and ran in 1984 for the House of Representatives in a decidedly Republican district.

Kulp married Charles Malcolm Dacus in 1951, divorced him in 1961. In an interview for Boze Hadleigh's book *Hollywood Lesbians* (1994), she spoke of her orientation, saying, "I'd appreciate it if you'd let me phrase the question. There is more than one way. Here's how I would ask it: 'Do you think that opposites attract?' My own reply would be that I'm the other sort—I find that birds of a feather flock together. That answers your question." Kulp died of cancer in 1991.

EDWARD CARPENTER

❦

AUG 29 1844 – JUN 28 1929
(AGED 84)

EDWARD CARPENTER was an English socialist, philosopher, and poet. Carpenter was an advocate of vegetarianism, anti-industrialism, women's rights, clean air, and the value of manual labor. His advocacy for overt homosexuality was done in part through his writings, books such as *Homogenic Love and Its Place in a Free Society* (1894) and *Iolaus: Anthology of Friendship* (1902), which is most likely the first anthology of gay writing in English.

He was a friend of Walt Whitman's and the inspiration for E.M. Forster's novel, *Maurice*, a gay happy ending written in 1913-1914, but only published posthumously in 1971. The story was sparked by a visit to Carpenter and his 22-years-younger working-class partner George Merrill, whom Carpenter met in 1891. Forster's diary entry from 1912 records that Merrill, "... touched my backside—gently and just above the buttocks. I believe he touched most people's. The sensation was unusual and I still remember it, as I remember the position of a long vanished tooth. He made a profound impression on me and touched a creative spring."

Merrill died suddenly in 1928. Carpenter died of a stroke 13 months later. They are buried beside one another at Mount Cemetery in Guilford, Surrey.

LEONOR FINI

AUG 30 1907 – JAN 18 1996
(AGED 88)

Argentine-Italian artist LEONOR FINI was a self-taught painter who exhibited with the male-dominated Parisian surrealist movement of the 20th century. Born in Buenos Aires and raised in her mother's home of Trieste, Italy, Fini spent months as a teenager with her eyes bandaged shut due to an ocular ailment. When the bandages were removed, with no formal artistic training, she felt a need to express her inward visions to the outside world.

Kicked out of every school she attended, Fini was the first woman to ever produce an erotic male nude, in 1942. Referred to as the "female Dalí," Fini never identified herself as a surrealist. Using her personal totem, the cat, she explored issues of matriarchy, lesbianism, and androgyny in her art.

Openly bisexual and anti-marriage, Fini once stated she preferred *ménage à trois* relationships: "I've always preferred to live in a sort of community—a big house with my atelier and cats and friends, one with a man who was rather a lover and another who was rather a friend. And it has always worked."

Until her death at age 88, she lived in her Parisian apartment with her two lovers and her 17 beloved Persian cats.

MARINA TSVETAEVA
(MARINA CVETAEVA, MARINA IVANOVNA EFRON)

OCT 8 1892 – AUG 31 1941
(AGED 48)

MARINA TSVETAEVA is considered one of the finest Russian language poets of the 20th century. In 1912, she married Sergei Efron, with whom she had two daughters and a son. However, the family lived during the Russian Revolution of 1917, which dismantled the Tsarist autocracy, after which Efron then joined the White Army (against the communist Bolshevik Red Army).

While separated from her husband during this Civil War, Tsvetaeva had a brief affair with fellow poet Osip Mandelstam, and a longer relationship with poet Sophia Parnok. In 1919, during the Moscow famine following the Revolution, Tsvetaeva's daughter Irina died of starvation. In 1922, the family emigrated to Berlin, then Prague, then Paris by 1925, where they lived in poverty.

With the approaching rise of fascism in Europe, Tsvetaeva's family returned to Russia in 1939. There, her husband and surviving daughter Ariadna (Alya) were arrested for espionage, due to the daughter's fiancé being a government spy against the family. Efron was executed in 1941, and Alya sent to a labor camp. Tsvetaeva and her son were forced into exile, where Tsvetaeva committed suicide by hanging. Her daughter ultimately spent 16 years in Soviet prison camps. Her son was killed in WWII.

SEPTEMBER

ETHEL WATERS
(ETHEL HOWARD)

OCT 31 1896 – SEP 1 1977
(AGED 80)

When ETHEL WATERS was 17, she sang two songs at a nightclub's costume party, and was so impressive she was immediately offered professional work at a Baltimore theater. She toured the vaudeville circuit, working the same clubs as blues singer Bessie Smith, who demanded to be the only blues singer, so Waters sang ballads and popular standards of the time. Waters went on to sing the blues with Duke Ellington, and was the first female black performer on Broadway with her role in Irving Berlin's *As Thousands Cheer* (1933), later becoming the highest paid performer on Broadway. Waters worked as a singer for Jack Denny & his Orchestra on the radio, started working in films, and was nominated for an Academy Award for her role in the film *Pinky* (1949).

Waters lived with dancer Ethel Williams. Waters and Williams performed together as "The Two Ethels," and had a sexual relationship as well. They were known to argue in public, and the relationship ended when Williams married tap dancer Clarence "Dancing" Dotson.

Waters once lost tens of thousands of dollars in a home robbery, and had ongoing problems with the IRS. She died of kidney failure in conjunction with uterine cancer.

BRYHER
(ANNIE WINIFRED ELLERMAN)

SEP 2 1894 – JAN 28 1983
(AGED 88)

English novelist, poet, memoirist, and critic, BRYHER is best known by her pen name for her historical fiction like *The Player's Boy* (1953), *The Roman Wall* (1954), and *The Coin of Carthage* (1963). She was a part of the Parisian expatriate group of artists that included Ernest Hemingway, James Joyce, and Gertrude Stein.

Bryher was the daughter of shipping magnate Sir John Ellerman, reported to be the richest Englishman who ever lived. She took the name Bryher from her favorite of the Isles of Scilly to keep her work separate from her family name's status.

Bryher spent most of her life with poet Hilda Doolittle

(H.D.), each of them occasionally taking on other lovers. Bryher married American author Robert McAlmon for convenience in 1921, and divorced him in 1927. That same year she married Kenneth Macpherson, a writer who was H.D.'s lover at the time, with whom she built a home and studio in Switzerland. They formally adopted H.D.'s young daughter, Perdita, in 1928, the same year H.D. aborted another child, fathered by Macpherson. In 1947, Bryher and MacPherson divorced. Bryher discontinued living with H.D., but maintained their relationship until H.D.'s death in 1961.

Bryher died at her home in Vevey, Switzerland.

RICHARD I OF ENGLAND
(KING RICHARD THE LIONHEART)

SEP 8 1157 – APR 6 1199
(AGED 41)

King of England from his September 3rd, 1189 coronation until his death 10 years later, RICHARD I gained the epithet "Cœur de Lion" (Lion-hearted) because of his military prowess during the Third Crusade. Living mostly in France, Richard was seen as pious and heroic in England, and has retained his unique sobriquet throughout history.

The source suggesting King Richard had a homosexual relationship with King Philip II of France is a contemporary recording from Roger de Hoveden: "[T]he king of England, remained with Philip, the King of France, who so honored him for so long that they ate every day at the same table and from the same dish, and at night their beds did not separate them. And the king of France loved him as his own soul; and they loved each other so much that the king of England was absolutely astonished at the passionate love between them and marveled at it."

Richard broke an engagement with Philip's sister in 1191, enraging him. However, they successfully joined forces to overthrow Richard's father. Their relationship ultimately ended in a literal shouting match over the Seine regarding their battles for territory. Richard died of a battle wound soon after.

MARY RENAULT
(EILEEN MARY CHALLANS)

SEP 4 1905 – DEC 13 1983
(AGED 78)

Eileen Challans worked as a nurse at the Winford Emergency Hospital in Bristol, and at Radcliffe Infirmary's brain surgery ward in Oxford, while she wrote her first novels under the pseudonym MARY RENAULT. Her third novel *The Friendly Young Ladies* (1943) featured a lesbian romance as part of a love triangle. When her novel *Return to Night* (1947) won the MGM prize, she moved to South Africa and connected with a community of gay expatriates. Renault may be best known for her historically accurate novels on Alexander the Great, Greek heroes, and Ancient Greek life, all of which depict homosexual relationships.

Renault met Julie Mullard in nursing school and they lived together in Durban, South Africa, where they hosted parties for fellow expats. They became official citizens of South Africa and joined Black Sash, a non-violent women's movement against apartheid. They traveled to Greece and across Africa, but never returned to England. After a wet winter in Cape Town and a persistent cough, Mullard convinced Renault to be seen by a doctor. When the doctor told Mullard that Renault had lung cancer, she begged the doctor not to tell Renault anything. Renault died prior to a scheduled lung operation.

FREDDIE MERCURY
(FARROKH BULSARA)

SEP 5 1946 – NOV 24 1991
(AGED 45)

Born in the British protectorate of Zanzibar, FREDDIE MERCURY was the lead-singer of British rock band Queen, known for such hit songs as "Bohemian Rhapsody," "Somebody to Love," "We Will Rock You," and "We Are the Champions." Mercury had a four-octave voice so unique it's been scientifically studied. He's included in multiple music Halls of Fame.

A 2012 biography by Lesley-Ann Jones states that the once-married Mercury's greatest loves were women, but that "with his sex life, he could only really satisfy his needs with men." Described by a former lover as "mostly gay," Mercury claimed the love of his life was Mary Austin, whom he met through Queen's guitarist Brian May. In a 1985 interview, Mercury said, "All my lovers asked me why they couldn't replace Mary, but it's simply impossible. The only friend I've got is Mary and I don't want anybody else."

Mercury's last romantic partner was Jim Hutton, who moved into his Garden Lodge mansion. They shared the home with Mercury's pet cats, whom he loved so much he would call home to talk to them while on tour. Mercury died of AIDS-related bronchial pneumonia. By request, his final resting place remains unknown to this day.

BAYARD RUSTIN

MAR 17 1912 – AUG 24 1987
(AGED 75)

Raised Quaker, BAYARD RUSTIN was a conscientious objector to WWII who brought his values of pacifism, communism, and socialism to the African-American civil rights movement. Professionally a nightclub singer, Rustin organized the 1963 March on Washington that Martin Luther King called the "greatest demonstration for freedom" in American history. He was praised by President Reagan, and posthumously awarded the Presidential Medal of Freedom by President Obama.

Openly gay, in 1953 Rustin was jailed for having sex with two men in a parked car. Before the March, Senator Strom Thurmond called Rustin a "Communist, draft-dodger, and homosexual." Roy Wilkins

of the NAACP agreed: "I don't want you leading that march on Washington, because […] I'll have to defend draft dodging. I'll have to defend promiscuity. The question is never going to be homosexuality, it's going to be promiscuity and I can't defend that." Nevertheless, on September 6th, 1963, Rustin appeared on *Life* magazine's cover with A. Philip Randolph as official leaders of the event.

Rustin met Walter Naegle in 1977. Though 37 years Naegle's senior, they had a decade-long relationship until Rustin's death from a perforated appendix. Naegle said, "He was an extraordinary person, but our everyday lives were quite ordinary."

VALERIE TAYLOR
(VELMA NACELLA YOUNG, VELMA TATE)

SEP 7 1913 – OCT 22 1997
(AGED 84)

VALERIE TAYLOR was a schoolteacher and secretary, selling poems, short stories, and articles on the side. She was paid $500 for her first novel, *Hired Girl* (1953), and used the money to pay for her divorce. Taylor became well known writing lesbian pulp fiction, noting, "There was suddenly a plethora of them on sale in drugstores and bookstores... many written by men who had never knowingly spoken to a lesbian. Wish fulfillment stuff, pure erotic daydreaming. I wanted to make some money, of course, but I also thought that we should have some stories about real people."

Taylor was an activist for feminism, gay welfare, elder rights, the disabled, and became a member of the Women's International League for Peace and Freedom to protest the Vietnam War. Taylor was also a member of the Daughters of Bilitis, a lesbian civil rights organization, and contributed to their magazine, *The Ladder*.

Taylor met Chicago attorney Pearl M. Hart at a Mattachine Society speaking engagement. Taylor called Hart "the love of my life," and they stayed together until Hart's death in 1975. Taylor was inducted into the Chicago Gay and Lesbian Hall of Fame in 1992. She died in 1997 in Tucson, Arizona.

SIEGFRIED LORAINE SASSOON

SEP 8 1886 – SEP 1 1967
(AGED 80)

English poet, writer, and decorated soldier, SIEGFRIED SASSOON was one of the leading WWI poets, along with his friend, Wilfred Owen, whom he met while in a military psychiatric hospital. Sassoon was awarded the Military Cross for his bravery at bringing in wounded soldiers while under rifle and bomb fire. His manic courage in the face of the horror and misery of war earned him the nickname "Mad Jack," and the confidence of the men he led. After the war, Sassoon moved into prose, writing the anonymously published fictionalized *Memoirs of a Fox-Hunting Man* (1928), followed by *Memoirs of an Infantry Officer*

(1930), and *Sherston's Progress* (1936). In later years he wrote genuine autobiographies as well.

Sassoon referred to his homosexuality as his "dark secret." He had several affairs with men, the most engaging of which was with artist and cross-dressing socialite Stephen Tennant, whom Sassoon described in his diaries as "the most enchanting creature I have ever met."

Sassoon married in 1933, had one son, George, whom he adored, though his marriage broke down after the end of WWII. He converted to Roman Catholicism later in life, and died from stomach cancer one week before his 81st birthday.

GENERAL LIANG JI
(BOZHUO)

DIED SEP 9 159 AD
(AGE UNKNOWN)

GENERAL LIANG JI inherited the post of General-in-Chief after the death of his father in 141 AD. With his sister Liang Na (Dowager), he decided over the enthronement of three emperors (often by poisoning the previous one), and the fate of Han China for more than 20 years.

Liang Ji kept a considerable harem, but was also enthralled and intimidated by his wife, Lady Sun Shou, who once slashed the face of one of his mistresses. He also had a beloved slave boy, Qin Gong, who was said to be favored by both husband and wife. Put to work as one of their most ruthless agents, Qin Gong was ultimately tasked with the killing that would bring the Liang family's downfall.

During a power-play after the death of his sister, Empress Liang Nüying, Liang Ji was stripped of his offices by Emperor Huan, and he and his wife were exiled. They committed suicide on September 9th, 159 AD, after which many of their associates and supporters were overthrown, arrested, or killed. The Liang family property was sold off, fetching a price so high it's said the empire was able to halve taxation on its entire populace for an entire year.

277

EMILY ELIZABETH DICKINSON

DEC 10 1830 – MAY 15 1886
(AGED 55)

American poet EMILY DICKINSON briefly attended Mount Holyoke Female Seminary before returning home and becoming a recluse for the rest of her life. On September 10th in her 52nd year, a visitor recorded 'meeting' Emily by writing, "I sang there, & the rare, mysterious Emily listened in the quiet darkness outside." Largely unpublished during her lifetime, Emily became known when her sister Lavinia began publishing her poems after her death. Heavily edited by her family, Dickinson's poems would not be available in their original forms until 1955.

Emily expressed herself most intensely through correspondence: with family friend Joseph Lyman, editor Samuel Bowles, the Reverend Charles Wadsworth, and her closest friend and advisor, Susan Gilbert. In 1882, she wrote, "Dear Sue—With the exception of Shakespeare, you have told me of more knowledge than any one living—To say that sincerely is strange praise." Thought to be an amorous interest based on the intimacy of Emily's letters, Susan later married Emily's brother Austin in what was ultimately an unhappy union. Emily and Lavinia remained unmarried.

After the death of her mother and of Susan's youngest child Gilbert (Emily's favorite) from typhoid fever, Emily died of kidney disease in 1886.

FRED EBB

APR 8 1928 – SEP 11 2004

(A G E D   7 6)

FRED EBB graduated New York University with a bachelor's in English Literature, and earned a master's in English from Columbia University. He worked as a baby shoe bronzer, and at a hosiery company, before co-writing the lyrics of the musical revue *Baker's Dozen* in 1951. His musical collaborators included Phil Springer, Norman Martin, Paul Klein, and most successfully John Kander. Kander and Ebb's second collaboration, *Cabaret* (1966), won eight Tony awards, and when adapted into a movie, won eight Academy Awards. Other Kander and Ebb shows include *Chicago* (1975), *70, Girls, 70* (1971), and *The Rink* (1984).

Ebb died of a heart attack in 2004. At the time he and Kander had been writing *Curtains: A Backstage Murder Mystery Musical Comedy* (2007), which Kander finished with librettist Rupert Holmes.

Ebb was uninterested in discussing his homosexuality publicly, and said any statement he and Kander wished to make about homosexuality had been made through their songs. At Ebb's memorial, fellow librettist and colleague Terrence McNally started his speech by joking, "What do you say about a homophobic, anti-Semitic gay Jew?"

Ebb was interred in a mausoleum marked "Together Forever" with close friends Edwin "Eddie" Aldridge and Martin Cohen in Green-Wood Cemetery.

EDITH "EDIE" WINDSOR
(EDITH SCHLAIN)

JUN 20 1929 – SEP 12 2017

(AGED 88)

EDITH WINDSOR received a master's in Mathematics from NYU in 1957, joined International Business Machines Corporation (IBM), and implemented operating systems while continuing her education at Harvard. In 1968, Windsor was made Senior Systems Programmer at IBM, their highest level technical position.

She married her older brother's best friend, and their marriage lasted less than a year. Windsor met Thea Spyer, a psychologist, at a Greenwich Village restaurant in 1963, and they danced all night. After hearing Spyer was at a friend's house in the Hamptons in 1965, Windsor invited herself to the party and asked Spyer if her dance card was full: "She said, 'It is now,' and I grabbed her and then we made love all afternoon." They were engaged in 1967 with a diamond brooch, and married in Canada in 2007.

After Spyer died in 2009, Windsor was unable to claim the federal estate tax exemption for surviving spouses due to Section 3 of the Defense of Marriage Act, and filed a lawsuit against the government seeking a refund. Windsor was issued the refund, and the Supreme Court issued a 5-4 decision that Section 3 was unconstitutional. Windsor remarried Judith Kasen in 2016. Windsor died in 2017.

NANCY BROOKER SPAIN

SEP 13 1917 – MAR 21 1964
(AGED 46)

NANCY SPAIN started wearing mannish clothes at her all-girls boarding school, where she played lacrosse, hockey, tennis, and cricket. Spain acted in BBC radio roles and was a sports reporter for the *Newcastle Journal*. She served as a driver and later in the press office of the Women's Royal Navy Service during WWII. Spain went on to publish several books, some non-fiction, some fiction, including a series of detective novels that took place at a boarding school similar to her own. Spain was best known for column-writing for the newspapers *Daily Express* and *News of the World*, as well as her radio broadcasts and panelist roles.

Spain was reported to have had affairs with Marlene Dietrich and Lena Horne. She lived with her partner Joan Werner Laurie, a magazine editor and publisher. Her choice of clothing and living arrangements were seen as bohemian by then. Spain and Laurie died in a plane crash in 1964, along with three others while on approach to land at Aintree racecourse. Upon her death, friend Noël Coward wrote in his diary, "It is cruel that all that gaiety, intelligence and vitality should be snuffed out, when so many bores and horrors are left living."

ISADORA DUNCAN
("MOTHER OF MODERN DANCE")

MAY 26 1877 OR MAY 27 1878 – SEP 14 1927
(AGED 49 OR 50)

Born in San Francisco, ISADORA DUNCAN lived her adult life in Western Europe and the Soviet Union. She was a trailblazing dancer and dance instructor, who studied Greek mythology to inform her techniques, which led to barefoot performances in tunics and major success. She had sold-out shows, gave private performances, and went on tours around Europe where she was adored by audiences and fellow artists alike. Her style and choreography placed emphasis on the female form, defying the conventions of the time. Her students were dubbed the "Isadorables."

Duncan bore two children defiantly out of wedlock, both of whom drowned in 1913 when their car careened into the Seine. She had a third child in 1914 who died shortly after birth. She married briefly in 1922, to the poet Sergei Yesenin, who later committed suicide.

Bisexual, Duncan had passionate affairs with both men and women, the scandalousness of which eventually began to overshadow her professional reputation, as did her frequent public drunkenness. She died when a long scarf she wore in an open-air car became entangled with one of the wheels, strangling her. In medicine, a lethal strangulation injury caused by entanglement with machinery is known as Isadora Duncan Syndrome.

CHAVELA VARGAS
(ISABEL VARGAS LIZANO)

APR 17 1919 – AUG 5 2012
(AGED 93)

Isabel Vargas Lizano was born in San Joaquín de Flores, Costa Rica. Her parents divorced, and she was left in an uncle's care before leaving for Mexico at 14 to pursue a musical career as CHAVELA VARGAS. She would eventually be called "the rough voice of tenderness."

She sang on the streets, dressed in masculine clothing, smoked cigars, and drank heavily. She sang the *canción ranchera*, a traditional male-dominated Mexican music style. Vargas dressed in a red jorongo, sang accompanied by guitar rather than mariachi, and slowed the tempo down to better play the tension and humor of songs.

Vargas recorded over 80 albums, and performed on September 15th, 2003 at Carnegie Hall to a sold-out crowd that brought her back for encore after encore.

Vargas came out publicly in her autobiography, *And If You Want to Know about My Past* in 2002. She had an affair with Frida Kahlo, boasted of sleeping with Ava Gardner at Liz Taylor's wedding, and denied rumors of carrying off peasant women at gunpoint. Having faced prejudice, Vargas said, "What hurts isn't being homosexual, it's that people throw it in your face as if it were a plague."

Vargas died of respiratory problems.

EMMELINE FREDA DU FAUR

SEP 16 1882 – SEP 11 1935

(AGED 52)

FREDA DU FAUR was an Australian mountaineer. In 1910, she was the first woman to climb New Zealand's tallest mountain, Aoraki Mount Cook. She climbed wearing both pants and a skirt, the one beneath the other.

Du Faur met her lover, Muriel Cadogan, while training at the Dupain Institute for Physical Fitness, where Cadogan taught rope techniques. After climbing New Zealand's five highest peaks between 1909-1913, du Faur moved with Cadogan to England, where the onset of WWI prevented any European climbing, but du Faur's book, *The Conquest of Mount Cook*, was published in 1915.

Cadogan experienced a nervous breakdown in 1929, and du Faur checked her into a hospital for treatment. The women were soon forcibly separated, and Cadogan was held until her family arrived. Cadogan died on the voyage back to Australia, possibly from having received electroshock treatments. Du Faur returned alone to Australia and settled in Dee Why, Sydney. Unable to find answers about Cadogan's death and still mourning, she committed suicide by carbon monoxide poisoning in 1935, just days before her birthday.

Du Faur was the first to climb two of New Zealand's South Island peaks; she named them Mount Du Faur and Mount Cadogan.

RODDY MCDOWALL
(RODERICK ANDREW ANTHONY JUDE MCDOWALL)

SEP 17 1928 – OCT 3 1998
(AGED 70)

RODDY MCDOWALL worked as a child model when he was just a few months old, appeared in British films as a boy, and had his first major role in 1938 with *Scruffy*. He became a U.S. citizen in 1949, where his film credits included *Lassie Come Home* (1946), *My Friend Flicka* (1943), *Cleopatra* (1963), and several *Planet of the Apes* films. He continued to work on television, onstage, in voiceover roles, and on the radio. In 1961, he won an Emmy for Outstanding Performance in a Supporting Role by an Actor or Actress in a Single Program for his appearance on *NBC Sunday Showcase* (1959-1960). McDowall also pursued his passion of photography and published several photography books, including *Double Exposure* (1966).

McDowall ran with Hollywood pals like Liz Taylor and Rupert Everett, hosted parties in his Los Angeles bungalow which featured terrible food and great gossip, and prior to an FBI raid in 1947, he held one of the biggest collections of pirated films and television series. He was extremely discreet about his personal life and never married. McDowall's rumored gay affair list includes Tab Hunter, Montgomery Clift, Merv Griffin, and Rock Hudson. McDowall died in 1998 of lung cancer.

GRETA GARBO
(GRETA LOVISA GUSTAFSSON)

SEP 18 1905 – APR 15 1990
(AGED 84)

Swedish-born American film star of the 1920s-1930s, GRETA GARBO received an Academy Honorary Award in 1954 for her "unforgettable screen performances." After a 20-year movie career, Garbo retired after 1941, and lived in New York City, making no public appearances. She received three Oscar nominations for her best-known films: *Anna Karenina* (1935), *Camille* (1936), and *Ninotchka* (1939).

Garbo never married. At least two men proposed, but to one she wrote, "I will probably remain a bachelor all my life," a statement reminiscent of her line in *Queen Christina* (1933), "I shall die a bachelor."

Probable affairs include actress Marlene Dietrich, writer Mercedes de Acosta, actress Louise Brooks, and heiress Marion "Joe" Carstairs. In a letter to lifelong friend Mimi Pollak—whom she called Mimosa—Garbo wrote, "I dream of seeing you and discovering whether you still care as much about your old bachelor. I love you, little Mimosa." When the married Pollak announced a pregnancy, Garbo wrote: "We cannot help our nature, as God has created it. But I have always thought you and I belonged together." When the child was born, Garbo sent congratulations that said, "Incredibly proud to be a father."

Garbo died of renal failure in 1990.

ANNE BONNY
(ANNE CORMAC)
C.1698 – APRIL 25 1782?
(AGE UNKNOWN)

MARY "MARK" READ
C.1685 – APRIL 28 1721
(AGED 35-36)

ANNE BONNY AND MARY READ were female pirates and crew-members of John "Calico Jack" Rackham's ship, which flew the skull-and-crossed-swords flag known today as the Jolly Roger.

Anne Cormac, born illegitimate and disguised as a boy, married sailor James Bonny in 1718, and set off with him to the Bahamas. Anne spent her time carousing with pirates, one of which was Jack Rackham, for whom she held special affinity. She left Bonny to join Rackham's crew. She mostly lived as a woman, Rackham's lover and helpmate.

Mary Read was also an illegitimate child, dressed as a boy by her mother to gain financial support from her grandmother, and lived comfortably as a man, often going by the name Mark. Teenaged Read served as a "powder monkey" on a British man-of-war, next joined the army, and married a soldier until his death before returning to sea.

Eventually captured by Rackham's ship, Read revealed her gender to Anne, but joined Rackham's crew as Mark. By some accounts lovers, these women marauded together until October 1720, when their ship was captured, the crew tried, but Anne and Read's executions stayed due to pregnancies. Read died of fever in prison. Anne's fate remains unknown.

JACK EDWARD LARSON

FEB 8 1928 – SEP 20 2015
(AGED 87)

JACK LARSON started off as a contract player for Warner Brothers. He achieved early success playing Jimmy Olsen on *Adventures of Superman* (1952-1958), but found the high visibility of the role led to typecasting and a lack of opportunity. Larson moved into playwriting, became the first playwright to win a Rockefeller Foundation grant, and wrote the verse play *The Candied House* (1966). Larson wrote the libretto for Virgil Thomson's operatic production of *Lord Byron* (1972) and wrote the text for the dance piece *The Relativity of Icarus* (1974).

Larson had a relationship with actor Montgomery Clift during the 1950s. His longtime companion was director James Bridges, whom he met on the set of *Johnny Trouble* (1957). Together they formed a production company, and lived in a Frank Lloyd Wright-designed house. Larson said, "It was obvious to anyone that since we lived together we were partners. We always went places together. We never pretended. I always did what I felt like doing."

Bridges died of kidney failure in 1993, and Larson created the Bridges/Larson Foundation to honor his memory, giving grants for arts and culture and higher education. Larson died peacefully at his home in 2015 at the age of 87.

EDWARD II OF ENGLAND
(KING EDWARD OF CAERNARFON)

APR 25 1284 – SEP 21 1327
(AGED 43)

The first English king to hold the title Prince of Wales, EDWARD II immediately recalled his lover, Piers Gaveston, from exile in France, where Edward I had banished him for being a bad influence on his son. Gaveston was given the earldom of Cornwall, a title previously conferred to royalty, thus beginning the noble-class resistance to Edward's rule. The barons had Gaveston exiled twice, but he returned to England each time, and was eventually captured and executed in 1312.

By 1315, after Edward led an army into Scotland and lost control of the country, his cousin Thomas of Lancaster became the leader of the baronial opposition. Edward had new favorites by then, Hugh le Despenser and son; when he gave them territory in Wales, Lancaster banished both men, causing a fight that ended with Lancaster captured and executed by Edward in 1322.

Edward revoked the restrictions placed on him after that, but his devotion to the Despensers alienated his queen, Isabella, who became the mistress of an exiled baron in 1325. Together they led an invasion that deposed Edward (enthroning his son instead) and executing the Despensers. Within a year of being dethroned, Edward died in prison, probably by violence.

ANNE LISTER
(GENTLEMAN JACK, FRED)

✦

APR 3 1791 – SEP 22 1840
(AGED 49)

In 1804, ANNE LISTER studied at the Manor House School in York, where she roomed with her first love, fellow student Eliza Raine. Lister inherited the family estate, Shibden Hall, after her aunt's death in 1836, and she made her income from tenants, town properties, and shares in industrial ventures. Lister was the first woman to climb Mount Perdu in the Pyrenees, and had the first official ascent of the highest Pyrenean summit, the Vignemale.

Lister was a dedicated diarist from 1806 to her death in 1840, partially in Greek and mathematical code. In October of 1820 she wrote, "I love, and only love, the fairer sex and thus beloved by them in turn, my heart revolts from any other love than theirs." Lister dressed in black and had a mannish appearance. She had many female lovers, including Isabella "Tib" Norcliffe, Marianna Belcombe Lawton who gave her the nickname Fred, and widow Maria Barlow. She held a marriage ceremony with heiress Ann Walker in 1834.

Lister died after a bite from a fever-carrying tick in the Caucasus mountains, and Walker spent seven months transporting Lister's embalmed body back to England to bury her in a church in Halifax, West Yorkshire.

GERALDINE ENDSOR JEWSBURY

AUG 22 1812 – SEP 23 1880

(AGED 68)

GERALDINE JEWSBURY'S first book *Zoe: The History of Two Lives* (1845) was one of the earliest Victorian novels to explore religious skepticism, and to doubt that marriage is a woman's sole purpose in life. Jewsbury's later works continued to forge this path, questioning female roles in society, and pushing back against stereotypes about how women should behave.

Jewsbury also wrote children's books and anonymously penned as many as 2,000 book reviews in the literary magazine *The Athenaeum*. She worked as a publisher's reader for Bentley Publishers and Hurst and Blackett house, and used her position to promote fellow female writers.

Jewsbury wore men's clothing and had relationships with men and women, including actress Charlotte Cushman and New Zealander Walter Mantell. Jewsbury had a long, passionate relationship with Jane Carlyle, wife of essayist Thomas Carlyle, with whom she had originally corresponded. In 1841, she wrote to Jane, "I love you, my darling, more than I can express, more than I am conscious of myself […] I feel towards you much more like a lover than a female friend!" Though their relationship may not have been consummated, Jane Carlyle became jealous over Jewsbury's other affairs. Jewsbury died in 1880 of cancer.

ESTHER ENG
(ESTHER NG, NG KAM-HA)

SEP 24 1914 – JAN 25 1970
(AGED 55)

After seeing the positive response of a documentary on the Chinese resistance, Ng Yu-Jat founded a film studio and employed his daughter, ESTHER ENG, as a co-producer. Eng worked in the film industry as a producer, writer, distributor, and director of films including *Minᶎu Nuyingxiong* (1937), *Duhua Fengyu* (1938), and *Nuren Shijie* (1939). She was the first female director to direct Chinese-language films in the U.S., and worked in San Francisco as well as Hong Kong.

Eng went on to open a restaurant in New York City to employ her childhood friends, who wished to remain in the United States rather than return to Communist China. Eng's restaurant, Bo Bo's, was hugely successful and she opened four more New York restaurants.

Eng wore men's suits, kept her hair cut short, and lived openly as a lesbian. A Chinese newspaper in 1938 mentioned that she was "living proof of the possibility of same-sex love." Eng was known to have ex-girlfriends managing restaurants and was rumored to have a relationship with the opera singer Wai Kim Fong, who often appeared in Eng's films. Eng died of cancer in 1970. The documentary *Golden Gate Girls* (2013) focused on Eng's life and works.

THOMAS "TOM" TRYON

❦

JAN 14 1926 – SEP 4 1991
(AGED 65)

TOM TRYON served in the Navy during World War II, and afterwards attended Yale, where he received a degree in Fine Arts. He studied with Sanford Meisner at the Neighborhood Playhouse, and understudied in the Broadway musical *Wish You Were Here* (1952)

He appeared in a number of television roles, most notably as Texas John Slaughter in the series of the same name as part of *The Wonderful World of Disney* from 1958-1961. His film work included *I Married a Monster from Outer Space* (1958), a Golden Globe-nominated performance in *The Cardinal* (1963), and an appearance in the docudrama D-Day film *The Longest Day*, released on September 25th, 1962.

Tryon started working on a movie script which ended up being his first novel, *The Other* (1971). He devoted himself to writing full-time, producing several novels, short story collections, and novellas. He was drawn to horror stories, mysteries, speculative fiction, and the darker tales of Hollywood.

Tryon married Ann L. Noyes in 1955; they divorced in 1958. He had a relationship with actor and interior designer Clive Clerk, and male pornographic film actor John Calvin Culver (better known as Casey Donovan). Tryon died of stomach cancer at age 65.

GLORIA EVANGELINA ANZALDÚA

SEP 26 1942 – MAY 15 2004

(AGED 61)

GLORIA ANZALDÚA, descendant of Spanish explorers, grew up in the Rio Grande Valley of southern Texas. Due to a rare endocrine condition, Anzaldúa began menstruating at three months old, and felt stripped of her sexual identity from the trauma and alienation. She read and wrote to escape the pain, graduating from Pan American University with a bachelor's in English, and receiving a master's in English and Education from the University of Texas at Austin.

While at university, Anzaldúa witnessed a lesbian couple having sex in a friend's dorm room, and while she was initially terrified, she was assured by a friend that the behavior was normal. Afterwards Anzaldúa discovered her own queer identity, later describing herself as a Chicana dyke-feminist.

Anzaldúa wrote *Borderlands/La Frontera: The New Mestiza* (1987), co-edited *This Bridge Called My Back: Writings by Radical Women of Color* (1981), and frequently contributed queer, Chicano, and feminist work with speeches, lectures, and writings. Among her accolades, Anzaldúa received the National Endowment for the Arts Fiction Award in 1991.

Anzaldúa died from diabetes complications in 2004, while working toward her doctorate in Literature from the University of California, Santa Cruz. Her degree was awarded posthumously in 2005.

HILDA "H.D." DOOLITTLE

SEP 10 1886 – SEP 27 1961
(AGED 75)

American poet, novelist, and memoirist HILDA DOOLITTLE published under the pen name H.D., and was part of the early 20th century avant-garde poets. Briefly engaged to Ezra Pound, he idolized her in his collection, "Hilda's Book" (1905), and she recalled their relationship in *Her* (1981).

Bisexual, H.D. fell in love with Frances Gregg, sailing to Europe with her in 1911, later writing about it in her lesbian idyll, *Paint It Today* (1922). H.D. then married fellow poet Richard Aldington in 1914; their marriage broke up during WWI, and was the subject of H.D.'s autobiographical novel, *Bid Me to Live* (1960).

In 1918, she had a child with Cecil Gray, and soon after met the most significant love of her life, Annie Winifred Ellerman, known as Bryher. In 1927, Bryher entered a marriage of convenience with H.D.'s lover, Kenneth Macpherson, adopted her daughter, Perdita, and moved to Switzerland with this new family unit to make silent films. H.D. explored herself by starting psychoanalysis sessions with Sigmund Freud, who described her as "the perfect bi-[sexual]."

H.D. suffered a mental breakdown after WWII. She was honored by the American Academy of Arts and Letters in 1960, and died the next year in Lausanne, Switzerland.

HERMAN MELVILLE
(HERMAN MELVILL)

Aug 1 1819 – Sep 28 1891
(AGED 72)

HERMAN MELVILLE was a sailor aboard the whaling ship Acushnet until he and a mate jumped ship in the South Pacific. Melville dramatically adapted this part of his life in his first novel *Typee* (1846). He went on to write other homoerotic sailing novels including *Mardi: and a Voyage Thither* (1849), *Moby-Dick; or, The Whale* (1851), and *Billy Budd, Sailor (An Inside Narrative)*, published posthumously in 1892.

Though he achieved early success in his writing, Melville was unable to recapture it, and lived off of his wife's allowance. Melville had a very one-sided relationship with fellow author Nathaniel Hawthorne: dedicating *Moby-Dick* to him, moving to his town in Massachusetts, showing up to his house uninvited, and writing him intimate letters, saying, "Well, the Hawthorne is a sweet flower; may it flourish in every hedge." He recorded that Hawthorne's influence "expands and deepens down, the more I contemplate him; and further, and further, shoots his strong New-England roots into the hot soil of my Southern soul." Their friendship fell apart when Hawthorne pulled away, and Melville eventually died of cardiac dilation at his home in New York. It wasn't until the late 1910s when his work started to be appreciated again.

TONY CURTIS
(BERNARD SCHWARTZ, ANTHONY CURTIS)

JUN 3 1925 – SEP 29 2010
(AGED 85)

TONY CURTIS was beaten by his schizophrenic mother when he was a child, and was once placed in an orphanage with his brother for a month when money was tight. After a stint with a neighborhood gang, Curtis was sent to a Boy Scout camp by a neighbor to straighten out. His first acting role was in a high school play.

Curtis was contracted by Universal Pictures and acted in over 100 films in a variety of genres, including *Some Like It Hot* (1959), *Spartacus* (1960), *The Sweet Smell of Success* (1957), and his Oscar-nominated performance in *The Defiant Ones* (1958). Curtis

found a second career as a surrealist painter, and named Magritte and Picasso among his influences.

Curtis was married six times and had six children. Curtis spoke of his younger days in Hollywood, saying, "I was 22 when I arrived in Hollywood in 1948. I had more action than Mount Vesuvius; men, women, animals! I loved it too. I participated where I wanted to and didn't where I didn't. I've always been open about it." Curtis had an affair with Marilyn Monroe, later noting, "That dame's pussy tasted like champagne!" Curtis died in 2010 of cardiac arrest.

TRUMAN GARCIA CAPOTE th
(TRUMAN STRECHFUS PERSONS)
SEP 30 1924 – AUG 25 1984
(AGED 59)

American novelist, screenwriter, playwright, and actor, TRUMAN CAPOTE was born in New Orleans but grew up in Monroeville, Alabama, a neighbor and childhood friend of Harper Lee (author of *To Kill a Mockingbird*, 1960). He got fan mail from Andy Warhol, a rivalry from Gore Vidal, and endorsed Patricia Highsmith into the Yaddo artists' retreat, where she wrote her first novel. Capote gained fame with his books *Other Voices, Other Rooms* (1948), *Breakfast at Tiffany's* (1958), and *In Cold Blood* (1965).

Fictionalized in the movie *Capote* (2005), the writing of *In Cold Blood* was a problematic mixture of fiction and fact based on the slaying of the Clutter family of Holcomb, Kansas, and the crime's aftermath. Capote never completed another novel before his death in 1984, nearly 20 years later. He died of liver disease brought on by alcoholism and drug abuse, behavior that his longtime partner Jack Dunphy said in his book, *"Dear Genius..."* *A Memoir of My Life with Truman Capote* (1987), was kept mostly in other spheres of Capote's life. Capote is as much remembered for his work as his personal presence, both aspects of which he very carefully crafted to bring him fame and acclaim.

OCTOBER

DOROTHY EMMA ARZNER

❧

JAN 3 1897 – OCT 1 1979
(AGED 82)

DOROTHY ARZNER originally set out to become a doctor, and worked in the ambulance corps during WWI. After the war, Arzner visited a movie studio and changed careers to the film industry. At 22, Arzner started off as a stenographer for the Famous Players-Lasky Corporation, better known by its later name of Paramount Pictures. Arzner quickly moved through the ranks as a screenwriter, then a film editor. She threatened to move to Columbia Pictures unless a directorial job was offered to her, and Paramount agreed.

Arzner was the only female director of the 1930s, directing silent movies and talkies. She created the first boom mike for the movie *The Wild Party* (1929) by having a microphone rigged to a fishing rod. Arzner was the first woman to direct a sound film and the first woman to join the Directors Guild of America. She has a star on the Hollywood Walk of Fame.

Arzner had relationships with actresses Alla Nazimova and Billie Burke. Her partner of 40 years was choreographer Marion Morgan, who created sequences for some of Arnzer's movies. They lived together in the Hollywood Hills, and then in La Quinta. Morgan died in 1971, and Arzner in 1979.

JOE CAMPBELL

NOV 4 1936 – OCT 2 2005
(AGED 68)

JOE CAMPBELL knew he was gay at a young age, and was often bullied and harassed in school for playing with the girls instead of the boys. When he was 19, Campbell was hanging out with his friends in Jacob Riis Park beach and met Harvey Milk. "It was a selection basically," Campbell said. "Harvey selected me and I was in the market to be selected." He quickly moved into Milk's New York apartment. Milk wrote Campbell romantic poems and notes when they were apart, correspondence Campbell donated to San Francisco's Gay and Lesbian Center in 1993.

Campbell was friends with Ondine, one of Andy Warhol's stars, and fell into Warhol's scene. He appeared in *My Hustler* (1965) as Joe the ex-hustler, or the Sugar Plum Fairy. This nickname was used for Campbell in Lou Reed's song "Walk on the Wild Side," an ode to Warhol Factory superstars.

Campbell had a relationship with Billy Sipple, an ex-marine who became famous for stopping a presidential assassination attempt and was publicly outed, in part by Harvey Milk. Sipple left Campbell, and a distraught Campbell attempted suicide.

He died in 2005 in the company of his partner of 29 years, Stanley Jensen.

GORE VIDAL
(EUGENE LOUIS VIDAL)

❧

OCT 3 1925 – JUL 31 2012
(AGED 86)

American author and intellectual GORE VIDAL was best known for his books *The City and the Pillar* (1948), *Myra Breckinridge* (1968), *Burr* (1973), and *Lincoln* (1984). He wrote so extensively about American history in his *Narratives of Empire* series, he liked to quip, "How can I be anti-American? I'm the country's official biographer."

An occasional actor, he ran twice for political office, in 1960 and 1982, losing both times. He engaged in scintillating on-screen debates with Norman Mailer, Truman Capote, and William F. Buckley Jr. He held many bitter feuds: with those men, John Updike, and fellow gay author Edmund White.

In his memoir, *Palimpsest* (1995), Vidal boasted that by age 25, he'd had more than 1,000 sexual encounters with both men and women. His conquests included actress Diana Lynn, an engagement to Joanne Woodward, an affair with her eventual husband Paul Newman, Tyrone Power, Jack Kerouac, Rock Hudson, and a three-way with Noël Coward and his partner Graham Payn.

For 53 years Vidal had a live-in companion, Howard Austen, but often said the secret of their relationship was that they didn't have sex. Vidal died of pneumonia in Los Angeles, where he moved after years of living in Italy.

HADRIAN
(EMPEROR PUBLIUS AELIUS HADRIANUS, CAESAR TRAIANUS HADRIANUS AUGUSTUS)

JAN 24 76 – JUL 10 138 AD
(AGED 62)

The 14th Emperor of the Roman Empire between the years 117-138 AD, HADRIAN is best remembered today for building Hadrian's Wall, a defensive fortification on the northern limit of Britannia. He inherited the Empire in its prime, and instead of carrying on further expansion and conquest, started withdrawing troops and shoring up their territorial borders. That cease of forward movement brought about an era of peace.

Hadrian had an unhappy, politically arranged marriage to the Empress Sabina which produced no children. He had several male lovers, his favorite being the Greek youth, Antinous, who accompanied Hadrian on his travels throughout Rome's vast empire. Antinous died when he was barely 20 years old, drowned some unrecorded day in October while traveling on the Nile with Hadrian's men under unknown circumstances (accident, religious sacrifice, suicide, and murder have all been speculated).

Hadrian wept openly at the boy's loss. He proceeded to deify Antinous, erecting statues of him throughout Rome, and naming the Egyptian city Antinopolis after him, which was located east of the Nile not far from where Antinous drowned in the year 130 AD.

Hadrian is believed to have died of heart failure in 138 AD, at the age of 62.

RUTH CHARLOTTE ELLIS

JUL 23 1899 – OCT 5 2000
(AGED 101)

RUTH ELLIS was an African-American woman known to be the oldest surviving open lesbian. Her father was born in the last days of slavery, was self-educated, and became the first African-American mail carrier in Illinois. Ellis's mother died when she was hardly a teenager.

Ellis completed high school along with two of her brothers, an accomplishment that fewer than 7% of African-American schoolgirls were able to do at the time. In the 1920s, she moved to Detroit with Ceciline "Babe" Franklin. According to Ellis, Franklin was handy around the house at remodeling, while Ellis learned to run her own print shop. Eventually they grew apart. "We were just two opposite people," Ellis said. "She liked to drink, go to bars, gamble. I never did all that. Mine was concerts and things like that, going to church and church things. [...] We went our separate ways, but we stayed together over 30 years. That's what I want these girls to do now, instead of breaking up after two or three months."

Franklin died in 1973, while Ellis went on to become an activist and an inspiration, before dying in her sleep at the age of 101.

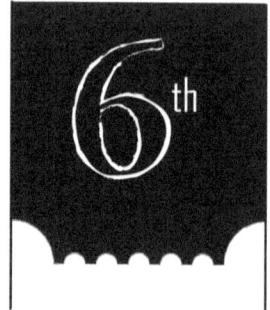

ELIZABETH BISHOP

FEB 8 1911 – OCT 6 1979
(AGED 68)

ELIZABETH BISHOP grew up on her grandparents' farm after her father died, and her mother was committed to an asylum. She studied English at Vassar College and though she had planned on attending medical school, she was guided by poet Marianne Moore to pursue poetry. Her first book, *North & South* (1946), won the Houghton Mifflin Prize for poetry. She won the Pulitzer Prize for Poetry in 1956 for *Poems: North & South—A Cold Spring* (1955), and the National Book Award for *The Complete Poems* (1969) in 1970.

Bishop was not interested in being known as a female poet. She turned down being in a women's poetry anthology by writing, "I don't like things compartmentalized like that."

Bishop's first love was Vassar classmate Louise Crane. She met Brazilian architect and designer Lota de Macedo Soares and had a relationship with her from 1951 until 1967, when Soares committed suicide after a nervous breakdown. Bishop met secretary Alice Methfessel while teaching at Harvard, and they moved in together. Bishop pushed Methfessel to find someone her own age in 1975, but they reconciled and reunited in 1976, and were together until Bishop's death in 1979 from a brain aneurysm.

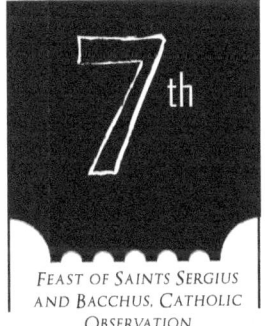

SAINTS SERGIUS AND BACCHUS

DIED 303 AD

(A G E S   U N K N O W N)

Christian saints who were martyred in Syria—BACCHUS in Barbalissos, and SERGIUS in what is now Resafa—Sergius and Bacchus were close friends and officers in the Roman army. Secretly Christian in faith, they were discovered when they refused to join in offering sacrifice to the Roman god Jupiter. In punishment, they were dressed in women's clothing and led in chains through the army camp and the nearby town. Bacchus was then beaten to death, while Sergius was later tortured and beheaded.

With the more recent publications *Same-Sex Unions in Premodern Europe* (1994) and *The Passion of Sergius and Bacchus* (2014) exploring the use of the Greek term *erastai* (lovers) that was used in the oldest text of their martyrology, Sergius and Bacchus have become important to the gay and gay Christian community as a heroic, romantic couple. Historian and Yale professor John Boswell suggests they were an early example of *adelphopoiesis* (brother-making), a form of same-sex union, the same sort of covenant that would have united the biblical David and Jonathan.

They are the patron saints of desert nomads and among the patron saints of Syria. October 7th is their feast day.

INTERESTED
LESBIAN DAY

SAPPHO
(PSAPPHO)

C. 630 – C. 570 BC
(AGED ~60)

Greek poet from the island of Lesbos, SAPPHO's lyric poetry is widely and almost exclusively known for its focus on the beauty of women and the love of girls. In the late 1800s "lesbian" came to mean erotic relationships between women, and was claimed as a medical term along with "sapphist" and "sapphism." In 1890, it was used to describe tribadism as "lesbian love," and by 1925 it was recorded as the medical equivalent to the male "sodomite."

Little is known of Sappho's life other than she was born to a wealthy family, had brothers, and probably went or was banished to Sicily. A leading theory is that she participated in a *thiasos*, a ritual education group for women, making Sappho akin to a schoolteacher, and possibly a composer of songs for a chorus of girls. Her death is unknown.

A poem translated by Mary Barnard begins:

I have not had one word from her

Frankly I wish I were dead.
When she left, she wept

a great deal; she said to
me, "This parting must be
endured, Sappho. I go
                    unwillingly."

I said, "Go, and be happy
but remember (you know
well) whom you leave shackled by
                    love [...]

AILEEN WUORNOS
(AILEEN CAROL WUORNOS PRALLE, AILEEN CAROL PITTMAN)

FEB 29 1956 – OCT 9 2002
(AGED 46)

AILEEN WUORNOS was an American serial killer, responsible for the shooting deaths of seven men in Florida between 1989-1990. Working as a prostitute at the time, Wuornos claimed that these were not murders, but homicides committed in self-defense after each man either raped or attempted to rape her.

Wuornos's father was schizophrenic, incarcerated from the time of her birth until he hanged himself in 1969. Her mother was married to him at age 14, divorced him two years later, and then abandoned Aileen and her older brother to the care of her parents. Wuornos claimed she was sexually assaulted by her brother, her alcoholic grandfather, and his friends. She became pregnant at age 14, and was thrown out of the house at age 15. Her son was given up for adoption, and Wuornos started working as a prostitute.

In 1986, Wuornos met hotel maid Tyria Moore at a Daytona gay bar called Zodiac. They moved in together, Wuornos supporting them both with the money she made from prostitution, and referring to Moore as her wife. Up until her execution, Wuornos claimed she was still in love with Moore. She was executed by lethal injection on October 9th, 2002.

YUL BRYNNER
(YULIY BORISOVICH BRINER)

JUL 11 1920 – OCT 10 1985
(AGED 65)

Best known as the King of Siam in the Rodgers and Hammerstein musical *The King and I* (1951), YUL BRYNNER played the role over 4,000 times on stage. He won two Tonys and an Academy Award for the film. He also starred as Rameses II in Cecil B. DeMille's *The Ten Commandments* (1956), *Westworld* (1973), and its sequel *Futureworld* (1976).

Born in Vladivostok, Yul Brynner emigrated to the United States with his mother in 1940. His first Broadway performance was in Shakespeare's *Twelfth Night* in 1941, and in 1942 he modeled nude for homosexual photographer George Platt Lynes.

Brynner ultimately had four wives and five children, as well as numerous affairs with male and female talents including: actor Hurd Hatfield, authors Jean Cocteau (*Les Enfants Terribles*, 1929) and Manuel Puig (*Kiss of the Spider Woman*, 1976), actresses Marlene Dietrich, Judy Garland, and Ingrid Bergman, among others. Brynner was described as so vain that he was "never far from a full-length mirror."

Brynner began smoking at age 12, and died of lung cancer at age 65. After his death, an anti-smoking commercial was released with Brynner saying, "If I could take back that smoking, we wouldn't be talking about any cancer."

11th

ANNA ELEANOR ROOSEVELT

OCT 11 1884 – NOV 7 1962
(AGED 78)

American politician, diplomat, and activist, ELEANOR ROOSEVELT was the niece of President Theodore Roosevelt and the wife of President Franklin Delano Roosevelt (FDR). Eleanor changed the role of the First Lady, giving press conferences and writing a newspaper column during her husband's tenure in office. She later served at the United Nations under Presidents Truman and Kennedy, focusing on human rights and women's issues.

Orphaned at age 10, in 1905 she married distant cousin Franklin D. Roosevelt, and had six children (one dying in infancy). In the 1930s, Eleanor had a close relationship with aviator Amelia Earhart, whom she once snuck out of the White House with to attend a party. Roosevelt also had a close relationship with reporter and lesbian Lorena Hickok, and was close friends with many lesbian couples, including Nancy Cook and Marion Dickerman, and Esther Lape and Elizabeth Read. Sending letters to Hickok to provide insight for a biography, Eleanor wrote such endearments as, "I want to put my arms around you & kiss you at the corner of your mouth."

Eleanor died of heart failure in 1962. She's remembered as one of the most outspoken women to have ever lived in the White House.

JOSEPHINE HUTCHINSON

OCT 12 1903 – JUN 4 1998
(AGED 94)

JOSEPHINE HUTCHINSON was 13 when she appeared in her first film, *The Little Princess* (1917). She studied at the Cornish School of Music and Drama in Seattle, acted in New York City, and moved to Hollywood, securing a contract with Warner Brothers studio.

Hutchinson appeared in several Warner Bros. films, but may be best known for her role in a Universal Pictures film, *Son of Frankenstein* (1939), where she played Elsa von Frankenstein. She also had roles in *Love is Better than Ever* (1952), *North by Northwest* (1959) and worked steadily in television productions.

Hutchinson was married three times. She joined the Civic Repertory Theatre company in 1926, and met actress Eva Le Gallienne. By 1927, Hutchinson and Le Gallienne were involved in an affair, and were together for several years. "Le Gallienne was my teacher in both love and work," Hutchinson later reported. "It was good and normal and healthy. There was never any sense of shame connected with our relationship." When Hutchinson's first husband initiated divorce proceedings, newspapers falsely reported that Le Gallienne was named in the paperwork. Hutchinson was dubbed Le Gallienne's "shadow," a codeword for lesbians at the time. Hutchinson died in 1998 of natural causes.

NILS ASTHER
(NILS ANTON ALFHILD ASTHER)

JAN 17 1897 – OCT 13 1981
(AGED 84)

NILS ASTHER spent a year as a foster child in Limhamn, Sweden until his parents married. His first acting lessons came from Augusta Lindberg in Stockholm. He was cast in the gay silent film *Vingarne* (*The Wings*) in 1916, and found work across Europe before leaving for Hollywood in 1927.

Asther was six feet tall, dark-haired, and devastatingly handsome. He appeared in the silent films *Topsy and Eva* (1927) and *Wild Orchids* (1929) before transitioning to talkies. Asther was blacklisted for a studio contract breach, and though he returned to Hollywood in 1940, his career was never the same.

Asther retired from acting in 1963 and took up painting.

Asther married actress Vivian Duncan in 1930; they had a child and divorced two years later. He met WWII Navy soldier and stuntman Ken DuMain in the early 1940s. After DuMain failed to recognize any of Asther's movie credits, they ended up in bed together. DuMain said, "When I left, he slipped a bill in my hands—fifty dollars. I felt like a hooker. But he said, 'I would like to see you more often. Here is my number. Call me whenever you're in town.'"

Asther died in 1981 in Stockholm.

LEONARD "LENNY" BERNSTEIN

(LOUIS BERNSTEIN)

AUG 25 1918 – OCT 14 1990

(AGED 72)

LEONARD BERNSTEIN first learned music on his cousin Lillian Goldman's unwanted piano. He studied at Harvard University and the Curtis Institute of Music before becoming Music Director of the New York City Symphony. Bernstein became a major figure in orchestral conducting, and his eclectic composing fused elements of different genres and styles together, successfully creating a bridge between classical and popular music. Bernstein's Broadway compositions include *On the Town* (1944), *Peter Pan* (1950), and *West Side Story* (1957).

Bernstein was the first conductor to give television lectures on classical music. He was President of the London Symphony Orchestra, and had honorary membership to the Vienna Philharmonic Orchestra. He founded the educational institute The Academy for the Love of Learning with fellow musician Aaron Stern.

He married Chilean actress Felicia Montealegre in 1951, and correspondence published in *The Leonard Bernstein Letters* (2013) details the arrangement, with Montealegre writing to Bernstein, "[Y]ou are a homosexual and may never change." She accepted him as he was. They had three children together, and Bernstein continued to pursue relationships with men, including musician Tom Cothran, with whom he later cohabitated. Bernstein died in 1990 from a heart attack brought on by progressive emphysema.

PAUL-MICHEL FOUCAULT

OCT 15 1926 – JUN 25 1984
(AGED 57)

French philosopher, critic, and historian, MICHEL FOUCAULT theorized predominantly on the relationship between power and knowledge, and how institutions utilize both for social control. He held a series of positions at French universities before his election to the ultra-prestigious Collège de France in 1969, where he was Professor of the History of Systems of Thought until his death.

Foucault operated from a hatred of bourgeois society and culture, with a natural sympathy for groups at the margins of the bourgeoisie (artists, homosexuals, pri-soners, etc.). From the 1970s, Foucault was active politically, often protesting on behalf of marginalized groups. He founded the Groupe d'information sur les prisons (GIP) in 1970 to expose France's terrible prison conditions, which was joined by Gilles Deleuze, Jean Genet, and Jean-Paul Sartre.

Foucault's first biographer, Didier Eribon, noted that while he was a "tortured adolescent," he'd become "a radiant man, relaxed and cheerful" in the 1960s, a man whom his colleagues described as a dandy. By 1969, Foucault was "the very figure of the militant intellectual."

An early victim of AIDS, Foucault died in Paris in 1984. After his death, Foucault's life-partner Daniel Defert founded AIDES, the first AIDS awareness organization in France.

OSCAR WILDE
(OSCAR FINGAL O'FLAHERTIE WILLS WILDE)

OCT 16 1854 – NOV 30 1900
(AGED 46)

Irish playwright, novelist, and essayist OSCAR WILDE attended Oxford from 1874-1878. His plays satirizing British society include *Lady Windermere's Fan* (1892), *A Woman of No Importance* (1893), and *The Importance of Being Earnest* (1895). His conversational wit brought him fame, wealth, and notoriety, and his romantic relationship with Lord Alfred Douglas brought his downfall.

Wilde married Constance Lloyd in 1884, and had two sons. Canadian journalist Robbie Ross was most likely Wilde's first male lover in 1886, when Wilde was 32, an age referenced and then later obscured in his novel *The Picture of Dorian Gray* (1891). After reading this novel, Douglas became obsessed with meeting Wilde, and their tempestuous relationship brought ire from Douglas' family.

In 1895, Wilde initiated a libel suit against Douglas' father over a note accusing Wilde of posing as a "somdomite" [sic]. The defense prompted Wilde's prosecution for gross indecency. Wilde's conviction resulted in two years hard labor, subsequent exile, and an early death in Paris.

Ross became Wilde's literary executor, and Douglas became a Catholic. Wilde's wife died in 1898, son Cyril died in WWI, and son Vyvyan Holland produced descendants who still do not bear Wilde's name. Wilde's grave is covered in kisses.

ALBERTA HUNTER

APR 1 1895 – OCT 17 1984
(AGED 89)

ALBERTA HUNTER left home in Memphis and moved to Chicago at the age of 11, to pursue a career in music. At the Panama Club, Hunter sang the blues in an upstairs venue, and frequently drew a crowd away from their main theater. She was known for her singing in multiple languages, as well as her improvisational skills, where she "would stand and make up verses and sing."

Hunter worked with King Oliver and his band, toured Europe in 1917, and produced several records. She appeared as Queenie in the first London production of *Show Boat* in 1928, and entertained in the USO's first black show. After her mother died, Hunter fabricated a high school diploma, enrolled in nursing school, and worked at Goldwater Memorial Hospital for 20 years. Hunter returned to music in 1977 after her hospital retirement, and continued to perform until her death in 1984.

Hunter was briefly married to union official Willard Townsend. They separated months later, and divorced in 1923. Hunter met Lottie Tyler, niece of comedian Bert Williams, while in Chicago. They sailed for France together in August 1927, and were friends and lovers for many years.

JEAN-JACQUES-RÉGIS DE CAMBACÉRÈS

(1ST DUKE OF PARMA, 1ST DUKE OF CAMBACÉRÈS)

OCT 18 1753 – MAR 8 1824

(AGED 70)

French nobleman, lawyer, and statesman during the French Revolution, JEAN-JACQUES-RÉGIS DE CAMBACÉRÈS is best remembered as one of the authors of the Napoleonic Code, which is still the cornerstone of French civil law today.

Born in Montpellier, Cambacérès was a moderate. He supported the 1799 *coup d'état* that saw Napoleon installed as First Consul, while maintaining safe distance, reportedly saying, "Gentlemen, don't expect me to support your revolution by force. I don't even know how to shoot." Cambacérès was Second Consul to Bonaparte, and his principal adviser on judicial matters from 1800-1814.

A well-known homosexual and lifelong bachelor, Cambacérès was the butt of Napoleon's jokes on the subject, and was also dubbed as 'Tante Urlurette' in society, an effete sort of 'auntie.' Cambacérès was as discreet as possible, but still gluttonous, pompous, and haughty; notably affected in his mannerisms, it made him subject to ridicule. According to Cambacérès, "A country is governed by good dinner parties." He was known for having the best dinners in France.

Cambacérès died wealthy and was buried with military honors in Père Lachaise Cemetery. However, the municipal council of his home town voted against erecting a statue honoring Cambacérès in 1859 due to 'moral' objections.

DIVINE
(HARRIS GLENN MILSTEAD)

OCT 19 1945 – MAR 7 1988
(AGED 42)

Glenn Milstead, better known by his stage name, DIVINE, was an American singer, actor, and drag queen, as well as the childhood friend of independent film director John Waters. While working as a ladies' hairdresser in Baltimore, Divine and the rest of Waters's acting troupe, the Dreamlanders, produced the films *Mondo Trasho* (1969), *Pink Flamingos* (1972), *Female Trouble* (1974), *Polyester* (1981), and *Hairspray* (1988), among others.

From the cult appeal of these films, Divine went on to do new recordings of old disco songs, and to take on theatrical roles, including avant-garde shows with The Cockettes, a San Francisco drag collective, and roles in Tom Eyen's plays *Women Behind Bars* (1975) and *The Neon Woman* (1979).

Due to his weight, Divine had a multitude of health problems, including sleep apnea, which led to exhaustion, depression, and a dependency on marijuana. Divine was preparing for his first role out of drag for the television show *Married... with Children* (1987-1997) when he died in his sleep of an enlarged heart. He's buried at Prospect Hill Park Cemetery in Towson, Maryland, where his grave is often covered in gifts of flowers, makeup, plastic pink flamingos, and kisses and messages left in lipstick.

ARTHUR RIMBAUD
(JEAN NICOLAS ARTHUR RIMBAUD)

OCT 20 1854 – NOV 10 1891
(AGED 37)

ARTHUR RIMBAUD was a French poet of the Symbolist movement. Restless and rebellious, Rimbaud left his mother's home at age 16 to tramp through Northern France and Belgium, the next year traveling to Paris to meet poet Paul Verlaine, who'd been impressed by Rimbaud's poems.

Rimbaud and Verlaine began a turbulent sexual relationship. In March of 1872, Rimbaud returned home as Verlaine attempted to reconcile his marriage, but by May, Verlaine abandoned his family again. He and Rimbaud lived together until April of 1873, Rimbaud writing and Verlaine becoming increasingly emotionally taxed by their tempestuous relationship. Rimbaud abandoned Verlaine again, returning home to begin writing *A Season in Hell* (1873). They met once more in July, in Brussels, where a quarrel ended with Verlaine sentenced to two years in prison after firing a gun at Rimbaud, who was struck in the wrist.

Rimbaud stopped writing poetry at age 21. He crossed the Alps on foot and became the first white man to travel to the Ogaden region of Ethiopia, where he set himself up as a trader until a tumor developed in his knee. On returning to France, his leg was amputated, and he died of cancer at age 37.

CHEVALIER D'ÉON
(CHARLES-GENEVIÈVE-LOUIS-AUGUSTE-ANDRÉ-TIMOTHÉE D'ÉON DE BEAUMONT, LEA DE BEAUMONT)

OCT 5 1728 – MAY 21 1810
(AGED 81)

Charles de Beaumont, the CHEVALIER D'ÉON, studied civil and canon law from the Collège Mazarin in Paris, graduating in 1749. He was appointed as a royal censor for history and literature in 1758.

D'Éon joined the Secret du Roi, King Louis XV's secret network of spies. While on a mission to meet with Empress Elizabeth, d'Éon was able to cross the Russian border dressed as a woman, and became Lea de Beaumont, maid of honor to the Empress.

D'Éon also served as a captain of dragoons, and drafted the Seven Years War peace treaty. Rumors circulated of d'Éon's sex, and d'Éon petitioned the government for gender recognition, claiming to be female from birth, and that being raised as a boy was an inheritance issue. The order for appropriate dress was approved in 1777 and on October 21st, d'Éon was presented in court transformed from French male uniforms to gowns and bracelets, performing fencing demonstrations in skirts.

D'Éon was paralyzed after a fall and died in poverty in 1810. In the post-mortem, the surgeon examining d'Éon's body found male sex organs and feminine characteristics, such as a "breast remarkably full." D'Eon is buried at St. Pancras Old Church.

CHRISTINA ALEXANDRA, QUEEN OF SWEDEN
(KRISTINA AUGUSTA)

DEC 18 1626 – APR 19 1689

(AGED 62)

Pope Alexander VII described CHRISTINA as "a queen without a realm, a Christian without faith, and a woman without shame." Thought to be male at birth because she was born "hairy" with a "hoarse voice," Christina's father King Gustav II Adolf was still happy, saying, "She'll be clever, she has made fools of us all!" Officially titled as King at her coronation, Christina was known around Europe as "the Minerva of the North."

With admiration for the virgin queen Elizabeth I of England, an "insurmountable distaste for marriage," and an intimate relationship with lady-in-waiting Ebba Sparre (whom she once introduced as her "bed-fellow"), Christina announced in 1649 that she would not marry, and named her first cousin Charles Gustav as her heir. His coronation occurred on October 22nd, 1650, making him her official successor.

Instead of reigning until her death, Christina abdicated her throne in 1654, amid widespread displeasure at her beheading of Arnold Johan Messenius and his son, who had jointly accused her of being a "Jezebel." Christina left Sweden in men's clothes for Rome, as she'd secretly converted to Catholicism. She traveled in exile, returning continuously to Rome, where she died of a combination of opportunistic infections in 1689.

JEAN ACKER
(HARRIET "HATTIE" ACKERS, MRS. RUDOLPH VALENTINO)

OCT 23 1893 – AUG 16 1978
(AGED 84)

JEAN ACKER worked the vaudeville circuit, and performed stunts on horseback for westerns. After connecting with actress Alla Nazimova and becoming romantically involved with her, Acker was able to negotiate a contract player position with a film studio, receiving $200 a week. Acker appeared in starring roles in the 1910s and 1920s, but in the 1930s logged uncredited roles as an extra.

Acker married actor Rudolph Valentino in 1919 against Nazimova's wishes. On their wedding night, Acker locked him out of their hotel bedroom, and the marriage was never consummated. Though they di-

vorced, Acker sued for the right to be billed as "Mrs. Rudolph Valentino" and won. Valentino remained angry with her for years, but they mended their friendship before his death in 1926. Acker wrote a popular song about him soon after he died called "We Will Meet at the End of the Trail."

Acker also had relationships with actress Grace Darmond, self-proclaimed psychic and fakir Rahmin Bey, and was engaged to Marquis Luis de Bezan y Sandoval of Spain. Acker's longtime partner was the former *Ziegfeld Follies* girl Chloe Carter. Acker died of natural causes and was buried next to Carter in Holy Cross Cemetery, Los Angeles.

FRANCIS BACON

OCT 28 1909 – APR 28 1992
(AGED 82)

Irish-born British painter FRANCIS BACON is best known for his figurative paintings of brutality, isolation, and degradation. Bacon was expelled from home at 16 when his father caught him wearing his mother's underwear. Artistically self-taught, his unique style earned him attention, the first significant reception coming from his *Three Studies for Figures at the Base of a Crucifixion* (1944).

At age 43, Bacon met former RAF pilot Peter Lacy, saying later, "Being in love in that extreme way, being totally obsessed by someone, is like having some dreadful disease. I wouldn't wish it on my worst enemy." The day before his first Tate retrospective in 1962, Bacon learned that Lacy's body had been found after an alcohol-related death.

Bacon met George Dyer two years later, reportedly when Dyer broke into his studio to rob him. Their fraught relationship lasted until Dyer's overdose on October 24th, 1971, two days before Bacon's retrospective at the Grand Palais in Paris. Years later Bacon said, "If I'd have stayed with him rather than going to see about the exhibition, he would be here now. But I didn't and he's dead." After Dyer's death, Bacon's work got even darker.

Bacon died of a heart attack.

CLAUDE CAHUN
(LUCY RENEE MATHILDE SCHWOB)

OCT 25 1894 – DEC 8 1954
(AGED 60)

Lucy Schwob was a Jewish French illustrator, writer, and photographer. She and Suzanne Malherbe, her lifelong creative/romantic partner and step-sister, took the gender-neutral pseudonyms CLAUDE CAHUN and Marcel Moore around 1919. Cahun's earlier nicknames included Claude Courlis, after the curlew bird, and Daniel Douglas, after Lord Alfred Douglas. During the 1920s she settled with Malherbe in Paris, where the couple held artists' salons, and collaborated on works of writing, sculpture, and photography throughout their lives together.

Incorporating Surrealist elements into her work, Cahun photographed portraits of herself as a body-builder, a vampire, and a Japanese puppet, among other guises. David Bowie exhibited a collection of Cahun's photos in 2007, saying, "You could call her transgressive or you could call her a cross dressing Man Ray with surrealist tendencies. I find this work really quite mad, in the nicest way."

After the fall of France during WWII, Cahun and Moore became resistance workers and anti-Nazi propagandists, which caused their arrest by the Nazis in 1944. Sentenced to death, they nevertheless survived until the end of the war and were released. Suffering ill health after imprisonment, Cahun died in 1954. Moore committed suicide in 1972. They are buried beside one another.

KARIN MARIA BOYE

OCT 26 1900 – APR 21 1941
(AGED 40)

KARIN BOYE moved with her family to Stockholm when she was nine, where she attended the largest girls' school in Sweden. Boye studied Humanities at Uppsala University, and was said to inspire "distant adulation" from fellow students. Boye wrote novels and poetry, and is often considered to be Sweden's greatest female poet. Her best-known works include the poem "Yes, of course it hurts" (1927), her novel *Crisis* (1934) which explored the problems between religion and lesbianism she faced as a teen, and the Nazi-inspired dystopian novel *Kallocain* (1940).

At university, Boye had a short affair with poet Nils Svanberg. She later married and separated from Leif Björck, a fellow member of a socialist student organization. She met partner Margot Hanel during a stay in Berlin, after which they lived together for the rest of their lives, with Boye referring to Hanel as her wife. Boye died of an apparent suicide in 1941—after swallowing sleeping pills, she was found curled up by a boulder on a hill. Margot Hanel committed suicide shortly after.

Boye's boulder is now a memorial. A statue of her called *Karin Boye Standing Up* was installed outside the library of her hometown of Göteborg in 1987.

JUNE ARNOLD
(JUNE FAIRFAX DAVIS)

OCT 27 1926 – MAR 11 1982
(AGED 55)

American author JUNE ARNOLD studied at Vassar College before transferring to Rice Institute in Houston for her bachelor's degree. She received her master's in Literature from Rice in 1958. Her first novel, *Applesauce*, was published in 1966, followed by *The Cook and the Carpenter* in 1973 and *Sister Gin* in 1975.

Arnold's novels challenged a woman's role as a wife, depicted communities of women who supported each other, and detailed the complicated mother-daughter relationship. Arnold co-founded Daughters, Inc., a press that focused on publishing lesbian works. She helped organize the first Women in Print conference in August of 1976, and argued that women's presses weren't alternative, but the real thing and the press of the future.

Arnold married and divorced twice. After one of her five children died from accidental drowning, she moved her kids to Greenwich Village. There she was able to explore her identity as a feminist lesbian, and began a long-term relationship with attorney Parke Bowman.

Arnold died in 1982 of brain cancer. When initially diagnosed with only a year to live, Arnold reportedly said, "They've never dealt with a tough-minded woman. Darlin', let them hide and watch." Her novel *Baby Houston* was published posthumously in 1987.

SOTIRIA BELLOU

AUG 22 1921 – AUG 27 1997
(AGED 76)

SOTIRIA BELLOU began singing at age three while attending church on the Greek island of Euboea. Her father secretly bought her a guitar and paid for her lessons. On October 28th, 1940, Bellou moved to Athens to pursue her music career, a date that coincided with Italy's invasion of Greece.

Bellou's talent was discovered while she was working as a waitress in a club, singing *rebetiko* songs after she'd lost a bet with a customer. Bellou went on to record albums, collaborate on *rebetiko* composers' records, and work in famous Greek nightclubs.

Bellou joined the Greek Resistance and the Greek People's Liberation Army. She was arrested, tortured, and detained in prison for several months. She was beaten by right-wing extremists after she refused to sing their song request. At 17 she had an arranged marriage to a bus conductor and after enduring months of physical abuse, threw acid in his face and was sentenced to three years in prison, a sentence reduced to six months on appeal. Bellou presented herself as an *androgyneka* with slicked-back hair, gravelly voice, and mannish clothing. She enjoyed spending money on her many love affairs, drinking, and gambling. Bellou died from throat cancer in 1997.

DOMINICK JOHN DUNNE

OCT 29 1925 – AUG 26 2009
(AGED 83)

DOMINICK DUNNE served in WWII, receiving the Bronze Star for heroism. After the war, Dunne started out as a stage manager for television programs and ended up Vice President of Four Star Television. He was producer on films such as *The Boys in the Band* (1970) and *The Panic in Needle Park* (1971).

Dunne also wrote several novels, wrote profiles on true crime, and covered sensational court cases, including the trial and conviction of his daughter Dominique Dunne's killer. Dunne enjoyed hobnobbing with fellow celebrities, though this led to the occasional scuffle. One evening while dining at the Daisy on Rodeo Drive, Frank Sinatra, not Dunne's biggest fan, paid a waiter to punch him in the face.

Dunne married Ellen Beatriz Griffin in 1954. They had five children and divorced in 1969. In his later years, Dunne called himself "a closeted, bisexual celibate." He had a relationship with a man named Norman, who was a longtime family friend, and who stayed with Dunne while he was in treatment at a stem-cell clinic in Germany. Dunne died in 2009 of bladder cancer. Son Griffin confirmed Dunne's sexuality, saying, "I thought it's so typical of him to come out and then leave."

NÉSTOR ALMENDROS

OCT 30 1930 – MAR 4 1992
(AGED 61)

NÉSTOR ALMENDROS was a Spanish cinematographer who won an Academy Award for his work on 1978's *Days of Heaven*, where he created breathtaking vistas to depict early 1900s Texas.

Emigrating from Spain to Cuba in 1948, Almendros studied for a year in Rome, and taught for a time in the United States. He moved to France in 1961, where his work included François Truffaut's *The Wild Child* (1970) and the popular *Love on the Run* (1979). His work on *The Wild Child* was admired by Terrence Malick, writer and director of *Days of Heaven*, and his award-winning work there led Almendros to three more Academy Award

nominations for cinematography in *Kramer vs. Kramer* (1979), *The Blue Lagoon* (1980), and *Sophie's Choice* (1982).

Almendros' autobiography, *A Man with a Camera*, was published in 1984. His later work included documentaries about the human rights situation in Cuba, including *Improper Conduct* (1984), about the persecution of gay people, and *Nobody Listened* (1988), about the treatment of Cuban prisoners.

Néstor Almendros died of AIDS-related lymphoma in New York City at the age of 61. The Nestor Almendros Award for Courage in Filmmaking is awarded every year at the Human Rights Watch International Film Festival.

NATALIE CLIFFORD BARNEY

OCT 31 1876 – FEB 2 1972
(AGED 95)

NATALIE CLIFFORD BARNEY was a writer and poet who hosted a fabled literary salon in Paris. Openly lesbian, she published love poems to women under her own name as early as 1900. Among Barney's guests were Gertrude Stein, Djuna Barnes, W. Somerset Maugham, F. Scott Fitzgerald, T. S. Eliot, and Truman Capote. She had a 50-year relationship with her partner, painter Romaine Brooks. Her life inspired the character of Valérie Seymour in Radclyffe Hall's *The Well of Loneliness* (1928), the most famous lesbian novel of the 20th century.

Uninterested in fidelity, Barney had significant romantic relationships with poet Renée Vivien, writer and Duchess Élisabeth de Gramont, and Dolly Wilde, the niece of playwright Oscar Wilde.

Barney is better remembered for her personal life and reputation than her work. In 2009, a historical marker was erected in her hometown, the first in Ohio to note the sexual orientation of its honoree, reading: "Natalie, who knew that she was a lesbian by age twelve, lived an outspoken and independent life unusual for a woman of this time period. Her openness and pride about her sexuality, without shame, was at least one hundred years ahead of its time." She died of heart failure.

NOVEMBER

HANNAH HÖCH
(ANNA THERESE JOHANNE HÖCH)

NOV 1 1889 – MAY 31 1978
(AGED 88)

German artist and the only woman associated with the Berlin Dada group, HANNAH HÖCH is best known for her pioneering photomontage compositions. Her work often portrayed dichotomous images of gender norms: contrasting a female body with the crossed arms of a man as she did in a piece titled *Tamer* (c. 1930), or portraying women with doll parts, mannequins, and puppets. She published the large-scale photomontage *Cut with the Kitchen Knife Through the Last Weimar Beer-Belly Cultural Epoch in Germany* in 1919. During WWII, her work was routinely censored by the Nazis.

Höch had a stormy relationship with married artist Raoul Hausmann which inspired her short story, "The Painter" (1920), about an artist who experiences a spiritual crisis after his wife asks him to do the dishes. With Hausmann's refusal to leave his wife, Höch ended their relationship in 1922. In 1926, she began a relationship with author Mathilda "Til" Brugman, with whom she lived for the next nine years. In 1935, she began a new relationship with businessman and pianist Kurt Matthies, to whom she was married from 1938-1944. Höch lived in a garden house on the outskirts of Berlin until her death at age 88.

CASEY DONOVAN
(JOHN CALVIN "CUL" CULVER)

NOV 2 1943 – AUG 10 1987
(A G E D   4 3)

Calvin Culver worked as a school teacher, a waiter, a model, an escort, and a doorman at Cartier's while he pursued an acting career. He understudied in the off-Broadway play *And Puppy Dog Tails* (1969), originated the role of Brian in the Broadway play *Tubstrip* (1974), appeared in the Broadway revival *Captain Brassbound's Conversion* (1972), and played Leonardo in the 1973 Lincoln Center production of *The Merchant of Venice*.

Culver found success as CASEY DONOVAN in gay pornographic films, with the landmark success of *Boys in the Sand* (1971), the first gay pornographic film to gain mainstream credibility. Casey Donovan didn't limit himself to gay porn; he also worked in bisexual and heterosexual pornography.

Culver had a relationship with actor and writer Thomas Tryon from 1973-1977. He met actor Christopher Reeve at a Broadway audition, and Culver spoke of a two-month-long affair, noting, "Christopher was a great lover and I think I liberated him sexually. I didn't think he was gay but he seemed willing to try anything once. He was curious."

Culver advocated for safe sex and offered advice through his column "Ask Casey" for *Stallion* magazine in 1982. He died from AIDS complications in 1987.

AARON BRIDGERS

JAN 10 1918 − NOV 3 2003
(AGED 85)

AARON BRIDGERS was born in Winston-Salem, North Carolina. He originally studied classical piano, but after hearing jazz pianist Art Tatum, a fellow black artist, Bridgers switched to jazz piano.

He met his partner, jazz composer William "Billy" Strayhorn, through Duke Ellington's son Mercer, and they shared a love of all things French. Bridgers and Strayhorn lived together at 315 Convent Avenue, Manhattan for almost 10 years, before Bridgers moved to Paris to pursue his musical career and a more accepting community. Strayhorn would frequently visit Bridgers in Paris while traveling or on tour. Bridgers became a French citizen in 1974.

In the 1950s, Bridgers was house pianist of the Mars Club, a gay-friendly Paris cabaret. He appeared in the film *Paris Blues* (1961) as simply "Pianist." He also worked in other clubs and bars, including the Ringside, the Living Room, and Le Boeuf Sur Le Toit. His LP *Music for Dreaming* was released in 1950. He also played piano on albums for Jimmy "Loverman" Davis, and occasionally backed other artists. He retired from music in 1995, but appeared on the 1999 Duke Ellington tribute album *Ellington Moods* with the song "Phil," dedicated to Strayhorn. Bridgers died in Paris in 2003.

FRANCES FAYE
(FRANCES COHEN)

Nov 4 1912 – Nov 8 1991
(AGED 79)

As Frances Faye stated, "I was born on Stone Avenue in Brownsville and I've been stoned ever since." Her parents placed a piano in the living room as a decoration, and Faye fooled around on the keys, teaching herself to play by ear. At 15 she filled in as a piano player at a banquet and ended up with her first job. She soon became a successful solo act, playing the nightclub circuit and pounding the piano so hard, it would need retuning each week. Faye started recording albums in 1936, played on Broadway, wrote "Well All Right" for the Andrews Sisters, and appeared in the 1937 film *Double or Nothing*.

Faye's secretary and later manager Teri Shepherd became her lifelong partner. Faye would often sneak Teri's names into her songs and peppered her act with bisexual banter. Her 1958 album *Caught in the Act* showcased the hipper meaning of the word "gay" when she sang, "Gay, gay, is there another way?" Faye was arrested in 1955 for possession of marijuana. Charges were later dropped, but she worked jokes and songs about her recreational use into her act. Faye died after a series of strokes in 1991 at age 79.

LUIS CERNUDA
(LUIS CERNUDA BIDÓN)

SEP 21 1902 – NOV 5 1963
(AGED 61)

LUIS CERNUDA was studying law at the University of Seville when he was swayed by his literature professor Pedro Salinas to become part of Madrid's poetry scene. *Profile of the Air*, his first collection of poetry, was published in 1927. Though early reviews were negative and hostile, Cernuda continued to revise and publish poetry collections, including *Poems for a Body* (1950) about an intensely physical affair he had in Mexico with an unidentified man. Cernuda served in the Spanish War on the Republican side, and after a trip to England, found it was not safe to return to Spain. He lived in England, Paris, and Mexico for the rest of his life, never returning to his native country.

Cernuda was known for being a snappy dresser ever since college, and was remembered by a professor as appearing in "a well-cut suit, a perfectly knotted tie." Though Cernuda's early poetry was more surreal, he later changed his style to reflect his desires: love for the beauty of the male form. Just before his death, fellow poet and friend Federico García Lorca famously complained that Cernuda's poems set a maddening standard of sublimity. Cernuda died in Mexico of a heart attack.

339

JACKIE FORSTER
(JACQUELINE MOIR MACKENZIE)

NOV 6 1926 – OCT 10 1998
(AGED 71)

English news reporter JACKIE FORSTER worked as an actress in the West End, as well as in films, before she became a television presenter on the BBC. While on a lecture tour in Savannah, Georgia in 1957, she had a lesbian affair, but didn't see herself as a lesbian at that time. She went on to marry author Peter Forster in 1958. They divorced in 1962; she kept his name.

In 1969, Forster came out publicly, announcing, "You are looking at a roaring dyke." It had taken her 12 years since her first experience with a woman "to get rid of the feeling there is really something rather nasty and nobody else should know about it."

Forster served on the executive committee of the Campaign for Homosexual Equality, was a founding member of London's Gay Liberation Front, attended the first Gay Pride march in the U.K., co-founded the long-running lesbian publication *Sappho* in 1972, and was an active member of the Lesbian Archive and Information Centre. Forster died in 1998 of emphysema and was survived by her partner, Lace. She was still working ceaselessly as a volunteer to provide talking newspapers for the blind in the week before her death.

LISA BEN
(EDYTHE D. EYDE)

NOV 7 1921 – DEC 22 2015
(AGED 94)

Editor, author, and songwriter, Edythe Eyde created the first known lesbian publication in the world, *Vice Versa* (1947). Her motivation was to meet more friends, that the publication was "a way of reaching out to other gay gals—[...] when I had something to hand out [...], I no longer had any trouble going up to new people."

The project also helped her look busy working as a secretary at RKO Studios, until the company sold and her job changed, ending the *Vice Versa* publication after nine issues. In the 1950s, Eyde began writing for *The Ladder*, the first nationally-distributed lesbian magazine published by the Daughters of Bilitis. That is when she began writing under the pseudonym "LISA BEN," an anagram of "lesbian," after her first choice, "Ima Spinster," was rejected.

At age 36, Eyde entered into her one and only long-term relationship; they lived together for three years until her partner lost their money gambling, after which Eyde only casually dated. Eyde preferred to be known under her pseudonym because she feared being discovered by people who would "not understand." As a result, at the time of her death, no obituaries were published, nor was her legacy publicly acknowledged.

ABRAHAM "BRAM" STOKER

Nov 8 1847 – Apr 20 1912
(AGED 64)

Born in Dublin, BRAM STOKER was the personal assistant of actor Henry Irving, and author of *Dracula* (1897). While young, he frequently attended salons at Sir and Lady Wilde's home—the parents of Oscar Wilde—and married Florence Balcombe, a former sweetheart of Wilde's.

An admirer of Walt Whitman, in 1872 Stoker wrote him a letter that he would not send until four years later. Along with a full physical description of himself, he wrote: "If I were before your face I would like to shake hands with you, for I feel that I would like you. I would like to call you Comrade and to talk to you as men who are not poets do not often talk. I think that at first a man would be ashamed, for a man cannot in a moment break the habit of comparative reticence that has become a second nature to him; but I know I would not long be ashamed to be natural before you."

Deeply closeted, after Wilde's gross indecency conviction, Stoker penned articles advocating for discretion and censorship; he also invented his most famous character, the decadent nightmare, Dracula. Like Wilde, Bram Stoker died of complications from tertiary syphilis.

ERIKA MANN
(ERIKA JULIA HEDWIG MANN)

NOV 9 1905 – AUG 27 1969
(AGED 63)

Eldest daughter of *Death in Venice* (1912) author Thomas Mann, ERIKA MANN was an actress, writer, and war correspondent.

Along with the daughter of playwright Frank Wedekind, Mann starred in her also-gay brother's lesbian play *Esther and Anja* in 1925. She had two marriages of convenience, with the play's director Gustaf Gründgens in 1926, and poet W.H. Auden in 1935, to secure British citizenship and safe passage out of Nazi Germany. Auden arranged for her lover Therese Giehse to marry out of Germany as well. Auden and Mann remained married but separated until her death.

In 1933, she and Giehse founded the cabaret Die Pfeffermühle (The Peppermill) in Berlin but were forced out. In 1938, Mann published *School for Barbarians* about the Nazi's educational system. In 1939, she and her brother traveled to report on the Spanish Civil War. During WWII, she worked as a journalist in London, covering the Blitz. After D-Day she attached to Allied forces as they advanced over Europe.

Mann's brother committed suicide in 1949. Mann settled with her parents in Switzerland in 1952, and was further devastated by her father's death in 1955. She died after an operation to remove a brain tumor in 1969.

ANITA BERBER

❧

JUN 10 1899 – NOV 10 1928
(AGED 29)

Born in Dresden to the First Violinist of the Municipal Orchestra and his wife, an aspiring actress and singer, ANITA BERBER'S debut as a dancer was in February of 1916. She went on to tour through Germany and Austria as a solo performer, and with choreographer Rita Sacchetto's troupe. She modeled, acted in silent films, performed scandalous, depraved, occasionally nude dance routines, and in 1923 co-authored *Dances of Vice, Horror, and Ecstasy*, a book of poems, photographs, and drawings. One of her film credits is *Different From The Others* (1919), believed to be the first pro-gay film in the world.

Berber cut her hair in a bob, dyed it red, and dressed androgynously. Her accessories of choice were a sable coat, an antique brooch filled with cocaine, and a pet monkey around her neck. She married three times to gay and bisexual men, and pursued relationships with women in the Berlin scene, including a young Marlene Dietrich, and bar-owner Susi Wanowski who later became Berber's lover/manager/secretary. She was once imprisoned for six weeks for insulting the King of Yugoslavia.

Diagnosed with advanced pulmonary tuberculosis in 1928 after a collapse in Damascus, Berber died shortly thereafter while trying to return home.

ERNST RÖHM
(ERNST JULIUS GÜNTHER RÖHM)

NOV 28 1887 – JUL 1 1934
(AGED 46)

Born in Munich, ERNST RÖHM survived WWI with a permanently scarred face. After the November 11th, 1918 armistice, he found leadership potential in a young Adolf Hitler, who was known as "Röhm's boy" until the failed Beer Hall Putsch of 1923, when a proto-Nazi militia attempted to take Munich. This resulted in jail time for Hitler during which he wrote *Mein Kampf* (1925), and a suspended sentence for Röhm. After Hitler's release, he appointed Röhm leader of the SA (*Sturmabteilung* or "Assault Division"), a paramilitary organization whose intimidation tactics helped Hitler gain power.

Röhm was a known homosexual, and once brought a male prostitute to court for stealing his suitcase. He was part of the Nazi Party until he was targeted by Göring, Goebbels, and Himmler for his Brownshirts being too socialist: "brown on the outside and red on the inside." On the Night of the Long Knives, a deadly purge of Hitler's perceived opponents, Röhm was arrested by Hitler himself, and was later given the option of suicide. Röhm refused it saying, "If I am to be killed, let Adolf do it himself." Upon his execution, his final words hailed the man and the party that ordered his death.

LIZ SMITH
(MARY ELIZABETH SMITH)

FEB 2 1923 – NOV 12 2017
(AGED 94)

LIZ SMITH graduated from the University of Texas with a Journalism degree in 1949. She wrote for Texas newspapers before moving to New York to work as a proofreader, a typist, and a reporter. Smith became a news producer for NBC, was a ghostwriter for Hearst's Cholly Knickerbocker gossip column, and in 1976 had her own gossip column for the *New York Daily News*.

Smith was known as "The Grand Dame of Dish." She appeared on the afternoon news program *Live at Five* in 1979 during a writer's strike, and stayed for 11 years, winning a Daytime Emmy award in 1985.

Smith also worked for Fox News, *Newsday*, *Staten Island Advance*, and the *New York Post*.

Smith was married and divorced twice. She considered herself gender neutral, bisexual, and though she "wasn't a happy convert to any particular sexual thing," she thought that her "relationships with women were always much more emotionally satisfying and comfortable [than with men]." When her memoir *Natural Blonde* (2000) was seen as her coming out, she said, "Honey, I don't think I have ever really been in." Smith had a longtime relationship with archaeologist Iris Love. Smith died of natural causes in 2017.

LEM BILLINGS
(KIRK LEMOYNE BILLINGS)

APR 15 1916 – MAY 28 1981
(AGED 65)

New York advertising executive LEM BILLINGS was best friend to American President John F. Kennedy. Roommates at Choate prep school and Princeton University, on a summer trip through Europe in 1937, they bought a dachshund together named Offie. Billings was an usher at Kennedy's wedding, and dined in the White House with the President and Greta Garbo on November 13th, 1963, nine days before Kennedy's assassination. It was the last time they would meet.

According to David Pitts, author of *Jack and Lem* (2007), Billings once propositioned Kennedy by writing on toilet paper, a common Choate practice to ensure the evidence could be easily destroyed. A 1934 letter from Kennedy says, "Please don't write to me on toilet paper anymore. I'm not that kind of boy." Most of Kennedy's letter was about his hospitalization and health, with this comment in parentheses.

Billings' sexuality was a known secret. Billings said, "Jack made a big difference in my life. Because of him, I was never lonely. He may have been the reason I never got married." Historian Sally Bedell Smith described Billings as "probably the saddest of the Kennedy 'widows.'" Billings died in his sleep at age 65, survived by his siblings.

LOUISE BROOKS
(MARY LOUISE BROOKS)

NOV 14 1906 – AUG 8 1985
(AGED 78)

LOUISE BROOKS started her theatrical career as a dancer at the Denishawn modern dance company in Los Angeles in 1922. She was dismissed from the company in 1924, with one of the founders telling her it was "because you want life handed to you on a silver salver." In 1925, Brooks found work as a featured dancer with *Ziegfeld Follies* on Broadway, and was signed to Paramount on a five-year-contract. Brooks starred in 17 silent films, eight sound films, and retired in 1938. Brooks popularized the bobbed haircut and became an iconic figure as a flapper. She published her memoir, *Lulu in Hollywood*, in 1982.

Brooks had a two-month affair with Charlie Chaplin, spent a night with the "charming and tender lover" Greta Garbo, married and divorced director Eddie Sutherland, and married and divorced Chicago millionaire Deering Davis, disappearing on him after five months and leaving only a note. She also had relationships with CBS founder William S. Paley and businessman George Preston Marshall. Brooks didn't consider herself lesbian or bisexual, once claiming, "I had two affairs with girls—they did nothing for me."

Brooks died of a heart attack in 1985, after years of suffering from arthritis and emphysema.

MARGARET MEAD

DEC 16 1901 – NOV 15 1978
(AGED 76)

MARGARET MEAD'S first anthropology field assignment was in American Samoa in 1925, where she focused her findings into the bestselling book *Coming of Age in Samoa* (1928). She studied and taught at several universities, became assistant curator of the American Museum of Natural History in New York City, was executive secretary of the National Research Council's Committee on Food Habits during World War II, and received 28 honorary doctorates. She was known on campuses as the woman with the cape and walking stick, and known to the world as the most famous anthropologist of her time.

Mead was writing about the fluidity of human sexuality and the constrictions of gender roles as far back as 1933. Mead was married three times, all to fellow anthropologists, and had a relationship with her anthropology professor Ruth Benedict. Mead worked closely with fellow anthropologist Dr. Rhoda Métraux, collaborating with her on several books and articles. They lived together in a house in Greenwich Village, and later an apartment on Central Park West. Personal correspondence released after Mead's death indicated their sexual relationship.

Mead died of pancreatic cancer and posthumously received the Presidential Medal of Freedom from President Jimmy Carter.

349

GLENN LAWRENCE BURKE

NOV 16 1952 – MAY 30 1995
(AGED 42)

GLENN BURKE was a basketball star at Berkeley High School, but his first professional sports offer came from Major League Baseball. Burke signed with the Dodgers in 1972, and was touted as the next Willie Mays. His teammates called him "the life of the team" because he was always dancing and joking. Burke was credited with inventing the high five in 1977, when he ran up to congratulate teammate Dusty Baker after a home run.

His team accepted him and his sexual orientation, but management felt differently. Traded to the Oakland Athletics, he received very little playing time and was isolated from the other players. Burke left baseball due to prejudiced treatment and injuries, saying, "I had finally gotten to the point where it was more important to be myself than a baseball player." Burke came out publicly in 1982, participated in the Gay Games, and played third-base in the San Francisco Gay Softball League. Burke's use of the high five became a symbol of gay pride in San Francisco.

Burke was hit by a car in 1987, and his injuries led him to drug addiction and life on the streets. Burke died in 1995 of AIDS complications.

ROCK HUDSON
(ROY HAROLD SCHERER JR.)

NOV 17 1925 – OCT 2 1985
(AGED 59)

Born in Winnetka, IL, ROCK HUDSON worked as a golf caddy, an aircraft mechanic, and a truck driver before his acting career. He was picked up by Hollywood agent Henry Willson, who created the name Rock Hudson and took him to 'straight' school, drilling in him how to walk, talk, dress, and act.

Hudson quickly became leading-man material. He was Oscar-nominated for the film *Giant* (1956) along with co-star James Dean, and received four Golden Globe awards. Hudson found work in westerns, dramas, and rom-coms, most notably with gal pal Doris Day. He also starred in the television series *McMillan & Wife* (1971-1977). Offscreen,

his romantic encounters included James Dean, Jack Coates, Tom Clark, Armistead Maupin, and Lee Garlington, who called Hudson a "gentle giant." Hudson married secretary Phyllis Gates in 1955. After three years, Gates filed for divorce citing mental cruelty.

Hudson was diagnosed with HIV in 1984, and confirmed in 1985 that he had AIDS. His admission gave a name and a face to the disease and helped destigmatize the victims. Hudson died from AIDS-related complications in 1985 at his home in Beverly Hills. The posthumous biography *Rock Hudson: His Story* (1986) named Garlington as his true love.

FREDERICK II OF PRUSSIA
(KING FREDERICK THE GREAT)
❧

JAN 24 1712 – AUG 17 1786
(AGED 74)

At age 16, FREDERICK II was intimate with his father's Scottish pageboy. He planned on fleeing Prussia for England to escape the cruel King Frederick William I, alongside his close friend and probable lover Hans Hermann von Katte, but once this plot was discovered, they were imprisoned, and the king forced Frederick II to watch Katte's decapitation. On November 18th, 1730, Frederick II was released from his cell and granted a royal pardon.

Frederick II ascended the throne in 1740, and during his reign he secured the end of the Seven Years' war, found success in leading the Prussian army, engineered the First Partition of Poland, and was a patron for the arts. After a battlefield defeat, Frederick wrote, "Fortune has it in for me; she is a woman, and I am not that way inclined."

His father married him to Elisabeth Christine of Brunswick-Bevern, whom Frederick II only met on her birthday each year, and separated from as soon as his father died. Frederick II wrote an erotic poem to Italian philosopher Francesco Algarotti, lived with Voltaire, and had a relationship with his valet who had "a very pretty face."

Frederick II died in an armchair in 1786.

WOMEN'S
ENTREPRENEURSHIP DAY

GISÈLE FREUND
(GISELA FREUND)

DEC 19 1908 – MAR 31 2000
(AGED 91)

GISÈLE FREUND received her first camera as a graduation present from her father in 1929. When the Nazis came to power in Germany, Freund escaped from Berlin to Paris with film negatives strapped to her body. Then, as the Nazis invaded Paris, she escaped to Free France.

Freund became known for portraits of artists and writers, with her photo of James Joyce gracing the cover of *Time* magazine in 1939. Before photographing someone, she studied their work and spent hours discussing it with them. She used color when others preferred black and white portraits, as color was "closer to life."

Freund was the first woman to receive the Grand Prix National des Arts from France, was elected President of the French Federation of Creative Photographers, and helped found a relief action committee for French artists. She was refused a United States visa, thrown out of Argentina, and lived in Mexico before returning to France in 1953.

She married Pierre Blum for a French visa in 1935. Freund was a lesbian, wore masculine clothing, and often photographed lesbian and bisexual women. Freund was close with Adrienne Monnier, Sylvia Beach, and Frida Kahlo. She died in 2000 at the age of 91.

SELMA LAGERLÖF
(SELMA OTTILIA LOVISA LAGERLÖF)

NOV 20 1858 – MAR 16 1940
(AGED 81)

SELMA LAGERLÖF was brought up by her grandmother, who raised her on fairytales. After studying at the Royal Women's Superior Training Academy in Stockholm, Sweden, Lagerlöf began writing her own fantasy fiction. Her first novel, *Gösta Berling's Saga* (1891), won a magazine contest for publication. She continued to write stories and novels that captured the imagination of children and adults alike, and her work was translated and read across the globe.

Lagerlöf was the first female writer awarded the Nobel Prize in Literature in 1909, and the first woman to be inducted into the Swedish Academy's membership in 1914. Near the beginning of World War II, Lagerlöf sent a gold medal she'd received from the Academy in 1904, along with her Nobel Prize, to the government of Finland to fundraise for the war effort. The Finnish government returned her medals with thanks and raised the funds by other means.

Lagerlöf met writer/translator Sophie Elkan in 1894 and they fell in love. Lagerlöf also maintained a relationship with teacher and city council member Valborg Olander, whom she met in 1898. Lagerlöf went back and forth between these women, with a fair bit of jealousy on both sides. Lagerlöf died in 1940.

QUENTIN CRISP
(DENIS CHARLES PRATT)

DEC 25 1908 – NOV 21 1999
(AGED 90)

Born Christmas Day in Surrey, England, QUENTIN CRISP was a rentboy, artist's model, writer, actor, and raconteur. He's best remembered for his effeminate presentation, his witticisms, and his memoir, *The Naked Civil Servant* (1968), which was made into a television movie starring John Hurt in 1975. Crisp's personal presence sustained a long-running one-man stage show where he told anecdotes and amusingly answered audience questions.

While picking up American G.I.s during London's wartime blackouts, Crisp found a love for America itself. His first visit's stay at NYC's Hotel Chelsea coincided with a fire, a robbery, and the murder of Nancy Spungen by Sex Pistols bassist Sid Vicious.

Crisp eventually moved to NYC, supported himself by writing movie reviews, and accepting every dinner invitation he was offered. Crisp would "sing for his supper" by regaling his hosts throughout the meal. He also took minor film roles as they came.

His dislike for Princess Diana and flippancy about AIDS were marks against him, but fascination for Crisp came from the likes of Sting, Boy George, and Andy Warhol. In Crisp's own words: "Life was a funny thing that happened to me on the way to the grave." He died of a heart attack.

ANDRÉ GIDE
(ANDRÉ PAUL GUILLAUME GIDE)

NOV 22 1869 – FEB 19 1951
(AGED 81)

French author and winner of the 1947 Nobel Prize in Literature, ANDRÉ GIDE is known for his revolutionary support of individual freedom in defiance of conventional morality.

Gide traveled to Northern Africa in 1893, embraced his attraction to boys, and rejected puritanical morality. Having befriended Oscar Wilde in Paris, they met again in Algiers in 1895, and joined up for several sexual encounters with young boys. Gide wrote of one instance, "No scruple clouded my pleasure and no remorse followed it. But what name then am I to give the rapture I felt as I clasped in my naked arms that perfect little body, so wild, so ardent, so sombrely lascivious?"

Gide considered himself a boy-loving pederast as opposed to an adult-attracted sodomite. Gide wrote about sexual matters in diaries, autobiography, and *Corydon* (1924), Socratic dialogues on homosexuality.

Gide's 1895 marriage to his cousin Madeleine was un-consummated and largely estranged. He was elected mayor of the commune of La Roque in 1896, and worked for Red Cross soldiers' convalescent homes during WWI. In 1923, he sired a daughter, possibly his only sexual encounter with a woman. He considered communism in the 1930s, wrote in the 1940s, and died in 1951.

VIRGINIA CHARLES PRINCE
(ARNOLD LOWMAN)

NOV 23 1912 – MAY 2 2009

(AGED 96)

VIRGINIA PRINCE was an American transgender activist, publisher of the magazine *Transvestia*, and founder of the Society of the Second Self for heterosexual crossdressers. Prince began cross-dressing at age 12, and by age 18 won a church Halloween costume contest, having successfully passed as a woman for the first time.

Prince earned a PhD in pharmacology in 1939, and in 1941 married a woman, with whom she had a son. She came to accept herself with the help of a psychiatrist, but still divorced due to her transvestism. She lost the support of her family, and started going by the name Charles Prince (after her father and the street she grew up on) to hide her civilian identity from her activist work and publications. Prince's goal with *Transvestia* was to contradict any perceived connection between cross-dressing and sexual deviation.

However, Prince was a controversial advocate in the transgender community due to her insistence on exclusionary definitions, her support for conventional norms like traditional family and marriage, and her stereotypical gender portrayals. In an attempt to normalize transvestism, Prince sought to exclude fetishists, homosexuals, and transsexuals from the group.

Prince died in her hometown of Los Angeles at 96 years old.

WILLIAM CLARK GABLE

FEB 1 1901 – NOV 16 1960
(AGED 59)

Called The King of Hollywood and best known for portraying the debonair Rhett Butler in *Gone with the Wind* (1939), CLARK GABLE'S screen persona was equal parts "man's man" and "ladies' man." Gable won an Academy Award for Best Actor in the comedy *It Happened One Night* (1934), was nominated for his role in *Mutiny on the Bounty* (1935), and ultimately appeared in over 60 motion pictures, including starring opposite Joan Crawford in Fred Astaire's debut film, *Dancing Lady*, released November 24th, 1933.

Clark Gable was a notorious womanizer. After two failed marriages, he married actress Carole Lombard in 1931, had an illegitimate and unacknowledged child with Loretta Young in 1935, and an affair with Lana Turner around 1941. After losing Lombard to a plane crash in 1942, he joined the army before marrying twice more, finally to Kay Williams, who was pregnant with a son when Gable died from a heart attack in 1960.

Clark Gable: Tormented Star (2008) claims a young Gable used sex for career advancement with both women and men. Essentially "gay for pay," his encounters reportedly included aspiring actor Earle Larimore, whose aunt had influential Broadway connections, and actors Rod La Rocque and Billy Haines.

VAJIRAVUDH, RAMA VI OF SIAM
(PHRAMONGKUTKLAO, KING OF SIAM)

JAN 1 1881 – NOV 25 1925
(AGED 44)

KING VAJIRAVUDH was the 6th monarch of Siam from 1910-1925, and is best remembered for his progressive reforms, and as a writer of poetry and plays. His sexual preferences were known in his court, as he had lavish parties with male courtiers and an inner circle of Siamese transvestites who functioned as his advisors. Political scientist Thongchai Winichakul asserts that Vajiravudh "is one of the worst kept secrets among Thai —." Vajiravudh promoted social reforms including making monogamy the only legal form of marriage, founding Siam's first university, and making primary education free and compulsory.

Educated at the University of Oxford, with a great love for Siamese literature, English poetry, and Russian ballet, Vajiravudh also survived one assassination attempt, entered four brief marriages, and sided with the Allied Powers during WWI. Vajiravudh introduced Western narrative forms into Thai literature, personally translating three of Shakespeare's plays, as well as Agatha Christie's *Hercule Poirot* mysteries. He also created the character "Nai Thong-In," based on Sherlock Holmes: Siam's first consulting detective.

Vajiravudh died of illness within hours of the birth of his only daughter. The throne then passed to his brother, Prajadhipok. Vajiravudh has monuments at Sanam Chan Palace and Lumpini Park, Bangkok.

WINNARETTA SINGER, PRINCESSE EDMOND DE POLIGNAC

JAN 8 1865 – NOV 26 1943
(AGED 78)

Daughter of Isaac Singer, modern sewing machine developer, WINNARETTA SINGER lived out her youth in Oldway Mansion, a 115-room-estate in Paignton. She married Prince Louis de Scey-Montbéliard when she was 22, and their wedding night involved Singer climbing onto an armoire with an umbrella, and threatening to kill the Prince if he touched her. Their marriage was annulled in 1892. She married gay composer Prince Edmond de Polignac in 1893, and they enjoyed a friendlier, unconsummated marriage.

Singer and her husband began a musical salon in the music room of their mansion in 1894, which became a haven for avant-garde artists of the time. Guests included Debussy, Ravel, Isadora Duncan, Claude Monet, Chabrier, Marcel Proust, and Colette. Singer was also an accomplished pianist and painter, a patron of the arts, and commissioned several works from young composers.

Singer worked with Marie Curie in World War I to convert private limo services into portable radiology units to help aid wounded soldiers. She commissioned public housing projects, and assisted in the construction of Foch Hospital in Suresnes, Paris.

Singer was rarely without a lover. Her romantic affairs included Romaine Brooks, Violet Trefusis, Renata Borgatti, and Alvilde Chaplin. Singer died at age 78.

KATHARINE SUSAN ANTHONY

NOV 27 1877 – NOV 20 1965
(AGED 87)

Suffragist, socialist, feminist, pacifist, and author KATHARINE ANTHONY was born in Roseville, Arkansas. Anthony received a bachelor's degree in Philosophy from the University of Chicago in 1905, and taught at Wellesley College in Boston in 1907. She went on to teach public school in Arkansas before moving to Manhattan.

Anthony was best known for her biographies of great women in history, with works on Queen Elizabeth, Catherine the Great, Margaret Fuller, Louisa May Alcott, Dolly Madison, Mercy Otis Warren, and Susan B. Anthony. She also wrote *The Lambs: A Story of Pre-Victorian England* (1945) on British writers Charles and Mary Lamb, *Feminism in Germany and Scandinavia* (1915),

and *Mothers Who Must Earn* (1914) which outlined the abuse of women and children in workrooms and labor jobs.

Anthony's longtime partner was educator and Little Red School House founder Elisabeth Irwin, and together they raised a family of adopted children. While they lived in Manhattan, they maintained a summer home in Gaylordsville, Connecticut, where they referred to themselves the "gay ladies of Gaylordsville."

Irwin died in October of 1942. In 1965, Anthony died from complications of a heart attack at 88, and was buried next to Irwin in Morningside Cemetery in Gaylordsville.

JEFFREY LIONEL DAHMER

MAY 21 1960 – NOV 28 1994
(AGED 34)

Born in West Allis, Wisconsin, JEFFREY DAHMER committed his first murder at 18 years old, before serving two years in the U.S. Army as a combat medic. After an honorable discharge in 1981, he moved in with his grandmother before being hired as a mixer at the Milwaukee Ambrosia Chocolate Factory in 1985, where he worked from 11 p.m.–7 a.m. for six nights a week.

Dahmer's second murder was committed during a drunken blackout in 1987. After that, a pattern of luring, killing, and cannibalizing male victims between the ages of 14 and 33 emerged, until an escaped victim brought police to his Milwaukee apartment in 1991. Inside the police found: blue barrels full of decaying remains, a severed head in the refrigerator, painted human skulls displayed as decoration, and Polaroid pictures of nude boys and dismembered bodies.

Dahmer would inject bleach into the brains of his victims in an attempt to destroy their frontal lobes and free wills, to make them into compliant sex partners. These experiments inevitably led to their deaths. In 1992, Dahmer was sentenced to multiple life imprisonments, which he served until he was beaten to death at 34 by a fellow inmate in 1994.

BILLY STRAYHORN
(WILLIAM THOMAS STRAYHORN)

NOV 29 1915 – MAY 31 1967
(AGED 51)

African-American BILLY STRAY-HORN was sent to live at his grandparents' house for months at a time, to protect him from his alcoholic father. There he became interested in music, playing records on his grandmother's Victrola and hymns on the piano. Strayhorn worked odd jobs to buy his first piano, and was writing and composing music in his teens.

After hearing Duke Ellington perform in Pittsburgh in 1938, Strayhorn approached the bandleader afterward to demonstrate how he would have arranged a piece. Ellington was so impressed he invited Strayhorn to New York, and Strayhorn worked with him from then on. Strayhorn got the nicknames "Swee' Pea," "Weely," and "Strays" by his bandmates, and collaborated on many of Ellington's works.

Strayhorn met musician Aaron Bridgers in 1939, and they lived together until Bridgers moved to Paris in 1947. Singer Lena Horne had a close relationship with Strayhorn, and considered him the only man she really loved, saying, "he was everything that I wanted in a man, except he wasn't interested in me sexually." While in the hospital with esophageal cancer, Strayhorn submitted his final composition to Ellington in 1967, "Blood Count," and died in the company of his then-partner Bill Grove.

LAURA GILPIN

APR 22 1891 – NOV 30 1979

(AGED 88)

As a child LAURA GILPIN camped and hiked along the Colorado countryside. Gilpin was gifted a Kodak Brownie Camera for her 12th birthday and discovered a love of photography. She studied music at the New England Conservatory of Music from 1904-1908, leaving school when finances were no longer available. She raised turkeys at her family's ranch to support photography classes, and later attended the Clarence White School in NYC.

In 1916, Gilpin had a bout with influenza that required a nurse, Elizabeth "Betsy" Warham Forster. Forster and Gilpin became longtime companions and photography partners. Gilpin's involvement with the Navajo began in 1930, when she and Forster ran out of gasoline in a remote section of their reservation.

Gilpin became well-known for platinum printing, calling it "the most beautiful image one can get," and for photographing the American Southwest and its Native people. Her work was purchased by the Library of Congress, she served as chairman of the Indian Arts Fund in Santa Fe, New Mexico, and in 1974 Gilpin was presented the First Governor's Award for Outstanding Achievement in the Arts in New Mexico.

Forster died in 1972, and Gilpin in 1979. They are buried together in Colorado Springs.

DECEMBER

ALEISTER CROWLEY
(EDWARD ALEXANDER CROWLEY)

OCT 12 1875 – DEC 1 1947
(AGED 72)

In 1904, ALEISTER CROWLEY and his wife traveled to Cairo on their honeymoon. While there, Crowley claimed to hear a disembodied voice named Aiwass. Crowley wrote of the encounter, producing *The Book of the Law* (1904), and declared himself a prophet. The hashish-fueled creation of an occultist mysticism religion called Thelema occurred around 1907, with the membership organization A∴A∴ established as a ladder for rising through the spiritual ranks.

Crowley toured with fellow members to perform feats of magic and phenomenon. He often incorporated working elements of other secret societies to Thelema, including teachings of "sex magick,"

with anal sex techniques taught and performed at the highest levels.

Crowley was bisexual, preferring women over men. While at Cambridge, Crowley had a relationship with fellow student Herbert Jerome Pollitt, a female impersonator who went by Diane de Rougy. Crowley later wrote of their time together, saying, "The relation between us was that ideal intimacy which the Greeks considered the greatest glory of manhood and the most precious prize of life."

Crowley lived off membership dues, used heroin to treat his asthma, and died in December 1947 of chronic bronchitis. His partial auto-biography, *The Confessions of Aleister Crowley*, was published in 1969.

JOSEPH ISRAEL LOBDELL
(LUCY ANN LOBDELL)

❧

Dec 2 1829 – 1912
(AGED ~82)

Born Lucy Ann Lobdell and so skilled a marksman as to earn the nickname "The Female Hunter of Delaware County," Lobdell married George Washington Slater, and was abandoned by him after the birth of their daughter, Helen. Lobdell then left Helen with family and began living as JOSEPH ISRAEL LOBDELL.

Dressing in men's attire and dating women whenever possible, Lobdell eventually met Marie Louise Perry. Also abandoned by her previous husband, Perry married Lobdell, and for nearly 20 years they lived together, often in poverty. Very much in need of money, Lobdell succeeded in getting a widow's pension as the wife of George Slater, who had died during the Civil War. However, after receiving the pension, Lobdell was declared insane by a brother and institutionalized.

In 1883, Dr. P.M. Wise wrote an account of Lobdell titled, "A Case of Sexual Perversion," stating, "She considered herself a man in all that the name implies." Lobdell died at the Binghamton State Hospital, predeceased by all siblings. Dr. Bambi Lobdell, a distant cousin of Lucy/Joseph's, published *A Strange Sort of Being* in 2011, arguing that her ancestor was not a lesbian in male dress, as other scholars have speculated, but a transgender man.

BRIAN SAMUEL EPSTEIN

SEP 19 1934 – AUG 27 1967
(AGED 32)

Born in Liverpool of Jewish descent, BRIAN EPSTEIN had acting ambitions. He attended the Royal Academy of Dramatic Art (RADA), but felt he was "too much of a businessman to enjoy being a student." He liked the idea of producing better.

Epstein was managing a record store when he saw The Beatles perform in 1961. On December 3rd of that year, Epstein proposed the idea of managing the group, and all agreed to sign a contract with him; Epstein was 28. He tailored the band's image, had them dress cleanly and uniformly, with no smoking on stage and no swearing. He negotiated the band's appearance on *The Ed Sullivan Show* in February of 1964, which launched them into worldwide fame.

Closeted during his life, Epstein was discharged from the British Army for being "emotionally and mentally unfit" due to his homosexuality. He left RADA shortly after an arrest for "persistent importuning" outside a men's public toilet. He's said to have once propositioned former Beatles member Pete Best, and is suspected of a sexual encounter with John Lennon during a four-day trip they took to Barcelona in 1963.

Epstein developed a drug dependency, and died of a barbiturate overdose in 1967.

MANUEL RODRÍGUEZ LOZANO

DEC 4 1896 – MAR 27 1971
(AGED 74)

Born in Mexico City, MANUEL RODRÍGUEZ LOZANO expressed homosexual desire through his drawings and paintings, as can be seen in the 1933 Mexican edition of Federico García Lorca's *Oda a Walt Whitman*. Lozano's melancholy depictions of Mexico stand in contrast to the festive imagery of the Mexican muralism movement.

Lozano married Carmen Mondragón in 1913. After her father's involvement in the assassination of Francisco I. Madero, the couple went into exile. In Paris, Lozano entered the spheres of Matisse, Braque, and Picasso. His wife disapproved of his bohemian friends, and in 1914 they lost a child in infancy. They separated on return to Mexico in 1921.

Lozano's studio attracted younger painters, among them Abraham Ángel, Julio Castellanos, and Angel Torres Jaramillo, called "Tebo," with whom he became romantically involved. His relationship with Ángel drew particular attention when Ángel died at 19 from a cocaine overdose.

Lozano was later imprisoned for stealing engravings by Albrecht Dürer, which went missing after he requested them as director of the Escuela Nacional de Artes Plásticas. The engravings mysteriously reappeared in 1966; Lozano was likely scapegoated due to homophobia. The tenor of his art grew darker after imprisonment.

Lozano died of heart failure in 1971.

DAME LILIAN
CHARLOTTE BARKER

1874 – 1955

(AGED 81)

LILIAN BARKER trained to become a teacher at Whitelands College in Chelsea, and went on to specialize in educating delinquents and troubled children. In 1913, Barker was appointed principal of the London County Council's Women's Institute correctional facility where she served for two years before joining Britain's war effort at the Royal Arsenal in Woolwich. She worked as lady superintendent, oversaw 30,000 female workers, and taught cooking, semaphore, and munitions. She also set up the cookery section of the Women's Legion and fundraised to provide nurseries and convalescent homes for the women workers.

In 1923, Barker was appointed governor of the Borstal Institution for Girls at Aylesbury, a prison for young offenders. She was the first British female assistant prison commissioner, and instituted sweeping prison reform, focusing on education, rehabilitation, and guidance, which became the basis for modern British correctional facilities. In 1944, Barker was named a Dame Commander of the Order of the British Empire (DBE) in honor of her welfare services for women and girls.

Barker was working as a Sunday school teacher when she met fellow teacher Florence Francis. Barker moved in with Francis and her family in Hampstead. They remained together until Barker's death in 1955.

VINCENT PRICE
(VINCENT LEONARD PRICE JR.)

MAY 27 1911 – OCT 25 1993
(AGED 82)

VINCENT PRICE first appeared onstage professionally in 1934, and in 1935 he performed with Orson Welles' Mercury Theatre repertory company. Price found work as a character actor, a villain, and in horror movies like *House on Haunted Hill* (1959) and Roger Corman's *House of Usher* (1960). His favorite roles included Egghead on *Batman* (1966-1968), and Oscar Wilde in the stage play *Diversions and Delights* (1978).

Price established the first "teaching art collection," the Vincent Price Art Museum at East Los Angeles College. He served as commissioner on the Indian Arts and Crafts Board, and was an art consultant for Sears-Roebuck.

Price was also a gourmet cook, authoring several cookbooks with his second wife, Mary Grant.

Price was married three times and had two children. His daughter Victoria Price confirmed his bisexuality by saying, "I am as close to certain as I can be that my dad had physically intimate relationships with men. I know for 100 percent fact that my dad was completely loving and supportive of LGBT people."

Price's last major film role was appearing as The Inventor in *Edward Scissorhands*, which first premiered in Los Angeles on December 6th, 1990. Price died of lung cancer in 1993.

7th

HURD HATFIELD
(WILLIAM RUKARD HURD HATFIELD)

DEC 7 1917 – DEC 26 1998
(AGED 81)

Best known for his role in 1945's *The Picture of Dorian Gray*, American actor HURD HATFIELD also appeared in *The Left Handed Gun* (1958), and *The Boston Strangler* (1968). He appeared frequently on television, including on *Murder, She Wrote* (1984-1996) opposite his lifelong friend and *Dorian Gray* co-star, Angela Lansbury. Of his most famous role Hatfield said, "I have been haunted by *The Picture of Dorian Gray* [...] The decadence, the hints of bisexuality and so on, made me a leper! Nobody knew I had a sense of humour, and people wouldn't even have lunch with me."

Hatfield never married.

According to classmates at the Michael Chekhov Theatre Studio, Hatfield and Yul Brynner had an affair in 1941. Actress Jane Withers once said, "The most creative people [in Hollywood] usually turned out to be gay. I'd hear that someone I knew or worked with was gay, and I'd think, I knew there was something special, something different, about him! [...] Hurd Hatfield was very different."

It was through Lansbury that Hatfield was introduced to Ireland, where he bought Ballinterry House in Cork County in the 1970s. He died there at age 81 in his sleep, after having Christmas dinner with friends.

CHRISTIAN DIOR

JAN 21 1905 – OCT 24 1957

(AGED 52)

CHRISTIAN DIOR was born in Granville on the coast of Normandy, France. When he was young, he sold fashion sketches outside his house for change. Dior served in the French army until 1942, when he joined Lucien Lelong's fashion house and designed dresses for the wives of Nazi officers.

Dior founded his fashion house on December 8th, 1946, where he worked to create voluptuous silhouettes of women with boned bodices and hip padding. His post-war "New Look" debuted in 1947, which revolutionized women's dress with full skirts and extravagant fabrics.

He frequently consulted fortune-tellers before making decisions, from what dates to debut collections on, to whether or not he should go to the spa. Outside of the fashion world, Dior enjoyed cooking, with most of his recipes involving meat being cooked in Dom Pérignon.

Dior remained deeply closeted and was unlucky in love. His last partner was Jacques Benita, a Moroccan singer three decades younger than Dior, whom he showered with affection and lavish gifts. Dior died of a heart attack after choking on a fish bone, or during a card game, or after a strenuous sexual encounter, depending on the report. The exact circumstances of his death are undisclosed.

EDITH CRAIG
(EDITH AILSA GERALDINE CRAIG, AILSA CRAIG)

DEC 9 1869 – MAR 27 1947
(AGED 77)

EDITH CRAIG worked for the Lyceum Theatre company as a costume designer and actress under the name Ailsa Craig. Known for creating historically accurate costumes, Craig founded the Pioneer Players in London, a company that produced formerly banned plays and those that promoted feminism. Craig later produced and directed plays for several English theaters, and appeared in silent films. Deeply involved in suffragist groups, she also created productions to raise awareness for the movement.

Craig lived in a *ménage à trois* with artist Clare Atwood and author Christabel Marshall. Her brother Edward believed her lesbian lifestyle was due to her "hatred of men, initiated by the hatred of her father." However, composer Martin Shaw proposed to Craig and she accepted, though the marriage was prevented by Edith's mother and by Christabel Marshall.

Suffering from acute arthritis, Craig dictated her memoirs to childhood friend Vera Holme. The memoirs were lost in an attic, resurfaced in 1978, and published as *Edy was a Lady* in 2011.

Craig died of coronary thrombosis and chronic myocarditis in 1947. Her ashes were intended to be placed alongside Marshall and Atwood, but the ashes went missing, and a memorial was installed in the cemetery in remembrance.

THOMAS MANN
(PAUL THOMAS MANN)

JUN 6 1875 – AUG 12 1955
(AGED 80)

German author THOMAS MANN was once considered the literary heir to Goethe. His first short story "Little Herr Friedemann" was published in 1898, and he continued to write essays, short stories, and novels throughout his life. He was awarded the Nobel Prize in Literature for his novel *Buddenbrooks* (1901) on December 10th, 1929.

In 1905, Mann married Katia Pringsheim, daughter of a wealthy Jewish family, and they had six children. They emigrated to Switzerland before the first World War and to the United States just before the second, settling in Los Angeles. There Mann recorded monthly anti-Nazi speeches for the German people that were flown to London and broadcast by the BBC. In 1952, the Manns returned to Switzerland, disturbed by rising McCarthyism in America.

Mann's best-known work is *Death in Venice* (1912), about a male writer's obsessive, unrequited love for a young boy. Mann insisted it was not autobiographical. When his papers and diaries were posthumously unsealed, his sexual struggle was revealed: he had relationships and fascinations with men and boys, including 17-year-old hotel waiter Klaus Heuser, and violinist and painter Paul Ehrenberg, whom he called "the central experience of my heart."

Mann died of atherosclerosis in 1955.

CHRISTINE JORGENSEN
(GEORGE WILLIAM JORGENSEN JR.)

MAY 30 1926 – MAY 3 1989
(AGED 62)

From the biography *Becoming a Woman*: "On the afternoon of December 11th, 1952, CHRISTINE JORGENSEN did something no other transsexual had ever done before and few have ever done since. Dressed in her new suit and with all the right accessories and jewelry, she took a taxi to a downtown hotel to meet a group of reporters and to show the world what a transsexual looked like."

Born in the Bronx, New York City, Jorgensen was drafted into the army at age 19, and after discharge began taking estrogen in preparation for sex reassignment surgery. Obtaining special permission to undergo the surgeries in Copenhagen, Jorgensen returned to New York as a sensational story in the tabloids: "Bronx GI Becomes a Woman!" She gave interviews, posed for photos, and was open about her transition and how happy it made her. In a letter to friends she wrote, "Remember the shy, miserable person who left America? Well, that person is no more and, as you can see, I'm in marvelous spirits."

She worked as an actress, nightclub entertainer, and lecturer, saying later that she'd given the sexual revolution a "good swift kick in the pants." Jorgensen died from cancer at age 62.

TALLULAH BROCKMAN BANKHEAD

JAN 31 1902 – DEC 12 1968
(AGED 66)

American actress of stage and screen, TALLULAH BANKHEAD was the epitome of a temperamental, flamboyant actress. Primarily a stage performer in shows like *The Little Foxes* (1939), she had screen success with Alfred Hitchcock's *Lifeboat* (1994), and a famously uninhibited sex life. Sometimes considered more star than actress, she's credited with nearly 300 roles.

By 15 she'd moved to New York City, and quickly charmed her way into the famed Algonquin Round Table. Bankhead was noticed for having "close friendships" with many lesbian/bisexual women, not least because she began introducing herself with, "I'm a lesbian. What do you do?" She became well known for her brash, husky one-liners like, "I'm as pure as the driven slush."

She nearly died in 1933 from a hysterectomy, necessary due to advanced gonorrhea; she said upon discharge, "Don't think this has taught me a lesson!" She married once in 1937, divorced in 1941, and inspired Tennessee Williams' Blanche DuBois in *A Streetcar Named Desire* (1947), but by the time she played the role in 1956, Williams said her Blanche was "the worst I have seen."

Bankhead died of pleural double pneumonia, complicated by cigarette-induced emphysema. Her last words were reportedly a request for "Codeine...bourbon."

KUWASI BALAGOON
(DONALD WEEMS)

DEC 22 1946 – DEC 13 1986

(AGED 39)

Black Panther, member of the Black Liberation Army, New Afrikan anarchist, and defendant in the Panther 21 case of the late 1960s, KUWASI BALAGOON spent much of the 1970s in prison, escaping twice to return to BLA activity.

In 1981, he was captured and charged alongside David Gilbert and Judy Clark for participating in an armored truck robbery which resulted in the deaths of guard Peter Paige and police officers Waverly Brown and Edward O'Grady. Balagoon delivered a closing statement at his final trial, saying, "I will tell you now and forever that New Afrikan people have a right to self-determination and that that is more important than the lives of Paige, Brown, and O'Grady or Balagoon, Gilbert, and Clark. And it's gonna cost more lives and be worth every life it costs, because the destiny of over thirty million people and the coming generation's rights to land and independence is priceless."

He was bisexual, part of the queer liberation movement, and his personal philosophies often clashed with the groups he associated with, i.e. the strictly defined masculinity of the Black Panthers. Sentenced to life imprisonment, he died of AIDS-related illness in 1986, just days short of his 40th birthday.

CHARLES XII OF SWEDEN
(KARL XII, KING OF SWEDEN)
❧
JUN 17 1682 – NOV 30 1718
(AGED 36)

CHARLES XII was the only surviving son of Charles XI, then King of Sweden. Charles XII's coronation took place on December 14th, 1697, after his father's death from cancer in April of that year. Charles XII is credited with inventing an octal numeral system, managed to start the Russo-Ottoman War of 1710-1711, refused any opportunities to end the Great Northern War peacefully, and led his army through campaigns to attack any country with leaders he thought unworthy.

Charles XII had no children and never married, turning down one of his marriage candidates by saying he could never wed someone "as ugly as Satan and with such a devilish big mouth." He was particularly close with Maximilian Emanuel of Württemberg-Winnental, who volunteered for Charles XII's army at the age of 14, and whom he called his "Little Prince," his "best and truest friend," and "very pretty."

Charles XII laid siege to Fredrikshald, Norway in 1718 and was inspecting trenches when he was struck in the head by a projectile and killed. As there were no witnesses to the event, theories surrounding his death range from grapeshot fired from the nearby fortress, to a hired assassin sent by Charles XII's brother-in-law.

ELSA HILDEGARD, BARONESS VON FREYTAG-LORINGHOVEN

(ELSE HILDEGARD PLÖTZ)

JUL 12 1874 – DEC 15 1927

(AGED 53)

After her second husband staged his own suicide and ran off to Manitoba, Canada, ELSE PLÖTZ supported herself by working as an artist's model. She married German Baron Leopold von Freytag-Loringhoven in 1913. The Baron left to fight in World War I, was captured in France, and committed suicide.

She worked in a cigarette factory in New York, wrote poems with shocking titles including "Ejaculation," "Kissambushed," and "Phalluspistol," and made a film with Man Ray and Marcel Duchamp, the aptly titled *Elsa, Baroness von Freytag-Loringhoven, Shaving Her Pubic Hair* (1921).

She created sculptures from garbage collected from the streets, and mounted her own living collage on her skin. The Baroness strolled Greenwich Village with postage stamps on her cheeks, her head shaved and painted red, with outfits designed from found objects like tin cans, silverware, curtain rings, a birdcage, and a bustle with a battery-powered taillight.

The Baroness died of gas asphyxiation in her Paris flat, exact circumstances unknown. She was buried in Père Lachaise Cemetery in Paris. Her personal papers and works were preserved by lover Djuna Barnes, who wrote of the Baroness, "For 54 years, [the Baroness was] ridiculed, praised, loved, brutalized, being passionate, ridiculous, splendid and impossible."

ARTHUR C. CLARKE
(SIR ARTHUR CHARLES CLARKE)

DEC 16 1917 – MAR 19 2008
(AGED 90)

Growing up, ARTHUR C. CLARKE built his own telescopes to look at the stars. He served as a radar specialist in World War II, and received a degree with first class honors in Mathematics and Physics from King's College London in 1948.

Clarke wrote science fiction novels, novellas, and short stories, as well as nonfiction science essays and books. Along with Stanley Kubrick, he was co-writer of the screenplay *2001: A Space Odyssey* (1968), partially inspired by his short story "The Sentinel" (1951). Clarke didn't publicize his sexuality. His standard answer when asked if he was gay was, "No, merely mildly cheerful." Once unsuccessfully married, Clarke stated in a 1986 *Playboy* magazine interview that he'd had a bisexual experience, and Isaac Asimov reportedly put it even more plainly by saying, "I think he simply found he preferred men."

Clarke's partner was Leslie Ekanayake, a scuba diver whom he lived with in Sri Lanka. He dedicated *The Fountains of Paradise* (1979) to Ekanayake, calling him "the only perfect friend of a lifetime." Clarke was knighted in 1998, and died in 2008 of respiratory failure stemming from post-polio syndrome. He is buried in the Colombo Cemetery in Sri Lanka, next to Ekanayake.

BERTHA HARRIS

DEC 17 1936 – MAY 22 2005
(AGED 68)

BERTHA HARRIS was born in Fayetteville, North Carolina. She graduated from the Women's College of the University of North Carolina in 1959, and moved to New York City, her reason for the move cited as "to find lesbians." She later returned to North Carolina to raise her daughter, complete her master's degree, and her first novel *Catching Saradove* (1969). Her second novel, *Confessions of Cherubino* (1972), came out of her love of opera and the South.

Her novel *Lover* (1976) was written as Harris stated, "straight from the libido, while I was madly in love, and liberated by the lesbian cultural movement of the mid-1970s." In her introduction to the 1993 reissue of *Lover*, Harris stated "*Lover* should be absorbed as if it were a theatrical performance. There's tap dancing and singing, disguise, sleights of hand, mirror illusions, quick-change acts, and drag." Harris co-authored *The Joy of Lesbian Sex* (1977), and published a biography of Gertrude Stein in 1995 as part of the Lives of Notable Gay Men and Lesbians young adult series.

Harris was with partner Camilla Clay Smith for 24 years. Harris died in 2005 while working on her next novel, an unpublished comedy titled *Mi Contra Fa*.

"JOE" CARSTAIRS
(MARION BARBARA CARSTAIRS, "THE QUEEN OF WHALE CAY")

1900 – DEC 18 1993
(AGED 93)

"JOE" CARSTAIRS was born in London, the heiress to a family fortune in holdings of Standard Oil. Carstairs dressed as a man, smoked cigars, had tattooed arms, and was openly lesbian. In 1925, she purchased her first motorboat, and received a Steiff doll from her girlfriend, Ruth Baldwin, that she named Lord Tod Wadley. She doted upon this doll for the rest of her life, and also became a champion motorboat racer: she was dubbed "the fastest woman on water," and according to Sir Malcolm Campbell was "the greatest sportsman I know."

Carstairs carried on numerous affairs with the likes of fellow World War II ambulance driver Dolly Wilde, singer Mabel Mercer, and actresses Greta Garbo, Tallulah Bankhead, and Marlene Dietrich. In the 1930s she purchased an island for tax purposes, Whale Cay in the Bahamas, where she hosted many of her own lovers while forbidding extra-marital relations for the island's other inhabitants. She sold the island in 1975, but not before building upon it a lighthouse, church, school, and cannery.

Carstairs died in Naples, Florida in 1993. She was cremated with the doll Lord Tod Wadley, and had their ashes, along with those of Ruth Baldwin's, buried at sea.

JEAN GENET

DEC 19 1910 – APR 15 1986
(AGED 75)

Born to a prostitute and later becoming one, JEAN GENET was also a thief, a soldier, a vagabond, and eventually a writer. His well-known works include the novels *Our Lady of the Flowers* (1943), *The Thief's Journal* (1949), and *Querelle of Brest* (1953), as well as the plays *The Maids* (1947), *The Balcony* (1956), and *The Screens* (1961).

Genet began writing in prison, and became an outstanding figure in erotic and subversive literature. In his essay "The Aesthetics of Evil" (1949), Genet wrote, "My talent will be the love I feel for that which constitutes the world of prisons and penal colonies. Not that I want to transform them or bring them around to your kind of life, or that I look upon them with indulgence or pity: I recognize in thieves, traitors and murderers, in the ruthless and the cunning, a deep beauty—a sunken beauty—which I deny you."

Genet died of throat cancer at age 75 in the city where he was born, Paris. Upon his passing, former Minister of Culture in France, Jack Lang, called him "a black sun that enlightened the seamy side of things," and said "those who hated and fought him were hypocrites."

ELSIE DE WOLFE
(ELLA ANDERSON DE WOLFE, LADY MENDL)

DEC 20 1865 – JUL 12 1950
(AGED 84)

ELSIE DE WOLFE came home from school and pitched a fit when she found her parents had redecorated the drawing-room with horrid gray palm-leaf wallpaper. After some work as an actress, she found her true passion in redecorating her first home. Her first commissioned work as an interior decorator was The Colony Club, a Manhattan women-only social club.

She continued to work in interior design for prestigious private homes, threw fabulous parties, and became a prominent figure in design, fashion, and entertaining with her book, *The House in Good Taste* (1913). De Wolfe volunteered as a nurse in France during World War I, was mentioned in Irving Berlin and Cole Porter tunes, and was named the best dressed woman in the world in 1935. On her visit to the Parthenon, she was reported as saying, "It's beige— my color!"

She married British diplomat Sir Charles Mendl in 1926. They entertained together but lived separately. De Wolfe met theater agent and Broadway producer Elizabeth Marbury at a party, and they moved in together in 1892. Gossip columnists nicknamed them "The Bachelors." Marbury died in 1933 and named de Wolfe her heir. De Wolfe died in 1950 at her home in Versailles.

VIOLET FLORENCE MARTIN
(MARTIN ROSS)

JUN 11 1862 – DEC 21 1915
(AGED 53)

VIOLET MARTIN was born in Connemara, County Galway, Ireland. She enjoyed riding horses, hunting, and writing. Martin met her second cousin, Edith Somerville, in January of 1886. They moved in together, considered themselves married, and traveled across the country and abroad. Under the pseudonym Martin Ross, she and Somerville co-wrote stories and novels as Somerville and Ross, including *An Irish Cousin* (1889), *Some Experiences of an Irish R. M.* (1899), and *The Real Charlotte* (1889). Their works described turn-of-the-century Irish society with witty characters and subtle commentary on Irish politics.

Their collections of diaries and letters reveal early talk of sharing a hotel room in Paris, how dreadful it was dancing with another woman at a party, and Martin's dislike of Somerville's unsuccessful suitor. After describing a confusing case of mistaken identity incest in 1892, Martin wrote, "That sort of thing sets one wondering if Nature or we ourselves are wrong."

In 1898, Martin was injured in a riding accident and never fully recovered. She died in 1915, in part from those injuries. Somerville continued to publish under both their names, and died in 1949. They are buried alongside each other at Saint Barrahane's Church in Castletownshend, County Cork, Ireland.

"MA" RAINEY
(GERTRUDE MALISSA NIX PRIDGETT)

APR 26 1886 – DEC 22 1939
(AGED 53)

At age 14, "MA" RAINEY started performing in minstrel shows, and by age 16 she'd heard her first blues song and started copying the style in her performances. In 1923, she signed a deal with Paramount Records and was one of the first performers to record the music style, earning her the nickname the Mother of Blues.

"Ma" Rainey married Will "Pa" Rainey at the age of 18, but many of her lyrics contain references to lesbianism and bisexuality. In the 1928 song "Prove It On Me," the lyrics are, "Went out last night with a crowd of my friends. They must've been women, 'cause I don't like no men." The song has been cited as a watershed moment for its treatment of lesbian desire.

"Pa" Rainey died around 1919. "Ma" Rainey eventually returned to her hometown of Columbus, Georgia where she ran three theatres—the Lyric, the Airdrome, and the Liberty Theatre—until her death from heart attack at 53. Rainey was inducted into the Blues Foundation's Hall of Fame in 1983, the Rock and Roll Hall of Fame in 1990, and the Gertrude "Ma" Rainey House and Blues Museum opened to the public in her hometown in 2007.

CHRISTA WINSLOE

DEC 23 1888 – JUN 10 1944
(AGED 55)

German writer and sculptor, CHRISTA WINSLOE is best known for her play *Yesterday and Today* (1930), which was made into the German films *Mädchen in Uniform* in 1931 and 1958. The play is a semi-autobiographical account of schoolgirl Manuela, whose romantic feelings for her teacher become known, leading to her suicide. The 1931 movie was entirely written, directed, and performed by women and girls. It also rewrote the ending so that Manuela is saved by her classmates. The movie was blacklisted by the Nazi Government.

Winsloe was sent to a strict boarding school after her mother's death. She studied sculpting, and entered a marriage of convenience for 11 years, divorcing in 1924. She left Germany soon after the Nazis took power, lived throughout Europe and in the U.S., eventually settling with her Swiss lover Simone Gentet in a French village on the Côte d'Azur in 1939. There they aided other refugees fleeing from Germany, and Winsloe battled the isolation by writing manuscripts later abandoned in the lead-up to the liberation of Paris. During the chaos, she and Gentet were abducted and shot to death by Frenchmen, who claimed they thought the women were Nazi spies. All four men were acquitted.

DEAN ARNOLD CORLL
("THE CANDY MAN")

DEC 24 1939 – AUG 8 1973
(AGED 33)

Born in Indiana, DEAN CORLL'S family moved to Texas in 1950. His mother married a pecan nut salesman, and started a family business that would later become the Corll Candy Company in 1963. Following an honorable discharge from the army, Corll relocated the business next to an elementary school. Corll would give free candy to local children, from whom he culled two boys to be his procurers—David Owen Brooks and Elmer Wayne Henley. He started by paying them for sex acts, then $200 a pop for bringing other boys to his house to be tortured, raped, and killed.

When Henley brought a girl along with some male victims, Corll was enraged, and intended to kill Henley as well. Henley talked his way out of danger, and shot Corll dead. At least 28 victims were later identified. Brooks and Henley were sentenced to life terms in prison for their participation.

Corll's murder was seen as self-defense and brought no conviction against Henley. Henley stated, regarding Corll's death, "Dean had been training me to react, to react fast and to react greatly. [...] He'd of been proud of the way I did it, if he wasn't proud before he died."

CHRISTMAS DAY

GEORGE MICHAEL
(GEORGIOS KYRIACOS PANAYIOTOU)

JUN 25 1963 – DEC 25 2016
(AGED 53)

GEORGE MICHAEL formed the band Wham! with schoolmate Andrew Ridgeley in 1981, and their first album *Fantastic* (1983) reached #1 on the U.K. charts. Michael was one of the best-selling music artists of all time, with numerous accolades and awards to his name. Hit singles include: "Wake Me Up Before You Go-Go," "Freedom," "I Want Your Sex," "Faith," and "Father Figure."

Michael spoke about his sexuality in 1999, saying, "I thought I had fallen in love with a woman a couple of times. Then I fell in love with a man, and realized that none of those things had been love." His long-term relationships were with make-up artist Kathy Jeung, dress designer Anselmo Feleppa, art dealer Kenny Goss, and hairstylist Fadi Fawaz.

Michael anonymously donated millions to charities like Childline and Macmillan Cancer Support, and privately gave to individuals seeking IVF treatments and others in need. He worked at homeless shelters, raised awareness and funds for HIV/AIDS foundations, did the same for the Rainbow Trust Children's Charity, and campaigned for LGBT rights.

George Michael died peacefully in his sleep, in his Oxfordshire home on Christmas morning, at 53. Cause of death was determined to be natural causes from heart disease.

BABUR
(EMPEROR, ẒAHĪR-UD-DĪN MUHAMMAD)

FEB 14 1483 – DEC 26 1530
(AGED 47)

BABUR (meaning "Tiger") was an emperor of Central Asia, founder of the Mughal dynasty of northern India, and a descendant of the Mongol conqueror Genghis Khan and the Turkic conqueror Timur. The descendants of Timur all had equal claim to his kingdom, and without rules of succession, were left to fight amongst themselves for control.

Babur's diaries, *The Baburnama*, made him unique among the squabbling princes. There he described his victories and struggles in battle and rule, as well as his unrequited love for a boy, fittingly named Baburi: "I developed a strange inclination for him—rather I made myself miserable over him." Though already married, the young Babur was largely uninterested in his wife. Upon meeting this boy, however, he wrote, "Before this experience I had never felt a desire for anyone." Bashful and unable to meet his eyes, Babur recorded that on a chance face-to-face meeting with Baburi, "I was so ashamed I almost went to pieces […] When I fell in love I became mad and crazed. I knew not this to be part of loving beauties."

Babur was a soldier, conqueror, poet, diarist, and statesman. After his death, his dynasty was succeeded by his eldest son.

NELL PICKERELL
(HARRY ALLEN, HARRY LIVINGSTON)

1882 – DEC 27 1922
(AGED 40)

Identifying as a man from a young age, PICKERELL worked as a bartender, cowboy, and farmhand. Pregnant at 16, Pickerell left the child with family, and was known to the boy as "Uncle." Newspapers reported Pickerell as the woman who "favored male attire, […] only eighteen years of age, but incorrigible. The ambition of her life is to act like a man." Notorious for seducing women who'd later commit or attempt suicide, Pickerell was once arrested for taking a woman across state lines for immoral purposes; the woman was Pickerell's partner, and introduced as "wife." Contemporary headlines include:

"This Girl Refuses to Wear Skirts; Nellie Pickerell Acts, Talks and Dresses Like a Man, and says She Ought to Have Been One"

"Girl Tries To End Her Life; Pearl Waldron Falls in Love With Notorious Nell Pickerell"

"Police Baffled By Silence Of A Nervy Young Woman; Female After Month's Imprisonment; Refuses to Tell What She Knows About Big Robbery"

"Nell Pickerell Returning to Jail"

"Nell Pickerell Again"

In 1916, "Nell Pickerell is Stabbed by Father" reported that the 79-year-old Robert Pickerell "stabbed her in the chest and back." Pickerell recovered only to die in 1922 of syphilitic meningitis at age 40.

GEORGE DUREAU

DEC 28 1930 – APR 7 2014
(AGED 83)

Lifetime New Orleanian GEORGE DUREAU was a photographer and artist known for his charcoal sketches and black-and-white nude photography of unusual bodies: poor athletes, dwarfs, and amputees. His work inspired Robert Mapplethorpe, who invited Dureau to discuss photography after seeing a picture of Dureau's longtime lover, Wilbert Hines (nicknamed "Wing Ding"), whose arm was amputated at the elbow.

Dureau's work can be seen in museums, in bronze outside of the New Orleans Museum of Art, on 1999's Jazz Festival poster featuring his painting of Professor Longhair, and on a wall in Gallier Hall where many parade krewes will hold their courts before Dureau's Carnival mural.

Dureau was able to support himself as an artist while living in the French Quarter. He said, "I ran a little kingdom where I was an esteemed patriarch, and the blacks were like natives of my village." Dureau would find models by offering them rides in his pickup truck, and if they remarked on his photographs by saying, in Dureau's explanation, "What a coincidence! I have a missing leg, too!" he would ask if they'd like to be photographed. Dureau said, "Almost everyone on earth wants to be remembered." Dureau died of Alzheimer's disease.

ISOBEL GUNN
(JOHN FUBBISTER, MARY FUBBISTER)

C. 1780 – NOV 7 1861
(AGED ~81)

In summer of 1806, ISOBEL GUNN of Scotland's Orkney Islands disguised herself as a man and boarded The Prince of Wales ship on a three-year fur-trapping contract with The Hudson Bay Company, thus becoming a pioneer of feminism, and the first European woman to travel to Rupert's Land, now Western Canada.

She was also the first woman of European descent to give birth in the North West, for on December 29th, 1807, John Fubbister the fur-trapper complained of stomach pains. The head of the trapping post recorded the incident: "[He] requested I would take pity upon a poor helpless abandoned wretch, who was not of the sex I had every reason to suppose. But was an unfortunate Orkney girl pregnant and actually in childbirth, in saying this she opened her jacket and display'd to my view a pair of beautiful round white breasts. In about an hour she was safely delivered of a fine boy."

In 1809, seen as a woman of "bad character" and only offered work as a washerwoman, Gunn and her son were forced to return to Scotland. She lived in poverty, working as a stocking and mitten maker until her death in 1861, aged 81.

GIANNI VERSACE
(GIOVANNI MARIA VERSACE)

DEC 2 1946 – JUL 15 1997
(AGED 50)

Born in Italy to a dressmaker mother, GIANNI VERSACE embraced the art of clothing design. He moved to Milan at age 26, and after five years of designing, opened his first boutique in 1978. Longtime editor of *Vogue*, Anna Wintour, said of Versace, "He was the first to realize the value of the celebrity in the front row, and the value of the supermodel, and put fashion on an international media platform."

Versace met his long-term partner, model Antonio D'Amico, in 1982. They were together for 15 years before Versace's death. Versace was murdered outside his Miami Beach home at age 50 by a 27-year-old serial killer for reasons that remain uncertain. Police closed the case on December 30th that same year, putting all the unanswered questions to rest.

Versace's funeral was held in Milan Cathedral, attended by over 2,000 people including Diana, Princess of Wales, singer Elton John, and supermodel Naomi Campbell. Versace's will left D'Amico a pension of 50 million lire a month for life (about $31,000) and the right to live in any of Versace's homes. The Versace family contested the will, and D'Amico obtained only a fraction of the pension and restricted access to the properties.

SAMUEL MORRIS STEWARD

(PHIL ANDROS, PHIL SPARROW, DOC SPARROW, WARD STAMES)

JUL 23 1909 – DEC 31 1993

(AGED 84)

SAMUEL STEWARD received a PhD in English from Ohio State University. He was dismissed from teaching at the State College of Washington at Pullman after his novel *Angels on the Bough* (1936) was published, and featured unsavory subjects like a likable prostitute. Steward connected with Gertrude Stein in 1932, and found a literary circle of friends when visiting France, some of whom he slept with.

Steward met sex researcher Alfred Kinsey in 1949, and collaborated with the Institute for Sex Research by collecting, donating, and filming material for Kinsey. Steward wrote short stories, erotica, and pulp pornographic novels under the name Phil Andros.

Steward was mentored by master tattooist Amund Dietzel, and during the 1960s was the official tattoo artist for the Hells Angels motorcycle gang.

While a student at OSU, Steward had sexual encounters with straight young men who were interested in experimenting. After meeting Kinsey, Steward maintained a green metal card catalog called the "Stud File," which documented 746 sexual experiences and partners he'd had, including Rock Hudson, Thornton Wilder, and someone he labeled as a "one-eyed sadist." Cards contained encounter locations, dates, sexual activities, penis descriptions, and brief commentary. Steward died of chronic pulmonary disease in 1993.

Abbéma, Louise 210

Abbott, Berenice 217

Acker, Jean 323

Adams, Dr. John Bodkin 226

Adrian 71

Ai of Han 175

Ailey, Alvin 7

Akerman, Chantal Anne 113

Albee, Edward 80

Alexander the Great 220

Allan, Maud 261

Almásy, László 90

Almendros, Néstor 330

Andersen, Hans Christian 104

Anderson, Lucy Hicks 99

Anne, Queen of Great Britain & Ireland 230

Anthony, Katharine Susan 361

Anzaldúa, Gloria Evangelina 294

Arnold, June 327

Arzner, Dorothy Emma 301

Asther, Nils 313

Auden, W.H. 57

Babur 392

Bacchus , Saint 307

Bacon, Francis 324

Bacon, Sir Francis 111

Baker, Josephine 114

Balagoon, Kuwasi 379

Baldwin, James Arthur 236

Bankhead, Tallulah Brockman 378

Barker, Dame Lilian Charlotte 371

Barlow, R.H. 152

Barnes, Djuna 180

Barney, Natalie Clifford 331

Barry, Dr. James Miranda Steuart 225

Barthé, Richmond 30

Bates, Katharine Lee 204

Báthory, Countess Elizabeth 241

Beach, Sylvia 82

Beard, James Andrew 139

Bedford, Sybille 84

Behn, Aphra 118

Belinfante, Frieda 144

Bellou, Sotiria 328

Ben, Lisa 341

Bentley, Gladys Alberta 242

Berber, Anita 344

Bernstein, Leonard "Lenny" 314

Billings, Lem 347

Bishop, Elizabeth 306

Bogarde, Dirk 96

Bonny, Anne 287

Borden, Lizzie Andrew 188

Botticelli, Sandro 151

Bowie, David 146

Bowles, Jane 138

Boye, Karin Maria 326

Brando Jr., Marlon 105

Bridgers, Aaron 337

Brocka, Catalino "Lino" Ortiz 49

Brooks, Louise 348

Brooks, Romaine 135

Brown, Margaret Wise 157

Bryher 270
Brynner, Yul 310
Buchanan Jr., James 125
Burke, Glenn Lawrence 350
Burroughs, William S. 41
Bussy, Dorothy Strachey 224
Byington, Spring Dell 81
Byron, Lord 75

Cahun, Claude 325
Caligula 26
Calomiris, Angela "Angie" 32
Campbell, Joe 302
Capote, Truman Garcia 298
Carangi, Gia Marie 31
Carlini, Benedetta 8
Carpenter, Edward 263
Carstairs, "Joe" 384
Cashier, Albert D.J. 164
Cassidy, Jack 239
Cather, Willa 126
Cernuda, Luis 339
Chapman, Dr. Graham Arthur 10
Charles XII of Sweden 380
Cheever, John William 161
Cheung, Leslie 103
Christina Alexandra, Queen of Sweden 322
Clarke, Arthur C. 382
Clift, Edward Montgomery 131
Cobbe, Frances Power 107
Cohn, Roy Marcus 56
Cole, Jack 53

Colette 237
Corll, Dean Arnold 390
Coward, Sir Noël Peirce 163
Craig, Edith 375
Crane, Harold Hart 129
Crisp, Quentin 355
Crowley, Aleister 367
Curtis, Tony 297
Cushman, Charlotte Saunders 223
d'Aubigny, Julie 44
d'Éon, Chevalier 321

Dahmer, Jeffrey Lionel 362
Damer, Anne Seymour 162
de Acosta, Mercedes Hede 69
de Beauvoir, Simone 11
de Cambacérès, Jean-Jacques-Régis 318
de la Roche, Mazo 17
de Souza, Felipa 229
de Wolfe, Elsie 386
Dean, James Byron 110
Deckers, Jeanne-Paule Marie "Jeannine" 97
DeLarverie, Stormé 158
Dickinson, Emily Elizabeth 278
Didrikson, "Babe" 194
Dietrich, Marlene 140
Dillon, Laurence Michael 70
Dior, Christian 374
Divine 319
Dodson, Owen Vincent 189
Donovan, Casey 336
Doolittle, Hilda "H.D." 295

Douglas, Lord Alfred 88
du Faur, Emmeline Freda 284
du Maurier, Dame Daphne 147
Duncan, Isadora 282
Dunne, Dominick John 329
Dureau, George 394

Eastman, George 212
Ebb, Fred 279
Edward II of England 289
Elbe, Lili 73
Eliot, Martha May 50
Ellis, Edith 208
Ellis, Ruth Charlotte 305
Eng, Esther 292
Epstein, Brian Samuel 369
Equi, Marie Diana 215
Esmond, Jill 228

Fassbinder, Rainer Werner 178
Fassie, Brenda Nokuzola 143
Faye, Frances 338
Fini, Leonor 264
Fisher, M.F.K. 190
Flynn, Errol 248
Flynt, Althea 195
Forbes, Malcolm Stevenson 253
Forster, E.M. 3
Forster, Jackie 340
Foucault, Paul-Michel 315
Francis, Kay 15
Frederick II of Prussia 352

Freund, Gisèle 353
Frisbee, Lonnie Ray 174
Fukaya, Michiyo 127

Gable, William Clark 358
Gacy Jr., John Wayne 85
Garbo, Greta 286
Gedroitz, Dr. Princess Vera Ignatievna 121
Genet, Jean 385
Genovese, Kitty 207
Gide, André 356
Gielgud, Sir Arthur John 116
Gilpin, Laura 364
Ginsberg, Allen 124
Gittings, Barbara 231
Gluck 247
Gore, Lesley 52
Gore-Booth, Eva Selina Laura 198
Granger, Farley 95
Grant, Cary 20
Griffith, Emile Alphonse 39
Grimké, Angelina Weld 63
Guang, General Huo 120
Gunn, Isobel 395

Haarmann, Fritz 197
Hadrian 304
Hall, Radclyffe 246
Hampton, David 130
Hansberry, Lorraine Vivian 14
Hardy, G.H. 43
Harris, Bertha 383

Hart, Lorenz "Larry" Milton 136
Hastings, Beatrice 29
Hatfield, Hurd 373
Heap, Jane 145
Hester, Laurel Anne 249
Highsmith, Patricia 21
Hildegard, Baroness Elsa 381
Hirschfeld, Magnus 148
Höch, Hannah 335
Holiday, Billie 122
Holman, Libby 154
Housman, A.E. 94
Housman, Laurence 218
Nelson, Alice Dunbar 219
Houston, Whitney Elizabeth 115
Hudson, Rock 351
Hughes, Howard 214
Hughes, James Mercer Langston 37
Hunt, Richard 251
Hunter, Alberta 317
Hutchinson, Josephine 312
Hutchinson, Leslie Arthur Julien "Hutch" 252

Isherwood, Christopher 260

Jackson, Charles Reginald 108
James I and VI of England and Scotland 92
Jewsbury, Geraldine Endsor 291
Jex-Blake, Dr. Sophia Louisa 9
Ji, General Liang 277
Jing of Han 64
Johnson, Marsha P. 258

Joplin, Janis Lyn 186
Jordan, Barbara Charline 19
Jorgensen, Christine 377
Julius III, Pope 91

Kahlo, Frida 206
Käkikoski, Hilda Maria 33
Kanyon, Chris 6
Karl von Württemberg 74
Keynes, John Maynard 123
Kinsey, Alfred Charles 191
Kovalevskaya, Sofia Vasilyevna 76
Kulp, Nancy 262

Lagerlöf, Selma 354
Landowska, Wanda Aleksandra 205
Larson, Jack Edward 288
Laurent, Yves Saint 235
Laurie, Joan Ann Werner 89
Lawrence, T.E. 153
Leduc, Violette 109
Leopold Jr., Nathan Freudenthal 155
Liberace 40
Lincoln, Abraham 48
Lister, Anne 290
Lobdell, Joseph Israel 368
Lorca, Federico García 173
Lorde, Audre 54
Lowell, Amy Lawrence 45
Lozano, Manuel Rodríguez 370
Ludwig II of Bavaria 259
Lyautey, Louis Hubert Gonzalve 221

Mann, Erika Julia Hedwig 343
Mann, Thomas 376
Mapplethorpe, Robert 77
Marbury, Elisabeth "Bessie" 187
Marlowe, Christopher "Kit" 62
Martin, Violet Florence 387
McDowall, Roddy 285
McLemore, John Brooks 83
McQueen, Lee Alexander 47
Mead, Margaret 349
Melville, Herman 296
Menken, Adah Isaacs 183
Mercury, Freddie 273
Michael, George 391
Milk, Harvey Bernard 156
Millay, Edna St. Vincent 58
Mineo Jr., Salvatore "Sal" 12
Mishima, Yukio 179
Munson, Ona 184
Murphy, Gerald Clery 93

Nash Jr., John Forbes 181
Nazimova, Alla 171
Newman, Paul Leonard 28
Nopcsa, Baron Franz 137
Novarro, Ramon 42
Nugent, Richard Bruce 202

O'Leary, Jean 72
Orton, Joe 243
Owen, Wilfred Edward Salter 86

Parnok, Sophia 245
Pearce, Louise 244
Perkins, Anthony "Tony" 106
Pickerell, Nell 393
Pollack, James B. 209
Porter, Cole Albert 60
Price, Vincent 372
Prince, Virginia Charles 357
Pryor, Richard 250
Puig, Manuel 222

Rainey, "Ma" 388
Read, Mary "Mark" 287
Renault, Mary 272
Rich, Adrienne Cecile 150
Richard I of England 271
Ride, Sally Kristen 160
Rimbaud, Jean Nicolas Arthur 320
Rivera, Sylvia Rae 55
Roger, Neil Munro "Bunny" 177
Röhm, Ernst 345
Romero Jr., Cesar Julio 51
Roosevelt, Anna Eleanor 311
Roper, Esther 238
Ross, Robbie 159
Russo, Vito 211
Rustin, Bayard 274

Sackville-West, Vita 170
Sappho 308
Sarton, May 216
Sassoon, Siegfried Loraine 276

Schragenheim, Felice Rahel 78
Sergius, Saint 307
Shakespeare, William 128
Simcox, Edith Jemima 255
Simmons, Roy Franklin 24
Singer, Winnaretta 360
Sipple, Oliver Wellington "Billy" 38
Smith, Bessie 117
Smith, Gerald "Jerry" Sanford 16
Smith, Liz 346
Snell, Hannah 254
Solanas, Valerie Jean 172
Sontag, Susan 18
Spain, Nancy Brooker 281
Stanwyck, Barbara 22
Starr, Ellen Gates 87
Stebbins, Emma 182
Stein, Gertrude 227
Steward, Samuel Morris 397
Stoker, Abraham "Bram" 342
Strayhorn, Billy 363
Sylvester 79

Talbot, Mary Ann 169
Taylor, Bayard 13
Taylor, Valerie 275
Tchaikovsky, Pyotr Ilyich 141
Thomas, Martha "Minnie" Carey 4
Tilden Jr., William "Big Bill" Tatem 46
Toklas, Alice B. 132
Tom of Finland 142
Trefusis, Violet 65

Tryon, Thomas "Tom" 293
Tsvetaeva, Marina 265
Turing, Alan Mathison 25

Vajiravudh, Rama VI of Siam 359
Valentino, Rudolph 257
Vance, Danitra 213
Vandross, Luther 201
Vargas, Chavela 283
Vechten, Carl Van 185
Verlaine, Paul-Marie 98
Versace, Gianni 396
Vidal, Eugene Louis "Gore" 303

Warhol, Andy 240
Waters, Ethel 269
Waugh, Arthur Evelyn St. John 112
Whipple, Diane Alexis 23
Whitman, Walter "Walt" 165
Wilde, Dolly 196
Wilde, Oscar 316
Wilder, Thornton 193
Williams III, Thomas Lanier "Tennessee" 61
Windsor, Edith "Edie" 280
Winsloe, Christa 389
Withers, Thomas Jefferson 149
Wittig, Monique 5
Wojtowicz, John Stanley 256
Wood, Thelma Ellen 203
Woolf, Virginia 27
Wuornos, Aileen 309

X, Malcolm 59

Yang, Olive 192
Yatō, Tamotsu 119
Yourcenar, Marguerite 176

L.A. FIELDS

L.A. FIELDS is the author of The Disorder Series, the short story collection *Countrycide* (2015), and the Lambda Award finalists *My Dear Watson* (2013) and *Homo Superiors* (2016). Other achievements include a BA in English Literature, an MFA in Creative Writing, an abandoned PhD, a dayjob, and a calico cat.

TYSON KADWELL

TYSON KADWELL holds an MFA in Creative Writing – Fiction from Columbia College Chicago and a BA in English from the University of South Florida. Works have been featured in *Hair Trigger 36* and *Strange World* anthology. Nomadic living conditions make current residences in Maryland, Michigan, Illinois, Florida, and beyond.